EXPECTATIONS
OF A
KING

EXPECTATIONS
OF A
KING

THE CHOPPER RA!

ROBERT DAVIS

EXPECTATIONS OF A KING
THE CHOPPER RA!

iUniverse books may be ordered through booksellers or by contacting:

iUniverse
1663 Liberty Drive
Bloomington, IN 47403
www.iuniverse.com
1-800-Authors (1-800-288-4677)

ISBN: 978-1-4917-3679-1 (e)
ISBN: 978-1-4917-3680-7 (sc)

Library of Congress Control Number: 2014912177

Printed in the United States of America.

iUniverse rev. date: 9/15/2014

CHAPTER 1

The hot sun engulfed her face. Normally, she would wipe the sweat from her forehead, before it trickled down. This time she couldn't. Suddenly, a breeze rushed through her hair, momentarily, dissipating the heat. That breeze cooled her entire body, before fading away as quickly as it came. Danaaa appreciated that breeze.

She was aware of her warrior's clothing that clung tight, but flexibly to her body. She could feel her wrist protectors on her skin. They always kept sweat from saturating her hands, keeping her grip on her axes secure.

Danaaa could feel particles of dirt between her toes. Dirt had infiltrated her firmly tied slippers. Even though her slippers clung tightly in battle, dirt always seemed to find a way in. She'd never been more aware of that dirt than now. What she didn't understand was why she couldn't move!

Danaaa could see her five siblings and cousin Yin. They were known as the Hammer-Axe Six. The Ra, Danaaa was the youngest and thought the most deadly member. At the age of thirteen Danaaa was simply the quickest, most accurate and deadliest ax master that anyone had ever witnessed.

The title of Executioner was reserved for the highest skilled killing technicians. In battle, Danaaa would put intense pressure on an opponent, executing them swiftly, no matter how skilled they were. Consequently, she was called High Pressure the Executioner.

After looking at her siblings, Danaaa looked at the Tat. She didn't like them. There were nine Tat and they had a large brute with them. The Tat used telepathy to control people's thoughts and actions. The Tat had the Hammer-Axe Six frozen, motionless, using their mind control abilities.

Danaaa struggled mightily, trying to move, but to no avail. If she could only move Danaaa would cut the Tat to pieces with her axes. She couldn't so she stared at them, thinking how things got to this point.

Danaaa's oldest brother and sister, La and Dan were twins and dual leaders of the Hammer-Axe Six. The Ra, Ramala was called La by her family and was the Number One Princess because she was the oldest daughter to the queen of Ra Hayee, Ramala.

La forced everyone lower in rank to refer to her as their queen. She was ruthless, cunning and very ambitious. Her main goal was to have her mother relinquish the throne and publicly name La queen. Taking the southern jungle was the first step in achieving that goal.

The Ra, Dan was in line to become the first born king of Ra. In order to attain his title, Dan needed a great conquest that would give him solid credibility and the backing amongst all the warlords of Ra. Conquering the southern jungle would undeniably give him that. Dan was going use his siblings, warlords and warriors to achieve his goal.

Danaaa most always went along with her siblings plots, even though she didn't think this one was a good idea. Being there, Danaaa thought if the situation got out of hand, she could rectify things with her axes.

The Tat, realizing the plot, came to prevent the young Ra Rulers from entering the Southern Jungle. The Southern Jungle was the home of a large tribe called the Shinmushee. The Shinmushee and the House of Ra had been warring in the past. Right now there was an unspoken truce. The Tat knew war would negatively affect the entire region long into the future.

Because La's thoughts told the Tat she was going into the

Southern Jungle no matter what, the Tat knew they had to eliminate the Hammer-Axe Six. While looking at the Tat Danaaa saw the one who began to speak.

"Remove all of their heads!" ordered the Tat, Taz.

The brute ax-man lowered his head and then raised it.

"As you wish." he replied.

The Ra warlords were closest to the large brute. He started walking towards them.

"Wait!" yelled Taz.

The brute ax-man stopped, turned and looked at Taz.

"Eliminate the one they call High Pressure the Executioner, first. She is on the far end. Finish the others, afterwards." ordered the Tat, Taz.

The Tat considered Danaaa the most dangerous and wanted her eliminated, first. The ax-man tuned and ominously walked towards Danaaa.

The Hammer-Axe Six found themselves in a perilous situation. All were in a state of panic after seeing the large brute walking towards Danaaa. As the large brute walked past each of them, the Hammer-Axe Six made an extra effort to get free. It didn't work.

Once Danaaa saw the large brute walking towards her a strange feeling engulfed her. She thought about her mother and father. Danaaa wished she could see them, again. She also thought about her brothers and sisters. Would she see them, again, after their heads were removed?

Danaaa also thought about all of the people she'd chopped with her axes. It was strange to Danaaa that, like the people she chopped never had a chance, she was in the same predicament.

The large brute with the giant ax stopped in front of Danaaa and looked at her. Danaaa, who had been trying to force herself to move, became calm. She didn't know why, but nothing seemed to matter anymore.

The brute reared his ax backwards, aiming at Danaaa's neck for a clean removal of her head. Although, amazingly calm Danaaa could still feel and see things. Danaaa saw the sun briefly reflect off of the Axman's blade.

The brute swung his ax full force at Danaaa's neck. Danaaa wished she couldn't see that ax coming at her neck, however her eyes were rendered motionless. This is where I'll be-Jinn, I mean begin.

Danaaa's body was being mentally controlled by the Tat, Tira. Tira was twelve and a half years old and had a serious look of concentration on her face. She hardly ever smiled. She was dark skinned skinny and average height for her age. Her hair was pinned back in a ponytail, but not braided. Tira Tat was the youngest Tat and the most advanced in mental abilities. That's why the Tat had her controlling the most dangerous member of the Hammer-Axe Six.

While controlling Danaaa, in the same instant the brute swung his ax at Danaaa's neck, Tira was transported to a place that she'd only been, once. Tira was on another world, standing on a barren dirt landscape. It was dark however, the ground was illuminated by the bright stars in the sky.

Tira could see several giant black marble like statues, off in the distance. She blinked out of fear remembering these menacing statues from the last time she saw them. When her eyes opened the statues had moved closer, covering half the distance between her and them. Tira looked around for the portal to this dimension that was here the last time she was. That time, Tira was pulled back through that portal by an Elder Tat and that's how she escaped from this place. That Elder was no longer alive and Tira was here, alone, without help.

When Tira didn't see the portal, she panicked. Beads of sweat started rolling down the sides of her face. Tira quickly turned and looked at the giant statues. They hadn't moved an inch from where they were since she'd last blinked. Tira knew every time she blinked her eyes the statues moved, so she tried not to. Tira's eyes began to burn as she held out as long as she could. Seconds later, she blinked.

When her eyes opened the statues were close enough that she could see their angry faces staring at her. Tira decided to close her eyes and not open them, until she figured out how to escape from here. However, before she closed her eyes, Tira heard a voice say, "Don't do that! You got it all wrong! Keep your eyes closed and you'll be dead, before long!"

Tira quickly looked around. She didn't see anyone, nor did she recognize the voice she heard. Tira asked, "Who are you and what do you want?!"

Out of thin air, right next to Tira appeared Danaaa. Startled, Tira quickly turned and stared at Danaaa. Danaaa didn't have on the Warlord fighting clothes she wore in the other world. She was dressed regally.

Tira heard a strangely deep voice coming from Danaaa, saying, "Meet me Immortal Line! Just, a Jinn. Not something made up in your head. Blink twice more and you'll be dead!…Now, let's play a game!"

The strange voice terrified Tira as much as the giant statues. Tira didn't understand what was said to her and she didn't want to play any games. Tira just wanted out of here! Then Tira blinked. As her eyes opened in slow motion, she saw all of the giant statues now standing around her.

Tira tried desperately to remember anything from the last time she was here, that might help her now. Nevertheless, she was already in serious panic mode. All Tira could remember was what her Elder told her about these giant statues. He told Tira that they were something you don't come back from. Tira held out as long as she could, trying not to blink. Her eyes burned as she frantically looked at the statues and then at Danaaa. Tira repeated that several times, until finally she blinked.

This time when Tira's eyes opened she saw one of the giant statues in front of her moving. Its arms were slowly reaching for Tira. She tried to move but couldn't. Tira stared in horror as the giant statue's hands were just reaching her shoulders.

It that same instant, Danaaa appeared in front of the statue right in Tira's face. Tira stared into Danaaa's eyes. Danaaa, this time, in her own voice, yelled, "After Mommy and Daddy, I don't have to do anything anyone tells me, except for La and Dan!"

Danaaa quickly pushed Tira backwards, with both hand, in Tira's chest so hard that Tira fell backwards and onto her butt. When Tira landed she looked wildly around. She didn't see the giant statues, anywhere. Tira had been transported back to where the Tat and the Hammer-Axe Six were. The other Tat were startled by Tira falling backwards and on to her butt for, seemingly, no reason. They quickly looked at her and then refocused their mental hold on the Hammer-Axe Six and the Ra Warlords.

Tira saw the brute's ax quickly moving towards Danaaa's neck, less than two inches from connecting. She watched in amazement as Danaaa's head moved sideways, in the same direction the ax blade was moving. Then Danaaa's head moved underneath the ax, just as the blade sliced through the air barely above her head.

Tira was even more amazed when the two axes she barely saw coming out of Danaaa's holsters moved upward from Danaaa's squatting position. Danaaa was on the unprotected side of the brute where his arm had not come back from swinging his ax at Danaaa. The ax in Danaaa's right hand sliced through his side, just below his armpit. Danaaa kept turning around and the ax in her left hand came up and split the side of his neck open.

Although seriously wounded, he brought his ax back from the swing he'd taken at Danaaa a half second earlier, hoping to get a good strike in on Danaaa. Danaaa quickly moved behind the brute, jumped up and ploughed both of her axes, one each into both sides of his neck, until they met in the middle. Danaaa landed and then jumped backwards as the brute's head fell to the ground, just before his body did. Danaaa quickly slammed her axes into their holsters. Tira was still on her butt watching Danaaa.

The eight other Tat had been watching the ax quickly moving towards Danaaa's neck, when they noticed that Tira stumbled backwards and fell. None of the Tat knew how that could happen when she was standing still!

The other Tat were unaware what happened to Tira. Best the Jinn, Ruler of all Gin and Jinni had a spiritual connection with the twins Ram and Danaaa. Best the Jinn had plans for Danaaa so it used the Gin, named Just, to move Tira in between time. Therefore, no time had passed in their reality during Tira's hellish experience in that other world.

After seeing Danaaa had released herself from Tira's hold and quickly killed the brute in no time flat, the other eight Tat tried to compensate and stop Danaaa from moving. When Danaaa felt them trying, she turned and stared at them.

"I don't have to do anything you say! Stop trying to tell me what to do!" yelled Danaaa in a nasty tone.

Danaaa then turned and walked over to her twin brother Ram. She hit him with a powerful backhand slap to his face. Danaaa yelled to Ram, "We don't have to do what they tell us! But, you already know that!"

Ram's face stung where he'd been slapped. He instantly became angry. He tried to move but couldn't. Danaaa watched Ram for a second, before sending another powerful slap to his face. Ram caught Danaaa's wrist, just before her hand reached his face. Danaaa snatched her hand away from Ram. They stared at each.

Ram slowly reached for his ax handles. When Ram's hands touched his axes, Danaaa turned away, walking towards the eight Tat. Ram looked at Danaaa, only for a second, before walking towards Tira.

Tira was so shocked by what was happening that she hadn't gotten off the ground. When Tira saw Ram walking towards her, her feet dug into the grass and she started frantically pushing herself backwards. Just as Ram reached Tira he pulled his axes with amazing speed. He twirled them one super-fast revolution, before they were aimed down at Tira. Tira froze. While looking into Ram's eyes, she knew if she tried anything she'd be killed.

Danaaa pulled her axes again and twirled them one super-fast revolution. When her axes stopped, one was pointed at the Tat and the other was pointed at her Ra siblings.

"I can swing an ax real fast! Let them go, or I Chop, I Chop, I Chop I!" yelled Danaaa.

The other Tat looked at Tira. With her help they were sure they could control the other Ra enough to make them fight the two that were free. They communicated that to Tira, mentally.

"Let them go!" screamed Tira.

The other Tat hesitated, because they knew the Ra would kill them if they did so. Danaaa took one threatening step towards them. The Tat released their mental grip on the Hammer-Axe Six and their Warlords.

"Kill them all!" screamed La, the Number One Princess, once she was free.

The Ra Warlords and two Elite guards moved forward, axes in hand. That's when Danaaa took a step back towards them. She twirled her ax one super-fast revolution, stopping it, pointed at the Warlords and Elite Guards. Danaaa never looked at them while, in a voice that sounded like her own mixed with a freakishly deep voice, said, "They will not be harmed by the likes of you! Stand your ground, or die! I Chop I!"

Everyone stared at Danaaa. It was peculiar to everyone hearing that voice come from her. The Ra Warlords and Elite Guards didn't move. They looked at La and Dan to see what they should do next. La motioned with her hand that they should stand there. La curiously looked at Danaaa.

La had never seen Danaaa in control of things. It shocked her. La thought she would always be in control. Her twin brother Dan showed her that wasn't going to happen all of the time. Then La's other sister Shaya showed her that she was capable of being in control, also. La didn't like sharing the power to control a situation. Nevertheless, La realized, at this moment, Baby was in control!

La slowly moved towards Danaaa, but stopped in her tracks when she heard that strange voice come out of Danaaa and say to the Tat, "Go north to your home with the Japha. No harm will come to you. We will see to that. You are necessary. Never test us, again. Now go!"

The Tat all took a step backwards, after the bass in Danaaa's voice forcefully slammed into them. They looked over and saw Ram slamming his axes into their holsters. Ram extended his hand to Tira. Tira had been staring into Ram's eyes. They were just as scary as the statues she'd faced, earlier. Tira hesitated for a moment, before slowly extending her hand. Ram lifted her off the ground.

Once standing, Tira stared at Ram, not moving. Several of the Tat called to her in her mind. Tira didn't respond. Finally, the Tat, Tonia walked over, grabbed Tira by her arm and pulled her away. After watching the Tat walk away, all of the Ra walked over to Danaaa. The Ra Warlords and Elite Guards stayed back a short distance and watched Danaaa, closely. La and Shaya were the first to get to Danaaa, with their brothers behind them. They stopped and looked into Danaaa's eyes. None of them recognized those eyes as being Danaaa's.

Danaaa was still looking in the direction where the Tat finally disappeared. Shaya and La, not knowing what to do, started fussing over Danaaa's clothes, while fearfully looking into Danaaa's eyes.

"Baby, are you alright?" La whispered.

Danaaa's eyes slowly moved to La's. Once their eyes met, fear ran through La's entire body and her knees bent, slightly. Whoever was looking at La through Danaaa's eyes looked like they wanted kill La. La screamed, pleading, "Baby, it's me! It's La, your sister!"

In that same instant Danaaa's eyes changed back to the eyes everyone knew. Danaaa curiously looked at La.

"But, I already know that!" Danaaa yelled.

Everyone incredulously looked at each other, trying to figure out what just happened. Lastly, La looked at Dan. Dan nodded his head and urged La to question Danaaa. La looked back at Danaaa and said, "Baby, your voice and eyes were strange to us. Tell me, what just happened?"

While looking into La's eyes, Danaaa reflected on what just

happened. Danaaa said, "When I saw that ax coming at my neck I knew I had to get out of the way, or I would be dead. So, I did. I don't even know how I did it. It just happened. Once I could move, I made that brute pay!" Danaaa looked over at the dead brute's body.

Everyone looked at the dead brute when Danaaa did. It took them back to when they thought they would be dead soon after the ax-man took Danaaa's head. They felt they'd barely escaped death's grip. It was a scary and euphoric feeling, all at the same time. Still, La needed answers.

"Your voice and eyes, tell me about that?" questioned La.

Danaaa curiously looked at La as if she didn't know what La was talking about. Danaaa shrugged her shoulders and said, "I talk like I always talk. Sometimes I talk loud and sometimes I talk soft. But, you already know that! And I only know one way to look at things. You already know that, too!"

La was about to press further, when Danaaa yelled, "Stop questioning me about the way I talk and look at things! I just almost got my head chopped off! So did you! Can't you just be happy that we're alive and not dead?"

Even though Danaaa had just yelled at La point blank, La wasn't offended. La could see the stress and turmoil in Danaaa's eyes. Danaaa's eyes glossed over with a thin layer of moisture. While looking in Danaaa's eyes, La marveled at how there was never enough moisture to create a teardrop. Then Danaaa's bottom lip went crooked on one side. It started to shake where it hung crooked. La had seen this many times whenever Danaaa got cross. However, this was the first time La realized that Danaaa wasn't cross. She was just upset over almost losing her life.

La gave Danaaa a reassuring look. She then reached for and hugged Danaaa. Shaya wrapped her arms around both her sisters. La said in a whisper, "Baby, I am happy. I'm so very happy you're here with me, now. I don't know what I would have done if......"

La's throat got all choked up and she stopped talking. All three girls held each other in a circle, while looking down at the ground.

Danaaa watched as La and Shaya's tears hit the ground, making little impressions in the dirt.

It surprised the Ra girls when the Ra boys came over, hugging them from behind. The Ra Warlords and the two Elite Guards knew this was a private moment for the Royal Ra, so they turned away and surveyed the area, watching for danger.

"I thank the heavens that we all are unharmed." said Dan.

The Ra stood there for a moment holding each other, while La and Shaya shed tears, without making a sound. La lifted her head, first. Shaya and Danaaa lifted their heads after that. La took her sleeve and wiped the tears from Shaya's face. When La was done, Shaya took her sleeve and wiped the tears from La's face. Before Shaya could wipe the other side of La's face Danaaa was doing so with her sleeve.

The Ra boys backed away from the girls. The Ra girls smiled at each other and at the Ra boys. The Ra boys, except for Ram, smiled back because even though they didn't shed any tears they were thrilled to be alive, also.

Ram was pissed about being slapped by Danaaa and needed clarification on that matter. He stepped in front of Danaaa. They locked eyes.

"You slapped me!" said Ram.

"You needed it." Danaaa solemnly said.

"Never do that, again!" replied Ram.

Danaaa pressed her lips together in frustration.

"You would step to me! Ram, you're acting like a moronic buffoon! I wonder what your mouth would be saying if your head was rolling on the ground, after that ax-man's blade removed it!" she exclaimed.

Danaaa turned and marched over to La, before turning back and facing Ram. She was breathing heavily and her lip was crooked on one side. Ram saw all of that. He also saw La quickly grab Danaaa's ponytail, while Shaya fussed over Danaaa's clothes. Dan looked at Danaaa and then turned to Ram.

"It's best for everyone if you leave her be." Dan said.

Ram looked at Dan and then at Danaaa. He would comply, for now. Ram felt insulted by Danaaa's slap and her words. Nevertheless, he had clarification on that matter!

Once Dan saw Ram was under control, he looked at Bo and the other Ra Warlords saying, "We need to get to the Lower Houses as soon as possible. We'll rest there before we do anything else."

The Ra Warlords lowered their heads and then looked at La. Dan turned and looked at La. La looked at her sisters and nodded to Dan that they were ready to go. The Hammer-Axe Six, their Warlords and two Elite Guards started walking towards the Sixth Lower House of Ra.

"I'm hungry!" Danaaa yelled in a whining voice.

"Don't get started! We'll eat soon enough!" La immediately responded.

Everyone realized things were starting to get back to normal.

The Hammer-Axe Six traveled a short distance before they saw a large caravan moving towards them. It came from the direction of the Sixth Lower House of Ra. After everything they'd encountered today, the Hammer-Axe Six and their Warlords went on guard and readied themselves for battle. As the caravan got closer, they could see it was a Ra caravan. Once the caravan was close enough, they saw Tania and her guards on several of the leading Elephants. Days ago, La put Tania in charge of the Ra military caravan that was sent to the Lower Houses of Ra.

La watched as the caravan stopped. Tania, with guards following, walked up to La. They all got down on their knees.

"How may I serve my Queen?" asked Tania.

La was pleased, but suspicious as to why Tania was here.

"Tania, rise and come to me. Everyone else, stay there!" La ordered.

Tania got up, peeked at Bo and the other Warlords, before quickly walking over to La. La watched Tania, closely.

Once Tania got to La she never looked above La's chest.

"My Queen?" Tania meekly questioned. La saw the level of respect she expected.

"Walk with me." La replied.

La turned and started walking away from her brothers. Shaya and Danaaa started walking as soon as La did.

"Although, it's good to see the caravan, why have you come here?" La asked.

"When Warlord Stacia told me to go to the Lower Houses and tighten security, while stockpiling supplies, I did just that. Stacia also told me you were going into the Southern Jungle. I thought it best to travel a ways from the Sixth Lower House, just in case my Queen needed extra supplies. I hope my actions haven't offended my Queen." responded Tania.

La and her sisters stopped walking and gathered around Tania. That made Tania nervous. La looked at Tania for a moment. Tania submissively lowered her head.

"I expect you to do everything I ask of you, first, without failure. You said you have done that. I will see to what degree once we get to the Lower Houses. After that, I expect you to do extra things to please me. I am not offended." La said.

Tania looked up and saw that La was smiling at her. Tania smiled back.

"Let's get to the caravan. I'm starving!" La said.

The Hammer-Axe Six and their Warlords boarded the elephants and headed to the Sixth Lower House of Ra. They were going to eat and process everything that happened to them up to this point. Afterwards, they were going to proceed with their original plans of taking control of the Southern Jungle.

On the way, after having a good meal, everyone was resting on their platforms. The Ra girls were already asleep. Don, Yin and Ram were going in and out of consciousness. Dan was sitting, leaning back on the wall of the platform. A light breeze was slightly dissipating the heat of the day.

Although on the lead elephant, Dan could still smell the

elephants. It didn't bother him that much. He was used to it. He would stand and survey the surroundings, continuously. Even though he was tired, young Dan knew they weren't home, yet.

Although he tried, Dan couldn't forget that devastated feeling that engulfed him when he thought his siblings would be killed. There he was powerless to protect his younger siblings from harm as he always had. If Danaaa hadn't saved the day things would have been much worse. Danaaa was an entirely different subject that Dan didn't want to face, just yet.

Even if he had somehow broken the mental grip and one of his siblings had been killed, Dan knew he wouldn't have been able to live with himself, after that. He also realized if he somehow found a way to live with himself, his mother and father would blame him. If he survived their wrath, he would have no chance of ever becoming king of Ra. Dan knew he had barely avoided disaster. Dan told himself he would have to do better, next time

At eighteen years old the last two days were the strangest of his life, so far. The day before, while entering the Southern Jungle, they were confronted by a Lightning Jinn. Seeing that they were out matched the Hammer-Axe Six decided to put some distance between themselves and the Lightning Jinn, by running away at top speed. It embarrassed Dan every time he thought about that incident.

I mean, what the heck is a lightning Jinn and where does it come from? Dan didn't even know what a Jinn was. Also, the encounter with the Tat really baffled Dan. How does someone get in your mind and control your movements? Was someone trying to control his movements now? Was someone listening to his thoughts?

Dan was starting to confuse himself. He remembered that his father told him not to think too much about things he had no control over. Dan knew he was tired. So, he put the thoughts of those events in the back of his mind as much as possible. Dan promised himself that when they got to the Lower Houses of Ra and everyone was safe, he was going to find the answers to all these questions. He also was going to make a new plan to conquer the Southern Jungle.

—————— CHAPTER 2 ——————

I t seemed a short time passed when Dan noticed the caravan was slowing down. Then it came to a complete stop. Dan jumped to his feet and looked ahead. The forward guards looked to be having trouble with a small group of about twenty men. That the guards hadn't moved them out of the path of the Royal caravan already made Dan think 'What now?'

The rest of the Hammer-Axe Six were on their feet looking around. One of the guards came back and asked for permission to speak. La was annoyed because her sleep had been disturbed. She impatiently motioned with her hand and said, "Speak!"

"Shinmushee Butchers are blocking the road. They said someone wants to meet the, so called, King and Queen of Ra. They said they would leave, after that." said the guard.

Dan and La looked at each other and then dismounted from their elephants, along with everyone else. Neither of them knew how to deal with Jinns, or mind readers, but they could deal with Shinmushee Butchers. La's face got stern, while staring at Dan.

"Shitmushee Butchers!" exclaimed La.

"Let's take care of this!" said Dan, calmly and assuredly.

Dan and La looked at their siblings. Everyone looked refreshed and ready. It seemed the meal and short nap rejuvenated them. The Ra Warlords Ali, Hoban, Bo and their Elite Guards walked over. Dan motioned for everyone to follow him, as he walked towards the Shinmushee Butchers.

As they were walking, they noticed that all of the Shinmushee Butchers were walking away, leaving one man in a throne chair. The Ra entourage stopped at a safe distance, while they watched the Shinmushee Butchers move, away. The Shinmushee Butchers stopped, turned and watched.

Dan turned to his Warlord Bo and said, "Keep an eye on them, while we question this man. Let me know the instant they move."

Bo nodded that he would. Bo had several guards move to a better vantage point to watch the Shinmushee Butchers. The Hammer-Axe Six and their Warlords studied the man for a moment. They knew if he was left by himself, unprotected, they should consider him dangerous. But still, he didn't look to be a threat.

Dan could see that the man sitting in the throne chair was very old. His skin was dark brown and all of his hair was a silvery white, including his eyebrows. His face was fat, but wrinkly. In fact, his entire body seemed to be overweight and stuffed tightly inside his clothing.

Danaaa and Ram slowly and cautiously moved closer, circling the throne, studying it and sniffing the man, while everyone else studied him from a safe distance. The man's eyes barely moved as he watched everyone around him, without staring, or looking directly at them.

After Ram and Danaaa did their search, they rejoined La and Dan. As she reached them, Danaaa looked at La and shrugged her shoulders. Danaaa turned around, facing the old man. La took a step forward and cautiously started walking back and forth in front of the old man, while studying him, closely. La stopped with her body half facing the man and half facing Dan and the others. La looked at Dan and then at the old man. While looking at the old man, La put her hands on her hips and said, "Why, he's nothing..., but an old man!"

When La said that, the rest of the Hammer-Axe Six walked up and joined her. Staring at the old man, Dan questioned "Old man, why are you here?"

The old man's face got animated, excited and jovial.

"Why, I'm here? To see the, so called, King of Ra. I hear he likes a good challenge!"

La didn't like this. She knew her brother couldn't resist a challenge, no matter how dangerous. La quickly looked at Dan. Before she could warn Dan, Dan said, "I'm the King of Ra. What is this challenge you speak of?"

"A fighting contest on this very spot. A test of skills with weapons, or not. Make your choice, but careful which you choose, because that will determine how bad you'll lose…Now let's play a game!" replied the old man, with a jolly smile.

When Danaaa and Ram heard that last sentence it startled them. Everyone quickly looked at them, after seeing them jump.

"Baby, what is it?" asked La.

Danaaa eyes squinted.

"There's something strange about that old man!" Danaaa whispered.

Before La could say anything Danaaa took a step forward, did a quick lowering and rising of her head to the old man, to show respect.

"Who are you?" yelled Danaaa.

"I'm not the one who started this mess. I'll tell you the truth, if right you guess." He replied.

"This is nonsense! What does it matter who he is? Guards! Remove this man from the road, immediately!" ordered La.

Ra guards moved quickly up to where the throne area was. Nevertheless, the old man didn't move. Once the Ra guards touched the lifting handles of the throne, the old man sprang into action. He lifted himself over the back of the throne chair, with his hands, kicking his feet at the guards behind him, sending them flying through the air backwards and onto the ground. Without stopping and all in one motion, the old man twirled himself with lightning speed towards the front of the throne and planted his feet in both of those guards' chests before they could move. They went flying through the air just as the other Ra guards had. The old man sat back in the throne chair and looked ahead as if nothing had happened.

All of the Ra watched the speed and accuracy in which the old man moved. However, the one thing that stuck out in all of their minds was as he was twirling himself through the air, his belly hung and jiggled. It was the strangest thing to them that this man's body appeared to be out of shape, yet he moved like he was a fighting master! Regardless of the shape of his body, Dan knew the old man was powerful.

The Ra guards quickly got off the ground. They looked at La. La nodded her head for them to proceed. The Ra guards then pulled their Hammer-Axes. However, the man didn't move. If fact, he looked bored!

After looking at La once more and getting another nod to proceed, the Ra guards attacked. Everyone stared in amazement as the old man jumped up, with both feet landing on the seat of the throne chair, while in a squatting position. Barely moving, the old man blocked the axes coming at him and then he sent powerful counter blows with his feet and fist. He hit two of the guards so hard that before they went flying backwards, they dropped their axes.

This time the Ra guards received blows that were much more powerful. They were breathing heavily and slow to get up. La turned and looked at Dan like she couldn't believe what she was seeing. Dan already knew what he was seeing. Young Dan was seeing the greatest challenge of his life.

Dan took a deep breath and said, "Guards, step back!"

Happy that they didn't have to advance on the old man again, the guards quickly did as they were told. La knew what was coming next and grabbed Dan's arm, pulling hard on it. Dan firmly held his ground, ignoring La.

"The King of Ra, Hammer-Axe Champion Warlord Faster Cut, the Chopper Ra accepts your challenge! That's me, you know!" said Dan.

The old man raised his head arrogantly high and chuckled. La jumped around and in front of Dan, glaring at him.

"Are you insane?! This old man can't be taken lightly! You saw what he just did, didn't you?" yelled La.

While looking into La's eyes, Dan did know how dangerous this man was. However, that wasn't going to stop him. Dan remembered the old man said and showed everyone that if you didn't use weapons he'd beat you soundly, but if you used weapons, it would be that much worse. That was Dan's interpretation.

"Don't worry. I know what I'm doing." said Dan.

La's bottom lip instantly went crooked. She couldn't understand why Dan enjoyed putting himself in danger like this. La planted her feet firmly, with her hands next to her ax handles.

"I'll not allow this! You'll have to fight me, in order to get to him!" shouted La.

Dan's eyes slowly moved to La's hands and then back up to her eyes.

"After you beat me, I'm going to fight him, anyway. If I fight you, I'll be much weaker and easier to defeat. Calm yourself and let me do this. You're right about one thing. That old man is dangerous. Let me fight him, while you watch from here. Look for any weaknesses he might have. That's how we gain the advantage on him." Dan calmly said in a low voice that only La could hear.

La's eyes were very concerned.

"What about you? How long can you last without being harmed?"

"I'll be alright."

Dan reached for and hugged La. When La's body went off guard, Dan quickly lifted La and moved her to the side. He started walking forward, before La could react. Danaaa and her siblings moved to La's side. They concentrated on Dan and the old man.

"Watch the old man. Find his weaknesses as soon as possible." whispered La to her siblings. Dan stopped at a respectable distance from the old man and lowered his head. "Wise teacher, I thank you for the lesson I am about to learn." said Dan.

The old man's face wasn't as friendly when he looked Dan up and down.

"Wise teacher he called me, well that we'll see! The lesson you learn, you'll have to earn!" said the old man as he motioned, with his hand, for Dan to start whenever he was ready.

Adrenaline was pumping heavily through Dan's body and his brain. He quickly remembered everything he saw the old man do to the guards, earlier. Dan stared at him, cautiously moving closer. When Dan's Hammer-Axes got close enough to strike, he attacked.

Dan kept his Hammer-Axe strikes short, powerful and didn't fully commit to any of his swings. Dan also didn't swing at the old man's body. Instead, Dan's axes assaulted and harassed the old man's arms and legs. Because Dan wasn't fully committing to his swings there were no blocking, or counter-attacking opportunities. The old man had to move his limbs out of the way, or have them sliced by Dan's axes.

Dan increased the speed in which he attacked. Now the old Man was twirling himself around on his throne chair sending his fist and feet at Dan, while avoiding Dan's axes. Dan gave those powerful blows all the respect they deserved. He ducked and dodged all of them, resigned to the fact that blocking one of them would leave him to the mercy of the old man's power.

The old man saw that Dan was very quick. It was hard for him to mount a counter-attack, with Dan's axes in position to slice him. So the old man baited Dan, by moving to the other side of the throne chair. Dan moved around the chair with his axes in hot pursuit. Dan kept his axes attacking, where ever he saw the old man pivoting himself. Dan was planning on catching the old man when he had his weight on either his hands, or feet. Dan was going to attack the old man's balancing limb.

However, the old man was wise in fighting strategy. He was going to make Dan think he had the advantage. The old man moved in like he was going to counter-attack. Dan quickly moved his axes in position to make the old man pay. That's when the old man sent a powerful blow at Dan with his foot. Dan avoided it, but instead of attacking that foot, Dan stepped his speed up to another level and started swinging his axes where he knew the old man had to land on the throne chair. It shocked Dan that the old man avoided his axes by tucking and rolling onto the ground, instead of landing on the throne chair and getting sliced up by Dan's axes. The old man came out of his tuck and roll into a standing position, on guard, facing Dan.

The jolly look left the old man's face and was replaced by a stern serious look. Dan could see that the old man was angered that Dan moved him off his throne chair. Dan paused to plan his next attack. He certainly wasn't going to charge the old man without a new plan.

Dan raised his axes, as he cautiously moved closer to the old man. The old man stood perfectly still waiting on Dan. A second later, Dan attacked.

Dan decided that speed was his best advantage. Dan twirled his axes at the old man with lightning speed. Dan swung the ax in his left hand and had it blocked by the old man. Dan was instantly hit in the chest and then had the ax in his right hand blocked.

Now the old man was inside of both Dan's axes. Instantly, Dan was hit again in the chest, but this time, much harder. Dan was sent off of his feet flying backwards, before he knew what happened. When Dan landed he tucked and rolled to get more distance from the old man. When Dan got to a standing position he didn't have his axes.

Dan realized he dropped them when he was hit with that powerful punch. Dan could see that the old man hadn't advanced on him. That's when Dan felt the pain and shock from those two blows. Dan's face winced in pain as he stood on guard against the old man. He had never been hit that hard, before.

Dan quickly looked at his Hammer-Axes on the ground, before looking back at the old man. The old man motioned with his hand for Dan to go and pick up his axes. Dan had only been hit twice by the old man and he really didn't want to fight him, anymore. Then

Dan's ego told him that the old man said he would get a less severe beating if he didn't use weapons. Dan's fighting ego told him that, if he was careful, he could find a way to beat this old man, without using his Hammer-Axes.

Dan started dancing on his toes, moving to his left and right in quick erratic movements. The old man just watched as Dan cautiously moved closer. When Dan got within striking range he took a super fast swing at the old man. The old man tore into Dan with ten straight super fast blows, before Bo and Hoban arrived, getting in between Dan and the old man. The old man commenced to putting a beating on Bo and Hoban. Ali and several Elite guards jumped in to save Bo and Hoban from the old man's wrath. They were treated to the same ferocious blows as the others were.

Dan was down on one knee trying to catch his breath, while shaking off the cobwebs of being clobbered by the old man. Even though he'd been roughed up, Dan realized the old man had only hit him with body shots. Dan thought that if the old man really wanted to, a couple of well-placed shots to Dan's head would have finished him off for good. Dan also realized he was right when he figured the old man wouldn't hit him as hard, if he didn't use weapons. Dan knew if those ten shot would have been as powerful as the two he took, earlier, when he had his weapons, he would be seriously injured, if not dead.

Dan looked over at the fight. Now La, Yin, Don, Danaaa and Ram were involved in the fight and they all were using their Hammer-Axes. Dan looked and saw that the Shinmushee Butchers had moved closer from their previous position. When he looked back at the battle, he could see La was almost in trouble, even though Danaaa and Ram were trying to defend her.

For some reason the old man was zeroing in on La. Dan grabbed his Hammer-Axes and bolted in defense of his sister. Danaaa and Ram had worked their way into better attacking positions just as Dan arrived to join the fight. The old man had to use all his skills to block Danaaa and Ram's ax swings. Nevertheless, they both had super-fast returning swings that Dan didn't think the old man could avoid. Dan moved in the perfect position to strike. The old man was in trouble whether it was from Dan's axes, or Ram and Danaaa's axes.

In an instant, Dan blocked both kill shots from Danaaa and Ram aimed at the old man. Then Dan sent his hammers, backwards, as fast and as hard as he could at the old man's chest. The old man blocked both with his hands. Dan sent two more lightning fast hammer shots to the old man's chest. The old man blocked them both again, but took a step backwards from the force of Dan's blows. Dan quickly turned and sent his ax blades at the old man's hands and arms. That gave La, Danaaa and Ram time to regroup. They moved into position to attack. Dan, seeing that, half turned towards them and yelled, "Everyone, stand your ground!!"

That froze everyone for the moment. La looked at Dan to see what his plan was. Dan realized he'd lost track of the old man. He quickly turned around. Dan saw the old man heading back to his throne chair. When he got there he sat down. He looked at Dan and said, "The Ra are strong and very tough. But of this game, I've had enough!"

The old man clapped his hands. The Shinmushee Butchers walked up, on guards against the Ra. Dan held up his hand, motioning for the Ra guards not to attack.

La and the rest of the Hammer-Axe Six moved next to Dan.

"You're going to let him go, just like that?" asked La.

Danaaa lightly bumped La and then said in her whispering voice, "We have to let him go. He's done playing with us. If we attack him now, he'll be within his rights to kill." La incredulously looked at Danaaa.

"Within his rights! What do you mean?" screamed La.

Dan thought for a moment, looked at La and said, "She's right! Wait here!"

Dan ran around and in front of the throne that the Shinmushee Butchers were carrying. Several of the Shinmushee Butchers went on guard. The old man motioned with his hand for them to hold their position. The old man looked annoyed when he turned and looked at Dan. Dan saw the Shinmushee Butcher that gave him a sound beating some time ago. Dan lowered his head to that Butcher and then went down on one knee out of respect for the old man.

"Wise teacher, much respect to you and….and thanks for the lesson!" said Dan.

"King of Ra I don't have any more time to play! Move aside, get out of the way!" the old man said.

All of the Shinmushee Butchers looked as Dan lowered his head again and did as he was told. The Shinmushee Butchers lifted the throne chair and started walking, again. Danaaa ran over to Dan. She looked at the old man and yelled out, "Jinn Ja!"

The Shinmushee Butchers stopped.

"Be it, How." without turning around, the old man said.

"Be it, How? Jinn Ja, How?" Danaaa, excitedly, said.

The old man slowly nodded his head in agreement.

"Be it, Jinn Eco." said Danaaa.

"Eco Jin, Ram." said Ram as he moved next to Danaaa.

Without looking directly at either of them, the old man nodded his head, again.

After that, the Shinmushee Butchers started walking, carrying the old man, away. La and the others walked over to where Dan, Ram and Danaaa were. They watched, until the Shinmushee faded off into the distance.

Dan turned to Danaaa and Ram.

"What's Jinn Ja?"he questioned.

"But, he already told you, How." replied Danaaa, while looking at Dan

"How what?" asked Dan.

"Jinn Ja!" yelled Danaaa.

Both Dan and Danaaa stared at each other in confusion. La moved close to Dan and gently put her hand on his shoulder. She looked around, nervously, surveying the area. With concern in her voice, La softly said, "Dan, enough of this!"

Dan's eyes slowly moved from Danaaa's to La's eyes. There would be more time to revisit this, once they were safely at the Sixth Lower House of Ra. Dan turned to his Warlord Bo and said, "Let's get out of here!" Dan refused to get caught up in this nonsense, with Danaaa, out in the field.

After their encounter with the Hammer-Axe Six the Tat quickly moved north. Once they were a safe distance from the Ra, Taz looked at Tira and questioned, "I still think we should have made them fight each other! We had them right where we wanted them! We missed the perfect opportunity! What happened back there, that shook you and made you lose your will to control them?"

Tira stopped and looked at Taz. Tira said, "I didn't lose my will to do anything! We were lucky to get out of their alive!" Tira paused for a second, while staring at Taz. All of the other Tat gathered around Tira. With a concerned look on her face Tira said, "The young girl that I was manipulating has figured out how to travel to other dimensions with her guest spirit. Somehow, I was transported to a dimension, while you all were controlling her siblings. I had no idea of how to get back. My life was in peril, until the Ra girl pushed me back into this reality. That's when I fell backwards onto the ground. When I looked up, no time had passed in this reality."

Tonia said, "That's why it looked like you fell on the ground for no apparent reason!" Tira nodded in agreement and then said, "That's right. Until we find out how to travel and return from different dimensions, we can't deal with the Ra."

Taz calmed down after hearing that. Still, he asked, "Is there anything else you can tell us about High Pressure the Executioner? That's what they call her, right?"

Tira nodded in agreement. She thought for a moment and then said, "I know what her guest spirit said about itself."

All of the Tat stared intently at Tira. Taz asked, "What?"

Tira said, "It said it was from an Immortal Line. Then it said it was just a Jinn."

Taz said, "If it's from an immortal line that means this Jinn is an ancient sprit and not just a Jinn."

Tonia said, "But Tira said it said it was just a Jinn."

Taz said, "Maybe that was a figure of speech."

Tanya said, "If it's an immortal spirit it said exactly what it meant and we should take it as that."

Tone said, "Unless, it was using words to trick Tira."

Taz looked at all of the Tat and said, "All of those are possibilities. We have to figure out how to deal with Jinni. If we figure that out, the Ra won't stand a chance against us!"

Taz looked back at Tira and said, "You did good to get us all out of there, without any of us being harmed. Let's go home. We have work to do!"

Before the Tat left their sanctuary in Japha territory, on their way to eliminate the Hammer-Axe Six, they told Queen Japha, Jan they were going on a pilgrimage to the mountain where they used to live. Queen Japha, Jan wanted to send an armed escort, but the Tat refused. They said if she insisted, they would take one brute with them. The Tat assured Jan that he probably wouldn't be needed.

Jan had spies watch the Tat from a great distance. The Tat knew they were being spied on, but didn't care. Jan's spies had to return, once the Tat moved into Ra territory. That's all they could tell Jan. Jan was going to wait until the Tat returned and see if they told her anything about what they were really up to.

So when the Tat returned without the brute, Jan asked if she should send guards to investigate. The Tat told Jan that the brute gave his life for the Tat and the matter shouldn't be investigated. Jan didn't want to push the Tat, so she let it go. Jan was going to quietly see if she could find out what happened in Ra territory that got one of her best henchmen killed.

The Hayee, Jay was the proposed mate that the Hellcat, Queen Ramala picked for her daughter the Ra, Ramala, La. La had one private meeting with Jay. After that, Dan and La had Jay fight some of their Elite Guards to test his fighting skills. They wanted to see if he was capable of protecting the Young Queen.

Jay didn't like being roughed up and thought they went too far. He took three hundred of his guards and left the main city of Ra, seeking asylum in the territory of Ramala's Warlord Benobu. It seemed La didn't like the fact that Jay left, without informing her. Spies told her where Jay was. The Hammer-Axe Six went to Benobu's place to find Jay. When they got there, he wasn't. That's when La, Dan and their forces headed for the Southern Jungle.

Jay and his three hundred guards moved back to Benobu's territory soon after the Hammer-Axe Six left Benobu's territory on their way to the Southern Jungle. He and his guards were able to avoid Dan and La forces by moving to different Ra territories. Jay's father and uncles had a lot of influence with all of Warlords under Queen Ramala and her cousin Wana, who led all Warlords in the kingdom of Ra.

Because Queen Ramala hadn't called for Jay's head, or even inquired about him, these Warlords let Jay visit, without letting anyone know. Jay and his guards were family. That's why he was able to move freely through Ra territory as long as he didn't get too close to any of the areas controlled by Dan and La's Warlords, or Special Guards.

Once Jay was back in Warlord Benobu's territory Stacia requested Jay meet with her. Stacia was Benobu's Great-Grand Daughter. She was also Warlord of this territory in La's name. She knew if La found out about Jay being here, that would mean trouble coming from La.

Jay didn't know Stacia was La's Warlord. He showed up at the designated meeting place, only to find that it looked like a military camp. Jay had fifteen of his closest guards with him. Only three were allowed to enter the meeting hall.

Jay barely remembered Stacia from some of the family gatherings. When he walked in he saw guards everywhere. Jay looked towards the front and saw Stacia, her sister Lynn and two of Stacia's brothers sitting in a throne area. That surprised him. Jay and his guards started walking forward. Lynn ordered, "Hold it!"

They stopped and looked at Lynn. Lynn said, "You three stay there! Jay, come and sit here with us."

Lynn waved her hand, showing Jay the table where she wanted him to sit. Stacia, Lynn and her brothers came and sat down at the table with Jay. Stacia's guards surrounded Jay. Guards also posted around Stacia and Lynn. Jay watched all of this. He got an uneasy feeling in the pit of his stomach. However, he kept a cool and calm look on his face.

Once they were sitting, Jay was studied by Stacia and the others. Jay decided to break the uncomfortable silence. He said, "Looks like all of you have become very important around here. But still, all of this just for me?"

Jay smiled, but could see that everyone at the table had serious looks on their faces. Stacia said, "Our Young Queen put me in charge of running this territory. Cousin, you have put me in a very difficult situation, by coming here."

Jay went from uncomfortable to nervous. He wondered why his uncle Benobu hadn't warned him of this. While Stacia was talking, Jay was thinking. Stacia said, "My Grandfather is very close to your grandfather. He is also fond of you. Even with that, I have responsibilities here. La has been looking to question you on certain matters that I know not of. But you had to know that, because you seem to be avoiding her. So, tell me cousin, why is that and why have you come here?"

Jay looked at everyone at the table, stopping at Stacia. He said, "Congratulations on your promotion! Had I known, I would have never put you in this situation by coming here. Whatever is between the Young Queen and me, its best you not get involved. I love the Young Queen, as I'm sure we all do, but right now we don't see eye to eye. One day in the future, I might gain favor with her. There need not be casualties amongst family members, because of this. I came here to get supplies. If you will allow that, I will leave as soon as possible."

"You already know the favor I can gain with La by handing you, or your head to her. With no way of getting out of here, why should I let you go?" Stacia said.

Jay knew he had to be smart or he would be, at the least, fighting for his life. The next words that came out of his mouth would determine his fate. Jay thought for a quick moment and then calmly said to Stacia, "Our Queen is young and sometimes finds fault where there is none. Like with your Grandfather, who she blames for certain attacks on her. Until she gets a little older and wiser, it might be best for all of us to have allies that can help each other. If there ever comes a time when any of you need not be found, I will help in any way I can. Family should protect family, even if it's from family."

Stacia looked at Jay for a moment. She said, "Well put. But you know I can't help you in any way. If La found out about that she might take my head. Go and see Grandfather. No guards will harass you in any way. It's best for everyone if you're gone, before next day comes and I not know about it. If I see you when next day comes, I will be forced to hold you in a dungeon and send word to La as to what I should next do."

Stacia didn't have to tell Jay twice! Jay stood up and lowered his head to everyone at the table. When he'd done so and was about to make a clean getaway, Stacia smiled and said, "Cousin, the meeting is over. Don't be so formal! Come and give me a hug!"

Jay walked over, hugged Stacia and then everyone else. As he was leaving, Jay remembered what Stacia whispered in his ear, as they were hugging. She whispered, "Be safe and remember your words to me and my family, in case we ever need you."

Jay and his guards re-supplied and left that very night. They roamed the plains closest to the main city and between the main city of Ra and the Six Lower Houses of Ra getting supplies and food as needed. That's where most of Ramala's Warlords had territory. That's where Jay could move freely without La finding out where he was. Jay still had to make sure he stayed far enough away from the Six Lower Houses of Ra that La and Dan's scouts wouldn't see him. Because the second they did, it wouldn't be long before La knew where he last was.

—————— CHAPTER 3 ——————

When the Hammer-Axe Six first arrived at the Sixth Lower House of Ra, after their encounters with the so called Lightning Jinn, the Tat and the jolly fat old man, they were exhausted. It was late in the day, so they ate and were escorted to some of the most lavish resting areas this House had to offer. Because of the earlier events, there wasn't much talking. They didn't even meet with the Elders and other important families of this House. Dan and La ordered everyone to get a good night's rest. They would deal with formalities, later.

When next day came, Dan realized the extent of his injuries, while fighting the jolly old fighting master. His stomach muscles, ribs, chest and shoulders were very sore. It amazed Dan that he could actually feel each of the twelve blows he received from the Shinmushee Fighting Master that Danaaa called Jinn Ja.

Still, Dan went to first Day's training as always. Although sore, Dan managed to push Yin and his brothers when he spared with them. He suffered through it, telling himself this was punishment for not being good enough to deal with a Shinmushee Fighting Master.

La and her sisters got up and went through their first days training session. They stretched, sparred and then went to get cleaned up. After that, they went to have first Day's meal with the rest of the Hammer-Axe Six and their Warlords.

Everyone had a good meal. Dan stared at La, until he got

her attention. He then he looked at Danaaa, before staring at the guards. La realized Dan wanted to talk about Danaaa in private. La gave Dan a slight nod that she understood. She then went back to eating.

Messengers from this Lower House came into the doorway and looked at Bo. Bo was Dan's Warlord. He got up, went over and briefly talked to the messengers. When he was done he walked over to Dan. Dan motioned for Bo to speak.

"The Elders of this House are questioning why the Royal family hasn't paid their respect by having first day's meal with them. They're wondering if they've done anything that might have offended." said Bo.

"Send word to them that no disrespect was done. Let them know that the Royal family always eats first meal together apart from others. Also, let them know that starting today and until we leave, we will regularly have mid-day meal with them." replied Dan.

Bo lowered his head and then told the messenger to deliver the message.

When Bo returned, Dan said, "I will be having a private meeting with my brothers and sisters."

Dan looked over at his cousin Yin and said, "That means you, too."

Yin already knew that.

"We need plenty of privacy and don't want to be disturbed." said Dan.

Bo, Ali and Hoban all lowered their heads and then left the room.

The Hammer-Axe Six turned their attention to Dan. Dan looked at La. La turned to Danaaa and said, "Do you remember the story that Grandma told us, long ago, about the Jinn Eco Jin?"

Danaaa shrugged her shoulders and said in her whispering voice, "A little. Sure. What about it?'

La leaned closer to Danaaa asking, "Are you and Ram the Jinn Eco Jin that Grandma was talking about?"

Danaaa looked at Ram. She then back at La. Danaaa shrugged her shoulders and seemed slightly confused.

"No. I mean ….I don't know…. I mean, who knows? I only sometimes call myself Jinn Eco, when I tell myself to. I don't even know why. I just do!" Danaaa said.

La stared at Danaaa. La was determined to get to the bottom of this, so she turned to Ram and asked, "What about you? Who tells you to call yourself Eco Jin Ram?"

Ram's eyes slowly looked at everyone there, before returning to La's eyes. Ram shrugged his shoulders, while staring at La. La could see she wasn't going to get anywhere with Ram, so she turned back to Danaaa.

La collected her thoughts and then asked, "When those Tat had control of us, once you broke free, your eyes and voice were strange to us. It was like we didn't know you and you appeared not to know me, although I was standing directly in front of you. I feared you might harm me. That's when I called out to you. Do you remember that?"

Everyone, except for Ram, stared at Danaaa waiting on her response. Ram watched everyone's reaction to what La said. After reflecting and checking her memory Danaaa said, "I remember killing the brute and then the next thing I knew, you were yelling in my face, telling me it was you, when I already knew that! And like I said, I always talk and look at things the same way! But, you already know that, too!"

Danaaa was getting annoyed and it was showing. It appeared that Danaaa didn't remember anything when her voice and eyes were strange to them. Still, La wasn't getting the answers she needed.

"Tell me, what Jinn Ja is?" asked La.

"How." replied Danaaa.

"With words." La said.

"But, I already did!" exclaimed Danaaa.

"I asked you about Jinn Ja! Answer me that!" yelled La.

"I said, How!" Danaaa yelled back.

"Just tell me!" La shouted.

"How is Jinn Ja!" screamed Danaaa.

"How should I know?!!!" screamed La.

Now, both La and Danaaa were confused. La took in slow, angry, deep breaths, as she stared at Danaaa. Danaaa stared at La wondering why La kept asking the same questions.

Dan could see La was angry. He knew she was going to press further, until she got answers. Dan looked at Danaaa and asked, "Hey Stupid, who is I Chop I?"

Danaaa looked at Dan. She then looked at La and Shaya. Danaaa decided she wasn't going to take the chance that they wouldn't understand what she meant, this time. Danaaa quickly stood up. She launched herself up and backwards over her chair. When she landed on the ground behind her chair, Danaaa continued flipping backwards, until she got to her axes that were leaning on the wall.

Danaaa quickly grabbed her axes and started walking back towards the table. Danaaa twirled and spun her axes in super-fast revolutions as she was walking. Don and Shaya were sitting in chairs on opposite sides of Danaaa. When Danaaa reached the table, they leaned back, fearful of Danaaa's axes. Danaaa stopped her axes, instantly, pointing them at Dan.

"That's me!" Danaaa yelled.

There was a moment of silence. Shaya and Don were still leaning back in their chairs looking at Danaaa. They both slowly looked at La and then at Dan. Dan could see that Danaaa was agitated. Normally he would push her further to see how far she would go. After hearing that strange voice come out of her and seeing those eyes that looked like Ram's, if not worse, Dan thought better of it.

"Alright I Chop I, calm down!" said Dan.

While staring at Dan, Danaaa slowly put her axes on the floor, next to her chair. She sat down, while staring at Dan. Dan didn't break eye contact with Danaaa.

Shaya, now over the shock of Danaaa's ax play, slowly put her hand on Danaaa's shoulder. Shaya said in a very soft voice, "Baby, don't take offense. We're just trying to understand. If there's anything you can tell us about Jinns, please do so."

Shaya's voice drained most of the building tension out of the air. Everyone's eyes, except for Ram's, slowly moved back to Danaaa waiting on a response. Ram was still watching everyone.

Danaaa felt everyone staring at her. She took a deep breath and calmed herself. Danaaa cut her eyes sideways towards Shaya and said in her whispering voice, "What I know about Jinns, well, I'll tell you. Jinns are very dangerous. They can't be dealt with. When you spot a Jinn, get as far away from it as fast as you can. Just like me and Ram did when we saw the Lightning Jinn. Jinns like to play games that they control and know all the rules to. If you ask the Jinn it will tell you the rules to the game it's playing with you with. If you break the rules of the game, Jinn has authority to proceed against you with all its powers, if it chooses to. If you follow the rules, Jinn knows you can't beat it at its game. Jinn are powerful, unpredictable and unbeatable. That old man we met on the road is not a Jinn. He is a Jinn Ja. He has a Jinn companion. His Jinn companion protects him. That's because Jinn plays games through him. I can tell when a Jinn is around. I just know it. It's harder to spot a Jinn Ja, because the Jinn is within and without its host. When Jinn are within, I can spot the Jinn Ja. Also, Jinn chooses humans, humans can't choose a Jinn. So, never call on Jinn. That opens the door to a game that you can't win, and probably won't survive. Remember this, Jinns don't care for humans and will kill, or destroy them, most times, if it has authority to do that. But, Jinn will protect its human vessel, only because it likes to play certain games that it can't play without a human host."

Danaaa paused for a moment and then, in a strange voice that was not hers, said, "She has told you enough. Question her not, about us. If you question her further, we'll play a game. If we play a game, you'll lose!"

Everyone at the table froze in silence, incredulously staring at Danaaa. None of them knew what to do, or say. They certainly weren't going to question her any further, after being told not to. They didn't have to be told twice! Heck, they didn't even know what to do, right now!

Ram was still looking at everyone's reaction to what Danaaa said. After a long and very uncomfortable moment of silence, Danaaa, with her eyes still cut towards Shaya, said in her own loud voice, "Look at Ram! He looks guilty, like he just got caught stealing cookies, or something!"

Danaaa's eyes slowly moved to Ram. Everyone quickly looked at Ram. Danaaa was right. Ram did look guilty of something, but they didn't know what of. A great relief came over all of them, hearing Danaaa's regular voice.

Danaaa laughed, first. Then, they all laughed at what Danaaa said. That broke the stress of the moment. A moment later, Ram joined in with a laugh that was so sinister and full of bass, it stopped everyone else from laughing. They all stared at Ram for a moment.

"What's wrong with you?" La questioned, as she stared at Ram. Ram looked at La without responding. La looked at Danaaa. Once La was sure it was Baby she saw, La said, "Time for next training!" everyone slowly got up, resigned to that fact.

La let out a sigh of relief when she saw Danaaa walking towards her. She wasn't sure if Danaaa would listen to her, or not. When Danaaa did, La decided to listen to that strange voice. She was never going to question Danaaa about Jinns, or Jinn Jas. La never wanted to see those eyes, or hear that voice coming from Danaaa. La hoped she would never encounter any of them, ever again, in this lifetime. Wishful thinking!

Dan, Yin, Don and Ram split up from the Ra girls and went to their next training session. On the way they were greeted by their many relatives from this Lower House. Dan barely acknowledged them. He was trying to process this new information Danaaa had given them. It only confused him further. Even though he'd been warned not to say anything, Dan couldn't stop himself from thinking about Danaaa, Ram and Jinns.

Dan tried to inconspicuously peek at Ram, from time to time, while they were walking. Dan thought that as long as Danaaa and Ram were on their side, they wouldn't have any problems. Dan thought 'What if we run into a Jinn Ja that Ram and Danaaa can't beat?' Dan stopped himself. He had to stop thinking about things he had no control over. If that situation came about, he would deal with it then.

They were almost at the training courtyard when Don said in a frustrated voice, "I still don't know what a Jinn, or a Jinn Ja is!"

Dan stopped walking, turned and looked sternly at Don. When Dan stopped walking so did Don, Yin and Ram. Don looked at Dan and said, "Well, I don't!"

Dan quickly said, "Listen to me and listen well. Don't speak of those things, until when, or if I find the answers. Don't bring on more trouble than necessary!"

Dan looked at Yin and Ram. He said, "That goes for both of you, too!" Yin and Ram nodded in agreement.

La and her sisters went to a separate courtyard to train. It was screaming time. There wasn't a pit for them at the Sixth Lower House, so they screamed in a courtyard, facing the main city of Ra. Shaya and La kept looking at each other. They both had unanswered questions that they didn't want to discuss around Danaaa. La motioned for Danaaa to come to her.

"Baby, it's time for your tree flipping training. We will be at the compound when you finish. Get a good workout and then come there." said La.

Danaaa did a quick nod of her head and walked over to two large trees that were about twelve feet apart. She looked at them for a moment, before she got started.

When Danaaa was years younger she started jumping from tree to tree, flipping one, or two revolutions in between trees. She was so good at it now that it was as easy to her as jogging. Danaaa took a running jump and launched herself off of one tree, flipping one revolution and landing feet first onto the side of the other tree, launching herself off of that tree flipping before she got to the other tree. This went on for about thirty minutes. Danaaa could have gone longer, but she was wondering what La and Shaya were up to.

After getting a good ways away from Danaaa, Shaya stopped, looked at La and questioned, "What are we going to do about Baby?"

"Let's get Dan and talk about this." La said, while cautiously looking around. Shaya nodded in agreement and they went to Dan's training courtyard.

When Young Dan trained he put most everything else out of his mind. If there was no instructor, Dan would push his brothers and Yin as hard as he could. That didn't always sit well with them. However, Dan was the oldest, strongest and fastest of his siblings. That was always enough to keep his them from testing him.

Today Dan was pushing his brothers and Yin extra hard, because of everything that went on the last few days. Dan felt it was his duty to make sure they were prepared for anything they might encounter.

Dan had everyone playing a game of triple team sparring. That meant each one of them had to spar against the others. First, Yin, Don and Ram triple teamed Dan. Dan was good enough that he punished the three of them. As usual, Don and Yin thought that Dan went too far.

Ram didn't care. He got a few good punches in on Dan. Ram was sure when it was his turn to be triple teamed he would get a few more on Dan. Ram was good with that.

Next was Yin's turn. He fought hard and held his own. However, just to let Yin know the seriousness of a real battle, Dan put some extra heat on Yin that Yin couldn't deal with, while also defending himself against Ram and Don. Yin got angry and when Dan called for the match to be over, Yin fought hard against Dan a little longer. Dan warned Yin and the others that when he said the match was over to stop fighting, right away.

Now it was Don's turn. Dan led the attack as always. The others joined in right after that. Don fought hard, but he too got touched up pretty good by Dan. When Dan called for the match to be over, Don threw a few more punches, before stopping. Dan gave Don a warning in the form of a long stare. Don angrily stared at Dan for a moment. Don looked over at Yin and then he backed down.

Dan could see that things were getting heated. He knew if those two didn't take kindly to his roughness, neither would Ram. Dan didn't care. He needed these three to be as tough as possible. They didn't need like him right now. In Dan's mind, this might save their lives one day.

Dan, Yin and Don moved closer to Ram. Ram went on guard. Dan always attacked first and this time was no different. Ram was tougher than the other two, so Dan attacked him with lightning speed.

As Ram was blocking two of Dan's swings, Dan was caught off guard by a powerful kick to his chest from Yin on his right side and a punch to his jaw on his left from Don. The only other person to ever get a clean shot to Dan's face was La.

It took every ounce of concentration for Dan not to crumble from Don's powerful punch. Dan quickly looked at Ram to guard against attack. Ram, upon seeing that this fight turning personal, backed away. Dan realized Ram wasn't a part of this.

Dan had less than a split second to see that. He had to duck under another one of Yin's kicks that would have connected to his head if he hadn't. On top of that, Don wasn't throwing training punches. He was trying to take Dan's head off with the most potent attack he could muster.

OH, Heck NO !!! That his younger siblings would dare do this pissed Dan off. He was determined to put both of them back in their places.

Dan avoided Yin's kicks, while blocking Don's punches, trying to close in on Don. Dan was first going to teach Don a lesson for clocking him on his jaw. Then he would teach Yin a lesson he would never forget.

However, as Dan was getting closer to Don, Yin's kicks were getting closer to connecting on Dan. Dan had to slow his attack on Don, just to give Yin's kicks the defensive seriousness they deserved. Dan changed his strategy to punishing Yin to the point that he wasn't a threat. Then he would deal with Don.

Dan turned and went hard at Yin, while using his defense to keep Don from connecting. But it seemed if nothing else, Don and Yin had some extra determination in their fight against Dan. Dan was now finding it hard to focus his entire wrath on Yin. For the first time ever, against his siblings, Dan had to stop attacking. He was forced to use his defensive skills, also.

That fueled Dan's anger and he dug deep and gave this fight the seriousness it deserved. Yin and Don were determined they were finally going to put a stop to Dan's reckless bullying. That took this fight to a level that had never happened between the three of them.

After another twenty minutes of fighting, they stopped. Ram watched intensely as Yin and Don slowly circled Dan looking for any weakness they could take advantage of. Dan watched both of them, closely. Dan still couldn't believe he hadn't put these two down, yet. He could taste blood in his mouth from Don's punch. Dan was determined to make them pay.

Both Don and Yin had taken some pretty stiff blows from Dan. Still, they weren't going to give in, no matter what. Dan looked at Don. Then Dan's eyes slowly moved to Yin's eyes. Without thinking, Dan's tongue touched the inside of his jaw where it was bleeding from Don's punch. It was raw and painful. Dan's face tightened a little as his tongue moved across the torn flesh inside his mouth. Yin saw that and an evil grin came on his face.

That was all Dan needed to see. He attacked Yin with lightning speed. Yin blocked two blows, but was hit with four straight that sent him stumbling backwards, before Don could get close enough to help. When Don got in position to take some of the heat of Yin, Dan turned and instantly Don was hit with a hellish eight piece combination that had him sucking air. Yin had recovered and moved in on Dan just in time to receive another six straight blows from Dan.

Yin was in trouble and Dan could see it. Dan was about to advance on Yin when he felt someone moving on him fast. He was about to teach Don a lesson he would never forget. At the last second he saw it was La.

When La and Shaya ran onto the courtyard, Shaya ran to stop Don and La ran to stop Dan. Dan drew back his punch and stared at La. La wasn't sure what Dan was going to do, so she quickly moved close to Dan, grabbing his arms and locking them.

"Dan, control yourself! What's going on here?" pleaded La.

Yin saw La had Dan locked up and thought he had an advantage. Yin moved quickly on Dan. That's when La let go of Dan and sent a lightning fast kick that connected to Yin's jaw, before he could move. In the same instant that Yin stumbled, La sent another powerful kick, just as fast to Yin's chest, while he was off balance. Yin went flying backwards and on to the ground. He was only on the ground for a second, before he was back on his feet on guard against La.

Yin had fire in his eyes. He was determined to make La pay for that. La squared up her body, pulled out her ponytail and went on guard against Yin. La said in the nastiest tone she could muster, "Yin, calm yourself! If you attack me I'll put you in the dirt, like I would a Shitmushee!"

"Get out of my way! It's not you I'm after!" Yin angrily said.

Yin and La stared at each other, without moving. Shaya ran over and grabbed Yin.

"Yin, don't do this! La's not Dan! She'll hurt you, or worse!" pleaded Shaya.

Shaya said a lot in those short sentences. Yin knew Shaya was right. La would go every bit as far as she said she would, if she had to. Yin knew how ruthless La was. He also remembered that he'd never come close to holding his own in a fight with La. Even though Yin was angry, he didn't struggle against Shaya. He didn't mind fighting Dan, but Yin didn't want to get into a death match with his cousin La.

Once La saw that Yin didn't want any of her, she turned and looked over at Don. Don wasn't crazy enough to go through La to get to Dan. La then looked over at Ram. He was sitting on the ground watching everything. La turned to Dan and said in a serious, but soft voice, "I come here to talk to you and this is what I find?"

Before Dan could answer, La turned and looked at Don and Yin.

"Me, Dan and Shaya are going to have a short conversation, without you! Go get clean up and calm yourselves! When you get back I'll expect both of you to have better attitudes!" La ordered.

La looked at Ram and said, "You go with them!"

Ram looked at La for a moment, before he got off the ground and joined Don and Yin. The three of them walked off together.

While Yin, Don and Ram walked to the bathing hall, none of them said anything. Don and Yin were still angry with Dan. Ram was quiet, because he always was. Yin was the first to break the silence by saying, "The next time I see Dan, he's going to regret the day he was born! Don, we have to think of a plan to get him back!"

Both Don and Ram stopped walking. They turned and stared at Yin. Don was angry at Dan, but Yin sounded crazy. After staring at Yin for a short moment, Ram said, "Let it go. It was training."

Yin looked at Don. Yin's eyes went back to Ram. Yin knew he was out voted.

"I just meant that next time in training, I'll fight harder. That's what training is for, right?" said Yin.

Don slapped Yin on his shoulder and said, "Don't think about that. Let's just go get cleaned up."

Meanwhile, right after Don, Yin and Ram had left, Shaya walked over to Dan. She had concern on her face. La looked at Shaya and then looked at Dan.

"Tell me Dan, what happened that things got so out of control?" asked La.

Dan told La everything. When he was done, La said, "Do what

you have to, so that they're in top condition. But remember, if you push them too far, they will resent you. One day that resentment might turn on you when you least expect it. Clean up this mess you made, next time you see Don and Yin."

Dan stared at La as she talked. He knew she was right. Dan didn't want to talk about that any further, so he said, "You said you came here to talk to me about something. What is it?"

La paused for a moment, because Dan didn't respond to her liking. Nevertheless, she could see that it wouldn't take much to push Dan over the edge.

"What are we going to do about Baby and, and.. …..you know, that thing that told us not to question her about it?" questioned La.

Dan took a moment to think. He really didn't know what to do. He looked around and then looked at Shaya and La.

"It told us not to talk about it, didn't it?" asked Dan.

"That's not what it said. It said don't question Baby about it. It didn't say we couldn't talk about it amongst ourselves." responded La.

Dan stared at La. He wasn't sure about this conversation. He looked at Shaya for conformation on what La said. Although Shaya was nervous talking about this, she put on a reassuring face for Dan, in order to back up La's words.

Dan looked back at La and then back at Shaya. He said, "Alright, what we know is it seems Stupid can't remember some things that ….that…..thing says. That thing also seems to show up when Stupid needs it most." Dan looked at La and said "I don't know why, but it doesn't seem to like you."

La remembered the look she got from Danaaa and realized Dan was right.

"What if it tries to harm us?" La nervously questioned.

"I don't think it will. I just don't think it wants us to question Stupid about it." Dan replied.

"What does it want with Baby and Ram?" asked Shaya.

La and Dan looked at each other. After a moment, Dan said,

"We don't have the answers to that, yet. Let's just watch Stupid and look for any strange behavior. If we see something strange, we can talk about it, later, when she's not around. And whatever you do, don't play any games with her!"

La and Shaya looked at Dan like that was the last thing they were planning on doing. Dan asked, "Is there anything either of you have to add?"

Shaya thought for a moment and then shook her head no. La looked at Dan and said, "You should probably stop calling Baby, Stupid. Who knows if that thing might find that offensive? We don't want to take any chances that we may offend it."

Dan looked at La like she might be right. Still, that's what he always called his youngest sister. So, he said, "Alright, maybe."

After flipping, Danaaa walked towards the compound where they were staying. Danaaa always attracted attention where ever she was. When she wasn't with her siblings she received even more attention. Danaaa was famous and everyone wanted to see the famous young girl who'd done all those incredible things.

Although related to her, many Hayee hated Danaaa for killing their close family members, in battle. They tried to see if she had any weaknesses they could take advantage of. So, as Danaaa walked back to the compound, groups of men, women and children stopped and stared as she walked past. Danaaa was well aware of them. She could smell and see all of them staring at her, even though she appeared to be looking straight ahead.

Danaaa thought about the questions Dan, La and Shaya asked her. She always called herself Jenny-Co (Jinn-Eco) and I Chop I for as long as she could remember. Now Danaaa wondered why.

Danaaa always thought it funny when she talked to people in a strange voice. Danaaa would stop herself from laughing, even though she wanted to. She never knew what she would say, or when she would say it. It just seemed to happen on its own.

She also would tell herself to go places that always led to her killing assassins that were planning on killing herself, or her family members. It was funny that she always found them when she didn't even know where they were!

Danaaa wondered how she knew certain information. Danaaa didn't know about Jinns, or Jinn Jas, until she was asked about them. She knew about other things that no one taught her. She wondered how she knew so much about things she didn't know anything about!

Danaaa started confusing herself. There was too much to think about. She was coming up on the compound. Danaaa told herself she would find answers to all those questions, later.

When Danaaa got to the compound she didn't see La, or Shaya. Danaaa looked at the guards. They didn't look like they knew where her sisters were. Danaaa sniffed the air, until she caught their scent. Danaaa turned and headed in that direction.

When Danaaa walked onto the courtyard where La, Dan and Shaya were they stopped talking and turned towards her. Danaaa walked up to them. She looked at each of them and then looked around.

"Where's Don and Ram?" asked Danaaa.

"They went to get cleaned up. Come, let's go. We have to have a mid-Day meal with the Elders of this House." La said.

Danaaa made a crazy looking face and said, "Elders, Smell-ders, who cares?" Shaya giggled and La snickered. Danaaa managed to put her sisters in a silly mood. La was still smiling when she said, "Come and let's get cleaned up, anyway."

Dan went to get cleaned up and saw his brothers and Yin outside the bathing area. He stopped and looked at them. They only briefly looked at each other, before Dan went and got cleaned up. After Dan got cleaned up and dressed, he saw his brothers and Yin waiting on him. It surprised Dan, after the earlier events. Dan decided if they could get past this so could he. Dan decided he would have to find a better way to push his brothers in their training, without letting it get personal.

The Hammer-Axe Six met with their Warlords, afterwards.

Messengers came and told them where they would be having the mid-day meal. The location had been changed to an outdoor courtyard, because so many members of this Lower House wanted to see the Hammer-Axe Six.

The walk to the courtyard was energy filled. It seemed the Royal Ra had reached a new level of popularity. People were everywhere. They were cheering the young Rulers all the way to and into the courtyard. Although, the Elder members of this Sixth Lower House knew the Royal Ra were popular, even they hadn't anticipated this.

Once the Royal Ra were in the courtyard they were fussed over by all of the high ranking young members of this family. Bo, Ali, Hoban and other Elite Guards weren't enough to keep the young members of this House away from the Royal Ra. Finally, the Elders had their guards get most everyone away from Royal Ra so they could make their way to the Elders.

When the Hammer-Axe Six got to the Elders they lowered their heads out of respect. The Elders of this Sixth Lower House were beaming with pride as they gave favorable nods to the Young Rulers.

The reason everyone from this House were heaping praise on the Young Rulers was because all reports had the Royal Ra butchering Shinmushee Butchers. Still, no one had heard about the Hammer-Axe Six's encounter with the, so called, Lightning Jinn, the Tat or the Jinn Ja, How.

While everyone was praising them, each member of the Hammer-Axe Six reflected on those encounters. It weighed heavily on their minds. Even with that, they had a nice meal with the Elders of this House and met with all of the most important young members who would soon be running most of the affairs of this House.

Because the Hammer-Axe Six were distant cousins to everyone in this Lower House and there were so many of them, they had to rely on emissaries from this House to re-acquaint them with who they should be meeting with. This was the political part of being Rulers.

La and her sisters looked at it as socializing. Dan and his

brothers didn't mind having fun and talking with large groups of their relatives. But other times Dan looked at it as a necessary, but annoying and sometimes unpleasant part of Ruling.

Shaya told Dan and La that the younger members of all the Hayee and Ra families were the future to running the House of Ra smoothly. Dan already knew this. He listened to Shaya and acted as if she was enlightening him. Dan decided that if Shaya knew so much about diplomacy he was going to use her and La to do most of it, leaving him and his brothers time to do other things.

La was very smart and could adapt to a situation, if she wanted to. She was going to solidify all of the families in the House of Ra through the young family members. If that didn't work, La was going to eliminate every one that gave opposition to her. La didn't tell Dan and Shaya that for obvious reasons.

After mid-day meal the Hammer-Axe Six met more young relatives. Afterwards, a private meeting was set with the Elders before dinner.

There were sixteen Elders at this Lower House. All of these Elders were brothers and cousins to each other. They were great-great-Grandfathers, great-Grandfathers, Grandfathers, fathers and uncles to everyone in this lower House. They had seven of their Warlords attend the meeting with the Rulers from Ra. Dan, La and Shaya were the only ones to meet with these Elders. The other Royal Ra were left at the compound.

Once everyone was seated, Dan got right to the point. He looked at all of the Elders.

"What do any of you know about a Jinn, or a Jinn Ja?" asked Dan.

Dan had almost whispered his question. That made several of the Elders laugh. When they saw La and Dan staring at them with serious faces, they stopped. One of the Elders was still smiling, tickled that they would ask, when he said, "Young King, stories about Jinns are nothing but fairy tales made up by a much older generation of Hayee that are no longer living. That's how old those stories are. May I ask why this interests you?"

La was offended that the Elders didn't take this more seriously.

"It just does! Now, if you have any information that can help, your King is still waiting on a proper answer!" ordered La.

Instantly, La changed the mood in the entire room from pleasant to uncomfortably serious. Another one of the Elders looked seriously at Dan and La. He said "It is said that a Jinn will grant a wish, or sometimes up to three wishes to a person. The Jinn makes that wish come true. Once the wish is fulfilled, the Jinn makes that person pay a price for what they wished for. The person thinks what they wished for will make them happy, but the Jinn reveals to them all the negative things that comes along with that wish. In most cases, the person feels they were better off without whatever they wished for and begs the Jinn to take it back. That's when the Jinn will ask for something. Usually, it's something of value to that person and they have to make a choice. The choice of living with the consequences of the wish, or giving the Jinn what it asks for, living with that choice, in order for the Jinn to resend the original wish. We know nothing of a Jinn Ja."

Dan, La and Shaya all stared at the Elder as he talked. This was nothing like the story about the Jinn Eco Jin they'd heard from their grandma and it was certainly nothing like what they'd seen. This actually did sound like a fairy tale to them. After a short moment of silence in which Dan and La tried to think of something to say, Shaya asked, "Are there any other types of Jinns that you know of?"

The Elders all looked at each other and then shook their heads, indicating they didn't. Shaya thanked the Elders and told them that they had been most helpful. The Elders could see that the look on Dan and La's faces said different. The Royal Ra left with more questions, than answers.

Word got to the other Lower Houses that the Young Rulers were at the Sixth Lower House. By the next day, the Sixth Lower House was overrun with teenagers from other Lower Houses. The teenager ranged in groups of nine, up to one hundred.

Each clique of teenagers had its core members. Those were the dominant and most popular ones in that group. Then there were the members that fit that particular group's needs. The last members were brothers, sisters and cousins that followed and they couldn't get rid of. Also, each clique had its own like-minded thinking, which was different in some ways to other cliques.

Now, you add up hundreds of cliques and you have, what appears to grown-ups as, hoards of unruly teenagers and children roaming around, freely. The Ra Rulers knew that they had to bring all of these different cliques together as one armed force, willing to fight for the House of Ra. Besides bringing all of them together, they had to find common ground that would bond these teenagers no matter what their differences. The Hammer-Axe Six already had the advantage of having celebrity status with the teenagers.

What happened next? One of the largest gatherings held to date. It lasted almost a week. The Elders of this Lower House met with Dan and La several times, trying to delicately put into words that the extended gathering was putting a strain on this Lower House and its resources.

After one week Dan and La decided to go back to the first Lower House. But as not to be disrespectful, they decided to visit each of the other five Lower Houses on the way. No sooner than the young Rulers got to the fifth Lower House, they were met by heavier crowds. Teenagers followed from the previous House.

All of these young high ranking teenagers expected to be treated better than anyone else, like they would be at their own House. The problem was they weren't at home! Protocol says you have to respect the rules of the House you're visiting. Rules are usually lost on unsupervised arrogant teenagers. There were so many high ranking young members from all six Lower Houses that fights broke out.

After a few heated skirmishes, the Ra Warlords took control. Everyone was separated and threatened that they should calm down. The gatherings at the fifth Lower House went on for two days, before the Royal Ra moved on to the Fourth Lower House.

Dan was almost nineteen years old and loved partying. It gave him a chance to release the stress of everything and everyone he had to deal with, including rules and protocols. On the way to the Fourth Lower House of Ra the Ra Warlords Ali, Tania and Bo met with Dan and La about security. They were concerned about the increasing crowds. They wanted to use guards and Elite Guards to keep the crowds more orderly.

Because he didn't see their family members as a threat, Dan told the Warlords to do what they thought best, without being abusive to any of the young Ra. Ali and the other Warlords were in agreement.

With the Ra army at the gatherings, everyone controlled themselves for the most part. Hostilities from previous encounters still smoldered and left a slight undertone of tension between some of the young hot headed teenagers from different Houses. Confrontations didn't explode because that would put the teenagers before Dan and La to be judged for their actions. All of the teenagers knew how harshly La dealt with situations. That kept the teenagers under a level of self-control that was acceptable.

Dan and La decided to slow down the partying. They needed to get back heavily into their training routine. They never stopped their daily training. However, training was less than normal.

It took the Royal Ra another four weeks to get to the first Lower House. In that time, Dan, La and Shaya questioned the Elders of each Lower House about Jinns. They got six different explanations from the six different Houses. And all of those explanations didn't match anything they'd seen of Jinns and the Jinn Ja.

They couldn't find a connection with all the different stories they were hearing. It was getting frustrating.

After not hearing anything they thought could help, Dan, La and Shaya needed a break from investigating the Jinn matter. So, after they talked about it with their grandfather and their main fighting instructor, which got them nowhere, they decided to put the Jinn investigation on hold for the time being.

——— CHAPTER 4 ———

Dan and La had a large portion of the Ra military under their control posted north of the Six Lower Houses of Ra. The Southern Jungle was south of the Lower Houses. They put the warriors, guards and attack elephants north of the Lower Houses so that Shinmushee scouts wouldn't see the military buildup that was going on.

Groups of Ra guards swept the plains around the Six Lower Houses looking for Shinmushee scouts. When Ra guards found scouts they tortured and killed them. That kept the Shinmushee scouts from identifying the Ra military camped behind the Six Lower Houses of Ra.

Supply routes were set up to the military camps. One supply route came from Yee province to Wa province and to the plains before the Lower Houses. The other supply route was from Yee province to the main city of Ra and then to the military in the plains. The military was well supplied for the invasion of the Southern Jungle.

With all of the political duties Dan and La had going on, coupled with their training, they had to delegate more and more duties concerning the coordination of the military. Dan wanted to put his Warlord Bo in charge of the military outside of the Six Lower Houses. La wasn't comfortable giving Dan more power there.

La bargained with Dan and got the compromise of Bo controlling half of the forces and Tania, La's Warlord, controlling the other half. Both would report to Dan and La regularly and give them updates.

The two Elite Guards that survived the encounters with the Lightning Jinn and the Tat where put as Governing Warlords over the Six Lower Houses. They were responsible for reporting to Dan and La everything going on in the Six Lower Houses.

Dan then had a meeting with La and Shaya. He didn't tell them what it was a bout, until they were sitting at the table of their private meeting room. Dan looked at La and then at Shaya. He said, "Shaya, I was very impressed how you handled our military during the Anduku conflict. You're ready for more responsibility. In my name, you are chief emissary to the Anduku and all surrounding territory. That includes Yee province and all areas north of Yee not controlled by the Japha army. Put warlords in place that will report directly to you. You will have one thousand guards and one hundred attack elephants to assist you."

La jumped up and stared at Dan because they never discussed this.

"What's the meaning of this?" La exclaimed.

"When I'm done, if you don't understand, I'll explain further." Dan calmly said.

Dan challenged La's intelligence and ability to understand. La slowly sat down and stared at Dan letting him know to proceed.

"Shaya, you will report your progress to me and La. Don't stop at the main city. We don't need mother questioning your motives." said Dan.

Dan turned to La. He could see anger building in her eyes.

"This move will allow us to concentrate on the Southern Jungle." said Dan

"What if I don't agree with this?" La skeptically asked.

"I'm firm on this. However, if you have any suggestions, I'll entertain them."

La's eyes slowly moved to Shaya and studied her. Shaya didn't seem overly ambitious about this. That allowed La to think of how this might serve her. Besides, protesting wasn't going to help.

"We don't want Shaya getting into any unsavory situations. That would be disastrous. Send Baby and three advisers of my choosing and you will have my full cooperation." La said.

"Consider it done!" said Dan, realizing he avoided a battle over this with La.

"Give me Ram and Yin. With them, success is assured." requested Shaya.

"They're all yours." Dan replied.

Shaya went to work, right away. She selected strong and capable Elite Guards to be her warlords. After coordinating her forces, Shaya left for Anduku territory. She already had the Anduku prisoners that made an attempt on her life. Even though La said she wouldn't kill them, Shaya knew La would if she found their whereabouts.

Shaya set up a meeting with the Anduku Elders and their young military leaders. While talking to them, Shaya had Ram, Yin and Danaaa with her. She told the Anduku what she expected from them. After that, she handed over the Anduku prisoners. Shaya gave a strong warning to the Anduku that if they didn't cooperate, fully, she would be merciless with retribution. Shaya said it was best if it didn't come to that.

Shaya gave a warm smile to the Anduku Elders, Warlords, warriors and lastly to the released prisoners. She turned her back to the Anduku and said, is a soft sexy voice that was not meant to be, "My Warlords will tell you what I expect. Any concerns you have need be conveyed, right away. It is of the utmost importance that my orders are executed, without failure."

Shaya's army then moved north and east of Ra territory taking over or making treaties with the tribes in those areas. Most times Shaya made treaties and put military outpost in those areas. The few times Shaya couldn't negotiate a peaceful settlement, Ram and Yin were there.

The Owakuba tribe had close to eight hundred family members. Six hundred were warriors and warlords. They lived on a large area of flat land that had very little vegetation and few animals that the Hellcats considered worth anything. This tribe was much smaller when the Hellcats formed the House of Ra. They were considered an insignificant military objective.

With her military caravan on the outskirts of Owakuba territory, Shaya took an entourage of fifty to meet the Elders and warlords of this clan. Shaya plus nine were allowed to meet with the Elders. Ram, Yin, and Danaaa were amongst the nine. The other six were Shaya's toughest Elite guards.

They met in an outdoor area. There were ten Owakuba Elders sitting on carved tree stumps that looked like stools. Twenty hardcore warlords and a host of warriors, behind the Elders, made a strong presentation of force. Shaya studied that, as well as the stern looks she was getting.

Shaya was very pleasant and presented what she thought was a reasonable arrangement. She told the Elders that the Owakuba way of life would be unaffected. The only changes would be several Ra military outposts here. Shaya said that if there was anything the Owakuba wanted to negotiate for to allow this to happen peacefully, she would hear them out.

The Owakuba Elders were old school. Men talked about matters like this, not women. For a woman to be sent here, was taken as a sign of disrespect. The Owakuba thought Shaya had a very pleasant voice. However, they weren't taking her seriously.

One of the Elders smiled at Shaya and said, "I don't know why you're here. If your Elder wishes to talk to us, he should come, himself. We have been respectful. Playtime is over. You're a very pretty girl. Take your friends and go."

Shaya clearly understood the Owakuba Elders. Shaya lowered her head out of respect and said "The Owakuba are a great people and have a lot of pride. I can see that. I am going back to my caravan. I will give you two days to send a messenger saying you want to negotiate. If I don't hear from a messenger I will take my army and leave. Thanks for giving me this audience."

Shaya lowered her head and walked away. As she was leaving, the Owakuba Elders watched. They all thought Shaya was a very pleasant girl. It was a pity that she would be waiting for a messenger, when none would be coming.

The Owakuba warlords and warriors escorted Shaya's entourage to her fifty bodyguards and then watched them return to their caravan. They set up a defensive perimeter and fortified it with as many warriors as they could spare.

While securing the area, one of the Owakuba warriors alerted his warlord that three Ra were approaching. The warlord told the Elders. The Elders told the Warlord to tell the Ra that they weren't going to negotiate and they should return to their caravan. The warlord took fifty of his warriors to give the Ra that message.

The Owakuba walked up to the three Ra. Their warlord, in a stern tone, said, "Don't come any closer! Why have you returned?"

Danaaa didn't like the way this man talked to her. Who did he think he was? Danaaa angrily yelled "I'm here, a for, to protect the women, children and old men!"

Danaaa pointed her thumb sideways at Ram and Yin. She yelled, "Them two's here for some convincing!"

The second Danaaa finished her last word, the blade of Ram's Hammer-Axe sliced downward through the neck and chest of one of the warriors. Ram quickly sliced through the next warrior and then continued on a path of destroying every warrior within striking range. The Owakuba warlord attacked Ram and was killed within seconds. Yin attacked a second after Ram did. All of the Owakuba warriors that weren't being slaughtered by Ram attacked Yin.

Just as Ram and Yin were finishing off the first fifty warriors, waves of Owakuba warriors charged and attacked. Ram butchered every warrior he could. Yin found himself if a life and death struggle, where one mistake would cost him his life. Yin wildly swung his hammer-axes in every direction, making sure that didn't happen.

Danaaa was also attacked, but only shredded warriors when she had to. Ram was tearing through the Owakuba, effortlessly, headed towards civilians. While, fighting off warriors, Danaaa moved ahead of Ram.

Danaaa yelled warnings to the female Owakuba that they should stay in a group behind her. As Ram fast approached, Danaaa realized the Owakuba were too panicked to comprehend what she was saying.

After putting down several more Owakuba warriors, Danaaa blocked Ram's path to some Elders and women. Danaaa yelled to Ram, "We don't harm women and children! But, you already know that!"

"I'm doing some convincing!" Ram's voice boomed.

"Well, convince over there!!" Danaaa yelled as she pointed towards a large group of Owakuba warriors. Ram looked at the warriors and then quickly looked back at Danaaa. Danaaa stuck her tongue out at Ram. Ram angrily looked at Danaaa for a second. He turned and massacred the group of warriors Danaaa pointed to seconds, ago.

Yin and mostly Ram slaughtered well over one hundred Owakuba warriors, along with several warlords, before a messenger was sent begging Shaya for negotiations. Shaya quickly came and stopped Ram and Yin.

Negotiations went well, considering all the Owakuba warriors that had been killed. The Owakuba and Shaya were thankful that no Elders, women, or children had been killed, thanks to Danaaa. Danaaa was also proud of herself. Yin was proud that he had survived that hellish battle. Ram didn't like that Danaaa tried to stop him from doing what he was told to do. Ram didn't think about the women and children he may have killed if it weren't for Danaaa. However, Ram forgave Danaaa for getting in his way.

That half day's battle and negotiation wasn't enough to put Shaya off schedule. Shaya's army move northward, east of the main city of Ra and Wa province, until they arrived at Yee province three and a half weeks after leaving the Lower House of Ra. Shaya's victories were so swift and complete that no one was aware of what she had done.

Shaya knew her mother, the queen of Ra, along with Dan and

La had spies in Yee province. Shaya quickly re-supplied her army and moved north and east of the House of Japha occupying as much territory as she could.

Japha scouts reported to their warlords that the Ra army was moving north and east of Japha with an army. This information quickly got to the King and Queen of Japha. King Japha San sent his armies east and north of where Shaya's army was, while Queen Japha, Jania Jett sent messengers to her closest ally, the queen of Ra, telling her of the Ra army's activities. Nevertheless, it would be almost a week before the message got to the city of Ra.

In that time Shaya met with King Japha, San and queen Japha, Jania negotiating a truce and agreement that Shaya would stop all advances. However, Shaya stated she would not concede one inch of land she's already taken. Because it wasn't originally Japha land, the Japha allowed it.

Shaya fortified those positions with warlords, guards and attack elephants. She was careful to leave a soft border in which the Japha army could roam, without either side becoming confrontational.

Once Ramala received the message from Queen Jania, she ordered the halt of all hostilities and summoned La and Dan to the main city. Ramala was surprised when Shaya, Ram, Danaaa and Yin arrived. Shaya told Ramala everything she'd done. Ramala was shocked, surprised and also impressed with Shaya. After spending a day with her children, queen Ramala let them return to the Lower House of Ra.

When Shaya and Danaaa returned Dan and La got a detailed account from Shaya. Shaya also told them how she planned to make that territory more productive. Dan turned and smiled at La, letting her know he'd made a good decision, putting Shaya in charge. La smiled back at Dan and Shaya because Shaya told La exactly what La's spies told her.

La wanted to replace Shaya's warlords and put her own in place. Dan wouldn't even entertain that idea. Dan knew La would recklessly control that territory causing friction amongst the tribes living there. So, Dan said he would give La total credit when they took the Southern Jungle. La agreed, thinking it would get their mother to publically announce La as queen, just as Dan planned.

All Six Lower Houses had several Warlords each. Dan put his two Elite Guards as governing warlords over them. All of those warlords were responsible for reporting to the Governing Warlords. This was all done by Dan so his time wouldn't be consumed with the day to day hands on running of these Lower Houses.

La's Warlord Ali was in charge of keeping the first Lower House orderly now that the Hammer-Axe Six were here. All the Warlords here would be reporting to Ali. No matter what extra duties Ali was given, he always made sure that the toughest Elite guards protected the Royal Ra.

Hoban was La's Executioner. He was a large brute with exceptional killing skills. He was most always with, or near La. When he wasn't he made sure La, Ali and everyone else knew where to find him.

With that, the Royal Ra were being treated like the Royalty they were. For mid-day meals and dinner the Hammer-Axe Six ate at the finest homes of this Lower House. Each of the richest families submitted request to have the Hammer-Axe Six eat at their homes. La and Shaya, trying to accommodate and solidify all of the young families, had their messengers accept every invitation. They put every family on a schedule. Everyone important at this Lower House, whether young or old, got to spend time chatting over a meal with the young Ra Rulers.

Even though the Royal Ra had small breaks in the day from training, political and military meetings, the most time they had was after the last day meal. That's when they would wind down and relax. Because of the new security measures instituted, no one could get within fifteen feet of the Royal Ra, without receiving permission.

Most times the Hammer-Axe Six would spend evenings together. Because they spent most of the entire day together, they would split up for short periods of time. They rarely went anywhere alone.

Usually, it was Dan, Don, Ram and Yin in one group and the three Ra girls in another. Sometimes Dan would take time to himself. At those times, Dan ordered Yin to never leave Ram roaming alone. Yin promised Dan, but when Ram needed to prowl alone Yin didn't object.

Yin and Ram would pick a designated place to meet. Yin would stay out of sight until Ram returned. It worked, until guards told Dan and La in private that they'd seen Ram alone on several occasions. Afterwards, men went missing.

Dan gave Ram a stern warning, that if he had to hunt people it should be Shinmushee warriors and scouts patrolling around this Lower House. Dan was just saying that to make a point. However, Ram took it as a direct order. Ram was very comfortable with his role in the Ra family dynamics.

Don, Yin and Ram devised many ways to separately move around by themselves. Dan decided he wasn't going to waste time on something petty like watching his brothers every movement. That was enough freedom for each of them to become more of who they really were.

La would get tired of her sisters just like Dan would with his brothers. When La needed to be alone, she would charge Danaaa with never leaving Shaya's side. La told Danaaa no matter what, if she was not around, Shaya was not to be left alone. Danaaa was a hardened soldier for La. Shaya wasn't able to persuade Danaaa, otherwise.

After returning to the Lower Houses of Ra the Hammer-Axe males were getting more attention from females. Security checks were a way for the Royal Ra males to feel up females under the appearance of looking for illegal weapon. It was harmless interaction between teenagers. Everywhere Don and Yin went, if La and her sisters weren't present, groups of girls insisted on a security check.

This evening was no different. Dan, Yin, Don and Ram were walking through the city. Girls came running up, but were stopped by Bodyguards. Don motioned that the girls should be let through.

Most of the girls formed circles around Don and Yin asking to be checked. A few girls lined up in front of Dan, while no girls approached Ram. The girls in back of the others just suspiciously watched Ram, without being obvious. That's how it usually went.

Don did a few security checks. He still liked doing them, but it wasn't the thrill it used to be. Don, always looking for new ways to amuse himself, saw a girl nervously watching Ram and the action in front of her. Don pointed to her and ordered, "You there, let Ram check you for weapons!"

Everyone turned and looked at the girl Don was talking to. That girl looked around like she didn't know who Don was talking to.

"Yes you, I'm talking to you!" Don said.

All of the other girls took a step away from the girl Don singled out. She took another look around and then focused her look on Don. Her eyes said she didn't want to be a part of this. Don, enjoying this girl's discomfort, pretended not to understand. Don looked over at Ram and said, "Ram, check that girl for illegal weapons! If you find any on her let me know, immediately!"

Ram looked at Don and then slowly turned and looked at the girl. The girl's head jerked from Don to Ram and back to Don. She stared at Don. Dan saw that and decided Don was going too far.

"Alright, Ram. Stand your ground. Don, you've gone too far, this time!" said Dan.

Dan looked at the girl and said, "Rest assured, you won't be subjected to any more of this nonsense."

Don looked at Dan and then at the girl like he was disappointed in her. The look in Don's eyes made the girl speak, even though she didn't want to. She said, "Please my King, it's what I want!"

Everyone was about to leave, but stopped in their tracks upon hearing that. Dan looked at the girl and said "You don't have to do this. Are you sure?" The girl nodded that she was. She then turned to Ram and said, "Please."

Ram looked at Don. Don smiled and nodded his head that Ram

should proceed. Ram looked at Dan. He didn't see any opposition. Ram's eyes moved to Yin. Yin's evil grin urged Ram to do it.

Normally, Ram wouldn't let Don influence him, but Ram decided he wanted to see what it was like. Ram had seen Yin and his brothers do security checks of women enough times to know exactly what to do. Anyway, how hard could it be? Ram turned and walked towards the girl.

The Ra, Octavia only came here to watch. Her cousins always knew where to find excitement. Octavia found it fun hanging out with the popular girls. Octavia never wanted to get directly involved, but wanted to be present. That's why she always stood in the back. She tried not to let it show on the outside, but inside she was terrified.

When Ram got to her she didn't move. However, when Ram's hands first touched her skin she flinched. After that, her eyes got big and fearful as she was aware of every movement of Ram's slow moving hands as they did a thorough search of her body. Ram bent down and continued his search. Ram had never done anything like this before. The first thing Ram noticed was how soft and warm Octavia's thighs felt. When Ram got to the blade high on Octavia's thigh she nervously whispered, "That's my personal protection!"

Most girls of this day and time had blades strapped to the inside of their thighs for personal protection. Ram's hand moved higher and brushed lightly across Octavia's forbidden zone. Octavia's hand quickly and instinctively moved to guard against any further intrusion. But, Ram's hand was gone from that area before she could completely react.

Ram stood up and looked at Octavia for a second. Octavia nervously looked up into Ram's eyes and then quickly looked down at his feet. When she did Ram looked over at Don and said in his unusually deep voice, "She's alright."

Don smiled and said, "Good work Ram!"

Octavia let out a sigh of relief and then quickly ran over to the other girls. The other girls fussed over and congratulated Octavia.

They admired Octavia's braveness. No girl had ever been brave enough to do what Octavia had done.

Octavia was still a little nervous as she peeked at Ram and quickly looked away. Although she survived the ordeal, Octavia wanted nothing more to do with Ram. Ram was still just as scary to her as ever.

Dan looked around to see if anyone noticed their antics. Once satisfied, Dan said, "Come on! We've wasted enough time here. Girls, get to your next training! And say nothing about what happened here today!"

All the girls chorused, "As you wish, my King!" and then they left.

Of course, that's not what happened. Word got around to all of the young girls that Octavia stood up to Ram. That was the way the story was told. That made Octavia very popular and slightly feared by everyone who hadn't witnessed what happened and was hearing the story second hand. Still, the girls who witnessed it thought Octavia the bravest girl ever.

CHAPTER 5

That same evening La gave Shaya and Danaaa time to explore the city without her. La loved her sisters, but Danaaa and sometimes even Shaya would become annoying. La would lounge around at the compound, alone, or with her cousins and childhood friends, Hestamiamay and her sister Falana.

Hestamiamay was called Hesta. Hesta was about the same age as La. She was a good looking freakishly strong tomboy, with extraordinary fighting skills. She also had an attraction to women. Hesta loved La and would do anything for her.

Hesta's younger sister was Falana. She was called Lana. Although, Lana was a year younger than Hesta, she was just as rough and tough as Hesta. Lana wasn't attracted to women. Lana was a controlled adrenaline junky when it came to fighting. She never started a fight but, she put everything she had into every fight.

La was sitting on some cushions meditating. Meditating was a technique her training instructors taught La to help keep her volatile personality in check. La had not completely mastered not flying into fits of rage. Nevertheless, meditating made La much more tolerable than she otherwise would be.

Without her sisters around La spent a lot of time thinking about her next conquests. The first was the Southern Jungle. La felt it wouldn't be long before she was ready to take that area by force.

La knew she would need an endless source of food, supplies and manpower to defeat the Shinmushee. The territory that Shaya acquired would fill many of those needs. La was impressed with the job Shaya was doing with her territory.

The second conquest on La's mind was being named Queen of the House of Ra. Oh, how La loved the sound of that in her mind! La wanted her Queen mother to publicly announce La as Queen of the entire kingdom of Ra. Still, La wondered if her mother would go back on her word of publicly announcing La as Queen, once La handed her mother the Southern Jungle.

Keep in mind, Queen Ramala never agreed to that. However, that's what La put in her own mind and believed it. La would get worked up over what she would do if her mother went back on that imaginary promise. La didn't want to do anything rash, but a promise is as promise, right? Even, if it was imagined by La's blind ambition. That was La's stance on this matter.

The third conquest in La's mind was Bo. La was almost nineteen. She was a late bloomer when it came to sexual urges. La was just too busy training herself to be a tyrant. Excuse me, a great Queen that her subject would admire. Yeah, right!

With that being said, every once in a while La's body was slowly letting her know it wanted to be dealt with. La knew exactly who she wanted to deal with her body. It was Bo.

Because Bo purposely derailed the interview to be La's mate, La had to be careful. Queen Ramala thought Bo was an idiot and not good enough for La after that interview. Young Dan didn't like that fact that Bo made a mockery of the interview. Bo was saved from Queen Ramala's wrath only because Bo was the best candidate to be Dan's Warlord. However, Dan was strict about Bo having minimal contact with La. Bo was good with that because although La was beautiful Bo didn't have feelings for La.

All of this made it hard for La to find time alone with Bo, so she could get him to like her. La was sure once she got Bo to like her everything would fall into place and they would have children. She would rule the House of Ra, while she and Bo lived happily ever after.

La's thoughts were interrupted when Hesta and Lana walked into the room. La's eyes slowly opened. She saw Lana lower her head and then dive on the cushions next to her. Hesta lowered her head, walked over and sat next to La.

"What took so long?" asked La.

"We checked on guards before coming in. Also, Hoban questioned us before letting us enter. Why does he still do that?" responded Hesta.

"Don't question me about Hoban. Just cooperate with him. He let you come here, did he not?" said La.

Hesta lowered her head. La lifted Hesta's chin and smiled at her.

"Enough about Hoban and protocol. Let's talk about something, else." ordered La.

Even though Hesta would sometimes over step her boundaries, she was good about not going far enough to annoy La. Hesta smiled at La and said, "I bet I can guess what you were thinking about!"

Hesta was well aware of La's fixation on Bo. La smiled and playfully pushed Hesta. Hesta said, "The way he's acting you're going to have to take control in order to gain an advantage on him."

La got a curious look on her face. She questioned, "What do you mean?"

Hesta stared at La and then said, "You're going to have to get him alone and get physical with him, starting with a kiss."

There was apprehension in La's eyes when she whispered, "But, I've never…." Hesta gently took La's hand and meekly whispered, "I know how. I can teach you."

La looked a little unsure. After a short pause, Hesta said, "When I'm done with you, Bo won't be able to resist you!"

La's eyes lit up. That's exactly what she wanted! She would try Hesta's plan if it would make her irresistible to Bo. La smiled and nodded in agreement.

Hesta stood up and extended her hand to La. La stood up and stared at Hesta. Up to this point La only experienced a mother's and father's kiss. Hesta realized that by La's reactions.

"Relax La, I'll show you how it's done." Hesta said.

Hesta gently put her hands around La's waist, moved close to La and gently pressed her lips on La's lips. La moved back slightly and looked at Lana. Hesta looked at Lana, but said to La, "She won't say anything. Isn't that right Lana?"

Lana nodded in agreement. Hesta turned back to La and said, "If she does, I'll kill her myself!"

La's eyes gave a cold hard stare to Lana letting Lana know if she said something and Hesta didn't kill her, La would. Lana lowered her head. After that, La turned back to Hesta, letting her know to proceed.

Hesta slowly moved closer to La and pressed her lips on La's lips. Hesta gave La a slow passionate kiss, without using her tongue. Hesta moved slightly back and said, "Now you try it."

La pressed her lips on Hesta's. Hesta moved back a little.

"You have to use your hands and body just like I did. Your hands have to lightly caress, while your body gently presses on his. That's how you create a special mood. Now do it like I did." explained Hesta.

La was a great student and there wasn't anything she couldn't master. La remembered everything Hesta had done to her and repeated it to the best of her abilities on Hesta. When La pulled back from Hesta, Hesta was almost in a trance.

"How was that?" asked La.

Hesta was caught up in that kiss and it took her a moment to gather herself. La's kiss was more pleasurable than Hesta expected. Hesta licked her lips.

"That was a good start. We'll keep practicing, until you're perfect. When you've mastered it, you can find the right time to use it on Bo." Hesta whispered.

La smiled at Hesta. They practiced kissing over and over, again. After La got comfortable, Hesta slipped her tongue into La's mouth. Hesta told La that was the advanced version of kissing and not to use that on Bo the first time they kissed. That after the first time she could use that technique, if she wanted to.

At first, all the subtle nuances of kissing were puzzling to La. But after practicing kissing training, La started to enjoy it. So did Hesta. Hesta enjoyed kissing La and hoped eventually they could take things further.

Lana tried to act as if those two kissing was normal. She knew the consequences would be dire if she didn't. She also knew her sister had a strong crush on La. Lana wondered where all this would lead to.

La was a warrior when it came to training. Training hard had always made her the successful at fighting. If learning kissing techniques meant getting Bo, La was going to put her all into this new training. And she did!

Meanwhile, Shaya and Danaaa were walking down the road, sightseeing. The toughest Elite Guards made sure no one got close to them. Danaaa was in a silly mood, so she kept pestering Shaya by slapping Shaya on her butt with Shaya's ponytail and sometimes with her own ponytail.

Danaaa loved bothering Shaya because Shaya would mostly beg Danaaa to stop. That allowed Danaaa to push and see what Shaya would do. Even though Danaaa was fourteen, she could tap into the child in herself and become very annoying.

This night Shaya was tolerant of Danaaa's pestering, because she was trying to think of a way to get what she wanted. Shaya's urges for sex had not gone away. However, she was monitored closely and couldn't slip away.

Shaya was seventeen years old. She started having sex when she was sixteen. Once she got some, getting more occupied Shaya's mind. But with La's watch hawk Danaaa with her, Shaya couldn't find any alone time. Half the time Shaya was good with that. Sometimes she could control her urges. Other times she couldn't or, didn't want to. During her weakest moments, Danaaa was there to keep her in check.

Shaya was walking and half ignoring Danaaa's antics. Danaaa hopped in front of Shaya and started walking backwards. Danaaa curiously looked at Shaya.

"Where are we going?"

"We're going to check on the guards."

Danaaa stopped walking. When she did so did Shaya. Danaaa gave Shaya a stern look and question, "Why?!"

Shaya's face got serious as she stared into Danaaa's eyes.

"You know guards sometime go places and do things that they shouldn't. Like when they came into our room at the palace." said Shaya.

"And like what they did to you!" Danaaa quickly responded.

Danaaa was referring to the guards Shaya had sex with. All of those guards ended up dead. Shaya tried not to break character when Danaaa said that.

"I'm not going to sit around and wait on them to do something else. That's why we're going to see what they're up to. You can sniff and see if you can detect trouble, while I take a good look around. That way, we can catch them before they do anything! Don't you think that's best?" questioned Shaya.

Danaaa stared into Shaya's eyes, while remembering when the guards came into their room, intent on harming them. Danaaa didn't trust guards after that. Danaaa would do whatever it took so that wouldn't happen, again. After reflecting for just a short moment, Danaaa nodded in agreement. After that they marched towards the guards barracks, although for different reasons.

When the bodyguards protecting the Ra girls heard Shaya say she was going to the guard barracks, they got nervous. They might be blamed for a negative outcome. They also didn't want to challenge the Number Two Princess on where she should be going.

One of the bodyguards sent another one ahead to make sure the guards were dressed and ready for a visit. Shaya was unaware of that. When Shaya and Danaaa got to the guard housing, all of them were dressed. Shaya and Danaaa inspected the guards. After Shaya got a good look at all of them, they left.

It surprised and disappointed Shaya that she didn't catch any of the guards half, or undressed. Shaya decided that she would try another time. Even though she enjoyed looking at the guards, it would have been more enjoyable seeing a few of them undressed.

To legitimize her actions Shaya questioned Danaaa as to whether she'd picked up on anything. Danaaa said she didn't. Shaya impressed upon Danaaa that even though they discovered nothing this time, that they should be vigilant in their watching of the guards. Shaya said that if something got past her, she would never forgive herself. Danaaa vowed that she would do her part to keep her siblings safe, as well.

After strolling a while longer, Shaya and Danaaa returned to their compound. Hesta and Lana had already left. When they walked up, La asked where they'd gone. She already knew, because her spies told her. La wanted to see if Shaya would lie to her.

Shaya was no fool. Shaya knew La had her watched, even though she sent Danaaa with her. Shaya told La they inspected the guard barracks and went for a short walk after that.

Because it was exactly what her spies told her, La didn't question further. She looked at Danaaa and then back to Shaya.

"We have a gathering to go to. Come, let's find Dan. I sent word to him that we would walk with them." La said.

Both sisters nodded in agreement. Danaaa did a quick hard jerk of her head to the left and then to the right. Her ponytail bounced high enough to land almost perfectly into La's hand. La grabbed Danaaa's ponytail and the three Ra girls left.

Dan and his brothers were on the other side of that same compound where his sisters were. The Ra girls got there just in time to see several girls gathered around their brothers. Once the girls saw La they quickly dispersed. La tried to remember their faces. If La saw these girls later, she was going to remind them of the proper etiquette when it came to her brothers and Yin. The Ra boys joined La and everyone went to the gathering.

Now that all of the Hammer-Axe Six were teenagers their personalities were becoming more evident. Even though they still viewed each other the same, all of them were changing. They were already Butchers of the highest caliber. Being Butchers was another reason why they were so popular, besides being the Young Rulers.

So, as usual, when members of this Lower House saw the Hammer-Axe Six and their bodyguards on the move, crowds followed.

La and Dan mostly ignored the crowds. Don and Yin watched the crowd looking at females as they passed them. Shaya tried to pay attention to La and Dan, while peeking at males that caught her attention. Danaaa and Ram watched the positioning of the bodyguards, as well as the crowd. These two were super sensitive to movement. Any false movements that could be interpreted as hostile would send these two immediately into action. That's one of the reasons La always held on to Danaaa's ponytail. There was no check, or balances for Ram. Ram was the attack dog, without a leash.

Once they got to the compound where the gathering was being held, they were led to a huge brightly lit courtyard. There were hundreds of people already there. Dan and La briefly looked at each other with smiles on their faces. This was going to be another fun night of partying!

Everywhere the Hammer-Axe Six went they were armed to the teeth with weapons. This time was no different. They were greeted by Elders who saw their weaponry and stared at it for a moment.

"Young King and Queen I would never suggest you not wear your weapons, but security is such that you don't have to." one of the Elders said.

"A King should never be without his weapons, when he's in public." responded Dan.

La smiled at the Elder and joined in with, "Enough of this talk. We're not here to talk about weaponry. We're here to have fun!"

The Elders lowered their heads, smiled and motioned with their hands for the Royal Ra to join them.

The Ra, Octavia was at this gathering. Octavia was the favored great-granddaughter of one of the Elders of this House. Her father was Warlord here. Her mother and sisters were amongst the highest ranking females of this House. However, Octavia rebelled against getting caught up in the politics of this House. Because, she was the youngest daughter, she was spoiled and mostly got her way.

Ram and Octavia saw each other shortly after Ram arrived. They stared for a moment, remembering their short security check encounter. Their attention went to others in the crowd after that.

Octavia thought about the stories she'd heard about Ram. She wondered if they were true. Octavia studied the rest of the Royal Ra for a few moments. She soon became bored with that and joined some of her other cousins in the festivities.

Almost immediately the Royal Ra were separated by their family members here. La and her sisters found themselves in negotiations with the high ranking females of this House. La questioned these females as to the importance of each member she saw or came in contact with.

Even though La knew the Warlords and who they were in charge of in the military, La wanted to know who the most important people were that had power without position. That way she could use Shaya to negotiate with them, if need be. Shaya paid close attention, smiled and asked questions that would give herself and La more information to work with. Danaaa watched La, the females and everything else around her, without saying a word.

Danaaa also watched Dan and her brothers. When she saw them leaving the courtyard with some of the females, Danaaa gave La and Shaya a hard look and then looked in the direction of her brothers. La and Shaya looked just in time to see them leaving. They were too far away to call out to them. La wouldn't do that anyway, unless their lives were in danger. In addition, this would be an opportunity to watch Bo, without Dan interrupting. La's thoughts were momentarily interrupted. It looked like a dance off was getting started!

Earlier, when Dan saw La was busy talking to the high ranking females of this House, he let the conversations with high ranking males move him and his brothers further away from his sisters. Once they were a good distance away, females started gathering around.

There were so many people that the Royal Ra men had to force their way through the crowds. That was when Don was at his best. Don not only had wondering eyes, he had wondering hands. While walking through a crowd Don's hands would find themselves lightly rubbing a thigh, fingers meandering along the curves of a round butt, or his hand getting caught in traffic between a females legs.

Don was so good at it that most times the females would take it as coincidental contact in a crowd. Other females, realizing where they'd been touched, would turn to see if they could identify the culprit. After seeing Don, most females figured it was him and didn't make a big deal out of it, because of who he was.

Don and Yin always got attention from females and this night was no different. Teenage females came over and pushed their way as close as they could. There would be no security checks if front of the Elders. However, because it was crowded there was a lot of inconspicuous touching.

Don was getting bored and it showed. These girls knew if they didn't keep Don's attention he would move to other girls that would. One girl realizing that, smiled at Don and said, "It's so crowded here I can hardly move. There's another room down the hall where we all can go, without being bothered."

That got Yin and Don's attention, immediately. Don looked at Dan, getting his attention. Seeing that Dan didn't object Don turned to the girl, saying, "That sounds like a good idea."

Several of the girls standing there chorused, "We want to go, too!" Don looked at each of the girls and then said, "That will bring too much attention."

The girl who originally made the suggestion said, "I have an idea." She pointed to three of the girls and motioned for them to move closer.

"We'll need a diversion. I want you three to go over there and start a dance-off." she said.

Those girls nodded in agreement and then walked away. She then pointed at two other girls.

"You two go over by that hallway and stand there. Don't move. When I get there I'll tell you what to do." She ordered.

These two girls looked at the one who spoke and then left.

"I want you to make your way slowly through the crowd. Go into that Hallway, two by two. When you get inside, wait on us." she said to six girls next to her.

Those girls slowly dissipated into the crowd, making their way over to the hallway. When the girl was done giving orders she turned and smiled at Dan and then at Don, seeking his approval. This girl barely paid attention to Yin and only peeked at him. She'd already seen Ram and tried not to be disrespectful in avoiding him, altogether.

Don, Yin and Dan were impressed. This girl looked and acted like a Warlord conducting a military mission. Dan and Don were smiling at her, while Yin had an evil grin on his face, anticipating what was going down. All three of them reexamined her body. It was tight, right and looked ready for a good wrestling, or a fight. The girl and her friends all were around twenty years old.

Because so many girls tried to get their attention, Dan and Don rarely remembered any of their names. It was the same with this girl. Don knew, just like himself, Dan and Yin didn't know this girl's name.

"What did you say your name was?" asked Don.

The girl had a beautiful smile, but her eyes had a deviously intense look to them. She looked at Don.

"I'm the Ra, Amalea. Everyone calls me Lea." she said.

When she said Lea, she wiggled her hips quickly, making her breast giggle, slightly. Dan, Don and Yin were slightly caught off guard by that short sudden quick movement. By the time their eyes had moved down to catch it, Lea's hips had stopped moving.

Lea saw that they weren't quick enough to see everything they wanted to see, so she said, "I said they call me Lea."

As she'd done before, Lea wiggled her hips when she said her name. This time, Dan, Yin and Don were quick enough to see.

When they looked back up at Lea she had that deviously beautiful look in her eyes that they'd seen, earlier.

Ram was the only one to see all of what Lea did both times, because of his field vision. Even though Ram wasn't looking directly at Lea, he could see her just as clear as if he was staring right at her. That's field vision.

Lea looked at Dan and then at Don.

"We'll be waiting in the hallway for you, if that's what you want." Lea said.

Dan nodded in agreement. Lea left after that. After she was gone, Don and Yin quickly looked at Dan. Dan smiled at them. These three couldn't believe the good fortune that had fallen on them. That was their interpretation of the situation.

Now, it was time to make this happen. They got serious looks on their faces. They looked over and saw that La was still in conversation and wasn't paying attention to them. If La saw them, she would scare the girls away. They looked at Ram like this was serious business. Ram stared back. Dan said to Ram, "Follow us."

Dan and his crew stealthily made their way to the hallway. Just before they got there they saw that the three girls had started the dance-off. The plan was working perfectly!

They walked past the two girls posted as lookouts. Dan turned around and saw that Ram was outside looking at something Dan couldn't see. Dan started to call out to Ram, but thought better of it. He didn't know if his sisters had spotted Ram. If he made Ram look in his direction, his sisters would know where he was. Dan didn't want to miss out on this opportunity, this night. He turned around and when he saw the girls waiting on him, Dan quickly forgot about Ram.

When Dan, Don, Yin and Ram were walking towards the hallway, something caught Ram's attention. It was the dance-off. Ram saw a Dance-off getting started out of the corner of his eye. That's when he saw Octavia join the three girls who'd started the dance-off as a diversion.

Once Octavia started dancing Ram stopped, turned and looked at her. He watched Octavia's dance movements, while his mind remembered how her body felt when his hands were touching her. That and the fact that Octavia could dance pretty good had Ram wrapped up watching Octavia dance. Octavia didn't see Ram watching her dance.

After going into the hallway Lea instructed the lookouts to alert her if they saw anyone heading in their direction. Lea then turned and led everyone down a hallway that led to another. They walked a ways, before turning into a room. It looked like a large lounging area to Dan and the others. They saw a table, some couches and chairs spread throughout the room.

Lea only gave them a few seconds to examine the room. She motioned for the girls to show some attention to Dan and Yin. Lea then moved close to Don

"Please, sit." Lea said.

Don looked behind him and saw a comfortable looking couch. He sat down. Don peeked over at Yin and Dan. They were occupied with girls. Don looked up at Lea, who was standing in front of him.

Lea smiled at Don, while staring at him with those devious eyes of hers. Her look made Don smile, without realizing it. Lea opened her blouse and pulled out her breast. She held them in her hands, presenting them to Don.

"Look at them. They're so firm, round and beautiful that even I can't keep my hands off of them." Lea whispered in a sexy voice.

Lea climbed on Don, straddling him, sitting on his lap.

"Go ahead, touch them. See how good they feel in your hands." she whispered.

Lea didn't have to tell Don twice! Don touched and gently rubbed Lea's breast. While he was doing that Lea started slowly grinding back and forth on Don's lap. She whispered, "What did I tell you? They feel spectacular, don't they?"

Don barely heard Lea. As his hands slowly rubbed, caressing Lea's soft firm breast, all he caught was the soft sexy tone in her voice. Don slowly nodded in agreement at what he thought he heard. Her breast did feel exceptionally good in his hands. They were warm, soft, yet firm.

Don was mostly affected by Lea's slow grinding on him. Her grinding sent a rush of blood and had Don rock hard. Both Lea and Don were aware that his hard stick was pressing upwards, underneath and between Lea's legs.

"Oh yeah, I like that." Lea whispered.

Don was so into Lea that he momentarily lost track of Dan and Yin. That rarely happened. Don peeked to make sure that his brother and Yin were alright. Both were receiving the same treatment. Don was about to give Lea all of his attention when he saw Ram standing in the doorway.

Lea saw Don looking at something behind her and quickly turned to see what it was. When she saw Ram, he looked like he wanted to join in the festivities. Lea paused for a moment, while watching Ram. She smiled at him. Lea turned and looked an order to one of the girls and then looked at Ram. The girl hesitated for a moment and then slowly walked over to Ram. She waved her hand, presenting one of the couches.

"Please." she meekly said, with her head lowered.

Ram saw the play that was going on here and wasn't opposed to it. He sat down on the couch and let the girl put on a show for him. At first the girl was very nervous. However, once she saw that she had Ram's full cooperation she felt more comfortable and put on a show for Ram that he enjoyed.

A few minutes passed when everyone heard footsteps in the hallway coming, quickly. All of the girls jumped off of who they were on and sat down on the couch beside them. They tried to look innocent, while making sure there clothes were back in place.

Just then, one of the lookouts came running into the room, with a panicked look on her face.

"It's Danaaa! High Pressure the Executioner is coming!" she excitedly said.

All of the girls jumped up and fearfully looked at the doorway. Dan, Don and Yin thought their behavior was over exaggerated. Nevertheless, the way Danaaa's brothers saw her was not the way others saw Danaaa. Others saw Danaaa as the murderous Butcher, High Pressure the Executioner.

—— CHAPTER 6 ——

When the Ra girl's dance routine ended, La looked directly at Bo and smiled. La had been watching Bo, while she danced. Occasionally, Bo would look at La. La wanted Bo to know she knew he had been watching her. When Bo saw La's smile he turned away. After that, the smile instantly left La's face. Cheers for the Ra girls' routine snapped La back into reality. A slight smile returned to La's face as she and her sisters waved to the crowd.

La slowly made her way over to Bo, with her sisters following. La lightly brushed her body against Bo, before turning and smiling at Bo. Bo took a step back and lowered his head.

"Relax, there's no danger here. Neither is Dan. Loosen up and have some fun. You do know what fun is, don't you?" La casually said.

"Yes, my Queen. However, I should keep an eye on things." answered Bo.

La gave Bo a sultry smile and said, "I'm sure you already are."

A moment passed and La got no response to her flirting.

"Shaya, you and Baby stay here, while Bo escorts me to the garden." La said.

Both quickly gave La suspicious looks. La grabbed Bo's arm and said to her sisters, "Don't protest, I'm sure Bo is capable of protecting me."

Shaya and Danaaa turned and looked a warning to Bo. Bo immediately turned, looked at and motioned for La's bodyguards to join them. La saw that and waved them off. She told them to stay and that she would be back after a short walk.

Once Bo didn't have a way out, he started walking with La. La stared a threat at anyone to look at her like she was out of line. No one did, until after La was gone. Then the looks were directed towards Shaya.

Bo and La walked down a hall and out into a garden. It had multi-colored flowers lining both sides of the pathway. The pathway led to benches surrounded by high manicured bushes. Once they reached the benches La slowly looked around the garden and then turned facing Bo. La stared into Bo's eyes and slowly said in a very soft sexy voice, "Finally, we're alone."

While looking into La's eyes Bo could see that although La's voice was soft, her eyes had an intensity that said she was in control. Bo smiled at La and then looked past her at the garden. He said, "It's nice out here. The garden is beautiful."

La slowly moved close to Bo, pressing her breast and hips firmly against him.

"Am I not beautiful, also?" La whispered in Bo's ear.

Bo took a step back and could see La was affected by their bodies touching.

"Of course you are." Bo said.

La slowly moved close to Bo and again she pressed her body firmly on his. She lightly pressed her lips on Bo's ear, again. La's voice was soft and sexy when she whispered, "Don't you like me?"

La forced her hips forward. La's heart was racing, while her body was heating up. La's actions made Bo hesitate. He could feel every inch of La's body where it touched his. La's body as well as her sensuality was affecting Bo's ability to think and do what he thought was right.

Nevertheless, he gently grabbed La's waist, while slowly backing away. La fought Bo's hands and forced herself back close to him. La's voice was soft with a hint of hurt in it when she harshly whispered, "You would reject me!"

Being tactful, Bo said, "You know King Dan would take my head if he found us together, alone. Besides that, you're Jay's mate. This is inappropriate!"

La impatiently whispered, "Dan doesn't have to know about us, until we see fit to tell him. Besides, I want you, not Jay!"

La pulled back just enough to stare into Bo's eyes and sternly whispered, "Don't you want me?!"

La's lustful eyes begged Bo for an answer. When he didn't she slowly leaned forward. La gently pressed her lips on Bo's mouth kissing him. She slowly manipulated her tongue into his mouth. La used every technique Hesta taught her.

La's attraction to Bo made La put an extra special effort and passion into this kiss. So much so that Bo was caught up in the moment. He couldn't force himself to pull away. Bo's hands moved around La's back and held her, firmly. While sharing a passionate kiss with La, Bo wondered how La learned to kiss like this!

Finally, Bo forced his mind back to reality. He slowly moved back from La. La's eyes had a trance like look to them as she stared into Bo's eyes.

"That was nice." La whispered.

"It was, but..."

"But, what?"

Bo hesitated and then said, "La, you're very beautiful and because of your attraction to me, I feel I am taking advantage of you."

"I don't mind! That's what I want!" La quickly responded.

After a moment of silence in which they both just stared at each other, Bo said, "La, I love you as my Queen and would do almost anything for you, but there couldn't be anything more than a physical relationship between us. You deserve more than that."

La's lip went crooked on one side and she looked down.

"So you're saying you could never love me as a woman, only as your Queen? The way you held me in your arm, tell me then, is that what I can expect as you Queen? If so, that will do just fine. And don't worry about Dan, or my Queen mother. All you have to do is be there for me when I need you. You can do that, can't you?" asked La.

Bo didn't answer. His silence was answer enough for La. After giving Bo a little more time to change his mind, La said, "I'm ready to join my sisters."

Bo lowered his head and said, "As you wish."

As they were walking back, La knew this wasn't what she wished. She wished Bo had the same feelings for her as she had for him. When they entered the courtyard, La saw her sisters. She made her way over to them, moving quickly, creating distance between herself and Bo.

Shaya immediately saw that La was annoyed. She fussed over La's clothes and adjusted then, although they didn't need it. That helped La focus on the crowd and everything else, while dealing with the rejection she felt from Bo.

Once La recovered and was a bit more focused, she looked around for her brothers. La remembered that they'd disappeared, earlier. If La couldn't get Bo's attention she wasn't going to stand around while her brothers were somewhere having fun.

La looked around once more and then they turned to Danaaa. La told Danaaa to sniff the air and catch their scent. La also told Danaaa to go and tell Dan that she was ready to go back to the compound. So that's what Danaaa did.

Danaaa followed the scent that led her down a hallway to a room. When Danaaa walked into the room where her brothers were, the first thing she did was scan the room. She took one deep sniff. She smelled lust and fear in the air. The look on Danaaa's face turned stern and very serious. All the girls in the room stared at Danaaa with fear in their eyes.

Dan, who wasn't happy to see Danaaa, said, "What are you doing here, Stupid?" Danaaa didn't look at Dan. Instead, she looked at each of the girls.

"That depends if these girls want to leave on their own, or if they need me to help them! Believe me, they don't want that!" exclaimed Danaaa.

Before Dan could blink all of the girls were up and running out of the room. After watching the last girl bolt through the doorway, Dan, with a disappointed look on his face, turned and stared at Danaaa.

"La said to come and get you so we can go back to the compound!" yelled Danaaa.

Dan, Yin and Don got up and gave Danaaa an angry look. She had interrupted their fun. With no girls, it really was time to go. Ram just looked at Danaaa. It didn't bother him that they had to go. He knew Don would find a way to put himself, Yin and Dan in another situation like this. Ram was good with that.

On the way back to the compound La questioned Dan and her brothers as to what they were doing. Dan, not thinking he was responsible for explaining what he was doing, answered, "We were having fun. No need to concern yourself with it, any further."

La only looked at Dan for a moment. She could see that she wasn't going to get a clear picture of what went on from Dan, Don or Yin. La didn't ask Dan anything else about what happened earlier this night.

Once everyone was safely back at the compound the Ra girls went to their sleeping quarter. They changed and got ready for sleep. La turned to Danaaa.

"Tell me everything and everyone you saw." asked La.

La and Shaya listened as Danaaa told everything she saw. La asked Danaaa if she could remember all of the girls there.

"If I can't remember all their faces, I know what they smell like!" Danaaa said.

La got a crooked smile on her face.

"Good work Baby! When nest day comes, we'll pay those girls a visit. Now, let's get some sleep!" ordered La.

Down the hall Dan and his brothers were having a similar conversation. Three of them took turns giving an account of their experience. In their minds these stories were just as great as some of the battles they fought. Even though they couldn't get much out of Ram, they could see he enjoyed himself, too. This night's events created a stronger bond between all of them.

Yin got a serious look on his face and looked at Dan. Yin said, "You know La's going to question Danaaa about what she saw."

"Danaaa didn't see anything. By the time she got there all the girls were properly dressed." Dan said.

"Yeah, I know, but she saw all of the girls. That's the problem. If Baby can identify them La's going to put pressure on them to stay away." reasoned Yin.

Dan realized Yin was right. Then Dan got an idea. Dan usually didn't remember many of the girls' names he came in contact with. However, Lea made sure she would be remembered. When Dan tried to recall her name, he saw her hips wiggling in his mind and her name came right to him.

"That Lea has very good leadership and organizational skills." Dan said.

When Dan said Lea's name that same image of her hips wiggling and her breast giggling came into Don, Yin, and Ram's mind. They knew exactly who he was referring to. They nodded in agreement.

"We can't let her talents go to waste. When next day comes I'm going to announce Lea as one of my advisers." said Dan.

Don gave Dan a suspicious look like Dan was stealing his prized possession.

"Because I have so many other duties, Lea will report directly to you, Don. By making Lea my adviser, we won't have to worry about La intimidating Lea, or something worse. I don't need to be involved in your meetings with Lea, unless you need me. Of course, you will keep me informed on any important meetings Lea might set up for the four of us with some of her colleagues. I expect those meetings to happen, soon and often. There are a few things that need to be gone over and explored, with those girls, if you know what I mean." said Dan.

Don's look of suspicion turned into a smile. He knew what Dan meant and Don was certainly the right man for the job.

CHAPTER 7

B ack in the main city of Ra, Elder Dan, King of the House of Ra, was just coming from one of his training sessions. Elder Dan got some really good work in today. He was putting in extra training. Elder Dan got in the pool-like bath to relax his muscles. He always trained hard, but now he was more focused.

One reason was Dan looked at how things went, recently. Dan had been challenged by one of Ramala's personal Bodyguards the Hayee, Monty. That didn't worry Dan. He would have dealt with Monty, himself, if La and her sisters hadn't attacked and killed Monty the same night the disrespect was shown.

Elder Dan thought about Elder Yin. It rubbed him the wrong way how the Japha twins, San and Jan, King and Queen of Japha, came for a visit. Everyone later realized the real reason they came was to kill Yin and take Yin's head back to the Japha Elders. Yin's head was proof that one of the Japha's most hated enemies was dead. As crazy as Yin was, Dan missed him. After all, Yin was one of the original Butchers.

Out on the battlefield Dan couldn't afford to think about his comrades. Here in the main city of Ra he could. While soaking in a nice hot bath, Dan thought about all the Butchers that died in battle, building the House of Ra. One by one they were getting killed. Now there were only six of them left. The six were the Syn, Jara, Ma, Mangler, Chi, Dina and Dan, himself. Dan couldn't help but wonder who would be next. He put that out of his mind. Dan was going to keep training and try not to make any mistakes that might get him killed.

Dan was snapped back into reality, when Queen Ramala walked into the room. Dan always faced the doorway and saw her when she walked in. Ramala stopped once she entered. They stared at each other.

"You didn't wear yourself out training, did you?"

"Not a chance."

"Good!" Ramala said, as she hustled to remove her clothes.

Dan watched Ramala. He could see his Queen had something she needed taken care of. As soon as Ramala got undressed she jumped in the bath. Ramala climbed on Dan and wrapped her legs around his back. Dan was standing, leaning with his back against the border of the pool-like bath. He entered Ramala and started thrusting upwards. Dan had firm grip on Ramala's hips, rapidly forcing her downward, giving emphasis to his nonstop bucking.

Ramala was hit with powerful shockwaves of pleasure. Her fingernails dug into the back of Dan's shoulders and neck, clawing, trying to gain some control, while having none. Dan had complete control, until after ten minutes in.

Queen Ramala was thirty-eight years old. She was at the peak of her sexual sensitivity. In the past, King Dan most always initiated sex between these two. Now, Queen Ramala wanted sex anytime she could get it. Queen Ramala was using Elder Dan to help find her sexual identity.

Ramala was being pounded ferociously by her king. She was in a super heightened state of animalistic carnal awareness. Ramala put her hands on Dan's chest and started bucking downwards in rhythm with Dan's upward thrusting. That's when Ramala took control of the action.

Ramala started riding Dan so wildly that his feet started slipping on the bottom of the pool. He quickly reached behind and grabbed the edge of the pool, clinging tightly with his arms and hands. That allowed him to plant his feet. Dan looked up into the sex crazed eyes of his queen and knew he would have to endure her fury.

Ramala had always been vocal during sex with her screams of passion. Lately, she had taken to name calling. Dan ignored most of it, until he couldn't.

"I got you now you no good shit for brains whore! Yeah, take that! What now, asshole? Yeah, you idiotic buffoon, take that! Can your whores do this? Yeah, asshole!" Ramala screamed, while riding Dan, thrusting downwards.

Dan never could understand what pleasure Ramala got out of insulting him. He didn't care. He was enjoying himself.

Dan was unprepared for what happened next. Ramala lifted her hand off Dan's chest, quickly reared back and one at a time sent both her open hands at Dan's face. His arms and hands were behind him holding on to the side of the pool. Ramala managed to slap Dan several times over.

When Dan removed his arms to stop Ramala he slipped and they both fell under the water. Dan, angered by the turn of events, lifted Ramala and threw her out of the pool. In the seconds Ramala was clearing the water from her throat, Dan jumped out of the pool and was on top of her. Before he could say or do anything, Ramala reached for and inserted Dan's member into herself. She slapped him, while slowly thrusting upwards.

Before he could stop himself, Dan's hands were around Ramala's throat. When he realized that, Dan let go. He received another slap for his goodwill. Dan grabbed both Ramala's wrist, pushed down with his weight and started thrusting down into Ramala as hard as he could. Ramala screamed into several orgasms. Dan didn't stop, until he roared himself into one, also. He rolled off of Ramala breathing heavily, looking upwards, focused on nothing.

Of all the things Dan had done to Ramala sexually, he'd never hit her. He'd thrown her around, but was mindful not to hurt her. He wondered if all the things he'd done to her in the past made her this way. Dan needed answers.

"What was the hitting all about?"

Ramala didn't answer, right away. She slowly got up and started brushing away the dirt and pebbles that were clinging to her back and butt.

"All of the times you've twisted, turned and pinned me in ways that I had never imagined, did I once ask you the girly question you've just asked me? Am I complaining about the dirt on my back? Quit whining and admit you enjoyed it. Things might get a little rough around here from time to time. So, toughen up and quit crying!"

Dan watched, while Ramala grabbed her clothes and walked out of the bathing room. No good was going to come from insulting his manhood. Dan decided to take Ramala's warning and be ready, next time!

After the Hammer-Axe Six left the city of Ra, the Syn, Jara had a big chunk of her day to herself. Normally, Syn spent most of her afternoons training Ramala's girls and sparring with them. That was reduced to about an hour spent training Tara's two girls, the Terrible Two.

Now that Syn, Jara had more time to herself she thought about Cat a lot, just not as much as she used to. The Butcher Catismallianne, Cat is what they called her, was a very close friend to Syn, until her untimely death in battle.

Syn also thought about the Butcher Ma who, after her twin brother Yin's death, lived in exile at the female Monastery in the Northern House of Japha. Syn would send messengers with word of what she was doing, to Ma. Ma would send the messenger back with word that she was doing well, but that's all. Ma never gave the messenger any real information to send back to Syn. Syn missed Ma and said she would visit Ma, soon.

What Syn thought about most was her last serious fight. It wasn't against enemy Warlords, or rebels. It was her last sparring session with the Number One Princess, La. That sparring session had become serious and lasted long enough that both Syn and La had to increase their level of fighting to trying to kill each other.

However, neither could. Even though Syn tried, she wasn't able to put La down, before the fight was stopped. Syn knew if the fight had gone longer she would have to kill La, in order to win. Syn was glad it hadn't gone that far. The Syn, Jara was undefeated in battle. This was the closest she'd ever come to being defeated.

Syn didn't know whether that was a sign for her to retire and just train others. She thought long and hard about that. Syn decided she was going to spend her extra time training herself to the max to see what she had left.

At the female monastery the nuns did a great job healing Ma busted knee. Ma's knee was severely damaged in a fight with Queen Japha, Jan. Ma's knee had recovered enough to walk, but she couldn't twist and turn on that leg. The loss of maneuverability meant Ma was done as a fighter.

Ma settled into the life of a nun. She worked hard and didn't complain. Ma would clean, cook and do other menial tasked that she hadn't done since she left the monastery, long ago.

Ma thought about her twin brother every day. Sometimes the pain of his death was overwhelming. It was hard for Ma to forgive her Butcher friends for not telling her the truth about her twin brother's death. That's the reason Ma rarely corresponded with Syn though messengers. Ma would listen to the stories Syn sent through messengers. She appreciated them more than she would admit to herself. Still, Ma was short in her responses to Syn.

Ma would always respond when the Ra girls sent messages inquiring about her. She knew if she didn't respond her nieces would come North causing trouble. The other reason was because of the bond she had with Danaaa. Ma loved every time she got messages about Danaaa. She would always send a special message back to Danaaa.

Mangler and Dina were the only two Butcher members of the

Death-Squad still living. Dina was in Yee province with Chi. Now that the army was rebuilding Mangler mostly trained and ate well.

Mangler was a large brutish Butcher. Like Dan, Mangler was aware if he slipped up, he would be dead like his comrades. Mangler trained hard and tried to learn as much as he could about military tactics. He attended military meetings whenever allowed. Mangler watched everything from the positioning of the guards, to their training rituals. Mangler always made sure he followed Wana's orders to the letter.

Because of his service to the Hayee Hellcats, Mangler was a hero in the House of Ra. That allowed Mangler to do what he wanted, as long as it didn't go against protocol the Hellcats set forth. Mangler was good with that.

Chi was the smartest member of the Butchers and Dina was the smartest Death-Squad member. When these two were sent to Yee Province they created a close working bond. That bond grew into a relationship, and soon after that they started having children. Right now they had two boys and a girl being the middle child.

After the Warlord Han and his family, Chi was one of the most powerful men in Yee Province. He might well have been only second to Han, but La, the Number One Princess, set Han's children as controllers of Yee Province in her name. Shaya now controlled Yee province. Still, Chi was very smart. He was always plotting ways to gain more power.

After the deaths of Cat and the other original Butchers, along with the deaths of Nana and all of the Death-Squad members, except for Mangler, Dina knew what it was. She knew the Hellcats were going to use the Death-Squad and the Butchers, until they were all dead, or useless to the point that they would be easy prey for the many enemies they'd accumulated over the years.

Once Queen Ramala sent Dina to Yee Province to help Han and Chi, Dina picked up on what Chi was doing, right away. Dina used her smarts to make herself a valuable asset to Chi. Soon after that,

Dina used her ass-sets and feminine skills to make herself someone Chi didn't want to live without.

Now that Dina was Chi's mate and the mother of his children, as well as his personal adviser, Dina was guarded and treated as one of the most respected women in Yee Province. Although aware that she had to be careful, Dina didn't think she would suffer the same fate as her fallen comrades.

Even though she missed them, Queen Ramala always enjoyed the times when her six children were out of the city. It gave her more free time to plot and execute sex missions against Dan. She also spent more time with her Hellcat cousins Hayee, Tara and Wana.

Ramala's oldest twins, La and Dan were in the Lower Houses of Ra making plans to conquer the Southern Jungle. Wana's forces were on high alert, ready to back up the Hammer-Axe Six at a moment's notice.

Ramala also spent time training Tara's daughters the Terrible Two. Yani and Tammy were Hell on Tara and most everyone else. They rebelled against almost everything Tara told them to do. It didn't help that Tara also had a young son to care for. That usually drained Tara. She didn't want to fight her daughters on doing simple task.

Nevertheless, it pissed Tara off that the Terrible Two would do anything to please their favorite Aunt, Queen Ramala. All Ramala had to do was tell Yani and Tammy to do something once and they did it. Tara resented that and was determined to get her daughters to respond for her like they did for Ramala.

After a valiant effort Tara got smart. She swallowed her pride and used Ramala to get her daughters to do whatever she wanted. That plan worked so well that Tara pawned her daughters off on Ramala more and more. Ramala didn't mind because she loved Yani and Tammy.

The fact that these two girls would always do their best to please Ramala made them easy for her. It was a match made in Heaven. Ramala would even let the Terrible Two sleep over at her palace, giving Tara much needed breaks.

King Dan didn't mind because he liked the Terrible Two and they liked him. It also kept Ramala from focusing too much attention on everything Dan was doing. Still, they didn't call these two girls the Terrible Two for nothing. If you weren't Ramala, Dan or their baby brother, these two girls showed you how they got that name.

Queen Ramala also had to train one of the most powerful women in all of Ra, who didn't know how powerful she was. That young woman was the Ra, Trina. Once Trina became the proposed mate to the firstborn King of Ra, Young Dan, she was instantly catapulted to a new level in the Ra hierarchy.

Trina spent time with Ramala learning how to run a household by delegating duties to maids and servants, being an administrator. Trina would never have to cook, clean, or lift anything, if she didn't want to. Ramala made her do those choirs so she could see what they were like.

Trina didn't mind learning to cook for Dan, because she saw it affected him in her favor. Trina didn't understand was why Ramala was making her clean and do other menial task. Didn't Ramala know that's what maids and servants were for?

Ramala explained to Trina that if ever a time came when she didn't have the use of maids and servants, she would still be able to make sure her King had an environment that was comfortable. Ramala stressed to Trina that these things were very important, if Trina wanted to keep a certain level of control in her Household and with her King. Trina gritted her teeth and although she asked why, Trina always did her best to learn the lessons Ramala was teaching her.

Queen Ramala found it difficult teaching Trina fighting techniques. Trina's family already tried to pull the warrior spirit out of Trina. They found she just wasn't as physical as most Hayee girls. Everyone was good with that, even Ramala.

However, after young Dan left the city of Ra, Trina begged Ramala to train her, until Ramala gave in. It only took Ramala a week of evaluating Trina to realize Trina didn't have the heart of a fighter. That's when Ramala asked her childhood teacher Deen and the Syn, Jara to help. After seeing Trina in action, they both thought it a daunting task. All three saw the determination Trina was putting into her training. It made them continue training her.

Trina hated how young Dan treated her in their encounters during the mating process. That was time for them to get to know each other, before they actually became mates. Trina saw Dan as arrogant, immature, self-centered and disrespectful. He was all those things and more. That made Trina dislike him and it also angered her, because Dan wasn't polished enough to do better.

However, after an encounter with Dan, Trina would go home angry and think of everything that transpired. She would remember the things she didn't like, but she also remembered things she liked.

Back when Trina was put in a dungeon for disrespectful words towards Queen Ramala Dan came and rescued her. Young Dan escorted Trina home, when he could have had guards do it. It made Trina feel special, like Dan cared.

So, even though Trina didn't like Dan's attitude, she liked Dan. And with each encounter she had with Dan she liked him more, even though sometimes she didn't want to. Also, the more time passed without seeing Dan, she missed him. Trina was training hard, all to show young Dan that she could be as tough as he wanted her to be.

On this day Trina was on her way to have mid day's meal with Ramala, as she usually did. Trina had eight battle hardened female bodyguards that followed her everywhere and watched her every move. She also had ten Elite guards that protected the eight female guards.

The male guards couldn't be with Trina when she needed privacy, like when she was bathing, sleeping, or doing other private female things. That's why Ramala gave her female guards. No matter what, at least four of Trina's female bodyguards were with her at all times. Ramala made sure Dan's proposed mate didn't make the same mistake of having sex with someone else, like her daughter Shaya.

Trina and her escorts made it to Ramala's palace. The Elite Bodyguards waited outside, along with four of the female bodyguards. The four females that accompanied Trina never lost sight of Trina.

They walked through the halls of the palace, until they got to the eating hall. Yani and Tammy bolted over to Trina, once they saw her. Trina's bodyguards lowered their heads to the Hellcats and Dan. Afterwards, they moved over to the waiting table, watching Trina from there.

Anne was at the palace learning her role in the Ra hierarchy, too. The Ra, Anne was the proposed mate of Queen Ramala's youngest son, Ram. Besides teaching Anne Ruling etiquette, Ramala was training Anne to be one of her top spies. Because Anne was always snooping, she took to Ramala's training, easily. Both Anne and Trina knew their roles and acknowledged each other with a smile.

Trina lowered her head to everyone in the room, just before the Terrible Two got to her. Yani and Tammy stared at Trina, scrutinizing her. Being Queen Ramala's favorite nieces, the Terrible Two would bully, or pester almost everyone.

They were different with Trina. The Terrible Two would stare into Trina's eyes and see that she wasn't a threat to them. They felt they could abuse, or even beat the snot out of Trina and she would give them very little resistance. They didn't do it, because of that.

Trina would always say something to break the silent stare these two were giving her.

"What have you two been up to?" Trina said with a smile on her face.

Yani just smiled at Trina, while saying nothing. When Yani smiled, Tammy did so right after that.

"Don't concern yourself with such things. Come, let's eat." Tammy said.

Tammy had a smart mouth, even when she was being nice. Trina ignored Tammy.

As the three girls turned towards the table, Tara's son, Jett walked towards them on unstable legs. Trina met him and picked him up. She hugged and kissed him. Little Jett loved the attention he got from Trina.

"Put him down! Don't spoil him!" yelled Tara.

Trina put Jett down then lowered her head to Tara. Everyone had mid day's meal and was relaxing, while digesting their food.

"Queen Mother, with your blessing, can I visit Dan at the Lower Houses?" asked Trina.

Ramala looked at Trina for a moment.

"Dan and La are training hard, making plans to take Southern Jungle. That means war. I don't want you to be a distraction to Dan." replied Ramala.

"I won't be a distraction! I just want to see him before he goes to war! Please, it'll be a short visit and I'll return!" pleaded Trina.

Everyone at the table turned and stared at Trina because she interrupted Queen Ramala. Ramala stared at Trina, until Trina lowered her head.

"Sorry, for my disrespect, Queen Mother! It's just that….!" cried Trina.

Trina's eyebrows furrowed in frustration. Now, Trina didn't know what to say.

"At this point, you can't even defend yourself properly. Even though you have bodyguards, you can't always count on them. What would I tell your family if harm came to you?" Ramala questioned.

"If I train harder, will you allow a short visit?" asked Trina.

Ramala looked unconvinced, but hadn't said anything.

"I'll be able to defend myself properly, in no time! I know I can do it! Give me another chance! You'll see Queen Mother, I'll show you!" yelled Trina.

Trina's face looked full of hope and desperation as she stared into Ramala's eyes.

"We'll see." Ramala said, unenthusiastically.

Trina stood up and lowered her head to everyone at the table and then left for her next training session. She was followed by her female bodyguards.

"Nice work! I couldn't have done better myself. Well, maybe." Tara joked.

"Thanks." said Ramala.

Wana, who was barely paying attention, took a drink from her cup, turned and looked at her cousins.

"Why are you giving that girl false hopes? At defending herself, she can only hope to be marginal, at best." she questioned.

"Wa!" Tara and Ramala chorused.

"You've seen her in training. I'm just saying!" Wana nonchalantly said.

Ramala and Tara couldn't dispute Wana on that, so they changed the subject of conversation.

Ramala put Trina through more strict training. She even had Wana train Trina in military tactics and positioning of guards. Trina didn't complain no matter what training Ramala gave her.

Trina was on a mission to see young Dan and wasn't going to fail. Ramala saw at fighting Trina was marginal, even with extra training. Trina did better with Wana's tactical training. Ramala thought that even though Trina might never be capable of defending herself, she might be capable of directing the guards protecting her.

Ramala was very proud of La and Dan. La and Dan begged for and got Wana to give them more Elite Guards, guards and attack Elephants. Ramala warned them how dangerous it was to go charging into the Southern Jungle without a plan. That they were heeding her warning made Ramala confident that they would succeed. Ramala later found out that Shaya used those elephants and guards to take over new territory.

The Hammer-Axe Six had already been at the Lower Houses for just over four moons, or months, after leaving the Hayee, Benobu's territory. La and Dan sent messengers telling their Queen Mother Ramala that they would be moving into the Southern Jungle in three to four more moons.

Ramala wondered what plan could take so long to perfect. Ramala decided not to push her children, if they weren't ready. She decided that if they were going to be at the Lower Houses a while longer, she would allow Trina to visit Dan.

When Ramala told Trina that she would be going to see Dan, Trina was ecstatic. Ramala said that Trina could only stay for ten days. Ramala watched as Trina listened carefully.

"I expect a full report on all of my children's activities when you return. If I am pleased with your report there might be another visit with Dan." Ramala said.

"Queen Mother, I will give a detailed report when I return!" assured Trina.

Ramala looked at Trina, unconvincingly.

"We'll see." Ramala replied.

Ramala sent Anne to the Lower Houses with Trina. Between the two, Ramala was sure she would know everything her children were doing.

Dan and La lived up to their promise of giving the surviving Wa some of their ancestral land to live on, as well as certain privileges. The Hayee Hellcats took over the Wa territory, while building their kingdom and killed many of their relatives.

However, none of the Wa were as privileged as the Wa, Yaya. Yaya grew up in the House of Ra with the Royal children. The Royal children loved Yaya and considered her their big sister. Dan and La threatened all of Wana's guards that no harm should come to their big sister. Entire family would be wiped out as a consequence.

That gave Yaya the freedom to roam the plains, freely. She was allowed to stop at Ra checkpoints to get supplies and free meals. Yaya only had to worry about accidentally running into Wana, or Tara at a Ra checkpoint. Both of these Hellcats wanted Yaya dead. If Yaya ran into either one of them, she would be killed before La and Dan knew it happened.

So, when the Wa wanted to visit their Shinmushee brothers and sisters, they had Yaya escort them to and from the Southern Jungle. At first, it made Yaya nervous. However, after seeing that the Hayee and Ra guards were respectful, or at the least ignored Yaya and whoever she was with, Yaya became more comfortable escorting the Wa.

Getting the Wa safely to and from the Southern Jungle also made the Shinmushee treat Yaya respectfully. She still got the occasional suspicious stare, but it never lasted long.

When the Wa made a treaty with the Ra, they told La that they left the youngest five back in the Jungle for safety. In fact, there were actually seven young Wa that the Ra had never seen. All of them were cousins within a year of twenty-three years of age. They were about four years older than Dan and La. Yaya fit in well with this group because she was a couple years older than them.

Three of these Wa were females and four were males. The females were Jami, Uma and Gia. Jami was then tallest of the three. She had tight muscles on an athletic frame. Her skin was the darkest shade of brown. She wore her hair in two ponytail like braids, that hung down just past and over the front of her shoulders. Jami was a natural born athlete and took to fighting very well. Jami usually had a calm demeanor, but could become easily irritated, because of her strict upbringing at the all female monastery.

Uma was shorter than Jani, but taller than Gia. Uma was slim, but deceivingly powerful for her size. She was not as dark skinned as Jami. Her hair had two braided ponytails, just like Jami and Gia's. Uma was quiet, unless her cousins engaged her in conversation. She always watched everything, looking for the unexpected, because most of her life that's just what happened.

Gia was slightly shorter than Uma. She was dark skinned like Uma. Gia had a powerfully built frame that was just short of thick. She was very quick and the best fighter of the three Wa females. Gia had a very positive bubbly attitude. She would talk continuously, if you let her. Gia most always found the positive in every situation. She always felt she was blessed.

The males were Tay, Zandu, Boku and Chet. Tay was as dark as brown could get. He was average height for a man. He had good weight but wasn't the size of a brute. Tay was in excellent fighting condition. He was strong, fast and powerful. He had a playful attitude. Tay would joke around, but could get serious if the situation called for it.

Zandu was just as tall, black and big as Tay. Everyone called him Zan. Zandu was an angry young man because of all that his family had gone through. He hated the Butchers, the Hellcats and the Ra with a passion. Zandu had very good fighting skills. He was hard to deal with and if he was angry, his attitude was worse.

Boku was slightly shorter than Tay and Zandu. He was slim and very muscular. Boku had excellent fighting skills. He was strong and quick, although he didn't have the power that Tay and Zandu had. Boku was easy going, until it was time to fight. Boku had a chip on his shoulder, because most of their family was killed by the Ra army.

Chet was about the same height as Boku. Chet wasn't as dark as his cousins. Chet had a slightly thicker build than Boku, but wasn't as thick as the others. Chet was chiseled. He was very fast, strong and had very good power. His fighting technique was the best the Wa had produced, so far. Chet was also easy going. Like his cousins, he also hated the Butchers.

This night, the Wa were relaxing after a grueling day of training and other choirs. It was China, Nicko, Yaya, Jami, Uma, Gia, Tay, Zandu, Boku and Chet. Yaya said she was going to visit her Ra family at the Lower Houses of Ra. Yaya said it would be the perfect opportunity for the Wa to get to know the Ra better.

At first, all of the other Wa just stared at Yaya as if she was insane. After a moment, Gia and Tay said they'd go. Everyone else did after that. Zan, Jami, Uma and Chet already planned on visiting the Southern Jungle. They said they would travel with Yaya and the others, until it was time to split. Zan said they would meet Yaya and the others at the Lower Houses three days after their visit.

China and Nicko said they weren't going. The other Wa knew that China and Nicko rarely visited the Southern Jungle, anymore.

They also avoided contact with their Ra Rulers. They were content living their lives out on their ancestral land. The other Wa left early days, later.

Everyone traveling through the plains carried weapons to protect themselves. You never knew when you might run into unscrupulous Ra guards, or bandits. The Wa were armed with Hammer-Axes and machetes.

The Wa passed many Ra checkpoints on their way. When it was time for the Wa to split up, Zan looked at Yaya.

"You remember to let them know we will be coming." he said.

Yaya smiled and nodded that she would. Yaya wanted to bridge the gap between both her families.

When the Wa got to the first Lower House of Ra, they were told their escorts would arrive, shortly. It was several hours before Shaya, Don and Danaaa showed up.

The Wa watched as the three Royal Ra approached. When the Ra girls got close, they ran to Yaya. Shaya got there a split second before Danaaa. Boku was a little nervous. As Shaya reached Yaya, Boku pulled his Hammer-Axe. Danaaa's ax blocked Boku's, as it was coming out of its holster. Danaaa, with lightning speed, sent the blade of that same ax upward towards his throat.

Gia quickly grabbed Boku and managed to pull Boku backwards. Danaaa's axes missed contact with Boku's neck by less than an eighth of an inch. It was so close that Boku's hand grabbed his throat, checking to see where he'd been cut. Everyone was surprised he wasn't. The Ra bodyguards quickly moved towards the Wa. Seeing that, Shaya ordered, "Everyone calm themselves and don't make another move!"

In that same instant, the hammer side of Danaaa's Hammer-Axe slammed into Don's chest twice, before anyone made another move. Don had drawn his axes and was moving to attack the Wa. After being hit in the chest twice by Danaaa, Don took a step back and looked angrily at Danaaa, before going on guard against the Wa.

Danaaa swung her axes one super fast revolution and then

slammed them back into their holsters. Danaaa looked at Gia with her hands in a quick draw position, next to her axes.

With one arm still hugging Shaya, Yaya put up her other hand, letting the Wa know to back down. The Wa were already frozen, staring at the girl who'd swung her axes really fast! Shaya saw the Wa staring at Danaaa and said, "This seems to be a simple misunderstanding. It's good to see that you would defend Ya. We love Ya, too. We'd never harm her. Now, I'll introduce everyone."

Shaya paused for only a second and pointed.

"That's my brother Don. He's second, only to the Young King Dan." she said.

The Wa all looked at Don. Don expected them to lower their heads out of respect. When they didn't Don just stared at them. The Wa didn't know that they should lower their head to Don as a show of respect for his high rank. Shaya didn't make a big deal out of it.

"Here, you show respect by lowering your heads and raising them when you are introduced to anyone important. Here, that's everyone you meet." Shaya explained.

Shaya pointed to Danaaa, while still looking at the Wa.

"That's my sister. I call her Baby. You call her the Number Three Princess. She's High Pressure, the Executioner. I'm the Number Two Princess, Shaya. Baby loves me and won't let anyone harm me. She can swing her axes really fast! You be very careful with movements of any weapons that might be interpreted as a threat. She eliminates all threats, without hesitation!" Shaya said.

All of the Wa lowered their heads and then raised them to Shaya. Danaaa, while staring in the direction of the Wa, but not directly at any of them, yelled, "I Chop I!"

Upon hearing Shaya call Danaaa High Pressure the Executioner, the young Wa stared at Danaaa. They realized this was the girl that Nicko said killed the Wa, Massiko inside of a second. They didn't believe Nicko, then. However, after seeing Danaaa's quickness, they believed it, now.

"She's really fast!" Gia said.

"How fast she is, you don't even know! It's a good thing for him you were fast. She rarely misses!"

Gia lowered her head and raised it. Shaya smiled at her.

"Where's La and everybody else?" asked Yaya.

"Come, I'll take you to them." said Shaya.

On the way to see La and Dan Yaya found herself staring at Shaya, Danaaa and Don. They looked so different to her. The Royal Ra girls still had ponytails that reached down the back of their knees. Shaya looked regal and comfortably in control, while ordering guards. Shaya didn't have that clingy, unsure look that Yaya remembered.

The once playful Don looked like a hardened Butcher to Yaya. Don looked like he wanted to kill her Wa family when Shaya introduced them and they didn't lower their heads out of respect. She was glad he hadn't.

She looked at Danaaa. Danaaa looked strong and very healthy. Danaaa still had her baby face but she looked more mature. Yaya remembered that Danaaa was the most physical of her Ra sisters. Yaya never imagined Danaaa would become this great Executioner she kept hearing about. Yaya was there and saw when Danaaa killed Massiko and remembered she'd never seen anyone move so fast.

While they were walking Danaaa noticed Yaya was peeking at her, inconspicuously. Danaaa, who was walking next to and slightly ahead of Yaya, did a quick and sudden movement of her head and body to the left and then to the right. Danaaa's long ponytail slapped Yaya's butt. Danaaa then quickly moved in front of Yaya, while turning her body in one super fast revolution. Her ponytail slapped across Yaya's butt, again. Danaaa turned and started walking backwards in front of Yaya looking directly into Yaya's eyes.

"Now, you don't have to peek at me. You can look directly at me, until you see what you're trying to see!" yelled Danaaa.

Yaya smiled at Danaaa. She did look directly into Danaaa's eyes. It slightly scared Yaya, because even though she saw the playful Danaaa she'd always known, Yaya also saw a true Butcher. Something she'd never seen in Danaaa's eyes, before.

Shaya thought Danaaa was being annoying.

"Enough, Baby! Don't get started!" Shaya warned.

Danaaa quickly turned, moving closer to Shaya. Now she was facing the same direction as everyone else. Danaaa jerked her head and body. Her ponytail slapped Shaya's butt with pretty good force.

"Don't tell me what to do! Quit acting like La!" yelled Danaaa.

Shaya didn't respond. When she didn't, Danaaa moved closer to Shaya and leaned on Shaya's shoulder while they were walking.

"If you're going to act like La, I'll act like you!" yelled Danaaa.

Danaaa was starting to annoy Shaya. Shaya knew if she moved her shoulder Danaaa would find some other way to pester her. Shaya refused to react. Danaaa, seeing Shaya wasn't affected, only leaned on Shaya's shoulder a short while longer, before standing straight up and walking.

To the Wa, Danaaa acted more like a brat, than an Executioner. Even still, they couldn't deny how quick she was with her axes. The Wa watched and thought this silliness to be strange behavior for people that carried the reputation for being ruthless Butchers.

Shaya showed Yaya and her Wa family where they would be staying while visiting this Lower House. After that they went to see La and Dan. La never trusted the Wa. They were former enemies of her parents. She was less than cordial and less than polite, for Yaya's sake. La refused to let Yaya's family meet her at the Royal compound. La told Shaya that she would be at one of the courtyards.

When Shaya arrived with the Wa, Dan and La were already there. Yaya walked up to La and Dan. Hoban was standing next to La and moved his arm in front of her. La motioned with her hand for Hoban to move back, so he did. La and Dan moved closer to Yaya. She hugged them one at a time. Dan smiled at Yaya. Yaya noticed that La barely held her when they hugged. They both pulled back and looked at each other. Yaya could see a masked suspicion in La's eyes. La looked past Yaya.

"Your guest, tell me, who are they?" questioned La.

"These are some of my cousins that you haven't met." explained Yaya.

Yaya introduced them to La and Dan. La and Dan mostly ignored the Wa. The Wa felt awkward because Dan and La weren't as friendly as Shaya.

"Where's Yin and Ram?" asked Yaya.

"They'll be at the feast we're having later. I'm sure you'll see them there." La said.

"Ya you're free to walk around, but don't go too far. Always accompany your cousins if they want to explore the city. Our guards know you, but don't know them." said Dan.

Yaya nodded in agreement. Dan looked at Don.

"We have business to attend to. We'll see everyone, later." he said.

La looked at Dan and then at Shaya.

"Shaya, escort our guest to their quarters and then come see me, right away. I'll be at the compound. Baby, go with Shaya." ordered La.

La paused for a second and then La left. Yaya could feel a strange distance that had developed from not being around La. She hoped this visit would bring them close, again.

When the other young Wa got to the Southern Jungle they first paid respects to the local Elders. These Elders were the ones who accepted them into the Southern Jungle, allowing them to live and be trained there. The young Wa men were very grateful.

Afterwards, the Wa went to see the Shinmushee family they lived with while here. The family consisted of nine, having four boys and three girls. All of the children were older than the young Wa. Nevertheless, they treated the Wa very well. The Wa loved their big brothers and sisters.

The Wa saw the youngest girls, first. They all hugged. The girls started talking and soon saw the mother and father. They got down on their knees out of respect and then ran to greet them. The other sister arrived, later.

After a while the Wa realized that none of the brothers were here. They inquired and were told the brothers were out on scouting missions and weren't expected back for several days.

The Wa spent two days visiting the Shinmushee. They stayed as late as they could, hoping to see their Shinmushee brothers. They would try to see them, after visiting the Ra stronghold called the First Lower House of Ra.

It was about seven hours travel time from the Southern Jungle to the First Lower House. Maybe they would see their Shinmushee brothers on the way. Soon, they started seeing Ra scouts off in the distance.

Zan stopped walking. The others stopped and looked around, before looking at Zan. Once Zan had their attention he said, "Yaya said her Ra family would get word to the Ra guards that we're coming. We don't know if that happened. If it looks like there's going to be trouble pull your axes. Defend yourself at all cost, because that's what I'm going to do!"

They looked at each other and nodded in agreement. Everyone was on edge after seeing Ra scouts. Several groups of Ra scouts watched the Wa, while keeping their distance. The Wa kept moving forward.

Ra scouts were joined by several Ra warriors. The Wa went on high alert. The scouts and warriors moved in front of the Wa. When they were close enough to get a good look at the Wa they stopped. The Wa stopped and waited. They weren't going to pull their weapons, until they were sure they were going to be attacked. It was a very tense moment as both sides stared at each other.

"You look like Wa. Are you?" a warrior asked.

The Wa nodded that they were.

"Come, you are guest of the young Ra Rulers. They are expecting you." he said.

Relief came over the Wa. They wouldn't have to carve up these warriors and scouts. However, the Wa watched for any sign of attack.

The Ra warriors also watched the Wa, closely, because they had weapons. While walking, everyone suspiciously looked at each other. One false move from either side, real or imagined and there would be a bloodbath.

When the four Wa got to the first checkpoint they were examined and scrutinized further. The Wa felt they were being treated less than hospitable. The Ra guards at the checkpoint didn't care about how they treated the Wa. Their job was to make sure no threats made it past them. Even though the guards were callous, they weren't abusive. If Ra guards didn't harm the Wa, whatever they did would be seen as them doing their job.

As they got closer to the First Lower Houses the guards were less abusive. The Wa still got suspicious looks, but they were short and to the point. After that, the guards were almost pleasant. The Wa were even offered food and water, before continuing onward. The Wa respectfully declined. They weren't going to eat anything, until they saw Yaya and the other Wa.

The Wa were held outside the last checkpoint to the First Lower House. They were told their escorts would arrive soon. Jami smiled at one of the guard.

"Who is escorting us?" she asked.

The guards suspiciously looked at all the Wa, before focusing their attention to Jami. After a moment, the guard she questioned said, "You'll see soon enough."

None of the Wa liked that answer. Zan stared at the guard who'd responded to Jami. Jami saw that and quickly grabbed Zan's arm, pulling him away from the guards, facing her. Jami smiled at Zan.

"Don't get impatient. I'm sure whoever they send will be here soon enough." Jami said.

—— CHAPTER 8 ——

Trina and Anne had an uneventful trip to the Lower House of Ra. They rode on a plat formed elephant surrounded by guards on other plat formed elephants. They still had a clear view of the plains ahead of them.

Trina and Anne had become close because of the time they spent at Ramala's palace. Both were being trained on how to be good mates and mothers. They were also being trained as spies for Ramala. Over time, Trina was barely sufficient at spying. That's because Trina was only interested in finding out about things that interested her.

Anne was a natural at snooping and wanted to hear and see anything she could. She would hide out of site just to hear a private conversation. Anne was very stealthy when it came to that. Anne excelled enough to impress all three Hellcats.

Trina liked Anne because she was a wealth of information. Anne liked Trina because even though Trina was older and had more rank, she never used it on Anne. Anne also found that Trina was also had good information on things that interested Trina. Right now, Trina was mostly focused on young Dan.

After traveling the plains for a while, Trina's caravan came upon the military camp that was before the Lower Houses. It was immense. Both girls studied and took in as much information as possible, before they reached the camp. They discussed what they saw, until they were met by guards from the camp. The two girls stopped talking just as ten guards arrived.

The guards lowered their heads out of respect. One of the guards stepped forward.

"I sent a messenger letting young King Dan know of your arrival. King Dan will send word when he is ready for your caravan to arrive" the guard said.

Trina stared at the guard. After Ramala's training Trina was confident in her high rank, even though she didn't flaunt it. But if she had to use it, she would. Trina hadn't come here to wait at a check post, like a common visitor. She came here to see Dan.

Trina looked away from the guard, with her head arrogantly high.

"Listen well. I am here on authority of Queen Ramala. I'm sure you're doing what you think your King wants. Continue to do well for your King, but don't get in my way. Now, move aside. I will not be held up by the likes of you." Trina said.

The guards only looked at Trina for a moment, before slowly moving aside and motioning for other guards to let Trina's caravan through. Both Anne and Trina saw guards and messengers from the military camp moving quickly ahead of them, towards the First Lower House. Both girls gave each other a curious look. They watched the guards, for a moment, until their caravan started moving.

As the caravan moved forward Anne turned and looked at Trina. Anne marveled at the way Trina was assertive with the guards. Anne admired Trina for that.

Trina felt Anne looking at her. She turned and looked at Anne.

"For a moment I thought we were going to be stuck at that checkpoint. You really know how to handle guards." Anne said.

Trina quickly peeked around to see where the guards were and if they could hear Anne talking. When Anne saw Trina look around, so did she. The two girls looked at each other, again. Trina said, "Guards don't need to be handled. They already know what to do."

Then Trina lowered her voice so only Anne could hear.

"Sometimes they just need reminding." Trina whispered.

Anne slowly nodded at this revelation.

It didn't take long for Trina's caravan to reach the First Lower House of Ra. Bo, Tania and a host of Ra guards were there to meet them. Anne and Trina got down from the elephant they were riding on. Tania and Bo walked to them, lowering their heads out of respect.

Bo stood and watched as Tania talked to Trina and Anne. Tania gushed on about how much Anne and Trina would like this Lower House. She said that it had much to offer and that everyone would be happy to see them.

After listening to Tania a little longer, both girls realized they weren't going anywhere. It was almost as if they were being detained, discreetly by Tania's talking. Both girls looked at each other acknowledging that fact. Trina turned back to Tania and smiled.

"I'm sure we'll enjoy our visit. However, Tania, I need someone to take me to Dan, right away." Trina said.

Tania realized that Trina had changed since last she saw her. Trina had learned how to properly use her rank. Tania didn't have enough rank to disobey a direct order from the proposed mate of the King of Ra, so she didn't. Tania smiled at Trina and then lowered her head. When she raised her head Tania motioned for several guards to come to her. Tania said, "Take Trina to Dan."

Then Tania looked at Anne.

"These guards will take you to Shaya. She will instruct you on what she wants." Tania said.

Anne quickly looked at Trina. Trina smiled at Anne.

"We'll meet, later." said Trina.

Anne smiled at Trina and then turned to Tania. Anne smiled at Tania letting her know that was agreeable.

Trina and her four female bodyguards, along with her eight male bodyguards, were escorted through the streets of this Lower House. On the way everyone stopped and stared at the new visitors.

Trina didn't look at the crowd staring at her. She just looked forward searching for Dan. They turned a corner on to another road and that's when she saw him.

Dan was with his brothers and Yin. He had been alerted several times that Trina was here. He and his brothers had just finished a grueling training session. They were coming from the bathing hall. That's when Dan saw Trina and her guards coming around the corner.

Dan watched as the Ra guards and Trina's bodyguards moved aside. Trina looked Dan in his eyes for a brief moment. She then lowered her eyes to no higher than Dan's chest, as she started walking towards him.

Don, Yin and Ram looked at Dan, before turning their attention to Trina. They liked watching the interaction between these two. It was always an interesting show.

Dan felt them looking at him, but wouldn't acknowledged it. He was focused on Trina. Dan was trying to figure out this humble attitude he was seeing.

Trina walked right up to Dan. When she got to him Trina bent her knees and then stood up. She looked up into Dan's eyes and softly said, "My King."

Something about Trina's eyes always threw Dan off when she stared directly into his eyes. Also, her soft voice was very soothing to his ears. Dan stared into Trina's eyes for a couple of seconds. He was lost in them. Dan quickly realized everyone was watching him, waiting on him to respond. His eyes darted away from Trina's, before going right back to them.

If no one had been around, Dan would have snatched Trina up in his arms and held her, because he was happy to see her. He also would have given her body a good security check, along with some other things he'd learned here, since last time he saw Trina.

With everyone around, Dan wouldn't openly show how happy he was to see Trina. He thought that would make him look weak in the eyes of everyone here. So, Dan tried to think of what to say that would make him look strong and in charge, like everyone was use to seeing from him. Dan knew he couldn't be as strong as he wanted, while looking into Trina's green eyes.

Dan slowly moved his eyes from Trina's to the bodyguards she had with her. She never had bodyguards, before. Now Dan could focus. However, he just couldn't think of what to say, but knew he had to say something.

Dan looked back into Trina's eyes. That didn't help his thought process. Dan decided to play it safe. He said, "Why are you here?"

As soon as he said that, Dan realized it didn't sound like he thought it would. It sounded much harsher. But, since he'd already said it, there was nothing he could do, accept wait on Trina's response. Dan only had to wait a split second, before seeing a slight change in Trina's eyes.

Trina's eyebrows furrowed in confusion for a second, before she pulled herself together. She couldn't believe Dan would ask that. Normally, Trina would blurt out something at Dan, showing how displeased she was with his ignorance.

However, Ramala's teachings taught Trina that she would have to be humble and patient, even when Dan was being difficult. Ramala told Trina that would give her an advantage when dealing with Dan.

Trina interpreted Dan's not saying anything as him not being happy to see her. In fact, it seemed to Trina, from what Dan said, he didn't want her here at all. Now Trina was starting to get angry. She was a little embarrassed at what Dan said in front of everyone. Even still, she was trying to keep her composure. Trina was apprehensive about the answer she might get, but she had to know.

"I've come to visit you, before you go off to war. Does my being here displease my King?" asked Trina.

Dan liked that Trina was humbling herself before him. Relieved that Trina didn't take offense to what he said earlier, without thinking and nervously trying to be humorous, Dan said, "Not, yet. But, the day is still young!"

Trina didn't see humor in what Dan said. She remembered how he treated her before he left. It was still as if he didn't care about her. Dan managed to stir Trina's emotions, without knowing it.

"Well, I can leave if that pleases you!" Trina yelled, before she could stop herself.

Dan was instantly aware that everyone heard Trina yelling at him. She always seemed to fly off the handle over the slightest things. That's what Dan's mind told him. Dan didn't want to look like he was begging Trina, so he said, "Do whatever you want."

"I will!" yelled Trina.

She turned and walked away from Dan, with her bodyguards joining her.

Dan was confused and asked, "Where are you going?"

Trina stopped, turned and stared at Dan for a second.

"As far away from you, as possible!" she replied.

Trina quickly turned and walked away. Dan stared in anger, not saying a word. Yin broke the silence, saying, "That girl really gets you going, doesn't she?"

Dan quickly turned towards Yin, staring angrily at him. Yin threw up both his hand.

"Hey! Hey! Calm down. I was just saying!" Yin explained.

Dan cut his eyes back in the direction where Trina was, before looking back at his brothers and Yin.

"Let's get to mid day's meal before we're late!" ordered Dan.

Don, Yin and Ram started walking with Dan, not saying a word. They always knew when Dan was angry because he would sternly say something that seemed unordinary to them. How could the young King of Ra and his brothers ever be late to a meal? No meal would dare start without them. They all knew that!

—————— CHAPTER 9 ——————

Trina told her bodyguards that she was going back to the main city of Ra. She sent a messenger to tell Anne. Trina told the messenger to tell Anne to let her know if she was coming back with her, or staying here. Trina said that she would wait a short while at the caravan for a response.

The messenger got to Anne, who was with La, Shaya and Danaaa. La knew Trina was here to visit Dan. After hearing what the messenger had to say, La figured Dan and Trina had a disagreement. La questioned the messenger as to what he witnessed. He told La everything that happened between Dan and Trina.

As soon as La heard everything, she sent several of her Elite Guards to tell Trina that the Number One Princess requests an audience with her, right away. La told her Elite Guards that no matter what, she expected to see Trina before mid day's meal. And since it was time for mid day's meal, the Guards knew how urgent La's orders were. They left, immediately.

Not two minutes later Dan and the Ra boys walked up. As soon as Anne spotted Ram she headed towards him. Ram watched Anne as she stopped right in front of him. She studied him for a moment.

"You seem different. I just can't figure out what it is, yet." Anne said.

Ram just stared at Anne without saying anything.

"Well, one thing hasn't changed about you." Anne said, referring to Ram not talking. After a short moment, they both turned their attention to La and Dan.

La could see Dan was flustered because he barely made eye contact with any of his sisters. La walked up to Dan.

"Ready for mid day's meal?" questioned La.

Dan curiously looked at La, because that's why they always met here after training. Still, he didn't want La to see he was bothered by something, so he nodded in agreement.

"Have you seen Trina, yet?" asked La.

Dan put on his poker face and then said, "Yeah, I saw her, earlier."

La looked at the side of Dan's face and said, "What's that on your face?"

Dan moved his hand up to wipe his face. La smiled at Dan.

"Let me get it for you." La said.

Dan lowered his hand. That's when La whacked him across the face with an open hand slap. Dan quickly grabbed La by both her arms. La stared at Dan and said, "Unhand me this instant!"

"What was that for?"

"Because, you're an idiot! Now, unhand me!"

Just as Dan was releasing his grip on La, she snatched her arms away from him.

Dan looked in La's eyes and said, "If you have something to say, just say it without slapping me! No good is going to come from physical violence between us! You know that!"

La stared at her twin brother. The only thing La knew about the physicality that happened between herself and Dan was that she always won. She let that go, so she could say what was really on her mind. La stared at Dan.

"Alright, no more hitting. I'll tell you, then. My new sister comes before you and humbles herself. That you would treat her with mockery is unacceptable!" exclaimed La.

La softened her look and then said, "Don't make the mistake of thinking whores can take the place of a good young woman like

Trina. I wouldn't be saying this if it weren't best for you. I'll tell you this, also. When next you see Trina, swallow your pride and treat her with the respect she deserves. If not, get rid of her, or let me do it for you." La could see in his eyes that Dan didn't want that.

"Lose Trina and we'll see if you can find someone to replace her." La said.

"Is there anything else?"

"There is something on the other side of your face. I can get it if you want."

Dan made a quick move towards La. She ran and giggled, before stopping and turning back towards Dan. They both looked at each other.

"Come Dan, I'm starving. Let's get something to eat!" La said, while smiling.

Trina, along with her bodyguards were escorted, by La's Elite Guards, to the eating hall. On the way Trina was disappointed with herself for letting Dan get her upset. She just didn't understand him! While walking, Trina questioned herself. Why did Dan always seem less than happy to see her? Why was she expected, by everyone, to know how to deal with Dan? What would happen to her family if she didn't get this right? What did La want with her? Trina didn't have the answers to any of these questions.

Trina knew La must have found out about what happened between her and Dan. She wondered what La's reaction would be. She didn't have to wait for long. Once Trina arrived at the eating hall, La, her sisters and Yaya came out to meet her.

Trina and Yaya looked at each other after being introduced. Trina heard of Yaya, but didn't remember seeing her. Yaya smiled and said, "So you're the girl that mother has picked for Dan."

Trina's face showed the confusion going on inside of her, even though she forced a smile on her face. Everyone saw that.

La looked at Trina's guards and said, "Leave us."

The guards lowered their heads and did as they were told. Once they were gone, La turned and looked at Trina. Right after their eyes met Trina lowered her head.

"I'm trying my best with Dan! I just can't seem to get it right! Tell me, what am I doing wrong?" Trina pleaded.

All of the girls watched and studied Trina. La walked closer to Trina. All the girls knew what was coming next, including Trina. La raised her hand. Trina flinched in anticipation of getting slapped. However, La slowly put her hand under Trina's chin. She lifted Trina's chin, until Trina was looking directly into her eyes.

"In your confusion, you seem to have forgotten your place. Normally, I would slap you back into reality, or worse." La calmly said.

La paused for a second and then continued with, "Remember this, because I'll only say it once. When I summon you it's not because I want to hear what you have to say, unless I ask something of you. Other than that, you show your respect by listening to what I have to say. Is that clear?"

"Yes Mistress."

"Good!"

La took a step back from Trina and said, "Dan is one tough cookie. But, I can see, you already know that."

After a contemplative pause, La said, "My brother likes to show everyone he is in control. Don't let that bother you. Get him alone and that's how you'll really get to know your King."

La looked around and then looked back at Trina. La said, "Have mid day meal with me as my guess. After that you're free to go back to the main city, if you want. But I wouldn't expect you to give up so easily."

Trina smiled and shook her head that she wouldn't. After that all the girls followed La to mid day meal.

A feeling of relief came over Dan when he saw La talking to Trina. Dan knew La would know what to say to Trina, even if he didn't. Then he saw Trina walking with his sisters over to the table. Dan was going to see if Trina had a better attitude before he said anything to her.

Dan watched as Trina lowered her head to everyone at the table before sitting. There wasn't any talking while everyone ate. Everyone at the table ate, inconspicuously, looking at Trina and Dan. Dan was watching Trina, while trying to look like he wasn't. Trina was aware of everyone at the table, including Dan, watching her. It made Trina aware of every movement she made from using her eating utensils to chewing her food.

Trina tried to concentrate on her food. She refused to look at Dan. She didn't want to provoke him into saying something rude to her in front of La. Trina didn't know how she would respond to that.

After looking at her food for a while, Trina looked up. First she peeked at Dan's brothers and Yin, without staring at them. She then looked down at her food. The next time she looked up, Trina looked at some of the guards that were behind Dan and his brothers around the perimeter of the room.

Every time Trina looked up, she had to concentrate on not looking at Dan, even though she could feel him looking at her. Trina looked up again and this time she looked at Dan. He was staring right into her eyes when she looked at him. Trina's eyes quickly darted away from Dan's eyes, before slowly moving back to them. They stared at each other. Dan picked up his glass. He never broke eye contact with Trina as he lifted the glass to his mouth. He only broke eye contact with Trina when he tilted his head back, drinking from the glass. As soon as his head returned, Dan and Trina's eyes locked, again.

Everyone at the table noticed these two staring at each other without saying anything. Finally, Danaaa put her elbow on the table and her chin in the hand of that arm. She stared at Dan and then at Trina. Danaaa's head turned from one to the other, with a look on her face that said she was bored. Dan broke his gaze on Trina to look at Danaaa. Danaaa and Dan stared at each other for a moment.

"Why are you staring at me, Stupid?" questioned Dan.

"To see if I can figure out why you're staring at her! You're staring at her like your eyes can talk, but they can't! If you have something to say, just say it and quit staring! You know I don't understand eye talk!" Danaaa quickly yelled.

Two seconds later everyone at the table, except for Dan, erupted in laughter. Dan watched as La, Shaya, Danaaa and his brothers were all laughing. Trina tried not to, but started laughing right after everyone else did.

Dan hadn't laughed, because Dan didn't find what Danaaa said to be entertaining, as he usually did. Instead, he thought it was the craziest thing he'd ever heard from her. Still, it tickled Dan to see everyone laughing. He smiled. Then he looked at Trina. She was still laughing when she felt Dan looking at her. She looked at him and her laughter slowed to one of the most beautiful smiles Dan had ever seen on Trina's face. This time they stared at each other with smiles on their faces.

Upon seeing that, Danaaa threw up both her hands and said, "Look, they're doing it, again!"

"Danaaa, enough!" La quickly said.

Danaaa turned towards La. They locked eyes. Now, everyone's attention was on Danaaa and La, including Dan and Trina's.

While staring at Danaaa, La ordered, "Yin, Don and Ram you won't be going to afternoon training. I need to meet with you all, right away. Baby, you and Shaya will come, too."

Dan looked at La to tell him what this was about. La saw that, turned to Dan and said, "Dan, this doesn't concern you. In fact, while we're meeting, why don't you show Trina around the city, for me?"

Dan could see the play that was going on here. Dan appreciated the fact that La had effortlessly done something that he himself found so hard to do, even though that's what he wanted. Dan's eyes never left La's as he nodded in agreement.

La quickly motioned for everyone to follow her. Everyone stood up and left. Dan stood up and when he did, so did Trina. They watched as everyone left. Dan walked over to Trina. She lowered her head, looking no higher than Dan's chest. When Dan got to her he lifted her chin and said, "Things have been a little tense between us. It's probably my fault. Relax and let's have some fun."

That was the closest Trina was going to get to an apology from Dan and she knew it. Trina looked up into Dan's eyes with a radiant smile that said she agreed. Trina wondered how Dan could be so mean to her one minute and then be nice, like now. If only he'd said this, earlier. Trina was sure that meeting would have gone a lot smoother.

Trina's thoughts were interrupted when Dan lightly touched her arm and said, "Come Trina, walk with me."

After feeling Dan's touch on her skin and hearing the tender bass in his voice, Trina would have marched into the pit of Hell with Dan, if that's what he wanted.

The rest of the Hammer-Axe Six followed La. They wondered if she really wanted a meeting. After a short walk La stopped and turned towards Yaya.

"Members of your Wa family have arrived and are waiting on an escort. Don, Ram and Yin will go with you. Be careful that your family shows them the proper respect. Without me, Dan, or Shaya being there things could get out of hand, before anyone could stop it." La said.

Yaya looked fearful as she thought about that.

"Don't you think I should go, just so nothing happens?" asked Shaya.

"Only, if you want to." responded La.

"I don't mind hanging out with my big sister for a while." Shaya said, while smiling at Yaya.

La looked at Yaya and then at Shaya. La didn't trust that Shaya wouldn't find a way to slip away from the others and end up in an unsavory situation with some guards. La looked at Danaaa and said, "Go with Shaya and don't let her out of your sight. I expect both of you to find me, after you inspect our guest."

Shaya said, "We will, right Baby."

Danaaa looked at La and did a quick nod that they would. La looked at her sisters for a moment, before walking away. Yaya looked as La took no more than four steps, before La's Warlords Hoban, Ali, along with her bodyguards and Elite Guards walked up to La. After lowering their heads, they walked off with La.

Dan and Trina walked, while Dan's bodyguards and Elite Guards cleared a path for them to have some privacy. Dan made small talk showing Trina some of the sights of this Lower House. They stopped and turned towards the Southern Jungle, which was off in the far distance. It was picturesque. They looked, without saying anything.

While standing next to Dan, Trina noticed she was having a strange reaction to him. Trina could feel energy building between herself and Dan. Her heartbeat quickened as well as the pace of her breathing. It felt like Dan was pulling her towards him, even though he wasn't touching her. Trina slowly turned and looked at Dan, trying to figure out what she was feeling.

Dan, while standing next to Trina, also felt energy building between them. Dan felt that same energy pulling him towards Trina. He wondered if Trina felt what he was feeling. Dan certainly wasn't going to ask and risk the chance he might say the wrong thing. He tried to refocus on the scenery. Trina did as well. They both turned and looked at each other.

While looking into Trina's green eyes Dan couldn't think straight. They stared at each other, without saying a word. Trina's eyes increased the energy already building inside Dan. Dan said, "Let's go back to my place and get something to e......"

Before Dan could finish Trina interrupted, softly whispering, "Alright, let's go!"

She didn't have to tell Dan, twice! They turned and Dan motioned for guards to bring an elephant for travel.

In Trina's and Dan's mind that short ride seemed to take forever and at the same time they seemed to get to Dan's place in an instant. Dan and Trina kept staring at each other like they were in a trance like state. Dan never took his eyes off of Trina, while ordering the guards that he should not be disturbed.

Once the guards were gone, Dan looked around to make sure they had complete privacy. He turned back to Trina. Dan slowly said, "Come here."

Dan planned on showing Trina everything he learned, while here at this Lower House. However, as soon as Dan spoke, Trina started tearing off her blouse, as she walked towards him. She then lunged at Dan, taking him to the ground. After falling backwards and landing on his back, Dan knew it was on.

Trina was on top of Dan grinding her pelvis into him, while kissing him. Dan tried to maneuver so he could get his pants down, however Trina was forcefully wrestling Dan, completely into what she was doing. Since that wasn't working for Dan he forced them both over, rolling on top of Trina. Trina quickly wrapped her legs around Dan and continued to grind on him. The blood was flowing strong into Dan's stick and it only took Trina a second to locate it. She immediately started grinding on it.

Trina was like a wild animal on Dan. After another moment Dan realized Trina didn't know what she was doing. Slightly annoyed, Dan finally said, "Hey, slow down for a moment!"

Trina stopped and stared into Dan's eyes. While looking into Trina's eyes, Dan realized he said that a little more animated than he expected. He softened his tone a little and said, "Let me show you how it's done."

Trina tried to calm herself as much as she could and let Dan show her what he knew.

Dan slowly took off Trina's clothes, caressing her body with his hands as he did. Trina's body wasn't as hard as most of the girls and women that Dan had been with here in this Lower House. Trina's body was firm, yet soft. With every movement of Dan's hand, Trina's body quivered. Dan planned on taking his time with Trina. Dan was aware of Trina's reaction to his touch. The scientist in Dan pushed Trina's body into pleasurable territory she'd never experienced, before.

After taking off Trina's clothes, Dan moved back on top of Trina. He kissed her lips and slowly moved down, kissing her neck. Dan let his lips moved further down Trina's body, giving soft kisses along the way.

Trina was glad Dan had taken control. With Dan's body barely brushing against hers, while his lips lightly made their way down her body, Trina's awareness was heightened to a level that she'd never known.

Dan's lips made their way down to Trina's forbidden zone. After a light kiss, Dan's tongue gently manipulated the gates to that zone. Trina got the shock of her life and reacted, instantly. Her legs quickly tried to tighten around Dan's head. Dan reacted quickly, by putting both his arms inside Trina's thighs and pressing down and outward on them. That allowed Dan to move, freely.

Although Dan had control of Trina's legs, he didn't have control of her arms. Now Dan's tongue had moistened and was able to enter her love gates. Trina, trying to gain some control over a situation that had gotten totally out of control, leaned forward and grabbed Dan by the back of his neck with one hand, while grabbing a hand full of his hair with her other hand. She dug her fingernails in as far as she could, putting a death grip on Dan's neck while pulling his hair as far as she could from his scalp, trying to control Dan's movements.

Dan only put up with that for a second. He reached up and grabbed both of Trina's arms by her wrist. He then put her arms over her head on the cushion she was laying on, as his body moved on top of Trina. Then he slowly entered her tight, wet love gates.

With the first slow thrust Dan barely made it inside. He heard Trina moan as her eyes got big staring into his. The second slow thrust only put Dan slightly further inside Trina than before. That's when Trina ripped her arms away from Dan and dug her finger nails into his chest, trying to push him away.

Dan put both his hands on the outsides of Trina's shoulders on the cushion beneath her for support. He leaned forward putting more of his weight on Trina's hands, to offset her pushing up on him.

Then came the third slow thrust from Dan that put him even further inside Trina. With that thrust Trina let out a yelping cry, while her body squirmed downwards into the cushion. All the while, Trina's fingernails were digging deeper into Dan's chest.

All the teachings from older females he'd been with since coming to this First Lower House was kicking in. With that third thrust and Trina's reaction to it, Dan knew that was about as much as Trina could handle and still enjoy herself. So, with the next slow thrust Dan went in slightly less than before. It took all the concentration and discipline Dan had not to thrust hard and fast in Trina.

When Dan hit Trina with that third thrust she thought she'd had enough. She didn't want to know what the fourth thrust would bring. Her mind was racing just as fast as her heart was beating. Trina's mind was trying to make since of what was happening to her body. Then the fourth, fifth, and sixth slow thrust came from Dan. They weren't quite as deep as that third one and although Trina was breathing and moaning heavily, she was better able to deal with them.

After a few more thrust, Dan could also feel Trina was getting wetter. And although Trina was still tight, it wasn't like at first. The death grip inside of Trina's love gates was starting to slightly loosen. Dan took advantage immediately by hitting Trina with quick and powerful thrusts, while being mindful not to go in further than he knew Trina could take. But at the same time, he gave her more than she could handle.

At that time, Trina was just getting somewhat use to the slow thrusting. She had managed to time her breathing with the thrust and decided that was the best way to deal with it.

However, that plan was thrown out the window when Dan started rapidly pounding Trina. Trina's breathing was shot to hell. Now, no matter how hard, deep and fast she breathed she couldn't seem to get enough air into her lungs. And the sensation of the pleasurable pain she was getting was taking her mind higher and higher. Trina couldn't handle all of these things going on, simultaneously. The intensity was so great that she did what every woman usually did in a situation like this. Her body was thrown into spasms, as she started howling like a banshee!

Trina instantly removed her hands and fingernails from Dan's chest and dug them into his back, clawing into it. Somehow, someway she was trying to get a grip on Dan so she could slow him down, just a bit. Trina was soaring through the stratosphere of her emotions, while just trying to deal with what was happening to her. Then without warning Trina's body and mind started to heat up and race at a level she couldn't understand, or comprehend.

Dan felt the change in Trina, right away. He slightly slowed his pace, while thrusting harder. Trina panicked and started yelling to Dan that something was happening. Trina arched her pelvis into Dan several times before she dropped back down on the cushion. Trina had her first orgasm, even though she didn't know that's what it was. She was still clawing at Dan's back because he hadn't stopped thrusting inside her. A wave of sensitivity hit Trina and now she could no longer take Dan's thrusting. Since begging Dan wasn't working, Trina was bucking, wrestling and fighting to get Dan off of her. Dan wasn't going to be stopped, slowed down, or deterred by someone as inexperienced as Trina. He had Trina right where he wanted her and wasn't going to let her get away. Still, Trina struggled. That extra activity sent Trina into several more orgasms. As Trina's body ramped itself up, crashing through each orgasm, it sent powerful waves of energy into Dan's body.

Dan was aware that he had complete control of Trina's body. Her excitement and reaction to his movements were sending Dan higher and higher. Although mindful not to go as deep as he could, he went in a little further. Dan increased the pace and intensity of his thrusting.

Dan had a lot of practice with the more experienced women of this Lower House, at holding out and not releasing himself, too soon. But Trina was tighter than and just as wet as the best girls and women he'd ever had.

Dan felt himself getting to the point that he knew if he kept going he wouldn't be able to stop himself from releasing. So, after seeing what looked like Trina having several intense orgasms, Dan got off of Trina and rolled over on to his back, looking at the ceiling. Dan breathed heavily as he turned his head and saw Trina's body jerking in spasms, as she lay there also breathing heavily looking up at the ceiling.

Dan looked back up at the ceiling. Both lay there for a few moments, before Trina slowly turned her head and looked at Dan. She couldn't believe what he'd just done to her and the way it made her feel. Trina always wondered what the big deal was about sex, or boom booming as it was called. Now that she had experienced it, she was evaluating what happened. After a quick assessment all Trina knew was she wanted to do it, again. She stared at Dan with a smile on her face. Before she could say anything, Dan spoke.

"Time to go." he said.

"Let's do it again!" Trina quickly said.

"I've got things to do. We'll see each other, later, right?" Dan calmly said.

Trina didn't say a word, because that's not what she wanted. Dan turned towards her, waiting on a response. Trina looked disappointed. She wanted to ask Dan to stay, but didn't. After a moment, she nodded in agreement.

Trina's look of disappointment wasn't missed by Dan. He knew exactly what he was doing. The seasoned women of this Lower House taught Dan not being selfish and always putting on a good show, will leave a woman wanting more.

They got dressed and started to leave. Dan moved closer to Trina and motioned for her to follow him. Trina lowered her head. In that instant Dan grabbed both of Trina's wrists and put her arms behind her, while pinning her onto the wall behind her. Dan held Trina there without saying a word to her.

Trina's heart started beating faster as she wondered why she was being restrained. She struggled for a moment and then stopped.

Trina looked up into Dan's eyes and in a somewhat annoyed voice said, "I've cooperated, fully! What is this?"

Dan moved his lips to where they were lightly touching Trina's ear.

"Whatever I want it to be, so get use to it. No more storming off, trying to embarrass me in front of everyone. I know you enjoyed what we just did. Be a good girl and I'll give you more." Dan, slowly, but forcefully said.

The bass in Dan's voice sent a slight vibration in Trina's eardrum, as well as on her earlobe where Dan's lip was touching. Trina was affected and could barely focus on what Dan was saying. But still, she heard him. His arrogance appalled her. But his direct forcefulness caught her at a weak moment. Dan moved back and looked into Trina's eyes.

"You understand me, right?" said Dan.

Trina's mind wanted to say something that would let Dan know he couldn't talk to her like this and get away with it. But Trina didn't.

"Can't you say it nicer than that?" she said.

Dan shrugged his shoulders, like maybe and said, "So we understand each other, don't we?"

Now that Trina had a taste of Dan and they had shared something special, Trina wanted them to get along. She quickly nodded her head in agreement and then looked down, before looking back up into Dan's eyes. Dan, realizing Trina had given in to him, slowly released her wrist and moved back from her.

When Dan moved back Trina moved close to him, putting her head on his chest, wrapping her arm around and embracing him. Dan could see Trina was caught up in the moment. Dan slapped Trina on her behind. Trina's body stiffened, immediately.

"Come on, time to go." Dan said.

They turned and walked off, together. Dan told Trina he would see her later at the last day's meal. Trina forced a smile on her face and lowered her head, knowing that's what Dan expected in front of his guards. Dan instructed his guards to escort Trina to her bodyguards and then to where La was. Dan turned and walked away, while Trina left with the guards.

Dan was tickled on the inside at Trina's response to him slapping her butt, even though he didn't let it show on his face. Trina was angry and confused as to why Dan would treat her that way when she had totally given herself to him, cooperating in every way. Although, she didn't like it, Trina didn't let it show on her face. She was going to do her best to get along with Dan, in spite of Dan.

CHAPTER 10

Shaya, Danaaa, Don, Yin and Ram left with Yaya to meet Yaya's cousins, while Dan was spending time with Trina. Yaya asked if they could stop and see if her cousins that were already here wanted to go. Shaya didn't mind, so she agreed.

They met up with Gia, Tay and Boku who were lounging around, enjoying the day. Now that the Wa knew it was expected of them to lower their heads to the high ranking Ra, they did so.

As they walked to the guard outpost there was very little conversation between the Wa and the Ra. Yaya was the only one trying to engage both sides in conversation. That made the walk less awkward than it would have been.

Still, the Wa watched each of the Hammer-Axe Six without trying to be obvious. The one they watched the most was Danaaa, because she was a High Pressure Executioner!

Danaaa was respected, admired and hated for her fighting skills and accomplishments. Only thing was she didn't look like she'd done everything she had. If you witnessed it you believed it. If you hadn't, you had to try to wrap your mind around the many stories of her battles.

Even though most wanted Danaaa dead, they wouldn't attack her. At least, not until they could find a weakness that they could exploit to give them an advantage. That's why Danaaa was watched so closely by the Wa.

The Wa also watched the other members of the Hammer-Axe

Six because even though Yaya trusted them, the Wa didn't. When people related to the people who tried to eliminate your entire family are around you, it's impossible for that not to be in your thoughts.

Danaaa was use to everyone looking at her, or either outright staring at her. Most time, it wouldn't bother her, unless she was in an unpleasant mood. Today Danaaa was happy. When Danaaa was happy she was silly, pestering, or mischievous. Shaya, Don and Yin watched Danaaa as they watched everything else. They knew the key to dealing with Baby was to stop her nonsense as soon as, or before it started.

With that being said, Danaaa started amusing herself, by dancing, while they were walking. Don looked at Shaya like Danaaa was getting started and needed, a warning. Shaya shook her head like she's alright for now. Even though the Wa wanted Danaaa dead for killing their cousins, they couldn't help being amused by her every time they saw her.

It was well past mid-day when the Wa at the guardhouse were told that their escorts had arrived. The heat of the day and just standing around had the Wa slightly aggravated. Several guards looked at the Wa and pointed around the guard housing. The Wa cautiously walked in that direction. They saw Yaya and their other Wa cousins walking towards them with several well dressed teenagers. The well dressed teenagers stopped at a distance and watched as the Wa walked towards each other. The Wa saw large men with Hammer-Axes watching the teenagers and everything around them, without getting too close. The Wa figured they were bodyguards.

Yaya and Gia hugged the new coming Wa. As the Ra teenagers were walking closer, both Gia and Yaya whispered to these Wa. They told them that it was very important that they followed certain protocol, while here. They told them that lowering their heads to these teenagers, who were the young Rulers of Ra, was one of the protocols they would have to accept.

Zan gave Gia a quick and hard look. Gia stared back and sternly whispered, "Just do what we do! Follow our lead!"

All of the Wa hugged and greeted each other, before turning their attention to the Young Ra Rulers. Yaya introduced each of them. As she did, Gia, Yaya, Tay and Boku lowered their heads, also, just to let the others know it was right to do so.

Jami was introduced first. She watched the way the others lowered their heads and followed suit. Uma was next. She'd seen how it was done, so she fell right in line. Zan looked at these teenagers that were younger than he was. He already didn't like them, because he felt like he was forced to lower his head. After slightly lowering his head, without taking his eyes off of the Ra, Zan liked these teenagers even less.

Chet was last. He didn't want to lower his head, either. But Chet knew if Gia came running over to tell them this, he should cooperate for now. Chet slowly lowered his head halfway, without taking his eyes off of the Ra, just as Zan had done.

All of the Ra noticed that. Yaya did too and nervously hoped it wouldn't be an issue. Yaya smiled at Chet and Zan, saying, "Let me introduce you to my other brothers and sisters."

Yaya introduced the Ra one at a time. The new Wa stared at each of them as they were introduced. An uneasy distrust was thick in the air as Yaya was talking. It got even thicker when Yaya introduced Danaaa. Shaya saw the astonished look on the faces of the new Wa staring at Danaaa.

As usual, whenever Danaaa and Ram were present, one of the Hammer-Axe Six would give the same disclaimer. After that, if anything happened the Hammer-Axe Six could disavow responsibility, if need be.

"She's High Pressure, the Executioner. My brother Ram is worse than her. It's best if you're careful with sudden movements of weapons around them. They are extremely dangerous." warned Shaya.

Because Ram was so stealthy, the Wa hadn't heard the many

stories about him that was known by the Hayee and Ra. However, they did look at Ram when Shaya said he was worse than High Pressure, the Executioner. That was hard to imagine. Her battles were raised to the level of hardy believable.

After looking at Ram for a moment, the new Wa looked back at Danaaa. This was the girl they were told who killed their cousin Massiko in less than a second. Now that they were face to face with her, the hatred in their eyes was evident.

Zan wanted to kill Danaaa where she stood. He looked at everyone near Danaaa, sizing them up. He was sure he could kill her before the others could help. Jami, Uma and Chet started checking their surroundings.

All of the Riyal Ra noticed this. To them, it looked like the Wa were about to attack them. That's when Danaaa, who rarely ever looked directly at someone, turned and stared Zan directly in his eyes. Danaaa moved her hands to a quick draw position next to her axes. Shaya saw that and quickly grabbed Danaaa's ponytail, pulling on it. A second later, a silly grin came on Danaaa's face, but she never broke eye contact with Zan.

Zan took that as a challenge and was ready to respond. Gia moved quickly in front of Zan, facing him. She said, "You look hot and hungry. Don't stare! Their Executioner may take offense! We've seen her in person! She's really fast, instant heat and High Pressure!"

Zan, Chet, Uma and Jami knew Gia was warning them not to attack. Still, they didn't care. They'd trained all their lives to kill the Ra. If Zan attacked, Chet, Uma and Jami would back him with extreme force. The other Wa would help after that.

Shaya, Don, Ram and Yin watched the four Wa, closely. None of them liked these new Wa. They knew the Wa didn't stand a chance against Danaaa. Nevertheless, if they attacked her, Don and Yin, along with Ram, were going to cut them to pieces.

Yaya moved between Zan and Danaaa. Yaya looked at warning to Zan. She then turned to Danaaa with a smile on her face. Yaya said, "Baby, quit acting silly. Don't taunt. It's been a long journey for my cousins. They're very tired. Let them eat and get some rest. I'm sure they will be more pleasant, then."

Shaya knew if La had been here and saw what transpired, all of the Wa would be dead. To Shaya, they didn't seem to want to get along, like the other Wa. Still, Shaya looked at Yaya and said "It's best if you take them to get food and rest. Inform them of the protocol expected of them. You know what La expects."

Shaya looked at Don, Yin and Ram. It was time to go. Shaya pulled on Danaaa's ponytail. Danaaa quickly turned and looked at Shaya. Danaaa was only use to La pulling on her ponytail, so it irritated her whenever Shaya did it. Danaaa turned and looked at Zan, before having her ponytail pulled again, by Shaya. Danaaa turned back to Shaya and wrapped her arms around her chest in a huff. Shaya, almost begging, pleaded, "Come on Baby, it's time to go!"

Danaaa made an exaggerated movement with her head. That snapped her ponytail and made it lash against the arm, where Shaya's hand held Danaaa's ponytail. After that, they walked off. Shaya momentarily forgot about the Wa. She now had to watch Baby, hoping she wouldn't get out of control.

After Shaya and the other Ra left, Yaya hustled the Wa away. After walking a short distance, Zan angrily said, "Can you believe them! We should have.....!"

Almost instantly, Gia put her hand over Zan's mouth and said, "There's a time for talking. That time is not now!"

Zan snatched Gia's hand from over his mouth. Chet's eyes quickly scanned the area. He saw Ra guards everywhere. Chet didn't want to get into a battle with the Ra guards and not have the opportunity to kill one, or all of the Ra. Chet said, "Zan, she's right!"

Zan looked at Chet. After a few seconds, Zan nodded in agreement. Yaya watched and knew she had to get her Wa family out of the First Lower House as soon as possible.

Yaya and her Wa family walked back to the building they were staying at, while here in this Lower House of Ra. The five Wa that hadn't been here before found themselves looking around at the people and sights. The Ra and Hayee also stared at the newcomers. The Wa noticed that once they saw Yaya, the looks from these people were less scrutinizing. One thing for sure to the Wa that had never been here before was that this Lower House was a booming metropolis. There was business and new construction everywhere.

Yaya saw the five that hadn't been here marveling at the city. She said, "It's impressive, isn't it?"

No one answered although they agreed. After a short pause, Yaya said, "If you think this is impressive, you should see the main city of Ra. It's beautiful."

Again, no one said a word. They all just wished Yaya would stop glorifying things that had to do with the Ra. When Yaya changed the subject, that's when the other Wa slowly joined her in conversation.

When the Wa got to their quarters they found that food had been put out for them. Yaya and the Wa that already had been here went over to the table and grabbed some fruit. The new Wa looked around and then suspiciously stared at the food.

Gia said, "I know you're hungry. Come and get something to eat. The food is safe, see."

Gia took another bite out of the fruit she had in her hand. Tay said, "Yeah, they don't poison their enemies. They usually cut them to pieces."

The five new Wa moved over to the table. They were hungry from their travel. They tested the food and then began to eat. Even though the food was not poisonous the five new Wa were still on guard.

The Wa that were already here told the new five Wa that they had been treated very well and it seemed the young Ra Rulers weren't as ruthless as their parents. The new five Wa didn't care about that.

They asked if the others thought they could kill one or all of the Ra and make it back to the jungle. Yaya didn't like this conversation and told them. They ignored Yaya and told the five Wa that would be very difficult at this point and they should access the situation for themselves. The five said they would do just that.

Then, out of nowhere, Zan announced, "I'm going to kill that she devil they call the Executioner."

Gia turned and looked seriously at Zan. She said, "That Executioner is everything she's advertised to be. Besides the stories of her battles, we got to see just how fast she is. She had her axes to Boku's neck, before he could move an inch. Her blade missed his neck by next to nothing, as I quickly snatched him out of the way."

Boku looked at the five nodding that that was indeed true. They continued to talk, until it was time to meet the young King and Queen of Ra

The one thing the five Wa were appreciative of was the new clean clothes supplied to the by the Ra. They were move comfortable and better suited for fighting, as well as for daily wear. After changing clothes, the Wa made their way to the feast.

On the way to the feast, guards let Yaya know that the new Wa would first be introduced to La and Dan. All of the Elders and everyone else would get a good look at the new Wa. The feast would start after that.

The Wa were led into a large courtyard, filled with people of all ages, rank and dress. They could see the throne area, ahead. Boku said "That's the Ra Rulers."

The new five tried to get a good look at them, while watching the crowd they were moving through. It shocked everyone when the Hammer-Axes Six came down from the throne area to meet the Wa, before they got there.

Trina and Anne got up and started to go with the Royal Ra. La stopped and cut her eyes in their direction. They stopped in their tracks. Trina and Anne got the message. They weren't part of whatever was about to happen. They stood there and watched the Wa from where they were.

The crowd parted giving the Royal Ra all the room they needed. As usual, Hoban and Ali, along with several Elite Guards flanked the Hammer-Axe Six. They made sure no one, including the Wa got close to La and her siblings.

Once the Royal Ra were close they stopped. The new Wa looked them over. They had seen the others, so they figured who La and Dan were.

The Wa could see that they both were regally dressed. The two also had arrogance about them. That arrogance seemed magnified by ten when La looked directly at each of the new Wa. Even though the new Wa lowered their heads as they saw their Wa cousins doing, when they raised them, they saw the Ra Rulers looking unfavorably at them. That instantly put them on guard. But still, they weren't ready to draw their weapons, yet.

La and Dan were like their parents in the fact that they could read eyes, very well. Looking into the eyes of these new Wa, La and Dan could see slightly masked hatred. Dan didn't care about that. As he listened to Yaya as she introduced them, Dan knew that he could have these five eliminated at a moment's notice, if they started any trouble.

It was different for La. As soon as she saw the hidden hatred, she took offense. She had given them some of their ancestral land, which was taken from them by her mother, as a gesture of reconciliation. Now they dare come before her with this attitude!

La barely heard Yaya and didn't make an effort to remember any of the names she heard. As soon as Yaya was finished introducing the five Wa. La stepped forward, walking back and forth several times, without saying anything. She stared into each of their eyes as she passed them.

La stopped, while still staring at them. Once La stopped, Shaya and Danaaa rushed to her side. La quickly grabbed Danaaa's ponytail as it came flying in front of her. Danaaa's hands went to a quick draw position next to her axes.

Shaya took La's ponytail just above the five pound metal ball that was attached to the end of it. Shaya then put the thumb of the hand she was holding La's ponytail with, into her mouth and turned her head sideways, leaning it on La's shoulder, while staring at the new Wa. La was instantly annoyed by Shaya, as she always was, when Shaya did this.

That made La pause for an extra second. Once La felt Shaya's head on her shoulder, La's eyes moved slowly from the new Wa, towards Shaya and then slowly back to the new Wa.

La quickly regained her composure. La's tone was stern, but not angry.

"I can see that letting go of the past is very hard for some. Still, no actions can change what has already happened. All of you should be careful not to offend, or disrespect me. Disrespect won't be tolerated. Now, remember what I have said to you, because I'll not say it, again!"

Before anyone could respond, La let go of Danaaa's ponytail, turned and walked away. Dan and his brothers did so after that. Shaya and Danaaa stayed with Yaya and the Wa. Yaya looked at Shaya and questioned, "Why is La being difficult?"

Shaya looked at the five Wa, before looking back at Yaya. Shaya said, "Ya, you know La. She says exactly what she means. That's just how she is."

"But, Ya, you already know that! Now they'd better know it, too!" yelled Danaaa.

Shaya turned and stared at Danaaa for a moment, before saying to Yaya, "As long as everyone shows respect, everything will be fine. Now, let's eat!"

The Wa were trotted out and shown to the Elders of this Lower House. They were scrutinized and studied. The Wa also saw La and Dan watching them, inconspicuously. This made them uncomfortable. They were led to their table, where food was served.

Although they were being watched, everyone seemed to be going out of their way to be friendly towards the Wa. The five Wa that hadn't been here even found that some of the Ra knew the names of their Wa cousins. The Ra used their names when they greeted them, as they walked by. To the five new Wa it seemed that the Ra and

Hayee had somehow lulled their cousins into a false sense of security. These five Wa were determined not to let that happen to them.

Tay saw that his five cousins were highly charged waiting on something to happen. He said in a whisper that only they could hear, "Hey, relax. Nothing's going to happen here. Don't let everyone see your true intentions. That could derail our mission. This is where they relax and show their true selves. Use this time to watch and learn. If anything does happen, you know we'll be ready."

Tay smiled and looked at each of the five. The five looked at the ones that had already been here. They got reassuring looks from them all. Although still on guard, that was enough to calm the five Wa.

Zan, Jami, Uma and Chet could see that the Hayee and the Ra of all ages seemed to let down their guard and everyone was in a partying mood. Not long after the feast the dance-offs started up.

Tay and Boku had seen a dance-off before. They smiled when they saw Zan and Chet staring, enthralled in the movements of the Ra and Hayee females. Boku leaned towards Zan and said, "Nice, aren't they? If you think that's something, you haven't seen anything yet."

Both Zan and Chet looked at Boku for a second when he said that. They then turned their attention back to the dancing.

All of the groups of girls dancing knew that they had to step up their game, whenever La and her sisters were involved in the dance-off. Sometimes the three Ra girls wouldn't involve themselves in the dance-off. They would let the other girls compete against each other. This was not one of those times.

Anne and Trina liked to dance, but didn't involve themselves in the dance-off. They would just watch, until it was over and join in the dancing after that. They moved themselves to a better vantage point to watch the show.

The Ra and Hayee girls could always tell when La and her sisters were going to join the dance-off. The main clues were when they took off their weapon holsters and started stretching. That's when you saw the other groups of dancers putting on their best performances.

After a countless number of performances La and her sisters walked out. The entire place went silent as the crowd moved back even further, giving them as much room as they might need. The Wa stood their ground and ended up with a front row view of the Ra girls.

As always, the drummers and other musicians wouldn't start up, until they got their key from La, which came in the form of a look and nod of her head that she was ready. La did her signature move and the drums started pounding in a racing beat.

The Ra girls never failed to put on a show stopping performance. This time was no different. They started out with some outstanding synchronized movements that memorized the crowd. Then they did something that hadn't been done, up to this point. They moved closer towards the crowd, dancing around the perimeter. This gave everyone an up close and personal view of their best moves. The show La and her sisters put on was spectacular!

Once they'd danced the perimeter of the crowd the three Ra girls moved back to the middle of the area in which they were dancing. The five Wa watched the three Royal Ra girls, closely. The one thing they noticed was that even though all three girls were dancing in sync with each other, each had their own style.

La, while moving in sync with her sisters, appeared to be moving slower than her sisters. Her moves were very distinct and deliberate. La's hips and arms told a slow sultry seductive story to the beat of the drums with every movement she made.

Shaya's body, although moving in sync with her sisters, was moving twice as fast as La's. Shaya's body had an urgent energy that couldn't be ignored. Her body shook, shimmied and vibrated to every beat of the drums. Her hips shook so fast to the beat that she seemed to be using her arms to balance herself.

Danaaa, while not able to match the speed of Shaya's hip movements, had the fastest footwork and acrobatic movements that anyone had ever seen. Danaaa moved at least three times the speed of her sisters. While dancing in sync with her sisters, Danaaa's feet seemed to take three steps to every one step her sisters took. And still, whatever moves Danaaa made were always in time with her sisters. She would jump straight up into a flip, or a somersault and land on her feet in step with her sisters.

The Wa, just as everyone else, were astounded, watching all three girls, while sometimes settling in on the individual performance of one of them. The Ra girls ended their routine by quickly jerking their heads, while running away from each other. La grabbed Shaya's ponytail, while Shaya grabbed Danaaa's, at the same time Danaaa grabbed La's ponytail. Once the all three ponytails were extended, the girls were jerked with their bodies extending away from each other. They all were launched from the momentum of being jerked. Shaya and Danaaa flipped past each other going in opposite directions, while La flipped straight up, just high enough as to barely make it over both her sisters as they went under her in opposite directions. All three came down out of the air together, landing on their knees, with Danaaa and Shaya on both sides of La. All three girls put their left leg in front of them and lifted themselves to a standing position. They slightly lowered their heads. When they raised them the crowd erupted.

La and her sisters smiled and looked around the crowd, enjoying all the attention they were getting. It was another perfect performance. As they were turning, about to go back to their seats, Shaya noticed that heathen Wa, Chet staring at her. She remembered he and the others that had just arrived always looked like they wanted to kill her and her siblings. Shaya thought this group of Wa was trouble and she didn't care for them. Shaya was taking back control of her breathing, so she turned with her sisters and put it out of her mind, taking in all of the attention she was getting from everyone else.

Zan and Chet had seen dancing from the Shinmushee girls, but it was nothing like what they saw from the Hayee and Ra girls. And the performance they saw from La and her sisters was heads above the rest. Zan stared at all three Royal Ra girls as they walked away. Zan thought La's slow erotic movements were the best of all three girls. He wanted to see more of La and her dancing.

Chet watched all three Ra sisters. After studying them for a while, his eyes settled in on Shaya. Shaya was beautiful to Chet. Her movements were intoxicating to him. Chet peeked around. He was sure no one could see that he was affected by Shaya's beauty. He was going to keep that to himself.

They both were snapped back into reality by Boku saying, "Now, that was a show! They dance like that a lot around here. It mostly happens after a feast."

Zan and Chet tried to act like they were unimpressed, even though the other Wa saw they were.

"Alright, let's look around, before we head back for the night." said Gia.

Yaya smiled and stayed close to her Wa cousins, keeping a close watch on them. As the Wa walked around, they noticed that the Royal Ra men were gone. Dan, Yin, Don and Ram left once they knew most of the crowd was distracted by the Dance-Off. The Wa watched everything from the security, to the exits and many people around them. They watched the Royal Ra girls inconspicuously from a distance, trying to find a weakness they could exploit. They couldn't get close to them because of the people trying to mingle with La and Shaya.

One thing the Wa noticed was the huge bodyguard called Hoban was always lurking near La. He looked to be on the level of a Butcher. They would have to take that into consideration when plotting an attack. Also they noticed the one called Ali was always directing the other guards and checking their positions around the young Rulers.

As the night went on, the partying intensified. The Wa were satisfied with the information they'd gathered here. It was getting late, so Gia suggested they leave. Everyone agreed. It had been a long day. When they got back to their quarters they would discuss what they'd seen, so far.

They turned and started walking towards the exit. Zan turned back and took a long look at La. She was beautiful to him. He thought it a shame that eventually they would have to take her head.

When he was turning back, he bumped hard into a Ra male of about seventeen. Zan was solid and unintentionally knocked the teenager backwards, off balance. The other Ra and Hayee that were with the teenager grabbed him and steadied him as he was stumbling.

The teen ager looked angrily at Zan. It embarrassed him that he was knocked backwards, so easily. He snatched himself away from his cousins that were holding him up. Before anyone could stop him, the teenager took a quick step towards Zan and threw a lightning fast punch at Zan's face. Zan moved out of the way and countered with a powerful blow to the young man's chest that sent him falling backwards.

Offended that a Wa would dare do this, the teenager's older brother and a close cousins attacked Zan. As that was happening, other Ra and Hayee that were with the teenager started moving closer to Zan. The Wa moved to defensive positions around Zan. That was taken as threatening maneuvers. Instantly, Fights broke out and it was an all out brawl within seconds of that. By the time it got everyone's attention, the Wa were mopping up the floor with young Ra and some Hayee. La saw the fights, but refused to motion for her guards to stop it. La could see that the Wa were excellent fighters.

Shaya saw that La was willing to let this fight run its course. Shaya knew if La didn't stop this fight someone would be seriously injured, or killed. If a Ra or Hayee were killed their families would demand that the Wa be killed as retribution.

Within seconds of realizing that, Shaya turned to Ali and ordered him to end this now. Ali looked at La. La unenthusiastically motioned for Ali to proceed. Ali turned and ordered the guards to separate everyone. Everyone was separated shortly after that.

Everyone could see that the young Ra and Hayee took the worse of this fight. They had busted lips and bruises on their faces. The only visible signs that the Wa had been fighting was their clothes were a bit disheveled.

After seeing that, the Ra and Hayee who had been fighting started struggling, trying to get another chance at the Wa. But the Ra guards were well trained in crowd control and had the situation under control. By the time Shaya and Danaaa arrived at the scene the Ra and Hayee were begging to be let go so they could kill the Wa heathen scum, as they put it.

Shaya looked at Yaya, before turning and staring at the Hayee and Ra who were being held back.

"Everyone, control yourselves and be silent!" yelled Shaya.

A second after seeing the seriousness in Shaya's face the Ra and Hayee stopped struggling. They angrily turned and stared at the Wa. Shaya turned towards the Wa and said, "I don't know what's happened here, but rest assured we will revisit this first thing when next day comes. For now, everyone take your leave. You will be escorted to your quarters. I don't want any trouble from anyone. If so, it will be harshly dealt with, this night! Now go!"

On Shaya's words, everyone quickly dispersed. Shaya turned and saw that La was gone. In fact, everyone turned to see La's reaction to what happened, but found she was not there. Shaya didn't see Hoban, or Ali. Trina and Anne were already gone. They left, earlier, just after the dance-offs. Shaya and Danaaa quickly left. They went to find La. They were sure they knew exactly where she was.

— CHAPTER 11 —

The crowd slowly went home. Ra guards escorted the Wa to their quarters. The Wa got a few glaring looks, while walking, but no one started any trouble. No one wanted to deal with the wrath of La or, the Number Two Princess, Shaya.

Once the Wa were in their quarters they checked to see if the guards were gone, so they could talk. When they were sure of that Gia said, "There's going to be trouble when day comes."

Yaya tried to calm the situation by saying "Shaya is very fair. She will see that it was a misunderstanding and that young Ra just over reacted."

Zan said, "That's what you hope will happen!"

Everyone looked at Zan. Their faces showed that they agreed with him. Gia said, "We should leave as soon as possible, before things escalate."

Zan said, "What's this talk of running? Did you see what we did? Those Ra and Hayee were no match for us! That wasn't close to our best! I say we kill at least one of the Royal Ra, if not all of them, before we leave!"

Yaya had fear in her eyes when she looked at Zan and then the other Wa. She said, "If you attempt that, you all will be killed!"

The Wa were offended that Yaya had so little confidence in their skills and it showed. Upon seeing that Yaya frantically said, "La and Dan are nothing like the Ra and Hayee you fought, earlier. Trust me when I say this. If you make an attempt on any of their lives, they themselves will kill you on the spot, or hunt you down until they kill all of you!"

Tay looked at the others and then looked at Yaya. He said, "Seems to me you don't have any confidence in our skills."

"It's not that! I just don't want any of you to get killed! Is that so bad a thing?" shouted Yaya.

Chet looked at Yaya and said, "We all came here knowing that was a possibility. You should have known that, too. If they think we're going to grovel at their feet, they have another thing coming. My mission, since I was a boy, was to train so that I could kill the Hayee and Ra that were responsible for the deaths of our family."

Yaya said, "The young Royal Ra had nothing to do with that! All of you know that! When will this blind hatred of them stop?"

Zan said, "Tell that to all of the innocent Wa that lost their lives!"

Yaya started to say something else, but Jami put her hand on Yaya's shoulders and turned Yaya towards her. Jami looked Yaya in her eyes and said, "No more talk. It's time for rest. If that Shaya wants to revisit things when first day comes, as she put it, the Wa will be ready."

Yaya knew there was nothing she could say this night, so she started getting ready for rest with the others. Yaya tried to figure out how she could defuse the situation when next day came. She thought about that until she drifted into sleep.

When next day came, Dan slowly came out of the deep sleep he was in. He opened his eyes and looked around. It was just before daybreak. The two females that spent the night with him were still sleep. Dan smiled and took in a deep breath and then exhaled. He was proud of himself.

The day before, Dan had one of the best days of his life. That day started out with Dan having the best sparring session he could remember. Dan was untouchable, while on defense. He was unstoppable when on offense. Besides Dan, everyone else there realized that, too.

Dan's great day continued when Trina showed up. Dan didn't know if he would be fighting with Trina the entire time she was here, after their first encounter. Dan thought to himself that La seemed to know how to deal with Trina, even if he didn't. Dan was glad he had La as a negotiator, because whatever La said seemed to work.

Dan took it from there and gave Trina a new experience that seemed to put her in his pocket. After what he put on Trina, Dan thought he would never have another problem with Trina.

Dan's great day wasn't over, yet. He met with and strengthened the alliances he had with the best warriors of this First Lower House. These warriors would now be training with Dan's top Warlords.

The icing on the cake was when Don said he had two females he wanted Dan to meet at the feast. One was nineteen and the other was twenty-six years old. Don told Dan that both of them were more than a little crazy. That was all Dan needed to hear. Once Dan got a good look at the two females, he knew Don was right. The nineteen year old giggled and stared at Dan, while the twenty-six year old smiled deviously at him.

In Dan's short history of dealing with women he had formulated a theory. Dan's theory was the crazier the girl was, the better she was in bed. Even though that wasn't always true, it had been true in Dan's dealings, so far. The only thing about crazy females is that they're not only crazy when it comes to sex, they're crazy most all the time!

Anyway, Dan got what he was looking for with these two girls. Dan took them to one of his private dwellings. Once there, they worked Dan over separately, as well as together. Dan first let them do their best, playing the willing victim. Soon, Dan turned the tables on both girls. He took turns riding them well into the night. Yes, Dan thought that was a great day! He wondered when this day came, could it get better. He sure was going to do his part to make that happen!

Dan looked over and noticed one of the females was stirring. He saw her perfectly round butt cheek flex, as she moved to a more comfortable position. Dan was a little hungry, but thought he might just hit that in a minute, or two. Awe heck! Why wait?

Dan raised his hand and slapped the girl's butt cheek. The sound was so loud that not only the girl who had her butt slapped was awakened, but the girl who was sleep was also awakened by the sound. They both jumped up startled, although for different reasons.

Both smiled at Dan and moved close on him. He wrapped his arms around both of them as they started manipulating his stick. In seconds, Dan was at attention, ready for whatever these girls could bring.

Dan and the two females paused after hearing someone coming down the hall. They listened intently, until they heard a guard outside the door whisper in a concerned voice, "My King, Trina is on her way! She forced her way in and could not be stopped! She'll be here any second!"

They listened to more footsteps coming fast. The two females tried to move away from Dan, as not to look guilty, but Dan held them close to him. They relaxed, knowing their King wanted them by his side. Trina turned into the doorway, stopped and stared at the girls. Then she looked into Dan's eyes. Her eyes moved down to the sheet that was covering Dan's hard stick, as it pointed towards the sky, underneath. Trina's eyes moved back to Dan's eyes. Dan could see the shock, hurt, and anger on Trina's face.

"What's the meaning of this?!!" screamed Trina.

Dan decided to take control of the situation before it got out of hand. Dan said, "Quite frankly, you shouldn't have come here. Calm yourself. No good will come from getting angry. Leave now and I'll meet you at first day's meal. Be a good girl and I'll give you some, later."

Dan smiled to let Trina know that everything was alright. Well, everything wasn't alright and Trina wasn't looking for any good to come out of this! As soon as Dan said his last word, Trina headed straight for him. She stopped in her tracks when both females in the bed with Dan jumped up onto their knees, in a crouching position, facing Trina. The nineteen year old female, named Cammy, said, "You heard King Dan! He said leave! It's best if you do just that!"

Trina's eyes quickly darted to Cammy's eyes. Once they locked eyes Trina lost it. She took one long step and launched herself into a flying kick at Cammy. Cammy tucked and rolled sideways out of the bed, barely avoiding the powerful kick.

When Trina landed she quickly turned towards Cammy. Cammy was naked and looked at her clothes for a split second to see if she could make it to them, before Trina attacked. That split second cost Cammy. Trina attacked in that same second.

Trina managed to get two solid blows in on Cammy, immediately. Those two punches sobered Cammy up enough to take Trina seriously. Cammy was use to much more physicality than that. After Trina's second punch, Cammy tore into Trina like a mad woman. Before Trina, or anyone else knew what happened Trina was on the ground trying to ward off the raining blows Cammy was sending down on her.

Dan feared for Trina's safety at that point. Just as he was about to move into action and call for Cammy to stop, Trina's female bodyguards appeared out of nowhere. Instantly, Cammy was beaten and dragged off of Trina. The twenty-six years old girl moved to help Cammy but was attacked and beaten by just one of Trina's female bodyguards.

"Enough!" Dan yelled and after a few more punches to get their point across, Trina's bodyguards stopped pummeling Cammy and her cousin. The bodyguards threw both girls to the ground, over in a corner of this room.

Dan looked a stern warning to Trina's bodyguards. He then looked down at the two girls that were unmercifully beaten. Dan turned just in time to see Trina moving fast towards Cammy with a furious anger. Dan jumped up and grabbed Trina, restraining her. Trina, while trying to force her way past Dan, said to the two females, "Next time I catch you with my King, I'll kill you!"

Dan, while holding Trina, half turned towards Cammy and the other female and said, "Leave, now!"

Dan looked at Trina's bodyguards and ordered, "Wait outside with my guards, until you are summoned!" the female bodyguards lowered their heads to Dan and did as they were told.

The two females cautiously grabbed their clothes and then ran out of the room. Dan watched as they did so. He couldn't remember either of their names. That wasn't important, anyway. He had an unruly Trina in his arms.

Trina struggled to get away from Dan. She was no match for Dan's strength. So instead of trying to use her arms, Trina pushed her body into Dan's, while twisting and turning. All of this extracurricular activity forced a rush of blood back into Dan's stick. When Trina felt it she stopped struggling and looked up at Dan with disgust in her eyes.

Dan said, "That's why those girls were here, because of your attitude! If you're so disgusted by me, get out of my sight!"

Dan took Trina by one arm and slung her towards the doorway. Trina's legs stopped her as soon as Dan's hand let go of her arm. Besides being angry, now Trina was confused. With her back to Dan, Trina angrily explained, "I would have been here, for you, if only you'd let me! You know that! I never.....!"

Dan grabbed Trina's arm and pulled her close to him. He interrupted her, saying, "Then don't, now!"

Trina was confused as to what they were talking about. She wrestled a little and said, "Don't what?!!"

Dan yelled, "That's it! Get out!"

Dan slung Trina towards the door, again. Again, Trina's legs stopped her as soon as Dan let go of her arm. At the same time, Trina yelled out, "No!!"

"Just, go!!" yelled Dan.

Trina paused for a moment and then said "No, I won't!!"

Dan grabbed Trina's arm and pulled her close to him. Dan's stick was still hard. Trina could feel it. Dan whispered sternly, "Then, what?"

Trina stared at Dan as he waited on a response. Although, Trina was angry and confused about what was going on here, she didn't want Dan to think he had to turn to other females for what he needed. Trina pleaded in a whisper, "Don't be angry with me because your whores are gone! I'm still here!"

Trina pressed her hips on Dan and started slowly grinding. She was shocked when Dan quickly reached down and put one arm between her legs and lifted her up. With his other arm behind Trina's back, Dan turned and jumped into the air towards the bed.

Even though Dan had Trina firmly in his arms, Trina dug the fingers of one hand into Dan's neck, while her other hand reached behind her trying to soften the impact she knew was coming. To Trina's surprise, because Dan had her firmly in his grasp it eased her impact. Dan immediately ripped Trina's clothes off, with her assistance. Then, Dan put it on Trina something fierce. He rode her into several orgasms. However, Dan would not release in Trina. Dan knew that was just enough to keep Trina satisfied and under control, so he stopped. Dan told Trina to go get cleaned up and he would see her at first day's meal.

Trina had just gone through a wide array of emotions. She went through shock, anger, dejection, rejection, confusion, pleasure, pain, happiness and more pleasure. Trina was emotionally spent. She was happy, as well confused. Still, she didn't want Dan to see that. She needed time to think about what happened and how best to deal with Dan. Trina was stuck on Dan no matter what he did and she knew it. She wanted him to keep doing what he'd just done to her. However, she also didn't like his attitude and the way he treated her. So, when Dan told her to go get cleaned up and he would see her later, that's what she did.

After Trina left, Dan relaxed on the bed. Sexually, Trina was no match for Dan. He knew that. His father and females, much older than Dan, taught him how to control women, with a mixture of forcefulness and a good sex game. That really put Trina at a disadvantage with Dan.

However, Dan did have to admit to himself that sex with Trina charged him more than any other female he'd ever been with. Dan put that out of his mind. He had Trina right where he wanted her. Dan smiled and told himself. With a little more training Trina would be doing whatever he wanted, without pause.

Dan was snatched out of his daydream by the pounding of war drums. He immediately jumped up and looked at his Hammer-Axes. Dan quickly put on his clothes. Dan knew his sisters should be at first day's training session. He didn't know where his brothers were. All of them split up with females of their choosing the night, before. Dan quickly grabbed his Hammer-Axes and was out the door.

Dan was met by several of his guards. Before they spoke, he could see the seriousness on their faces. They told him of what they knew. Dan couldn't believe it, even though, he had to. Dan asked about his brothers and sisters. After that, Dan took a deep breath and a half second to calm himself, before leaving.

La was alone, meditating on how she was going to deal with the Wa and her Hayee cousins. La saw the fight last night and thought the Wa might be a bigger threat that she hadn't anticipated. She was debating killing them and being done with it.

Another thing La was thinking about was the dreams she was having about the Lightning Jinn. She would regularly dream about staring into the eyes of the Lightning Jinn and being drawn in. She remembered being in a trance, until Dan snatched her off of her feet, breaking her eye contact with that Jinn.

In La's dreams she would stare into those eyes, until she saw something. She would be startled out of her sleep when she did. Every time La dreamed about that Jinn, those eyes revealed more to her. La didn't tell anyone about her dreams, because the dreams scared her. La was afraid of Jinns and everything to do with them.

What terrified her most was that she didn't want one taking over her like what she saw happen to Danaaa. Even though the dreams scared La, she didn't feel like something was trying to take over her mind and body. La heard the war drums and jumped up. She wondered where Shaya and Danaaa were. La grabbed her axes and quickly left.

Don and Yin were out cold. They were in the quarters of one of the high ranking females of this Lower House. She was thirty years old. She invited Don and his brothers here to enjoy her company, along with three of her close female cousins, for the night. So, for most of the night, Don and Yin put it to these females. They also learned a few more things from these women to add to their ever increasing sexual repertoire.

When the war drums went off, they both jumped up and only looked at each other for a second. Both quickly put on their clothes. Ram was with them when they came to this female's quarters, last night. He disappeared shortly after that.

Don was annoyed and wondered, if Ram knew something was going to happen the night before, why wouldn't he tell them? Yin thought about Ram and was annoyed, also. Yin wondered why Ram didn't take him along, this time. Don and Yin could see that besides being concerned for everyone, they both looked annoyed to each other. Neither knew it was because of Ram.

Right after getting dressed, Don and Yin headed for the front entrance. On the way, Yin suddenly stopped. Don stopped and looked at Yin. Yin looked at one of the guards in the hall and asked, "Where's the kitchen?"

Before the guard could answer, Don's face had an astonished confused look when he questioned, "What?"

"We haven't had anything to eat, yet."

"La and Shaya might be in harm's way! We have to get to them, immediately!"

While staring at Don Yin calmly said, "I know that. But, those are war drums. There's no telling what we might have to face. We both used a lot of energy last night. I'm not talking about a full meal. Let's just get a quick snack. That way we won't run out of energy."

Yin gave Don the only assurance an evil grin could give, which wasn't much. Don looked around and saw that this building wasn't under direct attack, yet. He wanted to get to La and Shaya as quickly as possible, but Yin made a good point. Don quickly nodded in agreement.

The guards escorted Yin and Don to the kitchen. They ate as much fruit and nuts as they could. Once they'd done that Don and Yin walked quickly towards the exit. They were met by females in charge here, who called their guards. One female told Don and Yin she would support them with guards. Yin and Don took a short moment, trying to figure out the best plan of action.

Don knew the war drums meant there was a threat from outside of this Lower House. Don knew once he and Yin met up with La and Dan, those two would make up a plan. Don was going to take his three bodyguards and find his siblings.

Yin, on the other hand, was a little pissed that Ram hadn't taken him on his secret mission. Yin, like his father, had a wild crazy side. The only thing that kept his angry wild streak in check was he had his mother's intelligence. Also, La and Dan would take nothing less than Yin staying in line. They weren't here, so Yin was going to think of a mission he knew would challenge himself and Don.

Before Don could respond to the female in charge, Yin said to her, "Stay here and protect this building with your guards. If there's a prolonged attack we may need a safe haven between battles. Once we find out what's going on, we'll let everyone know."

The female looked at Don to see if he agreed with Yin. Don thought Yin was on the right track, so he nodded in agreement. The female in charge started barking out orders, immediately. The guards and everyone else dispersed, going in different directions.

Don and Yin looked at each other and then headed towards the exit. Don knew his cousin well and looked at him suspiciously. He knew Yin was an adrenaline junky when it came to fighting. So, just as they were getting to the exit, Don reminded Yin, saying, "First, we get to La and Dan. We decide what to do, after that."

The Wa had been awake for a while. They were discussing what they thought might happen this day. They didn't have to wait long to find out. They were told that Shaya requested all of them to accompany her to see the Number One Princess and discuss last night's events. The Wa armed themselves and then went outside to meet Shaya.

Earlier, because La needed time to sort out her thoughts by herself, she sent Shaya and Danaaa to get the Wa and bring them to one of their small training facilities. La said that they would be questioned about their actions, there.

Shaya, although suspicious of La's intentions, decided not to question La. She would watch and try to persuade La, if necessary. Besides, Shaya had a plan. With it being this early, Shaya was sure she could catch some of the guards in a state of undress if she went to the guard housing. She thought it wouldn't hurt anything, since it was on the way to the Wa quarters. After they were far enough that La couldn't hear, Shaya told Danaaa her plans.

This time Shaya told Danaaa that only she could hear. Shaya's bodyguards wouldn't know where they were going, until it was too late. Shaya sent her bodyguards to fetch the Wa and meet her near the dungeons, which was halfway between the Wa place and the guards housing. By the time her bodyguards got back with the Wa, Shaya would have completed her mission.

No one, besides Danaaa and the guards at the housing would be the wiser. Shaya knew Danaaa wouldn't say anything to La, or anyone else. She also figured the guards would say nothing, knowing any gossip concerning the Number Two Princess was punishable, by death.

On the way to the guard housing, Shaya told Danaaa that this was the time that guards might be plotting something. She told Danaaa to remember that it was early in the day when they snuck into the palace and attacked, long ago. Danaaa's eyes squinted in contemplative memory at how sneaky the guards could be. So when they arrived at the guard housing and Shaya told Danaaa to check one building, while she herself checked another, Danaaa quickly nodded in agreement. Shaya went to one guard building, while Danaaa went to another.

The buildings the guards stayed in had entrances and many openings on all sides, which might be interpreted as windows. Shaya stealthily walked over and looked in. In this day and time, most of the guards slept with little, or nothing on. That kept them cool at night and allowed for a restful sleep.

When Shaya looked in she was not disappointed. She saw everything from naked bodies to the guards' hard sticks pointing as they slept. Shaya was so enthralled by what she saw that her mouth hung open as she stared. One of the guards felt someone looking at him and quickly turned to see Shaya. Shaya noticed his movement and stared at him. He had a curious look on his face upon seeing the Number Two Princess staring at him. Shaya quickly put one finger up to her lips and quietly, bit sternly said, "Shush!"

The guard slowly turned his back to Shaya and pretended to be sleep. Once Shaya had the situation under control she went back to staring at all the naked guards.

When Danaaa got to the other guard housing she looked in and saw that all of the guards were sleep. She was relieved that they weren't plotting anything. Then one of the guards turned over and Danaaa saw his rock hard stick pointing in her direction. She was shocked!

Still, Danaaa could see that he and the other guards were still sleep. For comparison purposes, as well as the curiosity of it all, Danaaa looked around and noticed that all of the guards were mostly naked. She knew Shaya was probably seeing the same thing she was. She just knew it!

"SHAAYYAAA!!!" Danaaa yelled as loud as she could, with her eyes blazing.

The guards in all of the guard buildings jumped up, upon hearing Danaaa's voice. Then Danaaa marched to where she knew Shaya was.

Upon hearing Danaaa yell Shaya knew the gig was up. Several of the guards saw Shaya quickly walking from one of the guard buildings. They hoped nothing happened. That's when they saw Danaaa march up to Shaya. Shaya saw Danaaa walking towards her. She could see that Danaaa was angry and annoyed. Shaya took control of the situation, saying, "Baby, did you find anything?"

Danaaa found and saw more than she was willing to admit. However, she said, "NO, I DIDN'T!"

"Neither, did I." Shaya quickly said.

Danaaa squinted her eyes, suspiciously looking at Shaya. After a short stare, Danaaa said in an annoyed voice, "Come, let's go!"

Shaya nodded in agreement and they both walked off. Shaya could feel Danaaa looking at her from time to time, but didn't care. Shaya had completed her mission of scouting the guards. That was only slightly satisfying for Shaya. Now that Shaya got a good look at all the shapes and sizes, Shaya was going to figure out how to complete the mission of finding alone time with certain guards she saw.

The Wa were being escorted to meet Shaya, so they could be taken to see the Number One Princess, La. They wondered why the guards didn't just take them. They figured it must just be some screwy protocol of the Ra. Nevertheless, they were on guard in case there was foul play.

Yaya, being with them, was nervous. She wondered what La had planned. And since Shaya wasn't here, Yaya couldn't get any for warning. Yaya and her Wa cousins walked for a short distance, before seeing the dungeons.

As the Wa approached they saw a large group of Hayee and Ra guards. The Wa remembered seeing some of them at the feast last night. The Hayee and Ra guards were tying two men to wooden posts. This was how they beheaded prisoners. As the Wa got closer they saw the young Ra they fought last night. Then they got a good look at the prisoners. They were Shinmushee. All of the Wa, including Yaya stared at the two prisoners who had already been badly beaten.

The young teenage Ra who was soundly beaten by the Wa the night before, turned and saw the Wa staring in his direction. He looked at the two Shinmushee prisoners, before looking back at the Wa. The teenage Ra said, "Don't worry about these two. They're dead. If not for Shaya and La, you would be, too!"

The other Hayee and Ra guards turned to see who their cousin was talking to. They were about to warn him about his taunting when they saw the Wa staring.

Trina had just come from Dan's place. She was so deep in thought that she was barely paying attention. She was following her bodyguards, going to meet the Royal Ra girls. She only looked up when she saw Anne running over to her. Upon seeing Trina's face, Anne asked, "What's wrong?"

Shaya and Danaaa were just coming in sight of the dudgeons. They could see the Wa, a lot of Hayee and some Ra guards. They also saw Trina and Anne, along with some of their bodyguards.

Once that teenage Ra taunted the Wa, Yaya knew it would only be a matter of time before hostilities broke out. She looked at Zan and Chet.

"Don't let him provoke you! You'll only succeed in getting yourselves killed!" pleaded Yaya.

Yaya saw in Zan and the other's eyes that it was already too late. Zan said in a low angry voice, "No one's asking you to help! Leave if you want!"

The two Shinmushee that were tied to the post, about to be beheaded, were the sons of the family that raised the Wa and acted as guardians while they were in the Southern Jungle. That's why these two brothers weren't in the jungle when the five visited their adopted family days, earlier. It only took the Wa seeing the two Shinmushee brothers tied to those post, before their minds were made up. Sometime you have to make a stand, no matter what the odds are. Without saying one word to each other, the Wa decided this was one of those times.

At that same moment, all of the Wa pulled their weapons and headed towards the Hayee and Ra guards. The second the Wa attacked the War drums sounded.

Upon hearing the war drums, every Hayee and Ra guard within sight turned. When they saw the Wa with their weapons already drawn, they rushed in to attack. The Wa were attacked from all sides.

Zan, Jami, Boku and Uma carved a path through the Ra guards, straight towards the two Shinmushee that were tied to the post. Chet, Gia and Tay formed a fighting perimeter at the backside of the four Wa that were now untying the Shinmushee prisoners. Boku and Uma instantly had to turn and attack guards that were already inside the perimeter when the fight broke out.

Yaya's eyes were wide and wildly staring at everything happening around her. She had her axes in hand but had not used them once. Reality hit Yaya when five Ra guards moved towards her. If they got past her, the guards could possibly separate the Wa into two fighting groups. That would give the Ra guards an edge in this battle. Yaya took a defensive step back. She really didn't want to engage the Ra guards. But once the Ra guards saw that Yaya hadn't stepped aside, they attacked her. After dodging and barely being missed by two axes, Yaya found herself in an intense battle.

When the battle erupted, Chet, Gia and Tay moved outward towards the Ra guards. When they did, that put Trina, Anne and their bodyguards inside the perimeter the Wa had created. The bodyguards instantly took defensive stances around Trina and Anne. That's when they were attacked.

Trina wasn't thinking about Dan, anymore. She saw axes swinging all around her. Trina saw Anne staring at the ferocious battles going on all around them. One of Trina's bodyguards cried out as he was split open from his neck down through his chest. After the second bodyguard fell, Trina grabbed Anne's arm and stared at her for only a second. In that second both girls knew what it was.

Both Trina and Anne pulled their axes, put their backs to each other and crouched in a defensive position. They saw one more of their Bodyguards fall to the axes of the Wa. Trina hoped Dan would get here before she had to use her axes. Anne also wondered why Ram wasn't already here, rescuing her. After that, both girls focused their concentration. They watched to see which Wa would get to them, first.

──── CHAPTER 12 ────

Now that the two Shinmushee were free, they grabbed axes off the ground, dropped by the dead Ra guards. Jami quickly looked around and yelled, "We got them! Let's get out of here!"

That's when Chet saw hammers coming towards him and the other Wa. He blocked the one coming at himself and then jumped in the air, intercepting and blocking the other hammers. When he landed, Chet had to duck under and block several axe swings, meant to slice him in half. In that same instant, Chet saw the girl who'd thrown those hammers.

Almost at the same time he saw the one called High Pressure the Executioner flying through the air in a tight ball, towards the center of the Wa, where Anne and Trina were. Chet was instantly engaged by several more Ra guards. He could still see the girl with the hammers, aiming and waiting on the perfect opportunity to throw them.

Danaaa got the attention of Chet and all of the other Wa as she landed next to Boku and Uma. Boku and Uma had managed to kill most of Trina and Anne's bodyguards. Once Danaaa landed next to Boku and Uma they turned and attacked her, immediately. Zan and Jami also moved towards Danaaa.

Danaaa was surrounded. Still, the second Boku and Uma attacked her, Danaaa swung her axes at both of them, continuously, really fast! That put Boku and Uma on defense, right away. The other Wa saw that and were amazed only for a second, before they knew those two needed help. Zan and Jami arrived just in time to help.

That's when the Wa found out how good Danaaa really was. She was moving extremely fast with not only her axes, but with her fancy footwork. She was running circles around the four Wa. So much so, that all of the remaining Ra guards moved back. They could see she had all four on defense.

Gia looked at Chet, who was with Tay, fighting Ra guards near Shaya. They both knew there was little or no chance of surviving, unless they got out of here, right away. Gia ran back towards the other Wa fighting Danaaa, while Tay and Chet forced a path towards the woods behind Shaya and her guards.

Zan knew they would be soon facing the entire Ra army, if they didn't quickly end this battle and leave with their Shinmushee brothers. Zan was determined that one of the Ra would die here today, if he was going to. Zan decided to sell out, in order to mortally wound, or kill the she devil they called the High Pressure the Executioner.

Zan moved ahead of the others and ferociously swung his axes at Danaaa. She was barely missed by two of his swings. That pissed Danaaa off. Then on top of that, while realizing she was pissed, she barely avoided two more of his swings. Danaaa knew the play that was going on here. Zan wanted to die first. Danaaa decided she was going to grant him that wish!

With three other Wa swinging their axes at Danaaa, she forced the action, with her axes, towards Zan. She blocked with her axes when she had to, but avoided most of the swings, so she could send her axes at Zan.

Zan and the other were swinging their axes for all they were worth at Danaaa. Still, they couldn't get an ax on her! Zan was doing everything not to get cut up by Danaaa. However, with axes still coming at her, Danaaa was putting more heat on Zan.

Danaaa's axes managed to maneuver their way through Zan's defense. She missed with the first, but caught Zan with a glancing slice that opened his flesh on one side of his chest. Zan was able to get a bit more room when the other Wa swung their axes at Danaaa.

Danaaa easily kept the others at bay, as she stayed close to Zan. Danaaa measured and realized how much closer she had to be so that the blade of her ax would go much deeper and mortally wound Zan the next time.

Danaaa worked her way closer and after some nifty maneuvering she swung her ax at Zan's chest. Inches from his chest, Danaaa's ax was blocked. Danaaa ducked under a powerful swing from Zan. She measured where his axes were and knew she could slice him before he had a chance to block.

Danaaa swung and again her ax was blocked. At the same time, another ax came at the wrist of her hand. Danaaa did a lightning fast tuck and roll away from the Wa. Zan and the other Wa swung wildly at Danaaa. They all barely missed her. The Wa quickly closed in on her. Just as they did, Danaaa saw the play that was going on.

Gia was using the speed of both her axes only to assault and defend the left hand and ax of Danaaa, while the other Wa attacked Danaaa from all angles. Danaaa knew she would have to eliminate this girl, if she wanted to kill Zan. So now, Danaaa's main goal was to kill Gia in order to get to Zan.

Once Danaaa decided what she wanted to do, it didn't take long for her to execute that mission. Danaaa spun away from the other Wa, towards Gia. Before the others could mount a defense, Danaaa was right on Gia. Danaaa quickly maneuvered her ax blades past Gia's blocking axes, seconds away from splitting Gia open. That's when Danaaa heard Shaya yell, "Baby, stop! Move back! If you harm them, he'll kill me!"

The instant Danaaa heard that, she launched herself backwards up into the air, landing a short safe distance from the Wa. She looked over and saw that one of the Wa had his ax up to Shaya's throat. Everyone who hadn't already seen Shaya stopped fighting and stared at her.

Chet, who had one arm around Shaya's waist and the ax in his other hand at her throat, lifted Shaya off her feet, while turning erratically, making sure none of the Ra Guards could get behind him to administer a fatal blow.

The Ra guards all took a step back from Chet. Chet cautiously made his way over to the other Wa. Once there, Chet slowly lowered Shaya letting her stand on her feet, with his ax still at her throat.

In the confusion Trina and Anne were quickly disarmed and had axes aimed at them by Tay and Boku. They were also taken hostage.

Danaaa walked over and cautiously followed Chet as he moved towards the other Wa. She watched for any opening that she could take advantage of. The only problem was that Chet had his ax blade right on Shaya's throat. Danaaa knew she would have to make one clean deadly strike that would take Chet down, without harming Shaya. When Danaaa didn't see that opening she looked Chet in his eyes and yelled, "Let her go!"

"Step back, or I take her head!" yelled Chet.

Danaaa's eyes went from Chet's eyes to Shaya's eyes. Danaaa could see fear in Shaya's eyes. Danaaa took a quick step backwards and looked angrily into Chet's eyes.

"What now?!" yelled Danaaa.

"We're getting out of here! If you try anything, I take her head!" said Chet.

"And we'll kill these two, also!" Tay added.

Danaaa had barely noticed that Trina and Anne were hostages. She peeked at them when Tay spoke. They weren't enough to keep her attention away from the ax at Shaya's throat.

Not even Yaya's begging for the three girls to be released got much of Danaaa's attention. Danaaa was aware of everything around her, but it was secondary to Shaya and Chet.

Staring at Chet, Danaaa didn't know the right words to make him let Shaya go. She also couldn't use her axes to resolve the situation. Danaaa took a quick look around and then looked back at Chet. Where was La? Where was Dan? Danaaa was sure one of them would know what to do!

Don and Yin came through the exit of the dwelling. Once there, both stopped and looked around. Don was glad he let Yin talk him into getting that quick snack. He could see it was going to be a difficult day. They saw that the guards of this dwelling had a defensive perimeter. Outside of that perimeter was a group of ten Shinmushee Butchers, backed up by what looked like an endless number of warriors. Don and Yin quickly drew their Hammer-Axes.

Don got a serious contemplative look on his face, while Yin's evil grin got nastier. In a low voice, Yin said to Don, "Nice! This is gonna be fun!"

Don half turned his head, while keeping his eyes ahead and said to Yin, "This is serious!"

"I know!" Yin calmly said.

"Well, just stick to the plan! We find La and Shaya, first! Then we see what to do next!" explained Don.

Don wondered why the Shinmushee hadn't attacked this home, yet. Instead, they waited until he and Yin came out. That puzzled Don. He quickly put that out of his mind and started studying the area that would soon be the battlefield. Yin got Don and everyone else's attention by clanging his axes together, taunting the Shinmushee. The evil grin on Yin's face got bigger. Don didn't waste time trying to stop Yin from taunting the Shinmushee Butchers.

After Yin's taunting one of the Shinmushee Butchers spoke, saying, "We'll kill everyone here, if we have to! But really, we just want you two!"

He looked directly at Yin and said, "Approach if you dare. I'm sure we can cut that silly grin off of your face!"

Don knew these Shinmushee were here to kill him and Yin. However, Don wondered how they knew where and who he and Yin were? And if they knew where he and Yin were, did they know where his other siblings were? Don hoped the others were safe. He knew the only way he'd find out was if he and Yin carved a path through these Shinmushee Butchers.

Yin was offended, but the evil grin didn't come off of his face.

He immediately started walking towards the Shinmushee Butchers. Yin yelled out, "Guards, move aside! We're going to give these Shitmushee what they're looking for! A quick trip to hell!"

The guards moved back, creating a new defensive perimeter, behind Yin and Don.

Don wanted to warn Yin that he was walking right into a trap. Since there was no time to warn Yin, Don marched right beside Yin towards the Shinmushee. Don and Yin moved slightly away from each other while walking. They were giving each other enough spacing to swing their Hammer-Axes freely without fear of cutting each other. Don took a step forward and said, "Alright, who's first?"

After Don said that the Shinmushee Butchers started spreading out surrounding Don and Yin. Don and Yin were extremely smart in their fighting strategies. They knew they couldn't be separated from each other, if they could help it.

Don was determined to get to his sisters. Yin was determined to kill as many of these Butchers and warriors as he could. A second later they were attacked.

Both of their battles went from zero to one hundred miles an hour in a split second. Both were fighting three Shinmushee Butchers each. Don forced his battle a little further away from Yin. Don wanted to make sure both he and Yin could keep an eye on all of the enemy combatants in their immediate area.

Meanwhile, Yin was attacking the three Shinmushee Butchers with what seemed to be reckless abandonment. He didn't seem to care about defense and was barely being missed by ax swings coming from the Shinmushee Butchers. The Shinmushee Butchers were trying to contain Yin with their ax-play, but had to mix in plenty of defense, because of Yin's accurately fast ax swings. As reckless as Yin seemed to be, the Shinmushee Butchers were sure they would be able to make him pay with his life.

What the Shinmushee Butchers didn't realize was this was the fighting style that Yin inherited genetically from his father and was what he was best suited for. Yin was the faster, stronger and smarter version of his father, because of his mother, Tara.

Yin was giving these three Shinmushee Butcher a fighting puzzle that they found hard to figure out. Yin's offense was erratic, unpredictable, while being extremely fast and accurate. So, within five minutes of their battle with Yin, the three Shinmushee Butchers had to turn up the heat on Yin. Within two minutes of turning up the heat on Yin, two of the Shinmushee Butchers were wounded. One of them, mortally.

Warriors helped the mortally wounded Shinmushee Butcher out of the battle, otherwise Yin would have finished him off. Several more Shinmushee Butchers joined the remaining two Butchers fighting Yin. The more heat that was put on Yin, the better and wilder his style of fighting became. Yin was now in a hellish battle with five Shinmushee Butchers. All of them intent on cutting him well!

Don was barely able to keep an eye on Yin. That was because he was under high heat from the three Shinmushee Butcher he was fighting. Don was fighting from one move to the next. Every one of Don's moves had to be his best leading up to his next move. His concentration was so focused that every once in a while he had to widen the scope of his vision beyond the three Shinmushee Butchers he was fighting. Don forced himself to do this, because he noticed other Shinmushee Butchers circling his battle, looking for an opportunity to strike.

With all of that going on, this was the most intense battle Don had ever been in. Well, it was, until several more Shinmushee joined in his battle right after Yin mortally wounded one of the Butchers he was fighting. Don kicked his fighting up to meet the challenge. Not one minute after that, Don, who barely saw Yin's strike on that Butcher, thought to himself 'Thanks Yin!'

After a few more moments of extreme fighting, Don realized it was hard to keep track of all the axes coming at him. He was in the Hell of axes coming at him from all directions. Don was near panic trying to keep those axes off his ass!

Then, out of nowhere, Don heard Syn, Jara's voice in his head. She said, "If you don't panic, there's always a way out of most every situation. Just stay calm, concentrate and keep your wits about yourself. That's how you figure things out."

Don remembered Syn, Jara telling him that in a training session in which she was beating the Hell out of him, unmercifully, with some high heat that he couldn't deal with. After she told Don that she still continued to beat the Hell out of him, but for some reason her words stuck in the back of his mind.

Still, Don saw his calm, his concentration and his wits at the door waving for him to come with them, because they were about to get the hell out of here! Don brought himself back from the brink of panic to a reasonably high state of urgency. He would stay there, in his mind, until he could find his way out of this situation, while fighting for his life.

Ali and Hoban were waiting on La when she was leaving the building. They quickly told La what they knew of the situation. Figuring Dan and her brothers could handle themselves, she inquired about her sisters. Ali, La's Warlord, told her that he'd sent extra guards to make sure they were protected. Still, that's where La was headed. After trotting a short distance La, Ali and Hoban were shocked by what they saw.

La saw her grandfather carrying Deen's bloody limp body, while Ra guards fought trying to protect their backs. La turned and saw Shinmushee everywhere. She looked back, with fear and concern in her eyes, towards her grandfather and yelled, "Grandpa!!"

La then bolted towards her grandfather. When she got to Roe, he said, "I'm alright, but Deen's badly wounded!"

"Master Deen!!" La screamed.

La saw Deen's clothes were soaked in blood. Deen's eyes were barely open. He saw La and focused his eyes on her. Deen's eyes seemed to light up upon seeing La. His voice was weak, but exited, when he said, "La, it's you!"

"Yes, master, it's me! Save your energy! We'll get you to safety!" La said.

Deen paused, breathing heavily. He refocused on La. Deen's voice was weak when he said, "Remember all that I …that I have taught you…..Mo…Most of all…...Have..mercy on….your enemies!"

Deen's head fell back. He was dead. La shook her teacher, trying to wake him. Once La realized he was dead she tenderly placed him on the ground and stared down at him. When Deen's head fell, so did La's heart.

The hurtful feeling of loss La felt quickly turned to anger. La thought 'Have mercy on my enemies, after this! If they can live after my ax blades slice through them to my liking, then mercy will be theirs to have!'

La was snapped back into reality when Roe put his hand on her shoulder and said, "La, we have to go!"

La looked up into Roe's eyes. A fierce anger engulfed her. However she was crystal clear about what needed to be done. She stood up.

"Get my grandpa to safety!" La ordered to Ali.

Roe looked into La's eyes. He feared what she might do. He said, "La, let's get everyone safely back to the main city!"

Ali motioned for guards to escort Roe. La looked her grandfather in his eyes. She gave him a warm smile full of concern and nodded her head in agreement. La gave her grandfather a kiss on his cheek. After that, La turned and bolted towards the Shinmushee. Ali and Hoban, along with La's bodyguards ran to aid her. La completely forgot about her sisters. She instantly started killing every Shinmushee in sight.

When Dan heard the war drums his bodyguards told him the Shinmushee were attacking the city from all sides. Dan went to make sure his sisters were unharmed. Where La and her sisters slept was in the opposite direction from where the Wa, Shaya and Danaaa were. But since Dan and his bodyguards didn't know that, he raced to where he thought they were.

Dan and his bodyguards met stiff resistance on the way. It didn't matter. Dan wasn't going to be stopped. He shredded every Shinmushee in his path. After a few intense battles he finally made it to where La was. Dan was briefed on what happened here. He asked about his other sisters, while watching La massacre Shinmushee. The guards had no information, yet. Dan decided it was time to get La under control so they could make sure all their siblings were safe.

Dan had his bodyguards push ahead of where La was fighting. That cut off her supply of Shinmushee. Before she could move past Dan's guards Dan stepped in front of La. It took a few second before La recognized Dan.

La angrily stared at Dan and yelled, "They killed Master Deen!"

"I just found out."

"Get out of my way! I'm going to kill them all!"

"Alright, but first we find Shaya and Baby."

La stared into Dan's eyes for a moment and then said, "Fine, let's go!"

They were about to turn around and saw the battle ahead of them taking a bad turn. Dan's bodyguards were being cut to pieces by Shinmushee Butchers. Ali suggested that they leave quickly if they wanted to get away. Dan and La looked at each other. It sounded like Ali was suggesting they run. Normally, La would see it as Ali trying to make sure they could get to Shaya and Danaaa. Because she was angry, La didn't.

La said, "We take care of this group, first! I don't want them sneaking up on me, later!"

Dan nodded in agreement. Ali and Hoban moved closer to La. Dan was next to a few of his bodyguards. That's when Shinmushee Butchers moved past the Ra guards, who were busy fighting other Shinmushee Butchers.

The Shinmushee Butchers walked forward. Just as Dan and La

were about to attack, one of the Butchers said, "Someone wants to meet you."

La and Dan paused. They thought it might be that fat old fighting master from the Jungle. They were wrong.

Dan and La were surprised when they saw four strange looking Shinmushee walking through the crowd of Shinmushee Butchers. There were three males and one female. Two other Shinmushee were carrying a large box that resembled a modern day coffin. A younger looking Shinmushee male was crouched in a squatting position with his feet on the seat of a throne chair that was being carried by several other Shinmushee guards.

The four walked a little closer and then stopped. La yelled, "You killed my teacher! For that, all of you die!"

The girl with the three men smiled at La and said, "If I'm right, tell me then. You must be the Young Queen of Ra. Are you not?"

La said in a nasty tone, "I'll not be questioned by a Shitmushee!"

The girl looked at the three men next to her and said, "See, I was right. That's her!"

La stared at the girl as she spoke. She peeked at the young man crouching on the throne chair, but was focused on the others that moved ahead of him. La watched both the crouching man and the girl who'd just spoke.

Dan watched all of the Shinmushee, closely. The three men and the girl all had axes in their hands, ready for battle. The one on the throne chair didn't. The man on the throne chair also looked strangely unconcerned with his surroundings. Dan took all of that in.

After seeing they were trying to identify La, Dan thought them to be the best Head Collectors the Shinmushee could find. However, Dan couldn't figure out what was in the box. Dan's thoughts were interrupted when the girl spoke, again. She looked directly at Dan and said, "You must be the King of Ra. Are you not?"

Dan was getting annoyed with this girl. He said, "Get to the point, or you'll be dead, before making it!"

The girl sarcastically said, "As you wish, King of Ra."

She smiled, looking at La and then back at Dan. She said, "You met my great grand-pappy a while, ago. He taught you a lesson you'll never forget."

Dan said, "So that fat old fighting master sent you here to die. What a pity!"

The smile left the girl's face, after Dan said that. Dan smiled at the girl. Once Dan smiled, the smile returned to the girl's face. She said, "Well, he was right about you. He said I'd be able to recognize you by your arrogance."

La took an aggressive step towards the girl. Both sides went on guard. Dan grabbed La's arm before she could take another step. La snatched her arm from Dan. La angrily stared at the girl. Dan moved slightly ahead of La and said, "As you can see, you don't have much longer to talk. Say why you're here, while you can!"

The girl said, "Why we're here, I'll tell you then. We're here to finish your lesson, as a gift to both of you."

"If we want anything from you, we'll just take it! As for a lesson, you're still talking!" yelled La.

Dan bumped La, while looking at the girl. He said, "I'll play your game. What lesson do you have for us?"

The girl looked at La, waved her hand, presenting the man on the throne and said, "First, a gift for you young Queen. He's one of grand-pappy's favorites. I'm his favorite, too. But, enough about me. Young Queen, I'd like you to meet Claw!"

Dan and La stared at the man crouching on the throne, who appeared to be in his young twenties. He looked to be in very good fighting condition. He had his hands up at his chest, pointing forward, like they were little bird claws.

When the girl introduced him, he seemed to come alive. He stepped down off of the throne, one foot at a time. He was still crouching on what looked to be unstable legs. He took an unstable crouching step, wobbling towards La, looking like a bird.

Dan and La curiously looked at each other, before erupting into laughter. While laughing, Dan could see that the girl was watching the strange man, closely. That's when Dan thought that they should take this, seriously. Dan said, "La, watch him closely."

La nodded that she would. A second later the young man jumped into the air, launching himself in La's direction. While in the air the young man let out a loud shriek.

Hoban stepped in front of La with his ax swinging towards where the young man would be landing. As he was coming out of the air, the young man extended one arm and placed his hand on the flat side of the ax coming at him. He pressed down only hard enough to send himself flipping over the ax blade with one of his feet aimed at Hoban's face. Hoban reacted just in time by ducking and moving to the side, just under the kick. That put the young man close enough to La that she swung her ax at him.

Now standing straight up, the man twisted his body just out of the way of La's ax strike, while extending his arm, reaching for the arm that La swung her ax with. La saw the counter move just in time and redirected her arm. Still, the cloth on the sleeve of her arm was ripped away. That shocked La, but she had a trick for this clawing birdman.

La plowed the ax in her other hand right at the chest of Claw. This time when his arm came clawing at her, La sent her other ax with lightning speed at his striking arm. Claw leaned back and his other hand came from his chest and grabbed at La's counter-striking arm. Again, La reacted in time not to be grabbed, even though cloth from that arm was also torn away. La's other ax came instantly came up, trying to carve that arm, but she just missed her mark by an eyelash.

Dan was watching and after seeing how quick Claw was without axes, Dan had seen enough. Dan quickly moved towards Claw. Claw was already inside of La's previous counter swing. Before Dan could get into position, or La could react, Claw struck out with both arms at the same time. La frantically avoided the left hand by moving to her right, while swinging her ax blade. La knew she wouldn't catch his arm before it struck, but she was going to chop it off as it was leaving.

Just as La anticipated, Claw got his free strike. La was surprised that even though Claw could have went for a more vital spot, La felt his powerful fingers digging into her shoulder. La twisted her shoulder just before Claw could get the full power of his grip on her. Still, the cloth from her shoulder was ripped away. La's other ax came up to take that hand and the cloth, clean from his arm, as it retracted.

La was surprised when Claw's other hand grabbed the ax handle of her fast approaching ax, while his other open hand slammed into La's chest with so much force that La was sent backwards, off of her feet.

La was strong, as well as stubborn. She held on to the ax handle that Claw grabbed. Consequently, as La's body was moving backwards, its momentum was stopped by her holding on to her ax handle. La's body was jerked back towards Claw. That's when Claw turned his body towards La's and he let go of the ax handle, sending a more powerful open palmed blow to La's chest.

This time the blow was so powerful that La let go of both her ax handles as she went flying backwards. La's arms swung wildly as she barely landed on her feet, stumbling backwards, trying to keep her balance.

Everyone, including Claw was surprised that La was able to keep her footing, after that powerful blow. The second thing that shocked everyone was that Claw had the rest of La's blouse in his hand. If not for La's chest protecting vest her breast would be completely exposed.

La had never been hit that hard in her entire life. While trying to take control of her breathing, La stared at Claw in anger, breathing heavily, while dealing with the pain from that blow. La didn't notice her blouse was gone, until she saw Claw throw it to the ground. He was attacked by Dan, Hoban and Ali, after that.

Dan had been trying to get into position to defend La. But the action between Claw and La was some of the fastest and ferocious he'd ever seen. Dan was only able to get into position after Claw's last blow on La. But when he saw the same blow that he received from the jolly old master administered to La by Claw, Dan knew he had to save his sister from whatever else was coming.

Dan kicked himself into a higher level of speed. His axes came at Claw's arms and hands much quicker than La's. Claw didn't have a chance to take advantage of La, while she was off balance. He was now doing everything he could to avoid Dan, Hoban and Ali's axes.

However, Claw was getting the most heat from Dan. La had been hit twice and Dan was offended. Dan took it personal and was disappointed that he couldn't get there in time to stop either blow. Dan was determined to right those wrongs. Each swing of his axes conveyed that.

The young girl saw that Claw was in trouble. She didn't want to take the chance that he could handle this battle on his own. The girl motioned for two of the three men at her side to help Claw. They quickly moved in and attacked Hoban and Ali. Ali and Hoban were quickly separated from Dan and Claw.

The other Ra bodyguards saw the play that was going on here. They rushed over to help Dan, while others ran over, taking up defensive positions at La's sides. The last man by the young girl's side looked at her. When she nodded her head he went to help Claw with Dan.

The bodyguards that went to help Dan and La's Warlords were met and attacked by Shinmushee Butchers. La watched everything that was going on. The situation had gotten out of control. She knew of only one way to turn things back in her favor. She looked and saw the young girl still staring at her, with a smile on her face. The girl had La's axes in her hands. La calmed herself and stared at the girl. La started taking air into her lungs.

La was only able to take in slightly more air than a normal breath. Not near enough to blast a scream. La's eyes got big with concerned after she tried again and felt pain when she tried to inhale, deeply. With intense fighting going on all around them, both La and the girl seemed to be mostly aware of each other.

The girl had a smile on her face when she said, "No screams

for you this day, Young Queen. You guaranteed that when you stubbornly took that second blow from Claw. How tough you are. I admire you for that. Your breathing would have return to normal in two days. By then, it will be too late!"

The girl threw La's axes to La after her last sentence. La caught her axes and went on guard. La knew even though she couldn't take in enough air to scream, she could control her breath enough to fight. She lifted her axes, pointing them towards the girl. La said, "Tell me, she who likes to smile! Before I kill you, what is your name?"

The girl quickly raised both her arms up and then down, towards the ground, at her sides. When she did, hooked blade came sliding out of their compartments, extending and locking over and past her hands. The girl's smile turned devious when she said, "My name, well, I'll tell you what I'm called! They call me Deadly Hearts! My given name is Shinmushee-La!"

—— CHAPTER 13 ——

La was shocked that this girl's name was that same as La's nickname. Still, La said, "Hooked blades are no match for axes!"

"When they're with me, they are!"

"We'll see about that! Guards, kill her!"

La's Elite Bodyguards attacked Hearts, immediately. The smile left Heart's face once she was attacked. La watched as Hearts moved with lightning speed right towards the first guard's ax swing. Hearts was barely missed when she leaned out of the way of one his axes. She then plunged her hooked blade straight into his heart, while blocking his other ax.

The other two Elite Guards attacked, swinging ferociously at Hearts. Hearts avoided, dodged and blocked all of the ax swings coming at her. When she saw the slightest opening, Hearts went on the offensive. She plowed her hooked blade threw the heart of that Elite Guard.

Before the other one could react, she had her hooked blade headed at lightning speed towards his heart. Well, he'd heard her name and also had seen the play that was going on here. This Elite Guard brought his ax up in front of his heart for the block, while sending his other ax at Hearts' neck. At the last fraction of a second, Hearts changed the trajectory of her blade and sent it up and threw the neck of the Elite guard. Almost at the same time she ducked under the ax swing aimed at her neck and then plowed her other hooked blade into his heart, as soon as his hand with the ax protecting his heart dropped. Deadly Hearts managed to kill three of La's toughest Elite Bodyguards inside of a minute and a half by expertly plunging her hooked blades through their hearts.

After seeing that, La quickly surveyed the battlefield. Hoban and Ali had been separated from Dan. They were fighting with Shinmushee Butchers and one each of the men that were by Deadly Hearts side. Dan was fighting with several Butchers and the last man that was standing by Hearts' side, along with Claw. All three were in death battles for their lives.

La's eyes settled back on Deadly Hearts. La pulled her ponytail with the weighted ball on it from around her back and let it rest going down her front past her knee. La had a crooked smile on her face as she started slowly circling Deadly Hearts.

"Looks like it's me and you!" growled La.

Deadly Hearts saw when La pulled out her ponytail. Hearts started moving cautiously in a circle with La, not letting La get an angle on her. Hearts smiled at La and said, "You misunderstand my intentions, young Queen. I'm not your gift. Claw is your gift. I'm gifted to the young King of Ra."

La yelled, "Why would you think I'd care?! I'm going.......!"

La stopped in mid-sentence and hopped back to a safe position as Claw came flying through the air, landing next to Hearts. Hearts' smile was both sweet and sinister, when she excitedly said, "Look Young Queen, your gift is here! Oh well, have fun!"

Hearts turned and walked over towards where Dan was fighting. La only looked at Hearts for a moment, before surveying the battlefield. She could see Shinmushee Butchers surrounding and watching Dan's battle. They were also doing the same with Ali and Hoban. After another quick look La saw that she too was surrounded by Shinmushee Butchers, who were watching her every movement. La quickly turned and focused her attention to Claw. This time Claw was standing straight up, not crouching. His hands were at his side and his fingers were stretched out like claws.

La thought about how hard she'd been hit by Claw. She didn't want to get hit like that, again. La didn't know how many more blows like that she could take, nor did she want to find out. La also hoped Claw couldn't see in her eyes the slight fear and apprehension inside of her.

However, La wasn't going to back down from a fight. She thought about everything she'd seen of Claw in their first fight. La knew she would have to do much better if she wanted to defeat him this time. La focused all of her concentration on Claw and then started circling him, looking for the slightest advantage she could jump on.

Claw stared at La, while she circled him. Not many could take blows like that from him and still be standing. Her chest protector must have absorbed some of the force of those blows, Claw reasoned to himself. Still, she was here, willing to fight, after that.

While Danaaa was watching Chet and the other Wa she could see Shinmushee warriors in fierce battles with Ra guards, all around. The Wa started walking away, with their hostages. Danaaa cautiously followed. Chet was walking backwards, facing Danaaa, so that he could keep his eyes on her.

Tay, who had his ax blade up to Trina's neck yelled to Danaaa, "Back away and stop following us!"

Danaaa yelled, "But, I'm not doing anything!"

Tay said, "Stop following us, or we take their heads!"

Danaaa yelled back, "Harm Shaya and I wound all of you, without killing you! Then, I'll make you all suffer in agony, for a long time, before you die!"

Tay yelled back, "We're not afraid of you!"

Danaaa yelled, "Yes, you are! Otherwise, you wouldn't be talking to me!"

Yaya looked at Danaaa and sternly said, "Baby, quiet, you're not helping!"

Danaaa asked, "When do they free Shaya?"

Yaya replied, "Once they get safely to the Southern Jungle, I'm sure they'll release her, right?"

Yaya looked at Tay and the others who had axes to the throats of their hostages. Zan said, "Maybe, maybe not!"

Shaya said, "Baby's not going to let you take me, without following. She won't attack, as long as I'm unharmed. If I'm harmed, all of you will die. So, let's figure out how we all can live."

Boku exclaimed, "Once the young King and Queen find out what we've done, they'll hunt us until the end of time!"

Danaaa yelled, "But, I already told you what happens, first! They can't hunt you, if I Chop I!"

"Baby, enough!" both Yaya and Shaya chorused at the same time.

There was a moment of silence. Shaya broke the silence by saying, "Make it safely to the Southern Jungle and then release me unharmed to my sister. If you do that, I assure you no retaliation from the young King or Queen will occur. Answer me this, so as to calm my sister."

Shaya slowly lifted herself on her toes while Chet held her tightly. Everyone noticed it. Chet shook Shaya once and then warned Shaya, saying, "Stop squirming!"

Almost the entire time that Chet had been holding Shaya closely, Shaya's body was having a reaction to Chet's body. It was partly because of the extreme fear Shaya was experiencing from having an ax to her throat. Her body was also reacting to being man handled and slung wildly around by Chet. Shaya's sensitivity to being touched by a man made her body squirm, investigating the feel of Chet's muscles.

After that, Shaya pressed her lower back firmly against Chet trying to identify where his stick was. Chet made that task difficult, because he adjusted himself every time he felt Shaya squirming. Chet thought Shaya's movements was her trying to find an advantage that would free her from his grip.

At first, he had no idea what she was really doing. Once Shaya pinpointed Chet's stick, that's when she lifted herself on her toes and squeezed her butt cheeks, letting them grab Chet's stick. Once Shaya did that, Chet shook her, loosening her grip, while giving her a stern warning.

Even with that, both Chet and Shaya knew that Shaya had managed to get a rise out of Chet. Right now, Chet couldn't let Shaya go, without his reaction being seen by everyone. Chet tried to threaten Shaya by jerking her when she put him at a disadvantage with her squirming. None of that worked. Once Shaya knew she had the advantage on Chet, she slowly lifted and lowered herself several more times. Once Shaya had Chet stiffly pressed hard against her, she stopped. Like I said, although everyone noticed, they didn't know exactly what was going on.

There was a moment of silence while the Wa were contemplating if they would, or should agree to Shaya's proposal. At the same time, the battles between the Ra guards and the Shinmushee warriors were getting closer and closer.

Before anyone said anything, Danaaa was attacked by several Shinmushee warriors. When she was attacked the Wa started slowly moving away, while Danaaa sliced up warriors. Danaaa saw that and kept her battle moving in the direction the Wa were going. Danaaa saw, out of the corner of her eyes, several large men moving through the crowd of the Shinmushee warriors. Danaaa avoided the swing of an ax, plunged her ax into that warrior and then took a quick peek at the men making their way towards her. Danaaa's eyes quickly darted towards Shaya and Chet. Danaaa quickly turned her attention back to the battle at hand. Very soon Danaaa knew she would be fighting, what appeared to be, Shinmushee Butchers.

At that same time, Dan was in a death battle with Shinmushee Butchers, the man who came with Deadly Hearts and Claw. Dan wasn't winning, but he wasn't losing, either. Then Claw removed himself from the battle with Dan by quickly launching himself in the direction Dan knew La was. Dan was forced to deal with his own battle, first. Otherwise, he might leave himself open for a fatal strike. Dan fought hard to create an opening that would let him get over to help La, before Claw got the best of her.

Dan saw the girl who'd been talking to him and La earlier

heading towards his battle. She turned and motioned to the warriors carrying the large box. They brought it over and stopped just short of where Hearts was. They put the box on the ground and then looked at Hearts for further instructions. Hearts turned towards Dan and said "How lucky you are, this day, young King. You get two gifts. The first one is from somewhere deep within our territory. No one really knows where she comes from."

"And the second gift?" asked Dan, while watching his surroundings.

Hearts smile got even more devious when she said, "Well, that would be me!"

Dan had been watching Hearts, closely. She was a beautiful girl. Her devious smile reminded him of Lea, but Hearts looked more like a hardened killer. Dan and Hearts stared at each other. A slight smile came on Dan's face as he thought that this girl couldn't seriously think she could best him in battle.

Without taking her eyes off Dan, Hearts waved to the warriors by the box. When she did, Dan watched as one of them opened a small window like door towards the top of the box. After that, all of the Shinmushee warriors quickly moved a safe distance away from the box. Even the Shinmushee Butchers moved back a little.

That surprised Dan and let him know that whoever was in the box was dangerous. Not four second after the wooden widow was opened everyone heard a scream coming from the box. After the scream, a voice from the box yelled, "Why is the sun on my face! I hate the sun!"

Hearts cautiously moved back away from the box. Hearts said, almost in a whisper, to Dan, "They call her Sunshine, because she hates the light."

A second later, the girl busted though, up and out of the wooden box. Once her body was fully exposed to the sunlight, Sunshine stretched out her arms, palms to the sky, while she looked upwards. She screamed out in agonizing anger. She yelled, "It's all over me! I hate the way it feels on my skin! Someone will pay for this!"

Sunshine turned and looked around. Her eyes stopped when she saw Hearts. Hearts sheepishly pointed to Dan. Sunshine turned and her eyes squinted in anger as she said, "So, it was you!"

Sunshine looked at two Shinmushee warriors. When she did they threw two fancy looking axes to Sunshine. She caught one in each hand, out of midair. Then Sunshine marched angrily towards Dan.

The Shinmushee Butchers and the other man that was fighting Dan all quickly moved further back to a safe distance. Dan thought about using that split second to bolt over to La's side. But when Dan saw La using a technique that he'd never seen before, he thought he might as well deal with the angry girl, first. He didn't want to lose track of an angry girl in a serious fight!

Dan was still trying to take this all in. Dan could see the girl called Sunshine looked to be in excellent fighting condition. She also seemed to have an uncontrollable amount of rage. Dan knew if Shinmushee Butchers were cautious, moving back from this girl, she must be taken seriously.

Dan watched as the girl came straight at him. She didn't seem to care that her axes weren't in a good position to block a strike. There was no way this girl could withstand the quickness and power of Dan's ax swings, with her axes being so low at her sides. Dan decided that he would use that to his advantage and quickly dispose of this girl.

Dan aimed the Hammer-Axe in his left hand at the Sunshine's neck, while he kept the Hammer-Axe in his right hand ready for any counterattacking move. Once Sunshine was in range Dan sent a quick and powerful swing of his Hammer-Axe to her throat. Sunshine only moved slightly, while Dan's blade barely missed her throat. The instant that blade moved past her throat Sunshine was moving towards Dan on the side where his blade hadn't returned from swinging at her. That made it impossible for Dan to counterattack with his other Hammer-Axe.

In that split second Sunshine had Dan out of position, Dan quickly let himself drop low to the ground and then he launched himself into a tuck and roll away from Sunshine. Dan came out of his tuck and roll facing where Sunshine had been. But she was not there. Dan's internal warning system shot off the scale.

Before looking to see where she was, Dan brought his axes up to blocking positions, as quickly as he could. Just as he did Dan felt the pressure of Sunshine's axes pressing on his axes. Dan thought that she would never get past his blocking axes with such a weak effort. But when both of Sunshine's axes gently glided off of Dan's and came straight at his chest, Dan was shocked. He barely avoided those shots by wildly jumping backwards.

This time Dan kept his eyes on that sneaky Sunshine. It was a good thing that he did, because Sunshine moved forwards just as fast as Dan had moved backwards. She was still in striking distance and swung her ax at Dan's shoulder that was closest to her. Dan moved dodging that swing and sent a counter swing at Sunshine meant to split her chest open or, at the very least, back her away. But Sunshine ducked under Dan's swing and launched herself, axes first, towards Dan's mid-section. Dan, being out of position, used every bit of his super-fast reactions just to get the flat side of his ax down in time to block a swing that would have split open the left side of his stomach.

Even with that block, while still in the air moving past Dan, Sunshine sent her other ax at Dan's arm that held the blocking ax. Dan realized that and moved as fast as he could out of harm's way. Still, Sunshine's blade sliced across Dan's forearm. In that same instant, Dan jumped towards Sunshine, hoping to chop her open as she landed. When Sunshine landed she brought herself to a standing position and was already facing Dan. Dan was amazed at how fast Sunshine was.

However, that wouldn't help her this time because Dan was right on top of her with his axes. Dan brought both of his axes flying towards the sides of Sunshine's neck, only to see her axes flying towards his chest. Dan knew his axes would sever Sunshine's head a half second before her axes plowed into his chest.

Dying with this crazy girl wasn't part of Dan's plan. Dan had to think fast. In mid swing Dan changed the direction of his axes and brought them down and inside of Sunshine's axes. Dan pushed outwards with both of his axes, knowing he would have an inside shot at Sunshine's chest when he sent his axes back at her off of the block.

However, Sunshine pressed hard against Dan's blocking axes and when Dan used his strength advantage to force her axes outward, Sunshine let go of her axes. Dan never expected that and the force he was using to push her axes outward made his arms go out further once there was no pressure on them. Sunshine took advantage of that be firing off a powerfully fast three piece combination. Two punches to Dan's kidneys and one to the side of his nose and cheek. That punch would have landed square on Dan's nose if he hadn't tried to slip out of the way.

Dan's eyes watered a little. He was pissed that this girl was able to do that to him. Sunshine tried to make a move towards her axes. That's when Dan attacked. Dan sent his axes at Sunshine with such ferocity that she was instantly in trouble. Hearts saw that and yelled, "Faster-Cut!" as she charged at Dan from his right side.

Dan was surprised that the girl fast approaching knew one of his nick-names. That got Dan's attention for a split second. That allowed Sunshine to avoid Dan by dodging his axes and running for her life. Still, Dan had to make yet another choice. Split Sunshine wide open or, turn and deal with the girl and her fast approaching hooked blades.

Dan decided he wasn't going to ignore the hooked blades. Besides, hooked blades are no match for Hammer-Axes. Dan could quickly finish off the girl with the hooked blades and then deal with the crazy girl called Sunshine.

Once Hearts reached Dan she gave him a flurry of swings from all directions with her hooked-blade. It took all of Dan's concentration to block every swing from her. Dan sent a counter swing at Hearts that would have split her neck open if not for Sunshine's blocking ax. Again Hearts hooked blades shot at Dan's heart from several angles. Dan avoided them, only after backing Sunshine up with ax assaults to her head and chest area. Sunshine and Hearts, as well as Dan were all going move for move, offensively and defensively. One mistake by anyone would likely lead to a mortal strike that would end this battle.

Dan was baiting Hearts by using his defense to block and dodge every swing coming from her. He was also quickly switching from a strong offense and then blocking, not dodging, defense on Sunshine, keeping her occupied and unable to mount a potent attack.

In a heated exchange between the three, Dan put high heat on Hearts and then turned to block a deadly swing coming from Sunshine. However, instead of blocking hard with his axes, like he'd done before, Dan dodged Sunshine by diving backwards, turning and sending his ax towards Hearts, who was moving fast in on Dan for a counter-attack strike.

Now Hearts and Dan were within striking distance of each other. Hearts hooked blade was already on its way towards Dan, while he was still in the air. Dan blocked, using his strength, forcing Hearts' blade downward. In that same second, Dan sent the hammer side of his ax back towards Heats chest. Hearts turned, while moving backwards and dodged the chest shot, but was hit hard by the hammer square on the front of her shoulder. Hearts was knocked backwards from the force of that blow. It was so powerful that Hearts arm drop as pain shot through her shoulder.

Once Dan's feet hit the ground, he was already turning back towards Sunshine swinging his ax. Sunshine anticipated and judged its distance for a counter-strike. Dan's ax sliced through the air just missing Sunshine's neck. As soon as his blade passed her, Sunshine charged forward, sending her ax towards Dan's chest. Dan wildly tried to avoid Sunshine's strike by moving to the side and backwards. Still, Sunshine's ax sliced through Dan's clothes cutting across his chest.

Even though Dan was cut across his chest, he sent his other ax straight at Sunshine's midsection. Sunshine, who was out of position, did the only thing she could. She jumped backwards into a tuck and roll away from Dan. He closed the gap and was right on top of her with a free shot at her.

As Dan was quickly moving in on Sunshine, Hearts came flying in front of and past him with her hooked blade aimed at him. That stopped Dan enough for Sunshine to come to a standing position. A half second later Hearts was also standing. Dan studied both girls. He had managed to wound both of them. Hearts was favoring her right shoulder. Dan knew he would be able to take advantage of that once the action started back up. Sunshine had cuts to her right shoulder and left forearm. She wouldn't last long.

But as Dan was watching both girls, he could see that they both were watching him. Hearts and Sunshine could see that Dan had been sliced across the front of his chest, his left and right forearms. The cuts weren't deep, but both girls thought that if they cut him once they could cut him again. Also they could see the bruising on Dan's cheek where he'd been hit by Sunshine's fist. Although they had to admit Dan was tough, they planned on finishing him off, here and now.

Near about the same time, La was slowly circling Claw. She looked at every inch of his body. He looked like a perfect killing machine to La. She was ready to attack, but needed some extra motivation after being hit so hard by Claw. So, La's eyes glared at Claw when she said, "Tell me, was it you who killed my Master Deen?!"

Claw's voice was rich and deep as it vibrated La's eardrums when he spoke. Claw said, "What would I know of your Master? My first encounter with any of you Ra was when I met you, earlier."

Claw looked over every inch of La's body. La could see his looks weren't intended to judge her fighting abilities. He was checking out her feminine assets. La was offended.

Before La could say anything, Claw said in that rich bass voice of his, "Don't worry, I'm not going to kill you. I'm just going to beat you into submission. Then, I'll drag you back with me and make you my sex slave. If you're lucky, I'll let you live when I'm done with you. If I do kill you, it won't be for a while. I can get a lot of use from that body of yours!"

After saying that, Claw chuckled a bit, while keeping a sharp eye on La. La found every word Claw said more offensive than the last. And after his first two sentences her lip went crooked on one side. With each sentence after that, La's lip went more crooked on that side, until it became an angry scowl.

No man had ever talked to La like that, before. The prospect of Claw actually doing what he said made La imagine it for a split second. That angered La even more. Didn't this arrogant Shitmushee know she and her body belonged to Bo, even if Bo didn't want it? La was not only going to kill Claw because she hated him for being a Shinmushee, La was fighting for her respectability. She also was fighting Claw to save her succulent goodies from being taken by him. La now had enough motivation to kill Claw.

Claw saw that La was thinking about what he said. It amused him when her lip went crooked on one side. Then he saw her eyes get very intense. Claw prepared himself, because her eyes said she wanted to kill him. Claw saw La make two over exaggerated movements with her head, just before she attacked him.

Claw saw La and her axes move at him with amazing speed. She was moving much faster than before. Claw barely moved out of the way of La's axes and was about to mount a lightning fast counter-attack when he saw out of the corner of his vision an object rocketing towards his skull. That made Claw take a defensive step backwards, just as the metal ball on the end of La's ponytail came whizzing past his face.

Claw was about to grab La's ponytail when he saw La coming out of a lightning fast spin, in which both of her axes were coming at him from two different angles. La's swings were tight and close to her body. There was no room for Claw to move inside and counter. So, he wisely took another step back, still giving himself room to attack. That's when La's axes quickly turned back towards Claw. He saw them and was shocked when he was hit in his upper back, just below his neck with a powerful shot from the metal ball on the end of La's ponytail. Claw reached out with lightning speed to catch La's ponytail as it was returning. He heard a guttural grunt from La as her ax blade nearly took off his hand as he was reaching for her ponytail. Claw had managed to move his hand back just out of the reach of her blade.

Almost instantly, La's other blade was coming at Claw's chest. Since this was coming straight at Claw he was able to quickly move his hand inside and block outward. At the same time, Claw sent a powerful blow towards La's chest. This time she would be in trouble, even if she had on a chest protector. But a split second before Claw sent that blow to La's chest, he was hit with that metal ball, again.

Because he was so close to La, Claw was hit on his lower spine. That took a lot off of the punch he threw at La. Still that punch connected to La's chest. It sent La backwards and away from Claw. As La was moving backwards, her ponytail was the last part of her moving away from Claw. He grabbed it and again was surprised at how fast La's ax blade moved towards his had in defense of the ponytail.

Claw let go of the ponytail as quickly as he grabbed it. He decided to move back a couple of steps from La so he could regroup. La was good with that after taking that punch to her chest. Although it didn't have the full force Claw had intended, it was enough to get La's full attention.

Claw also felt the power of La's metal ball. He was surprised that her metal ball could land with such accuracy and force, while she was swinging her axes. He tried not to let La see that he felt pain from both hits he took.

It didn't matter. La already knew the damage her metal ball could inflict, whenever it connected. Even though La couldn't tell how much Claw felt those blows from her metal ball, she could see anger in his eyes. It replaced the overconfidence she saw, earlier.

That scared La a little. She knew from the look on Claw's face that he didn't care about making her his personal whore, anymore. The look in Claw's eyes said he wanted to kill her.

A second later La attacked. She didn't want to give Claw time to think about how to deal with her metal ball. Within seconds of attacking Claw La's metal ball came rocketing at him from different directions.

This time Claw made sure he kept track of the metal ball, while avoiding La's ax swings. Claw stayed just out of harm's way. He was staying on defense, trying to find a way to get to La without being hit with that metal ball.

La quickly figured out that Claw wasn't making any offensive moves. That's when La turned up the heat on Claw with her axes and some very potent kicks. La only used her ponytail as decoy, because she knew Claw was focused in on it. Her axes and kicks played very well off of that. La was able to get a couple of decent kicks to Claw's mid section, without taking any counter blows from him. Every time La thought Claw was catching on to her technique, she changed it.

Claw wasn't affected by La's kicks that occasionally hit their mark. Claw was a hardened killer and had taken much more punishment than La was putting out. Still, it bothered him that she could stay a half step ahead of him with this strategy of hers. Even with that, Claw knew La was no match for him. He decided to prove that to her.

In that instant, La landed a powerful kick to the side of Claw's face. That kick enraged Claw. After avoiding several deadly swings by La's axes, Claw moved right into harm's way. La had two opportunities to slice Claw wide open. Her first swing was so fast that she thought she was slicing through flesh. She quickly realized that Claw caught her axe by the handle. La made an exaggerated move, while at the same time sending her other ax at Claw's wrist that was holding her ax handle. Claw's other hand grabbed that ax handle. Claw quickly forced La backwards and to her right. Her metal ball came flying past Claw's head, barely missing it. La realized

Claw had control of her axes, but not her hands. La let go of her axes and fired off four lightning fast powerful punches at Claw's face. Three of them hit their mark, before Claw blocked the forth.

La was still close to Claw and after he blocked her last punch La knew she had to get out of the way of her axes that were still in Claw's hands. But as she moved to evade Claw, he dropped her axes and grabbed the wrist of her arm that he blocked the last punch coming from her. Before La could react, Claw lifted her wrist, bringing her arm up. With lightning fast speed Claw hit La with three powerful blows from his other fist. One to the rib, one to the stomach and one to La's solar plexus.

The punches were so powerful that La winced in pain as she doubled over, falling towards the ground with her hands out in front of her so as not to fall on her face. However, before La's hands hit the ground she was shocked by Claw quickly moving in front of her. Claw squatted low and put both his arms underneath La's arm pits. He stood up and launched La into the air with his arms. While La was still rising, Claw punched downward into La's mid-section with so much force that La was sent downward hard into the dirt. She barely stopped her head from crashing into the dirt, underneath and behind her.

La was dazed and badly hurt, but could see Claw moving towards her, ready to finish her off. La tried to move but was dizzy and couldn't. La looked up at Claw. She tried to back away from him by scooting her body backwards. That was the best she could do. It was a worthless effort, because she had no control over her muscles. La feared for her life. Still, she refused to cry out for help. She looked at Claw with a crooked scowl on her face that said, 'Do your worse!'

Claw walked up to La. She had bloodied his nose and blackened one of his eyes. She hit him so fast and hard that Claw couldn't react, until after her third punch had already landed. No one had ever done that to him, before!

Claw stopped just short of La and stared angrily into her eyes. She was defenseless and he knew it. They stared at each other for a moment. Claw was going to enjoy killing her, after what she just did to him. That's when Claw blocked two spears heading right for La's mid-section. Then he blocked a third and a forth spear. Claw turned and gave a death stare at the Shinmushee Butchers around him. He yelled, "Don't interfere! She's mine!"

One of the Shinmushee Butchers excitedly said, "Hurry and finish her! We're under attacked!"

Claw quickly looked around. La was still trying to force her body to move. However, she couldn't. She looked around. La and Claw saw intense battles going on to the right of them. Seconds later, they saw Jay, Stacia and Lynn breaking through the perimeter. Once they saw La on the ground and Claw standing over her, they bolted towards them. They were attacked by more Shinmushee.

Claw looked back at La. They stared at each other. Claw knew he only had a moment to kill La, before help arrived. He wasn't going to waste this opportunity.

However, while staring into La's eyes Claw saw a light flash into his eyes from within La's eyes. When the light disappeared, Claw didn't move towards La. He just stood there staring into her eyes.

La wondered why Claw hadn't tried to kill her, after first looking like he would. She also wondered why he was just staring into her eyes. La wasn't going to look away. She didn't know if Claw was getting one last look, before he killed her. La was unaware of the reason why Claw just stood there motionless.

A second later Claw was attacked by Jay. Being attacked brought Claw out of the trance he'd fallen into staring into La's eyes. Jay mounted a very potent attack on Claw. Seconds later, Lynn and Stacia joined Jay, against Claw. Claw didn't understand what had just happened to him, but he was glad he was able to react in time to focus on these Ra that were attacking him, now.

While they were fighting Claw, Jay yelled to Stacia, "Get La to safety!"

Stacia ran to La. She helped La stand. Stacia could see by La's slowed reaction that she was badly injured. Stacia looked over and saw that whoever the man Jay and Lynn were fighting was very good. He was backing both of them up with a potent attack. Stacia quickly surveyed the area. More Shinmushee Butchers were fighting their way past her and Jay's guards. Stacia gave La a serious look and said, "All hell's breaking loose! We have to get out of here, while we can!"

La was very unstable on her legs. Stacia wrapped her arm around La's waist for support. La looked at Stacia with panic in her eyes. La said, "Where's Dan? Where's Shaya?!"

Stacia's eyes looked down, before they came back and met La's. Stacia solemnly said, "I've not seen either of them."

La exclaimed, "We have to find them, now!"

Stacia looked around. She then looked La in her eyes and said "Right now, we have to get you to safety!"

Stacia started forcing La away from the battles around them. La was hurt and still a little dazed, so she couldn't resist like she wanted to. They were just clearing the raging battles when two Shinmushee Butchers stepped into their path.

—— CHAPTER 14 ——

S tacia was dragging La with one arm, while on guard with her ax
in her other hand. When she saw the two Shinmushee Butchers,
Stacia quickly removed her arm from around La's waist, grabbed her
other ax and went on guard. La looked at Stacia and reached for one
of Stacia's axes. Stacia pushed La behind her just as she was attacked.

A fraction of a second later, several of Stacia's guards ran up
and attacked the two Butchers. Stacia stepped out of the battle and
quickly grabbed La. She took off towards an area that was clear of
the fighting. They were met by Hesta, Lana and two of the twelve
undesirables put under La and Dan's charge, here at this Lower
House of Ra. La stared at the two undesirables. La recognized the
two girls, immediately.

The first undesirable was Shara. Shara was a close cousin to
little Shit. Little Shit was an undesirable that had putrid body odor.
Shara didn't have that same putrid body odor as Little Shit, but
when Shara became very nervous she would get the horribly putrid
flatulence. And the more nervous she became the worse it got. The
Elders from this Lower House worked tirelessly with Shara building
her confidence. They trained her body for fighting and her mind
to keep her calm. Being a female warrior helped Shara to mostly
overcome her affliction.

The second undesirable was named Sheena. Sheena was the worse
habitual liar anyone had ever seen. She would lie about everything,
no matter how important, or insignificant it was. She would even lie

about her name, if you asked her it. So to combat her affliction the Elders from this Lower House made it a rule not to question Sheena. You only talked to Sheena with straight forward statements. Any questions asked of Sheena would lead to a round of unimaginable lies that she would back up with more lies.

The two girls said they were here to help in any way they could. Stacia looked at La and said, "Go with them. They will take you to safety, while I find Shaya and Dan."

La looked at the two undesirables. They looked ready to do their part. Besides, La realized she needed rest if she wanted to effectively fight, later. La nodded in agreement. Stacia gave a stern look at all four female warriors. She said, "Get La to safety! Let nothing stop you from achieving that!"

All four girls nodded in agreement. Stacia smiled at La and then hugged her. After that, Stacia ran in the opposite direction, towards the raging battles.

When Danaaa saw the Shinmushee Butchers moving closer to her she decided she didn't need the distraction these Shinmushee warriors were presenting. Danaaa put on a spectacular display of cutlery that left every Shinmushee warriors close to her dead in no time, flat. Others moved back a safe distance, waiting on the Shinmushee Butcher to take over.

The Wa had seen Danaaa in action before, but were astounded by what she'd just done. It looked as if those warriors weren't a challenge to her. Chet was so shocked by what he saw he had momentarily forgotten about Shaya's slow, unnoticeable to everyone else, grinding on him.

Trina and Anne didn't have axes to their throats, but were being closely guarded by Uma and Jami. One false move and they both would be dead. Both knew this and was making it very clear to the Wa that they weren't going to be a problem. Even though Trina and Anne weren't going to try anything, they both had weapons in the holsters around their waist.

The Shinmushee Butchers were now right there with the Wa and Danaaa. Danaaa realized that they looked a little different from Shinmushee Butchers she'd seen before. They stopped at a safe distance from Danaaa. There were six of them. All of them smiled at Danaaa except for two. One of the ones that were smiling said, "So you're the she devil they call High Pressure the Executioner. It was a challenge just catching up to you. Now that we've found you, it's time to put your legend to an end."

Danaaa was on guard, watching Chet and the Wa, while paying close attention to the Butchers facing her. Besides being angry and confused, because she didn't know how to free Shaya, Danaaa was annoyed that these men were bothering her. She cut her eyes at the one who spoke and said, "She's trying to get her sister! Get out of my way! We don't have time to play! But, if me you try to delay! You won't last past this day! I can swing an ax real fast! I Chop I!"

All six men thought, 'How strange this young girl talks'. One of the six men said, "Well, we wouldn't want to delay your trip to hell!"

They all pulled their weapons. That same man said, "We chop, too!"

None of the men knew they were actually addressing the Destroyer that resided within and without of Danaaa.

The Wa thought that this was the perfect time to put some distance between themselves and Danaaa. So, they started moving away from the impending battle. As soon as they started moving, Shaya stiffened her body, while trying to keep an eye on Danaaa. Her voice had concern in it when she questioned, out loud, to herself, "That's my sister! I'm not leaving! What's going to happen to Baby?"

Chet said, "You should be worried about what's going to happen to you!"

Shaya adjusted herself on Chet. Chet angrily said, "Quit squirming, before I give you what you're looking for! And I guarantee it won't be pleasant!"

That momentarily took Shaya's attention away from Danaaa.

Shaya smiled for a second. Chet didn't know Shaya wanted it any way she could get it!

"Chet, don't let her get to you! We'll only kill her if we have to!" Jami quickly said, because the other Wa weren't aware of what was going on between Chet and Shaya.

Danaaa saw the Wa moving away from her. Now, she was even more annoyed. She knew the longer she had to deal with these men, the longer it would take to catch up with Shaya. Danaaa was determined not to let this battle take too long.

Danaaa was quickly snatched out of her little Day dream when axes started flying at her from several directions. These men seemed to be quicker that the usual Shinmushee Butcher and Danaaa found herself on defense, right away. She quickly started countering off of the ax swings coming at her. That's when Danaaa almost had her arm chopped off. She quickly tucked and rolled out of the way of a powerful ax swing. That put her right into the path of several more ax swings. Danaaa wildly rolled in the dirt, avoiding those ax swings. She was met by several more axes aimed at her. Danaaa blocked and ran to the next group of axes coming at her. For the first time in her life, Danaaa was facing heat. Extreme heat, to be exact!

The Wa were leaving when a few of them peaked at the battle. They stopped in their tracks. The others stopped to see what they were looking at. They all saw the same thing. Danaaa looked to be in trouble. She was running and fighting for her life. They could see that Danaaa was making the most outstanding defensive moves they'd ever seen, just to stay alive. They watched in awe, wondering how much longer she would last.

When Shaya saw Danaaa's battle she panicked. After hearing Danaaa talk in the third party, Shaya was sure Danaaa would quickly kill those men and rejoin her. Right now, it didn't look that way. It looked, to Shaya, like Baby needed her help. Shaya struggled with Chet and was slightly cut on her throat. Chet had to move his blade back from Shay's neck, otherwise he would have cut deeply into it. Chet warned Shaya, saying, "Stop struggling or you'll lose your head!"

Shaya yelled, "I don't care!"

Gia came over and grabbed Shaya's arms, helping Chet. Uma also came over and helped. Once they'd restrained Shaya, they looked back over to Danaaa's battle. What they saw shocked them.

Danaaa was in the fight of her life. She was using all of her abilities to stay just out of the way of axes coming at her. But still, she wasn't getting any help from her Jinn Eco. She couldn't understand why, but didn't have time to think about that. She was too busy fighting for her life.

Danaaa never panicked while fighting. She was so into the fight that she used every ounce of her concentration, along with her extreme agility, to keep herself a fraction of a step ahead of these men. Seeing Danaaa put on such a display was the reason the Wa hadn't moved, yet.

The six men fighting Danaaa were specialist. They had watched several of her battles from a distance, studying her fighting style. They practiced long and hard devising a way to defeat her. This assault style was what they came up with.

The style they were using was a triple attack style. Two men attacked Danaaa relentlessly. The next two attacked every counter-attack move she made by trying to chop off the arm, or leg that was making the counter move. The last two men tracked Danaaa's movements and were responsible for cutting off her escape routes.

They knew she would be a challenge and had the utmost respect for this young girl that she hadn't been killed, yet. She hadn't gotten away from them, or even mounted an offensive attack. But, she had managed to avoid expertly placed swings from axes coming at her from all directions. They couldn't even figure out how she saw some of the ax swings she avoided.

Nevertheless, these men were determined to complete their mission. They turned up the heat on Danaaa. It looked like Danaaa was in real trouble, now. Danaaa knew she couldn't take this kind of heat for very long. She launched herself into the air trying to get some space so she could regroup. The two men that were always cutting off her escape route moved in for the kill. They kept enough spacing so that it would be near impossible for Danaaa to defend herself against both. Danaaa would have to choose her killer, by defending against one, or the other. Without thinking too much, Danaaa made her decision. She turned both her axes towards one of the men, while trying to make the other side of her body as less of a target as she could. She knew the man with the free ax swing at her would have to be worthless, not to get a decent chop in on her.

Coming out of the air, Danaaa did a super-fast block with one ax and a super fast chop to the neck of that man with her other ax. A spray of blood went shooting in the air from his neck as he fell to the ground. He was dead within seconds of that. When Danaaa's feet hit the ground she instantly went into a tuck and roll to get better spacing. The other men were right on top of Danaaa. For a split second she didn't understand why she hadn't been chopped. Then out of the corner of her eyes she saw Yaya fighting the man who almost had a free ax swing at her.

When Yaya saw that Danaaa was having trouble she bolted over to help. She arrived just in time to attack the man who she thought was going to kill Danaaa. Now that man was putting some serious heat on Yaya.

With one of them dead and another occupied by Yaya, the four men remaining were already swinging their axes at Danaaa. In an instant, Danaaa's ax plowed into one man, took the head of another and in the blink of an eye Danaaa was behind the man Yaya was fighting, plowing her ax so hard though his back, that her ax blade came out through his chest. It happened so fast that as she was pulling her ax out of the third man, the bodies of the first two she killed were just hitting the ground. Everyone was astounded by what had just happened. They barely saw Danaaa move. Everyone's eyes had only caught up to Danaaa when she was pulling her ax out of the third man she'd just killed. No one moved. They all just stared.

After Danaaa pulled her ax out of the third man she'd killed, he dropped to the ground. Yaya looked at Danaaa and besides being shocked by what Danaaa had just done, Yaya was shocked while looking into Danaaa's eyes.

Yaya was terrified. Then a strange voice came out of Danaaa's mouth that was unfamiliar to Yaya and said, "You dare interfere!"

Before Yaya knew it she'd lost control of her legs. She went down on her knees, but never broke eye contact, while looking up at Danaaa. In her own defense, Yaya screamed, "But, you're my sister! I love you! I couldn't just watch and let harm come to you!"

The last man had regrouped enough for an attack. He wasn't going to waste this opportunity. He saw the two girls talking and moved with lightning speed to attack Danaaa, while her back was turned to him. Before anyone could react he had his ax blade quickly moving towards Danaaa's back. His blade was a half inch from entering Danaaa's back when she did a back flip up and over him, plunging her ax blade into his back. She pushed it in further as she fell on top of him. Danaaa pulled her ax blade out of his back and slammed both her axes into their holsters. She grabbed the man by his hair and pulled his head back. She put her lips close to his ears and said in a low voice, "But I already told you! I can swing an ax real fast! I Chop I!"

Those were the last words he heard. It was said that only he should hear it, but since Yaya was close she also heard.Yaya was staring at Danaaa in shock when Danaaa's eyes moved back to Yaya's eyes. Yaya was terrified. Yaya didn't know if she was next. She and Danaaa stared at each other for another moment. That's when Yaya saw a change in Danaaa's eyes. Yaya yelled, "Baby, it's you!"

Danaaa still angry and annoyed with the situation yelled back, "But, you already know that! You know what I look like! Who else would I be?"

Yaya was confused, yet happy. She lunged at Danaaa and hugged her, tightly. Now, Danaaa was a little confused. She didn't remember seeing Yaya come over here. Danaaa thought she must have been too busy killing those men to see Yaya coming.

Danaaa realized she didn't actually remember killing these men. She checked her memory and only then did she remember what happened. By that time Danaaa and Yaya realized they were on their knees hugging over the dead man. They both hurried to their feet. They looked down at him and then they checked their surroundings. All of the other Shinmushee warriors were gone. They left once Danaaa killed the last of those men.

The Wa had never seen, or expected anything like this. They were brave and confident in their abilities. With that being said, they knew they were goners. Chet was so surprised by what happened that he let his ax drop from Shaya's neck down to his side. Shaya only noticed that when she saw Danaaa turn and look in her direction.

Shaya grabbed Chet's arm that was holding his ax. She quickly put it back up to her throat. Shaya saw Danaaa and Yaya making their way back over to them. Shaya whispered in a panicked voice to Chet, "Keep your blade up to my neck! Maybe that will stop her! But, whatever you do, don't provoke her by threatening to harm me!"

First of all, Chet wanted no parts of Danaaa. He barely saw her kill two men and his eyes only caught up with her after she'd plunged her ax through the back of the third man who was twenty feet away from the others! On top of that, the young princess was forcing him to keep an ax up to her neck, while telling him not to provoke the she devil. If putting an ax up to someone's neck wasn't provoking, Chet didn't know what was!

Chet tried to remove his ax blade from Shaya's neck. Shaya wrestled him to keep it there. Yaya and Danaaa walked up and saw this. They both interpreted it as Chet trying to force his ax blade through Shaya's throat. They thought Shaya was fighting for her life.

Danaaa's face suddenly got a sense of urgency to it. She quickly pulled her axes. Shaya saw that and panicked. Her scream was full of panic and concern when she pleaded, "BABY, PLEASE!!! DON'T HURT CHET!!!!"

Both Yaya and Danaaa stopped in their tracks. They looked at each other and then turned and stared at Shaya. Danaaa put her hands on her hips and looked at Shaya in disbelief. If fact, all of the Wa and everyone there stared at Shaya. Everyone was silent. No one knew how to respond to what they'd just heard Shaya scream.

Shaya took advantage of this opportunity. She said, "Baby, there has been a big misunderstanding! I realize what has happened here!"

Shaya had everyone's attention, while Danaaa suspiciously looked at her sister, folding her arms at her chest, with axes still in hand.

Shaya was saying, "The Wa had no intentions of hurting me, Anne, or Trina. They just wanted to leave. When they were attacked, they did what they had to in order to get away. Since there are no Ra guards, or Shinmushee around, I think they will be willing to let us go, if they are not harmed. I'll tell La that the Wa helped us escape from the Shinmushee and she will think them heroes. The Wa can tell the Shinmushee anything they like. That way, everyone wins!"

Danaaa looked at Chet, who still had his ax up to Shaya's neck. Chet forced his blade away. This time Shaya didn't fight him. Shaya, Anne and Trina all walked over to Danaaa. The Wa didn't try to stop any of them. The Wa looked at Shaya to see if this satisfied her plan. When Shaya got to Danaaa she looked into her eyes. Once Shaya was satisfied that they were Danaaa's eyes, she grabbed Danaaa's ponytail. Shaya then looked at the Wa and said, "It seems that this has all been one big misunderstanding. Rest assured I will say the proper words to put all of the Wa in good standings with my siblings. With that being said, Wa, you may go in peace."

All of the Wa thought that this was better than facing High Pressure the Executioner in battle. Without realizing it, they all slightly lowered their heads to Shaya, including Zan. They looked at Yaya who was still next to the Ra sisters. Yaya said, "I'm going back with my younger sisters. Once I know they're safe, I'll catch up with you." All of the Wa gave Yaya a favorable nod, although they didn't think these girls needed protection. The Wa turned and started walking away.

That's when Shaya screamed, "Chet!" Everyone turned and

looked at Shaya. Once Chet turned and looked at her, Shaya waved to him. She then put both her hands together with Danaaa's ponytail in them, while staring at Chet. The look on her face was hard to describe. Shaya had a smile on her face, while her eyes had a dreamy look to them, as she stared at Chet.

Chet shook his head like, 'That girl is crazy!'

Just as he was about to turn back around he saw Danaaa move to Shaya's side and administer an open hand slap to Shaya's face. That snapped Shaya out of her lustful daydream. Shaya stared angrily at Danaaa. Danaaa peeked at Chet and then turned and stared into Shaya's eyes. She grabbed Shaya's ponytail and pulled hard on it. Danaaa said, "Come, it's time to go!"

Shaya pulled hard on Danaaa's ponytail. Yaya yelled, "Shaya, Baby, stop this nonsense!"

Shaya, while looking in Danaaa's eyes angrily said, "She had no cause to slap me like that!"

Danaaa, while looking into Shaya's eyes, said, "If La had been here, it would have been worse! But, you already know that!"

Shaya did already know that. Shaya looked at Yaya and then back at Danaaa. Shaya pleaded, "Alright, I do know that! Just don't tell La! Now, let's go!"

Danaaa and Shaya roughly pulled on each other's ponytails, while Yaya, Trina and Anne followed. The Wa watched the Ra, until they were out of sight.

It was always strange to the Wa how the Ra girls could be regal one minute and unruly the next. Once the Ra were out of sight, all of the Wa turned and stared at Chet to make some sense of what had happened regarding Shaya. Chet said, "What?"

But, really, Chet already knew what. He just didn't know how, or why!

The fight between Dan, Sunshine and Deadly Hearts resumed after a short break. Dan turned the tides of this battle in his favor by turning his speed up to a higher level. So much so that several

Shinmushee Butcher joined in to keep the two girls from being killed. But still, that didn't matter. Dan was in a zone and he wasn't going to stop, until he finished off these two girls.

In the heat of battle, Dan managed to plow the hammer side of his ax into Hearts mid section. She stumbled backwards as Sunshine and the others fighting Dan gave her a moment to regroup, by keeping heat on him. However, Hearts was injured. Hearts cried out, "Claw!"

Claw was fighting Jay and Lynn. He had the advantage on them and was close to putting enough heat on them to finish them off. Claw heard Hearts cry out and instantly launched himself into the air in her direction.

When Claw landed he was next to Sunshine. Sunshine was intent on killing Dan. Claw grabbed Sunshine by her arm and slung her around to where she was facing Hearts. Sunshine angrily looked at Hearts and then back at Claw. Claw said, "Get her to safety!"

Sunshine snatched her arm from Claw. She stared at Claw for a moment. Sunshine had been put in her place many times before, by Claw. Because she had no chance of beating him Sunshine turned and then angrily stomped her way over to Hearts.

Dan moved towards Hearts and Sunshine, only to be intercepted by Claw. Claw still didn't have axes. That Dan had to use axes on an unarmed man didn't sit well with him. Dan threw his axes to the ground. Claw said, "I'm not here to fight you. Let me go back to the jungle and I won't fight."

Dan wasn't listening to that nonsense. If Claw didn't want to fight, he never should have come here in the first place. Dan attack Claw, immediately.

Dan found out, right away, that Claw was extremely fast. Dan had to increase his own speed in order to avoid Claw's counter-moves. However, Dan couldn't gain an advantage on this guy, no matter what he did. Jay and Lynn joined in the fight. Still, they couldn't take this guy down. More Ra guards showed up and joined the fight. All of the other Shinmushee had either escaped, or were dead. Claw was alone, fighting Dan, Jay, Lynn and close to twenty or so Ra guards. Still, they hadn't taken Claw down.

After a while Dan started to get embarrassed. He couldn't even take down Claw with all of this help. He knew, eventually his brothers and Yin would arrive to help. Claw would eventually get worn down and be killed. Dan knew if that happened, he would be a coward in his own mind. Dan stepped back and yelled, "Everyone, hold it! Move back and don't attack him on orders from your King! I will address this Claw fellow!"

Everyone reluctantly did as they were told. Dan made them move back even further. Once they'd done so, Dan looked at Claw for a moment. Claw had a black eye and a bloodied nose. Dan knew none of them had done that, because Claw already had those.

Dan also spotted his axes that he threw on the ground, thinking he was giving Claw half a chance to live. Dan walked over and picked up his axes. He put them in their holsters. He turned to Claw and said, "Where's my sister, you know, the one you were fighting?"

Claw answered, "Some Ra rescued her, even though they didn't have to."

It puzzled Dan when Claw said that. Dan asked, "You were going to kill her if you got the chance, were you not?"

Claw looked at Dan for a moment before saying, "At first, I had other plans for her. Besides, killing her is going to be near impossible with her skills."

Dan thought, 'That must be where Claw got his black eye and bloody nose from!'

Dan paused for a moment, while looking at Claw. Finally, Dan said, "Your skills are very good. Our fight was interrupted, by my people. Although their intentions were good, I don't need their help to defeat you. So, because it wasn't a fair fight, if you're still willing to leave, you may go. I'll catch up with you later and we'll finish our fight. Rest assured, it will be one on one."

Dan paused and then said, "Unless, your people think you need help."

Claw smiled. He said, "I'll leave young King."

Claw turned and started to walk away. He stopped without turning around and said, "You might not want to come looking for me. I won't be hard to find."

Dan said, "I'm counting on that! But, don't worry about me. I'll be alright. Oh, and by the way. Thanks for the sparring session. It was most enjoyable!"

Claw didn't respond. He started walking away. Guards cleared a path, while other guards ran ahead and told guards that this man should not be approached on order from the King.

After Dan watched Claw disappear he asked for an update on the situation. They told him what they knew. Still, it wasn't what Dan wanted to hear. Stacia told Dan about what she knew of La. He asked Stacia why she was here instead of protecting La. She answered, but it wasn't good enough for Dan. He stared at her for a moment and then ordered, "Find my sisters and report back to me as soon as you have done so!"

Meanwhile, the two undesirable female warriors were on each side of La, supporting, almost carrying her. Hesta and Lana were leading the way, while scouting for danger. They were moving towards the Second Lower House of Ra.

All was going well, until they spotted Shinmushee Warriors and Butchers ahead. They moved to an area they thought was safe enough to wait, until the Shinmushee passed by. But they were spotted by a group of about ten Shinmushee warriors. The warriors moved quickly to the girls' position. All four female warriors went on guard, creating a perimeter around La.

The Shinmushee warriors saw that and figured La had to be important for the other girls to do that. If they capture that girl, it could mean promotions for all of them. The Shinmushee warriors attacked, almost immediately.

La watched as the four female warriors fought ferociously. The female warriors took down eight of the ten Shinmushee warriors before one of the last two yelled out a distress call for help. The four girls carved him and his comrade to shred, a moment later. However, La and the other girls knew it was too late.

Two girls grabbed La and they all ran. They could see Shinmushee warriors a ways behind them. The female warriors looked wildly around. It looked to be hundreds of them. They were everywhere! They knew they couldn't kill all of these Shinmushee, without help. They needed a place to hide.

Just then, Lana pointed with her ax to a ravine. The ravine was down a small hill, just under the path, or road. The girls all ran and hid on the side of the hill, just under the road. If you were on the road you couldn't see them, but you could see enough of the ravine and everything else. It was the perfect hiding place!

A few minutes later, they heard the Shinmushee walking by in groups. They could hear them beating the bushes and rustling around looking for them. All of the girls stayed perfectly still.

The Shinmushee stopped beating the bushes. All the females wondered what they were doing. Then they heard one of the Shinmushee say "They must have slipped by us."

Another said in an animated tone, "No way! We covered every possible escape route! They have to be around here, somewhere!"

A couple of the warriors walked to the edge, just over where the girls were hiding. They looked over and couldn't see anything. One of the warriors said, "Well, they're not around here."

The warriors were unaware of the girls as little crumbs of dirt showered down on the girls from the men being so close to the edge.

When the warriors first started beating the bushes and walking around searching, the girls all made themselves as still and motionless as they could. They knew if dirt or small rocks started rolling down the hill, from any movements they made, that would give away their position.

La slowly looked to her right. She saw Lana and Sheena. They were calm, cool and collected with their axes in hand. La gave them a reassuring smile. Then La slowly turned to her right. She could see

Hesta was just as calm and ready as the others. However, when La looked at Shara, she saw that Shara was nervous and sweating like a thief caught red handed.

La gave Shara a reassuring look, letting her know that everything would be alright. As they heard voices above them, La could see that Shara was getting even more nervous. La was still looking at Shara trying to calm her. Crumbs of dirt came showering past the girls. La stared at Shara, as Shara stared back. Shara let out a short sharp fart. La's lip went crooked on one side. That's when Shara let out a loud boomer of a fart, relieving the pressure of the situation. At that moment, La wanted to kill Shara. If La weren't wounded, she probably would have. All of the girls noticed it was silent above them, after that.

When the Shinmushee warriors heard the first fart, they all got quiet and looked around at each other. When they heard the second, they tried to pinpoint where it came from. After a moment of silence the warriors started laughing, pointing and blaming each other.

A great relief came over La and all of the girls when they realized they hadn't been discovered. Even Shara was relieved. La's lip straitened itself out. La didn't need this girl getting anymore stressed than she already was. But just as the pressure of being nervous was too much, so was the relief of not being discovered. This time Shara let out a long stress relieving fart, while looking directly into La's eyes. La never felt more betrayed than at that moment. A second later, the girls heard one of the Shinmushee say, "It came from down there!"

His suspicions were confirmed when Shara let out another fart, conveying the stress she was dealing with.

All of the girls knew they were discovered. They readied themselves for battle. That's when Sheena jumped out and turned towards the Shinmushee warriors. She yelled, "Can't a Shinmushee female warrior get a little privacy, while she's taking care of her personal business!"

Sheena didn't look like and definitely wasn't dressed like female

Shinmushee warriors. In fact, she looked and was dressed exactly like a Ra female warrior. All of the Shinmushee could see that!

In his disbelief, one of the warriors yelled, "You're not Shinmushee! Why would a Shinmushee be dressed like a Ra??"

Sheena looked that warrior directly in his eyes and with a serious look on her face she said, "I'm on a secret mission from one of your top Warlords. It's very important that I not be interrupted!"

The Shinmushee didn't have Warlords. The equivalent to a Ra Warlord was a Shinmushee Butcher. They knew this girl dead wrong, lying. But they made the mistake of asking another question. A warrior nudged the warrior next to him, while asking the girl, "Tell me the name of this, so called, Warlord over you?"

Sheena said, "I told you, I'm on a secret mission! Why would I tell you?"

An angry look came on several of the warriors faces They were done playing with this girl. One of the warriors angrily growled, "Do you actually expect us to believe that bullshit?" Yet, another question.

Sheena said, "I don't care what you believe. If my Warlord finds that you have interrupted my mission, he'll have your head!"

Even though Sheena was calm, cool and collected while lying, Shara wasn't. While staring at the girl who was lying to their faces, the warriors were treated to another one of Shara's finest farts. They instantly knew it hadn't come from the girl they were looking at. One of the warriors asked, "What was that?"

Sheena said, "That was me!"

One of the warriors yelled out, "Bullshit!" as several of them jumped over Sheena, landing and facing the other girls hiding underneath the path in a small ditch.

They paused after seeing one girl had her hands draped around the neck of another girl. It was La trying to strangle the life out of Shara, the farter. Once La saw the Shinmushee warriors facing her, she let go of Shara's neck, turned and looked at them.

Without thinking and sure that the girl didn't have an answer for this, the same warrior questioned, "Who are they?"

Sheena calmly said, "Well, my Shinmushee brothers, since it seems you have discovered my mission, I might as well tell you."

La's mind was racing at to what to do next. But as she looked at the Shinmushee warriors, La realized that they were caught up in Sheena's web of lies. Since those lies got them this far, La was going to try to think of a way out of this, while Sheena kept a hoard of Shinmushee warriors at bay with her potent attack of deception.

Sheena was still talking. She was saying, "I've taken these Ra girls as prisoners to be slaves for my Warlord."

The warriors couldn't believe what they were hearing. They could see that all except one girl had axes in their hands, on guards against attack. One of the Shinmushee warriors incredulously exclaimed, "If they're prisoners, why are they still armed?!!!"

Sheena said, "Well, it seems you don't believe me. Come, follow me! I'll take you to my Shinmushee Warlord. He will explain everything!"

Sheena turned and quickly walked like she had purpose. That slightly confused the warriors. Half of them watched her, while only a few kept an eye on the other girls. Sheena took one more step and then raised her axes with lightning speed, carving up warriors closest to her. The other female warriors sprang into action the second Sheena did. It was a bloodbath as La watched her female warriors battling these Shinmushee. The girls had positioned themselves well and were carving up every Shinmushee warriors that came at them.

La had momentarily forgiven Shara. It seemed that when Shara was fighting, all of her nervousness went away. Shara was doing a great job protecting her Queen. Nevertheless, La knew they couldn't stay there forever. If Shinmushee Butchers found them they would be in serious trouble, no matter how hard these girls fought.

Then one of La's greatest fears was realized. She didn't hear everything he said, but definitely heard Claw ask, "Where are they?"

All of the Shinmushee warriors backed up from the female warriors. The girls regrouped to better protect La. La had fear in her eyes as she looked around, waiting for Claw to appear. However, it never happened. In fact, all of the Shinmushee warriors backed away, until they disappeared.

The girls helped La back up and over the ridge. They looked around and didn't see any Shinmushee warriors. A look of relief came on La's face. She looked at all of the girls like they had done well. La was even proud of the way Shara handled herself in battle. That was enough for La to forgive her for giving away their position, earlier. Lana said, "Come, my Queen. Let us get you back to safety." La nodded in agreement.

CHAPTER 15

Don and Yin were in intense battles with Shinmushee Butchers. Both had wounds, but nothing serious. They also dished out punishment, too. That made the Shinmushee Butchers put everything they had into killing these two. Still, they hadn't, yet.

Don couldn't remember fighting a battle for this long. The Shinmushee Butchers took breaks by letting other Butchers, who were fresh take their place for a while, before returning to the battle. Don and Yin didn't have that luxury. They had been fighting from morning to well into the afternoon. Both of them were fighting on pure adrenaline. Still, that would only take them so far. One mistake by either would surely be their last.

Then, without any warning, the Shinmushee Butchers moved back and disengaged Don and Yin. Don and Yin didn't advance. They were going to take this break, however long and try to rest, before the battle continued. The fact that the Butchers stopped their attacks made Don and Yin think more experienced killers were coming to fight them. They both readied themselves.

That's when they saw a man walk up. The first thing Don and Yin noticed was that he didn't have any weapons they could see. They also saw that someone had given this man a swollen eye and a bloodied nose. The man walked up and studied Don and Yin. He saw that they had been roughed up, too.

"You two must be really tough to still be standing." said Claw.

"Tough enough to take on any Shitmushee. What about you? You want some!" Yin said with an evil grin on his face.

Neither Don, nor Yin knew this was Claw. Claw looked at Yin. He could see that even though Yin was good enough to stay alive, he was reckless in his taunting. Don was annoyed at Yin's taunting but didn't let it show on his face.

Was Yin crazy? He was begging this guy for a fight! Didn't Yin know how long they'd already been fighting? Yin should be trying to figure a way out, instead of digging a deeper hole for them! Those were Don's thoughts. But since he was here with Yin, all Don could do was wait and see what would happen next.

After looking at Yin for a short moment, Claw smiled. Claw said, while still looking at Yin, "Alright men, back to the jungle!"

Claw turned away from Don and Yin. Yin said, "What's wrong, afraid you'll get beat?!"

Claw stopped in his tracks. He turned and looked at Yin. This time, there was no smile on Claw's face. He was all business. Don quickly put his hand firmly on Yin's shoulder and said, "Don't taunt! Let them leave! We need to check and make sure everyone else is safe!"

Claw's eyes went from Yin to Don when Don started talking. When Don was done talking Claw's eyes moved back to Yin's eyes. With an even more evil grin on his face, Yin slowly said, "You got lucky, this time! Now, run along!"

Claw smiled at Yin. Claw's smile was both sinister and devious. Claw slowly said, "Right!"

Claw didn't care for Yin, or his attitude. If the opportunity presented itself Claw decided he was going to kill Yin, plain and simple. Claw wasn't going to let that affect his decision making. He knew it was time to leave. Claw turned and walked away. The Butchers and warriors with Claw watched Don, Yin and the Ra guards closely as they made their exit.

After they were reasonably sure Claw and his men were gone, Don turned to the Ra guards and said, "Find all of my sisters and

Dan! Make sure they're safe! I'm going to La's place. When you have more information, get it to me!"

Don turned and stared seriously at Yin. Don didn't mind a fight, but he could see Yin was reckless and out of control. While Don was staring at him, Yin questioned, "What? What did I do?"

Don didn't answer. Instead, Don said, "Let's find the others!"

Don started walking. When he did, so did Yin. Yin, figuring Don was angry with his taunting, said, "I knew they weren't going to attack us at that point. That's the only reason I said what I said. I was just getting in their heads, is all I was doing! Don't get so serious over that!"

Both Don and Yin knew that wasn't the truth. They both knew Yin wanted that fight to go on as long as it could. Still, that was as close to an apology as Yin was going to give Don.

Once Bo and Tania heard from their scouts that war drums were going off in the first Lower House of Ra, they sent messengers to the main city of Ra and the other Ra strongholds, letting them know the situation. Afterwards, they sent all of the Guards and elephants at their disposal, racing towards the First Lower House. Claw and the other Shinmushee started retreating, once they got word the Ra army was headed towards them.

Tania and her forces were the first to reach La. Bo split from Tania and secured all of the territory in and around this First Lower House. Once he'd done that, Bo went to meet his King Dan for further instructions.

It was late in the evening when all of the Hammer-Axe Six along with Yaya met at the compound La was staying at. La and her sisters got cleaned up, before meeting with their brothers. Ram was the last to arrive. It was after dark when he returned. No one questioned him, because he looked beat up like everyone else. Nevertheless, they were glad to see Ram was alive. From the reports they got, it seemed the Shinmushee didn't attack any one, or anyplace, besides where the Royal Ra were. It was an assassination plot against the Hammer-Axe Six!

While eating, no one said a word. They looked at the bruises on each other from the battles they were in. They hadn't seen each other look like this since they were beaten by the Hayee, long ago, when they were young children. They also thought about what happened to themselves, in battle this day.

Yaya was happy to be here. This reminded her of old times with her Ra family. Even La made Yaya feel welcome. Yaya looked around the table at her younger brothers and sisters. She felt more at home, fighting next to Danaaa, than she'd felt in a long time. She wished she could stay with her brothers and sisters. She knew she couldn't do that because of her battle with the Ra guards.

Yaya knew her last battle to help save Danaaa would change the way the Shinmushee thought about her, also. She didn't care. Yaya would do it a thousand times over, if it meant saving Baby. Yaya though for a moment and looked at Danaaa. She wondered about that strange voice she heard from Danaaa. She was going to ask La about that later, when Danaaa wasn't around.

While eating La thought about Claw. The more La thought about her fight with Claw, the more furious she became. La's body was battered and sore. She was more than a few steps slower than normal. La's mind went over that battle a hundred times since it happened.

This was the first time La felt she'd been defeated in a fight. In all her other fights she either won, or chalked it up as training and sparring. Even when she fought Syn, Jara La told herself that she would have won that fight if her mother hadn't intervened. Wishful thinking!

But in La's mind she saw her battle with Claw, differently. La remembered how powerful Claws arms felt when he lifted her effortlessly off the ground, before knocking her back into the dirt. She also remembered being on the ground defenseless against Claw. And what nerve of Claw to stand over her reveling in victory! So much so that, even though he could have, he didn't kill her. Why wouldn't he? La just couldn't understand that!

La also thought about Claw saying he would make her his personal whore. That frightened La because she didn't think she could stop him. That gave La another strange feeling that she didn't want to think about. But, every time La winced in pain, she thought about Claw. And the more she thought about Claw, the angrier La became.

Dan wasn't thinking about the possibility that he could have lost his battle with Hearts and Sunshine. Dan knew he had them and if they hadn't run away, he would have finished them off. Dan thought about the fact that two girls could occupy him for that long. If he would have finished them sooner, he could have helped La and the others in their battles.

Dan could feel pain from both his wounds. It was nothing he hadn't dealt with before. Once he caught up with Hearts and Sunshine they would pay dearly for his pain. He also thought about that Claw fellow. That guy was so confident in his abilities he didn't use weapons. Even with that, they couldn't kill him. That bothered Dan more than the two girls. Dan wanted a rematch with Claw more than any fight before now. In Dan's mind, it was only a matter of time before he got it.

Shaya was watching all of her siblings. She could see La was very upsets. She was also watching Baby. Shaya hoped Danaaa wouldn't tell La everything she did. At least, not the part concerning Chet.

Shaya thought about when she first saw Chet. She didn't like him. That changed when Chet put his arm around her waist and pulled her close to his body. Shaya had a reaction to Chet that never happened when her guards held her.

Shaya could feel Chet's muscles pressing against her. Every time he lifted her off her feet and jerked her around, in defense of himself, Shaya was turned on even more. When she squirmed, looking for Chet's personal treasure and found it, Shaya wanted that treasure for her very own. Shaya was determined to get it!

Shaya knew seeing Chet would be next to impossible, after today's events. Looking at La and Dan, she somehow knew they would be on a mission, very soon.

Shaya didn't want to be a princess. She didn't even want other men, anymore. However, she reserved the right to change her mind about that! Right now, Shaya wanted Chet. Shaya was going to find Chet and be with him, forever!

While enjoying his food, Don was glad this day was coming to an end. He was exhausted and had been pushed to his limits. Those new Shinmushee Butchers were tough as hell! Still, he managed to come out of it with his life.

Don thought about if that fellow hadn't come along and sent the Butchers back to the jungle, how much longer would that fight have gone? The way it was going, would he have won? Don wasn't going to concede defeat in a battle that he didn't lose. Don could feel the aches and pains from his battle. He knew he had to get much better. Because, next time, he might not get saved, by the enemy deciding to leave on their own.

Yin was upset with himself for several reasons. The first was he didn't get to kill any of those new Shinmushee Butchers. Even though they didn't kill him, Yin felt they beat him up pretty good. The way Yin's body ached wouldn't let him ignore that fact. That didn't sit well with Yin.

Yin peeked at Don. If it weren't for Don, he would have, at least, been able to kill the unarmed man. Yin thought that man was too cocky for his own good. Yin decided he was going to teach that fellow a lesson, next time he saw him. Yin looked at Don, again. It was much more fun killing with Ram, than with Don. With Ram, you had to use every skill you had, just to make it back alive. And still, there was no guarantee you would. That was the thrill Yin was looking for. The same as it was for his father.

Ram sat there eating his food like nothing had happened. He didn't waste one moment thinking about what happened to him this day. He had just walked up and met everyone just as they were getting here. His clothes were ripped to shreds and he was battered and bruised. No one questioned Ram as to where he had been. Ram was thinking about how good the food and blood tasted. He wondered if there would be cookies, afterwards. Ram had a tough day and hoped someone made cookies. If not, it might be a tough night for someone!

Danaaa was angry, annoyed and confused by this day. She was angry and confused because Shaya made her promise not to tell La something she thought she should tell La. Danaaa was also annoyed because she wasn't smart enough to get the Wa to let go of Shaya, before Shaya did it on her own. Just like in the past, Danaaa's wits were no help. They were hiding, as usual! Danaaa still couldn't figure out how Shaya got them to let her go!

What also angered, annoyed and confused Danaaa was the fact that the voice in her head that she called Jinn Eco appeared and talked to the strange Butchers like it was going to help her fight them. However, as Danaaa found out, she was alone for most of that fight, even when she thought she needed help. Then, at some point, Jinn Eco showed up and tried to hide the fact that it was helping Danaaa by killing the Butchers without her being aware of it. Why, that sneaky bastard!

Jinn Eco was starting to remind Danaaa of her wits. Only being there when they wanted to and not when she needed them. But since Danaaa thought Jinn Eco was her own voice in her head talking to her, she wondered why she would do such a thing to herself. Danaaa was getting even more confused. Then the voice inside her head said, 'You will succeed with and without my help! That battle was part of training yourself!'

Danaaa, while looking at everyone, yelled out loud, "Well, that's just great! Now, I guess I'm training myself!"

Everyone turned and quickly looked at Danaaa. Danaaa gave them a confused look, while shrugging her shoulders, with both palms extended, facing the sky. No one wanted to go into that conversation, so one by one they slowly looked away from her.

Anne watched everyone, especially Ram. Ram always fascinated Anne. It seemed he was always in his own world. His clothes were torn and he looked bruised. Still, he acted as if nothing had happened.

Anne remembered how scared she was when she and Trina were surrounded. Anne was sure Ram would come and save her. She always thought that was going to happen, even though most times it didn't. Anne wondered if Ram really cared about her. She was going to find out.

Trina didn't know what to make of this day. Was this the life Dan wanted for them. If it was, Trina decided she didn't want any parts of it. I mean, who wants to spend every day, fighting for their life in battle? That's no way to live!

Still, as Trina looked at Dan, she knew he would soon be going after whoever was to blame for this ambush. That's just who he was. Trina loved Dan, but decided she was going back to the main city. Once there, Trina was going to live her life like she saw fit. She didn't want to spend her time fighting Dan's whores and fighting for her own life. Trina was going to let Dan whore around, battle and wage war, until he forgot about her.

Once they were done eating servants took the food away. The servants brought a large plate of cookies and sat it on the table. They put it close to Ram and Danaaa and then left the room. After the servants were gone La stood up and stared at everyone there. Her eyes were red and full of anger. La tried not to notice Ram and Danaaa eating cookies like there was no tomorrow. She turned and looked at the guard near the entrance and yelled, "Send them in!"

Jay, Stacia, Lynn, Bo, Tania, Ali, Hoban and several other top Warlords were waiting outside. Now they all walked in to see La staring at them. La could see that all of them were beat up just as bad as she was, or worse. Ali was wounded the worse. He was being held up by two Warlords.

Nevertheless, La yelled, "How could you let this happen?!!"

No one said a word. After realizing no one was going to freely take the blame, La yelled, "Look at us! Are you not guilty for allowing this to happen?!! Do you have the heads of those that did this? Should I take all of your heads because of your incompetence?! Well, somebody, ANSWER ME!!!!"

Ali snatched himself away from the Warlords supporting him. He took a step forward and went down on his knees. After that, the others joined him. Dan had been watching. He knew La had to blow off some steam, but he wasn't going to let her kill their Warlords.

Dan stood up. When he did La turned and looked at him. Dan smiled at La letting her know that it was his turn. La conceded by gently touching the bandaged wound on Dan's chest. Still, she didn't sit. She stood by Dan, staring at their Warlords, as he talked.

First Dan looked down at all of the Warlords. He said, "All of you, rise!"

They all slowly got to their feet. When Dan looked at them, it wasn't the same look they were getting from La. Dan looked at all of their wounds with concern in his eyes.

Dan said, "As you can see, your Queen sees this day's events unacceptable, as do I. However, I will say it is because of your bravery that I and my family are alive and here. I've seen and heard that you gave everything you had defending us."

La's eyes slowly moved sideways and down towards Dan. Of course, her lip went crooked on one side, right after that.

Dan paused for a moment, after feeling La's stare burning into the side of his leg. Dan continued with, "Make no mistake when I say that we all failed here this day. That an enemy could come into our stronghold, attack us and get clean away is unacceptable! The blame starts with me, first! Then I blame my sisters and brothers."

When Dan said that, La turned towards him on guard. That was a warning, letting Dan know she was offended. Dan was unshaken by La's actions. If she started a fight, the way this day went, he wouldn't be surprised.

Although, Dan was aware of La's movements, he never stopped talking. He was saying, "Lastly, I blame my Warlords and Top Elite Guards. All of you before me."

Dan paused and said, "I'm certainly not going to take my own head for what has happened, so I'm not going to take yours. But still, nothing like this can ever happen, again. It certainly can't go unpunished. Rest assured that whatever punishment is dished out, all of us here will receive it, as we are all guilty."

Dan paused long enough for La to say, as if she was disgusted with everyone, "Now get out of my sight!"

Dan turned and looked at La. La cut her eyes in Dan's direction, daring him to change her orders. He didn't. Dan knew there would be no reasoning with La right now. She was upset over today's events and needed to simmer down, some. Dan was going to put up with La, for a little while. The Warlords lowered their heads and then left.

La hadn't calmed down, yet. She looked at everyone still here and settled in on Ram. La stared at Ram, until he looked at her. Normally, La wouldn't stare into those creepy eyes and she rarely ever confronted Ram. However, while staring Ram in his eyes, La said, "You've been gone all day, only to return when night has fallen! Tell me, Ram! Where were you?!!"

Everyone turned and looked at Ram. Ram broke his stare with La and looked off to the side, like he was checking his memory. He thought about how this day began.

Ram was with Don and Yin last night. He was getting bored with the women there. So, Ram decided to take a walk. Once Ram left that residence, he was watched by guards. The Ra guards would watch Ram, without being obvious. They also didn't follow Ram. That's how you disappear. All the guards knew that.

Ram continued walking. He had no particular destination in mind. Ram walked until he got to the edge of Ra territory, facing the Southern Jungle. He stopped and looked at the jungle. A voice in Ram's head told him to go into the jungle. Just like Danaaa, Ram thought the voice in his head was his own. Ram looked straight ahead. Because of the trees it was pitch black in there. That didn't bother Ram. He could see when there was no lighting, at all. He started walking into the jungle. The Ra guards watched as Ram disappeared into the darkness of the jungle.

Once Ram entered the jungle he was in stealth mode. All of his predatory instincts became heightened. Ram stalked his way through the jungle, not knowing where he was going. He realized his destination, once he saw a camp ahead. Ram stealthily crept towards the camp. Ram got closer and realized he must have stumbled upon an invasion force. He studied everything he could about this group.

At that camp, everyone was resting. There were a few guards around the perimeter and a few others that were still awake. Claw was resting in a crouching position. Hearts was near him stretched out on the ground, while Sunshine was resting comfortably inside her box.

Claw detected something that the guards hadn't. He opened his eyes and whispered, "Someone is out there, just beyond the camp."

Hearts, as well as several of the Shinmushee Butchers jumped up. Sunshine just listened intently from inside her box.

Just as they all were getting ready to go and investigate, they heard, "Don't go out there. If you do, you won't make it back. Relax, we have a guest. Rest now, you will see him when day comes."

Everyone turned and looked at the man who'd spoken. If it had been anyone else, they all would have hunted whoever was lurking in the jungle. But instead, they all rested, while on guard, waiting for day to come. They all were curious as to who this visitor was. They would find out, soon enough.

Ram had been watching the camp when several people jumped up. They were joined by several more. Ram wondered what was going on. He was pretty sure he hadn't been detected. Ram watched and waited. If they came towards him, Ram was going to kill every one of them in the darkness of the jungle. Ram waited to see what they would do. When he saw that they calmed down and went back to resting, he waited. Once Ram saw they were sleep, he thought about how he could ambush and kill everyone in that camp. Then Ram told himself, 'Wait until day comes. Otherwise, you'll walk into your own death.'

That made Ram think. Ram had never said anything like that to himself, before. He decided to listen. He sat down, leaning back on a tree and rested. He was going to wait until day came, just like he told himself. After that, Ram was going to do what he did best, regardless of what he told himself!

Day came fast and Ram was awakened by the smell of food. He stood up and stretched. He was going to walk into that camp, kill everyone there and then eat the food they'd cooked. It was the perfect plan! Ram started walking towards the camp.

When the guards saw Ram coming, they alerted everyone in the camp. The guards were told to move back and not confront Ram. Heats, Claw and the Shinmushee Butchers stared as Ram walked right into the camp towards them. Hearts went on guard. A voice said, "Hold it!"

Ram turned and saw that jolly fat old man sitting on a throne looking at him. Ram also saw Claw crouched down on another throne chair. It was a strange sight to Ram. That man looked like a bird!

Ram quickly turned his attention back to the old man, while watching everyone around him. The fat old man smiled at Ram with that jolly smile of his. The old man said "Welcome, young Ra! I'm glad you could make it. I must admit, coming here didn't take much wit!"

Ram looked at Hearts and the other Butchers. He didn't care about what the old man said. Ram wasn't going to be distracted. Ram put his hands in a quick draw position, next to his Hammer-Axes.

The old man saw that and motioned with his hand, while saying to Ram, "Forget about them, just let them be. If it's a fight you want, come, try me!"

Ram thought the old man was trying to confuse him with words. Why should he listen to the old man? He could kill the others and still kill the fat old man, afterwards. Ram decided his own plan was best. Ram quickly pulled his axes.

Before Ram could attack, the old man was out of his throne chair and into the air, coming at Ram. Ram was extremely quick and jumped into the air, towards the old man. He was going to slice up the old man before he hit the ground.

As Ram and the old man moved towards each other, no one else moved. They just watched. Once Ram's Hammer-Axes were in striking range, he sent them at the old man. The old man blocked both shots coming from Ram and before Ram could get out of the way, he was hit hard by the old man. That punch sent Ram hard to the ground. Ram was only there for a split second, before he was on his feet with his axes pointed at the old man.

The jolly smile was gone from the old man's face when he said, while looking at Ram, "Some young people don't like to listen! They think they can kill, because they're here at now! Well, fight me then, because I'm How!"

Although, Ram didn't understand what the old man said, he decided to give him what he was looking for. A quick trip to hell! Ram peeked at the others. He would get to them, later. Right now, the old man dies! Ram charged the old man, swinging his axes, for all they were worth.

After avoiding about ten swings from Ram's axes the old man backed Ram up with two powerful shots to his mid-section. That only stopped Ram for a second. After that Ram was right on top of the old man, again. While fighting the old man, Ram heard Hearts say, "See you later grandpa! Have fun!"

Upon seeing Hearts and most everyone else, except for a few servants leaving, Ram tried to move to a better position to stop them from leaving. But, the old man turned up the heat on Ram, attacking Ram. Ram had to use all of his concentration to Artfully Dodge the old man. Still, Ram was punished here and there with powerful punches from the old man.

Ram didn't remember the old man fighting like this the last time they encountered him. Was he saving all of this just for Ram? He must have been because Ram was taking a slow but thorough beating from the old man. Still, Ram fought as hard as he could, not backing down.

Finally, Ram caught a break. He used it to go on a ferocious offensive tear. He managed to shred the old man's shirt to pieces and cut his forearm lightly, before the old man was able to create some distance between himself and Ram. The old man flipped backwards towards his throne, with Ram in hot pursuit. Once the old man got to his throne, Ram saw him grab two axes. That shocked Ram. Ram's first thought was 'That's not fair! He never used weapons, before!'

That thought only lasted a split second, before the old man turned on Ram and attacked him. Instantly, Ram was under some serious heat. The old man put Ram in a meat grinder and was shredding Ram, without killing him. Ram found that the old man was super-fast and used his power to bully past Ram's axes. Ram was unusually strong, but was in a dogfight with the old man. Ram had to use every ounce of his concentration and strength fighting this old man.

Then Ram smelled cookies. He peeked and saw some servants cooking. That's where the smell was coming from! Ram was instantly hit twice with the butt of the old man's axes. Ram thought that the old man probably could have sliced him open with the axe side if he wanted, because Ram was distracted by the smell of cookies. Ram was determined not to make that mistake again!

But as the fight went on, Ram's stomach told him it was past time for his first meal. Ram tried to ignore it. He had more pressing issues. Like this old man trying to kill him.

Then, out of nowhere, the old man hit Ram with the butt of his axes ten times, before Ram could do anything. Ram stumbled backwards, trying to keep his balance. Ram could feel the pain from each one of those blows, along with the sting of the many cut all over his body. He stared at the old man in anger. That's when the old man said, "Come, it's time for first day meal. When we're done, we can finish this deal!"

For the first time in his life, Ram was injured. If the old man was going to give him a chance to recuperate, Ram would take it. After that, the old man was dead! Ram slowly nodded in agreement. Both watched each other as they put down their axes and got something to eat.

Servants brought food over to the old man, first. They then cautiously took some over to Ram. Ram sniffed the food to see if it was poisonous. Once satisfied it wasn't, Ram started eating. The old man said, "You don't talk much. Are you the night stalker, Ram?"

Ram was busy destroying the food in front of him. After noticing the old man was waiting on an answer, Ram looked him and nodded yes. The old man kept talking to Ram but all Ram heard while stuffing food into his mouth was 'Jibber-Jabber this and Jibber-Jabber that.'

The old man saw that Ram was barely paying attention, but he kept instructing Ram. Servants brought cookies over to Ram. Ram tore into those cookies. They were delicious! The old man paused at seeing Ram eating cookies, before continuing to talk.

When Ram was done with his food and cookies is when the old man's words became clear to him. Ram realized the old man was telling him the mistakes he made, earlier. Sort of like his master Deen, the Syn, Jara and other Ra fighting teachers would do. Ram incredulously stared at the old man not understanding the old man's intentions. Didn't this old man know that Ram was going to kill him, shortly!

The old man stood up and stretched. Ram looked at his Hammer-Axes. He peeked at the old man once more and then dived towards his Hammer-Axes. The old man quickly grabbed his axes and attacked Ram. Ram got more of the same beating that he took before. Ram was now wondering why he didn't pay more attention to the old man when he was instructing him, earlier. Ram's beating lasted until the old man called for another meal. Ram was more than happy he had.

This time, although battered, bruised and hungry Ram listened closely to the old man. Ram focused on every word the old man said. Then as they were sitting there, the last thing the old man said to Ram was, "Now we fight without weapons!"

Ram couldn't beat this man with weapons. He certainly didn't know how he was going to beat him without them. But, the one thing about being Ram was none of that mattered. Ram was going to fight, anyway.

The old man beat Ram unmercifully, while instructing Ram on how to not get beaten so badly. Ram listened and found that what the old man told him mostly worked. Ram wondered how come the old man didn't tell him how to defend against a technique, before he used it on Ram.

Finally, the old man slowly backed away from Ram. Servants came over and wiped the sweat from the old man's face. When they were done the old man looked at Ram and said, "You fight well and your endurance is strong. Train from the memory of our fight and don't get it wrong. Remember and get it right. If you do, you'll be the only one who can defeat you in a fight. Now, go! I've tired of this game!"

If Ram hadn't been beaten into submission, he would have used this opportunity to attack the old man. Right now, Ram didn't know if he had the strength to make it back home.

Ram was in pain from head to toe. Still, he struggled and got down on one knee. He referred to the jolly old man by what Dan called him. Ram slowly said, "Much respect, wise teacher."

The old man seemed to be annoyed when Ram said that. He said, "Don't say that! The Ra seem to have a strange way of interpreting situations! Get yee, now, from my sight, before again you I'll have to fight! If I do, you won't survive this night!"

Although, Ram wasn't one to back down from a challenge, he decided to leave. Ram lowered his head to the old man once more and then left. Ram didn't care what the old man said, he was just glad that he was able to leave in one piece. Oh, and he was happy that he got to taste some of the best cookies he ever ate.

After walking a ways through the jungle, Ram saw the Shinmushee war party returning. As they got closer Ram could see that they'd taken a beating. They were on guard, the same as Ram, when they passed each other. However, no words were exchanged and no one attacked. They all were exhausted.

Ram thought these Shinmushee were lucky to be alive. Hearts, Claw and the other Shinmushee saw Ram. He was busted up pretty good. Still, they wondered why their grandpa let Ram go. They thought Ram was lucky to be alive, also.

CHAPTER 16

Ram snapped out of his short daydreaming memory. La was still staring at him waiting on an answer. Ram looked at La and said in his deep voice, "I got beat, like everyone else."

Even though La heard Ram she incredulously questioned, "What?"

Dan looked at La and said, "You heard him. It's quite simple. None of us were good enough this day!"

La didn't like either of those answers. She looked at her sisters. They stood up and moved to her side. La looked at Yaya like it was alright if she came. Yaya stood up. They left with Anne and Trina following them. Dan looked at his brothers and Yin. He shook his head.

Dan said, "Come, let's get some rest. We have work to do when first day comes." Don and Yin looked at each other. They knew what that meant. Dan was going to put them in the hell of training, until they couldn't take it anymore!

The next day was hell on everyone from the Warlords to the Hammer-Axe Six. Dan and La had everyone doing extra training from sun up to sun down. Once they were done training for the night the Hammer-Axe Six had a meeting. They all told of the battles they encountered the day, before.

Shaya told a grand story of how the Wa fought against their Shinmushee brothers in order to insure her and Danaaa's safety. La stared at Shaya for a moment. Spies had already reported to La that the Wa freed two Shinmushee prisoners. La didn't know about Shaya being taken prisoner. La decided Shaya must have pardoned the Wa for a good reason. Since Shaya was safe, La didn't want to know anymore.

Ra guards also reported that the Shinmushee Butchers that surprised and killed their Master Deen were the same ones Danaaa fought and killed. Shaya, Anne, Yaya and Trina all told La and Dan how amazingly fast Danaaa moved. Yaya even told how Danaaa's voice changed to one that was not familiar to her. La knew that meant Danaaa's Jinn killed those men.

After hearing what Danaaa's Jinn Eco did to the Shinmushee Butchers La asked Danaaa, "Can you get it to kill Claw and those girls?"

"No one touches those girls, except me! The next time I see them, they're dead!" Dan quickly said.

"Let me have a crack at the Claw fellow! I'm sure I can beat him!" Yin said.

Both Dan and La looked at Yin and said, "No you can't!"

Yin was offended. He said, "You don't know that!"

La said, "How can you beat him, when you can't even beat me?!!"

Yin, even angrier, said, "I haven't beaten you, because of my love for you. If it weren't for that!"

La growled, "Pretend we're not blood and try me now!"

La stood up. When she did, Dan quickly stood up and grabbed La. Dan said, "No good is going to come of that! Queen Ramala, you're losing control! All over one day's battles! That's not you. This isn't about us fighting each other. It's about defeating our enemies. Use your wits. Calm down and let's figure this out, together."

Dan managed to bring La down a couple notches. La peeked at Yin, only for a second. That let him know that they were going to revisit this, when Dan wasn't around. Yin was good with that.

La turned back to Danaaa and said, "Well, can you get it to kill for us?"

Danaaa, not liking the way La talked to her, said, "Why don't you ask? It seems to have special feelings for you!"

La stared angrily at Danaaa. La remembered that thing in Danaaa seemed to hate her. There was no way she'd talk to it. Shaya frantically said, "La, we shouldn't provoke it! We don't know what it will do! Please don't ask Baby to bring it out! Please!"

Now La could back down, by making it look like she was concerned for Shaya.

"Fine! We'll find another way!" La said.

After meeting with her siblings, La set up a private meeting with Jay. Danaaa and Shaya insisted on being there. Once La saw that her sisters weren't going to leave her side, La had the meeting with them present.

Jay walked into a small private garden, without his guards. He saw La sitting on a bench next to Shaya, while Danaaa leaned on a tree next to the bench, watching him. When La saw Jay she motioned for him to approach. Once Jay got close he went down on one knee and lowered his head. La and her sisters watched Jay, closely.

After a moment, La said, "Why you're here, I'll tell you, now. I remember well how you came to my aid and fought off the Shitmushee invaders and that Shitmushee Claw."

La seemed flustered after mentioning Claw's name. After a sort pause, in which La regained her composure, she said, "I commend you for that. However, I have instructed my guards to report to my Queen mother and everyone else that it was Bo that rescued me. You will do the same, if asked. If you wish to have continued freedom, as you've already been given, it is important that you cooperate fully."

La paused again, before saying, "Continue to do what's best for me and show up when needed as you did. That's all I require of you, at this time. Only next time I expect you there, sooner! Is that understood?"

Jay, realizing that La had not given him permission to rise, knew this was a direct order. Although he didn't agree with it, Jay said, "As you wish, my Queen."

La said, "Good! Now that we've taken care of that, you may rise and take your leave. I have other business to attend to."

Jay stood up, lowered his head to all three Ra girls and then left. Once Jay was gone Shaya gave La a hard stare. La quickly asked, "What? Did I miss something?" Shaya said, "Jay has been nothing, accept cooperative. He even showed up in time to save you. You could be a little nicer towards him."

La, annoyed that Shaya would confront her on this, growled, "That was nice! Don't take issue with me concerning Jay!"

La seemed angry over what Shaya considered to be nothing. Shaya, almost pleading, said, "Alright, I won't!"

La, not seeing any opposition from Shaya, said, "Come, let's go!"

Danaaa and Shaya moved to La's side. Danaaa made an over-exaggerated movement with her head and the end of her ponytail jumped up high enough for La to catch it in her hand. The Ra girls walked off after that.

The next day the Hammer-Axe Six got another surprise. Their father, along with Syn, Jara and Mangler had just arrived with a small army. Now, everyone had to go through the humiliation of talking about their battles. Everyone, except for Ram and La. Ram didn't talk much and used that to his advantage. Dan and Syn weren't going to spend a lot of time with Ram, getting nowhere.

La just refused to talk about it. That evening, Elder Dan didn't say too much to La. He could see that her eyes were angry and she wouldn't look directly at him, or Syn. Elder Dan and Syn were going to wait, until the next day to see if La's attitude changed. When Syn went to see the Ra girls at first training session, she found it hadn't. In fact, it was worse!

When Syn showed up at first day's training for the Ra girls, La stared at her, before she went back to stretching. La was in no mood to put up with the Syn, Jara. If Syn, Jara came here looking for a fight, that just what she was going to get. La decided that she was going to beat Syn worse than she had the last time they fought. That's because, over time, La made herself believe that she had beaten Syn, Jara that day. La told herself that she was going to give Syn, Jara a severe beating, this day!

Shaya looked at Syn, Jara and then back at La. Shaya saw La look at Syn and could almost see La's thoughts. Shaya instantly got nervous. Shaya also figured the only way to get La out of this funky attitude she was in would be to beat it out of her. Shaya knew Syn was just the person to do it. Only this time, Shaya couldn't run and get help from her mother, the only person who could stop La, if she got out of control. That made Shaya very nervous.

Danaaa also saw everything. She saw Syn walk in. She saw La's reaction to Syn. She saw Shaya's reaction to La and Syn. Danaaa kept stretching. She also kept watching, because she knew something was about to happen. She just knew it! And whatever it was, Danaaa didn't want to miss any of it.

Syn, Jara barely acknowledged Shaya and Danaaa. She walked right out on to the center court of the training area. All the while she kept her eyes studying La. It amazed Syn remembering the little girl she trained all those years. That wasn't who she was looking at now. Syn saw La as a hardened Butcher with a bad attitude and skills to back it up. It reminded Syn of herself and Ramala when they were La's age. Syn thought about that for a second. Still, when Syn got to the center of the courtyard, she said, "La, come."

La's lip went crooked on one side, as she quickly started walking on to the courtyard. La was determined to severely beat Syn for the beating she took from Claw. She stopped just short of Syn and went on guard, focusing all her concentration on the Syn, Jara. The concentration in La's stare made Syn proud as her teacher, but concerned that La would look at her this way. A second later everyone heard the distant rumbling of thunder.

Everyone except for La looked up and saw dark clouds off in the distant sky. They hadn't noticed them before now. This time they saw lightning strike, before hearing the thunder. The thunder was a little louder than before. La looked up at the sky along with everyone, else.

Then, La's concentration was broken when she heard someone yell, "Ramala!"

It was Elder Dan's voice. The only other voice La would recognize in a situation like this. La said, "Father, it's best if you not interfere!"

La's voice was soft, yet forceful, still showing a level of respect. Thunder rumbled in the background.

After looking up, Elder Dan walked out on to the courtyard. La's mind raced. She wondered if her father would attack her. La knew she was thinking crazy. Her father would never attack her. But still, La couldn't make herself go off guard. Again, thunder boomed in the background. The storm seemed to be getting closer.

Dan watched his eldest daughter as he walked towards her. He saw that his daughter looked to be ten times as intense as her mother. La also looked to be much more physically fit than her mother ever had been. La even looked more fit that Syn, Jara. Elder Dan couldn't see all that when he arrived the day before. But seeing La in her training clothes, showing most of her legs and arms, he could see that now.

In fact, all three of his daughters looked to be in outstanding condition. But what shocked Dan most was when he looked into the eyes of his oldest daughter. In all his years with her mother, Dan had never seen the intensity and fire in Ramala's eyes, than he was seeing in La's at that moment. Dan wondered what he and Ramala had created. Because this was his daughter, Dan knew he had to deal with her.

When Elder Dan got to La she demanded, pleaded and begged in a voice that sounded like she was giving an order and a warning, saying, "DAD!!!!"

La turned so that she was on guard against both Syn and her father. La was looking no higher than Dan's feet and her eyes were extremely angry. Elder Dan was shocked by this. He moved closer to La and gently put his hand under her chin, slowly lifting it so that they were looking eye to eye.

Dan saw a ruthless Butcher, mixed with a cunning intellect in La's eyes that made her mother look as innocent as a new born baby. All of that was hiding just behind the anger in La's eyes. Elder Dan wondered why he never saw that, before. Dan remembered how La treated everyone, except him. He figured it was a father's love that blinded him to who La really was. La was her mother one hundred fold. With all that, Elder Dan knew he was dealing with a woman and her emotions. He knew he had to be careful. He would use the only advantage he knew he had.

Elder Dan removed his hand from La's chin and gave her a big hug. That surprised La. With Dan hugging her, La couldn't see Syn. La tried to maneuver herself so she could keep an eye on Syn, but couldn't. Then, Elder Dan put on the perfect act. His voice was emotional and full of concern as he said, "When I heard that the Shinmushee attacked, I rushed up here to protect my precious La! I don't know what I would have done if you'd been harm! Those Shinmushee will pay for dearly for this! I'm going to kill every one of them, until I find out who's responsible for attacking my sweet little La!"

After hearing what Elder Dan said, La's emotions were completely turned in another direction. La was happy that her father was concerned enough that he was fawning all over her. La loved this kind of attention from her father.

However, La also didn't respect Elder Dan's fighting skills. She would never hurt his feelings by telling him that she could see past all of his moves and thought they were simple enough that others would, also.

What La didn't realize was that she had the advantage of watching her father's fighting moves all her life. Seeing them so many times allowed her to figure them out and see past them. A luxury that Elder Dan's enemies would never have.

From what she saw La didn't think her father would stand a

chance against Claw and that Hearts girl. So, with love and concern for her father in her voice, La exclaimed, "Dad, I'm alright! It was a tough battle, but that's all. You need not concern yourself with this! Please, let me handle it on my own!"

Elder Dan pulled La back a little and stared into her eyes. He said, "Are you sure that's what you want? I could easily...."

La interrupted her father, saying, "Please dad, it's what I want!"

Elder Dan reluctantly said, "Well alright, if that's what you want."

La gave Dan a reassuring look and said, "It's what I want. I'm not a child anymore, dad. We will deal with those Shitmushee."

Dan said, "Alright, I'll let you get back to your training."

La smiled at her father and nodded in agreement. Elder Dan looked up at the sky and then smiled at his other daughters. He said, "Looks like the storm is passing. See you at first day's meal."

Shaya and Danaaa looked up and it looked like the clouds were moving in another direction. They were relieved. After seeing the so called lightning Jinn, it always made the Ra girls nervous when storms came.

Elder Dan purposely didn't look at Syn. He turned and walked out of the training facility. Elder Dan realized that not only did he have to skillfully play his Queen Ramala in order to deal with her volatile personality. He now had to do that with, at least, one of his daughters.

La proudly watched her father leave the courtyard. She was glad she saved him from going after Claw and possibly getting himself killed. La's emotions had been totally changed by Elder Dan. The care and concern she felt now was nothing like the intense killing rage she'd felt, earlier. Once Elder Dan was out of sight, La realized Syn was behind her. La quickly turned, facing Syn.

Now, looking at La, Syn didn't see the intensity she'd seen earlier in La. Syn decided to take advantage of that. Syn cautiously moved closer to La. Then Syn did something that surprised La. Syn started talking to La. Once Shaya and Danaaa saw that Syn and La were talking, instead of fighting, they both ran over. They didn't want to be left out of anything that involved La. They looked at Syn. Syn gave them a look that said they could stay, as long as they didn't interrupt.

Syn, Jara started by telling La how her father and grandfather were killed. She told La how she felt and what she did, afterwards. Syn told how she raged, killing out of control, until she was deceived and captured. She said she was blinded by the rage that she felt after her grandfather was killed. Syn explained the mistakes she made, while raging out of control and how they led to her capture. She then explained how she felt, facing death, while shackled to a wall.

The Ra girls listened, intently. They knew a little about how their parents met Syn, but they'd never heard the story from Syn's memory and the details of her emotions. The Ra girls were enthralled by the story of the Syn, Jara. So much so that first day's meal was brought to them, while Syn continued to give her testimony, filled with what she was going through, emotionally.

Syn was very honest with the Ra girls. She even told them how she planned on killing their father and the other Butchers as soon as they freed her from that wall. Something Dan and the Butchers never knew. She told them that Cat and Ma were the only reasons she didn't. She also said that the Ra girls' father never knew that and although she didn't feel that way now, she hoped the Ra girls would never tell their dad and keep this conversation a secret. The Ra girls agreed that they would.

Mid day's meal was served at that same courtyard. The girls continued to listen to Syn. Syn told the Ra girls how she and Elder Dan met their mother. She told of her fights with their mother. She told them of how she felt love for each of them when they were born. It took the entire day for Syn to share her complete story, up to this point, with the Ra girls.

The story was so thorough that after Syn shared her thoughts on her last sparring session, slash fight with La, La went to her knee and begged for forgiveness. Syn was shocked by that. But she knew she had La in an emotional state that she could use to her advantage. So, that's when Syn finally told La she would be honored if La shared what happened in her battles, days before.

La was very smart and knew Syn was manipulating her. However, after not being so angry and now feeling companionship with Syn, La didn't care. She needed to talk about this, but didn't know how. So what if Syn figured it out for her. Syn was her teacher. It was her job to do that. La started out slow. She didn't stop until she told the entire story. She also used the technique she just learned from the Syn, Jara. The technique of telling how you felt on the inside, while you told what was happening to you and going on around you.

After using it, La liked the way this new technique made her feel. Sharing and talking about your problems helps you deal with them better than dealing with them alone. La felt like a weight had been lifted off of her shoulders. Syn stayed with the Ra girls over night.

After leaving his daughters in the care of the Syn, Jara, Elder Dan went to see his sons and nephew. He caught up with them at their training facility. They were just finishing a round of sparring. Elder Dan got to watch the last ten minutes. He evaluated as much as he could from what he saw.

Once the Ra young men were done, they went over to Elder Dan. As they were coming over, Dan could see that his young men were in top condition. He was proud of them. When he looked at Yin, all he could see was the late Elder Yin. Whenever Yin saw his uncle Dan he would always give him that evil grin he inherited from his father. Elder Dan hugged all of them. Then he instructed them on what he saw of their sparring.

Elder Dan knew these young men were all past his ability to spar with them. They were just that good. They all had more endurance, speed and extremely quick adaptability in battle situations, than Elder Dan knew he, himself, had. Elder Dan wasn't going to let his fighting ego get in the way of him helping them. So Elder Dan spent the entire day with the Ra young men, going over the battles they had. He instructed them on ways to improve their skills as well as how to increase their chances of quick and decisive victories.

All of the Ra young men listened to Elder Dan's instructions and theories. They seemed to be sound. Dan, Don and Yin were glad Elder Dan didn't try to impress his fighting skills on them by sparring with them. Just like La, they were well past Dan in their fighting skills. So much so that the last few times they did spar with Elder Dan, they held back as not to offend, or wound him. Elder Dan realized that and was good with it. Still, it was his job to help them as much as he could. And that's just what he did.

The next day, everyone met at first day's meal. It was rare that the Hammer-Axe Six hadn't seen each other an entire day. Dan and his brothers noticed the change in La's attitude. She was downright pleasant.

At first, Dan wondered how bad of a beating Syn put on La to break her attitude. After his spies, some of whom were servants of La's, told him that hadn't happened, Dan was a little disappointed. He never wanted to see someone outside the family beating La, but it was a good day if it had been done by the Syn, Jara. Dan guessed that his twin sister must be maturing. It seemed La didn't always need a good ass kicking to bring her back to normal.

While digesting first day's meal, La told young Dan that their father and the Syn, Jara weren't here to take over their battle with the Shitmushee. She told Dan that they were just advising them and would be leaving as soon as next day came. Young Dan knew La was updating him on the results of her full day's meeting with Syn. Dan, in turn, did much of the same, telling La, in so many words, what their father talked about to him. Elder Dan and Syn both found it amusing the way La and Dan communicated in code to each other.

After first day's meal young Dan met with his father in private. It was about Trina. Trina left the First Lower House of Ra without telling young Dan. His guards told him and that's how he found out. It annoyed Dan that she left. Mostly, because he didn't get a chance to hit that before she left. It pissed him off, because after all he did, he thought he had Trina wrapped around his finger, like he had so many females in this Lower House.

Young Dan's eye brows furrowed in contemplation when he said, "Just when I think I've got Trina figured out, she does the unexpected. How can I keep her under control?"

Elder Dan said, "What has she done that you think you need to control her?"

Dan said, "She went back to the main city, without telling me."

Elder Dan looked at his son. At first when everyone told Elder Dan his son looked, acted and had the same mannerisms as he did, Elder Dan didn't see it. As time went on Elder Dan started noticing it was true. Elder Dan was more than twice the age of his oldest son. Now he could see a lot of himself, when he was that age, in his son. A lot of it Elder Dan saw as immaturity and didn't care for. Elder Dan had a strong fascination with women. He also knew his son was the same, but was more blatant, because he could be.

Elder Dan asked, "Do you love that girl?"

The question caught young Dan off guard. He wasn't ready for that, so he replied, "What do you mean?"

Elder Dan just looked at young Dan. He wasn't going to play word games with him. He'd already asked a question and expected an answer.

When Young Dan saw his father looking directly at him, without saying anything, he knew an answer was expected. Dan looked away from his father and said in a lower voice than normal, "I don't know, but I do like her."

Elder Dan said, "When I saw Trina, in the main city, she seemed to want to see you, at all cost. I wonder what you might have done to make her run from you. Can you think of anything?"

Young Dan thought about the beating Trina took. He didn't want to admit that, so he said to his father, "Nothing that stands out."

Elder Dan was sure his son had done something after that statement. Elder Dan said, "Dan, you have a lot of power and control. It comes with your position. I'm not saying you have to be perfect, because it's human to make mistakes. Everyone can't be a King. You have that by birthright. Still, sometimes you should think about how what you do affects others. Search your mind and see what you've done when she was around. Then, think if you were her how that would make you feel."

Young Dan said, "I'm not a woman, so I'll never really know how she feels."

Elder Dan said, "I don't expect you will. But you can be smart about not letting her see everything you're doing that she might find offensive. That is, if you want to keep her."

Young Dan didn't respond this time. Elder Dan said, "Remember this son, women are attracted to men in power. So, they will always be around you. I'm not saying don't have your fun. Just be smart. You'll see women tend to come and go. Especially, when times get tough. But to have a Queen that will have your back, until the end, well that's worth all the women you can ever have."

Dan questioned, "How do I know she will have my back, no matter what?"

Elder Dan said, as a matter of fact, "Because she loves you enough to come here trying to please you. And, besides, your mother's been training her to do just that."

Elder Dan paused and then said, "But you're a King, now. You do whatever you want. However, you should always do what's best."

Dan thought about what his father said. It made a lot of sense. Everyone seemed to think Trina was perfect for Dan. But, Dan wasn't sure.

Elder Dan knew that was more than enough for his son to digest. He stood up and started to leave. Elder Dan stopped and asked, "What are you going to do about the Shinmushee situation?"

"We will train, until we are good enough to take the Southern Jungle."

"How long do you think it will be before you're ready?"

"We'll go over the techniques used against us. Once we've

mastered counter attacks, we'll leave. That should be, maybe two cycles of the moon."

"Don't rush it. And think about this. They have also seen your techniques. Whatever time you have to train, so will they."

Young Dan stared at his father. He hadn't thought about that, even though it was obvious.

Elder Dan added, "When the Hellcats find out what happened to their childhood teacher they're going to want heads. I know you told me the ones who killed him, Danaaa killed. That's not going to matter to them. What matters to them is that this happened in the territory you are Warlord over. That means you and La have to answer for this."

Young Dan said, "I know."

Elder Dan was about to leave when Dan said, "Dad, there's one more thing."

Elder Dan turned around and looked at his son. Young Dan told him something that Elder Dan needed verification on. Elder Dan told his son to get one of his top spies here, immediately. Dan knew who his father was talking about. It was La. La would tell her father everything about everybody, except herself, if he asked. Young Dan was going to bring Shaya along, just in case his father needed more than La's word.

Elder Dan ended up staying an extra day while La, Dan and Shaya told him about their dealings with Jinns and the strange voice that would sometimes come from Danaaa. At first, Dan watched his children closely, trying to see if they were pulling his leg. He stared into their eyes as they talked. All three seemed to be genuine.

For a moment, Elder Dan wished he'd never come here and heard this crazy story because he didn't know anything about what they were telling him. When they were done all three looked at Elder Dan. Elder Dan didn't know what to say, so he said nothing. They waited, until La finally said, "Dad, what should we do?"

Elder Dan looked at La. He said, "What you have here is a

puzzle that the three of you will have to figure out. Keep everything that you have witnessed, so far, in your mind. Just like a puzzle, all the pieces will eventually come together and fit. Right now, you don't have all the pieces. Be patient. Don't rush things. You've been doing a good job of collecting the facts. Keep it up. I'm sure you will find the answers, eventually."

All three stared at Elder Dan. Didn't he know that's what they were already doing? They thought he might be able to, at least, steer them in the right direction. Even though he didn't, they placed what he said in their minds. What they didn't realize was this was Elder Dan's way of saying he had no idea how to help them. And that they were pretty much on their own.

Elder Dan and Syn left early in the next day. Once they were on their way, Syn congratulated Dan on how well he handled La. Syn joked, saying, "At first I thought we might have no choice, but to kill her."

Dan looked at Syn and said, "Don't joke like that."

Syn said, "You know La has serious anger issues."

Dan said, "She's her mother's child. You know that. I suspect there's not a lot we can do, except keep her in a calm state of mind."

Syn said, "Then you better teach Dan and Shaya that little trick you used on her."

Dan said, "Don't under estimate them. I'm sure they already know how to deal with La."

Syn questioned, "What makes you so sure?"

Dan said, "Because, La's been at the First Lower House for a while now. I'm sure this isn't the first time La's been angry. We haven't heard of her massacring any families here, so I think she's manageable."

Syn stared at Dan to see if he was joking. A chill went down her spine, thinking of what La might be capable of. Dan didn't mention what his children questioned him about. Still, he thought about it on the way home.

Once Elder Dan got to the main city of Ra, Queen Ramala

grilled him on everything that happened. Queen Ramala wanted to match up what she heard from her spies in the First Lower House to what she would hear from Dan, to what she'd been told by Anne and Trina. Anne and Trina arrived back at the main city days before Elder Dan had.

While lounging in their private sleeping quarters Dan asked Ramala, "What do you know about Jinns?"

Ramala turned to Dan and asked, "Why?"

"Just curious." Dan said.

Ramala paused, not saying anything. She wanted to see if Dan would push her on the issue. She was trying to read if this had something to do with his trip to the First Lower House.

When he didn't, Ramala said, "The only thing I know about Jinns is the stupid old fairytale my grandmother told me a long time ago."

"Huh. Is that right? Tell it to me." Dan said.

Ramala instantly got suspicious and asked, "Why?"

Dan looked at Ramala and gave her a look like he was bored. He said, "Forget it. I didn't think it was going to be that big a deal."

Ramala quickly said, "It's not."

Ramala climbed over Dan and rested her head on his lap. Once she got comfortable, she told him the story her grandmother told to her.

After hearing the story, Dan thought, 'What have these blood drinking Hayee got me and my children involved in?'

Dan couldn't wrap his mind around any of this. He needed to marinade on it. But before he got a chance to do that, Ramala looked at him and asked, "How do you propose to pay for that information you received?"

"What's your price?" asked Dan.

He didn't have to ask twice. Ramala climbed on Dan and rode him, until she had an orgasm. She rolled off of Dan, looking at the ceiling. Ramala looked over at Dan, with a smile on her face. Her smile said, 'Payment in full!'

—— CHAPTER 17 ——

The next few days, Ramala was cold and callous towards Trina, even though she let Trina have meals with her. Ramala told Trina that she was disappointed that Trina didn't handle situations better with the young Dan. She told Trina that she had to be smarter and sometimes stern when it came to Dan.

The way Ramala was treating Trina, Trina thought that Ramala didn't want her there for mid-day meals. So, Trina decided not to go. Once Trina didn't show up, Ramala summoned her and set her straight. Ramala backhand slapped Trina and told Trina that her Queen Ramala would tell her when and where to be. That if she had any questions about that, she should ask them now. After being slapped, Trina wasn't about to tell Ramala that she was trying to distance herself from the royal family. Ramala stared at Trina.

At first, Ramala was sure this girl was perfect for her eldest son. Now, she was having doubts. If Trina made Ramala look bad for picking the wrong mate for her son, Ramala was going to make Trina and her entire family pay for that.

After not seeing Dan for only two days, Trina's body and mind missed Dan. She couldn't stop thinking about him, even when she wanted to. So, while standing there looking at the disappointment in Queen Ramala's face, Trina begged, "Queen Mother, please instruct me on how to deal with Dan! I need help! Just give me another chance! This time, I won't fail you!"

Ramala didn't know whether this girl was begging to save her life, or because young Dan had twisted her mind so. It didn't matter to Ramala. In the end, she knew this was best for her kingdom. Ramala said, unenthusiastically, "We'll see."

Days earlier, after passing Ram in the jungle, Claw and the other Shinmushee went to see the jolly old man, who was their great-great-great grandfather. He was so old that everyone just called him grandpa, whether he was, or not. They all lined up in front of him and then went down on their knees. Hearts cried out, "Grandpa, we failed!"

The jolly old man looked down at all of them from his throne chair. He said, "How have you failed when you are still alive? You just learned a tough, yet valuable lesson. Don't talk of failure to me. I'll know when you've failed, because you'll be dead!"

"All of you, on your feet!" he then ordered. They all instantly stood up and were at attention, looking forward.

The old man could see that all of them had been battered and bruised. But what surprised him was when he looked at Claw. One of his prized pupils had a blacked eye and a busted nose. The old man could tell by Claw's slow, measure steps that his body was also injured. The old man didn't know it was because of the two blows Claw received to his spine from the metal ball on La's ponytail. He looked away from Claw in disgust. He then noticed six of them were missing. After not seeing them, the old man looked a question to Hearts. She shook her head with tears in her eyes.

The old man stood up and walked off his throne. He said, "I told you not to go looking for trouble with those Ra. But you insisted on going, anyway. I came with you, to keep you from going too far, not figuring this. Look at you, now!"

The old man looked at Sunshine. She was calmer because she was in the shade of the jungle and not in direct sunlight. Still, he could see she was angered by what happened, earlier. Sunshine looked down, before looking back up at the old man. After looking at Sunshine for a moment, the old man turned his back to and took a step away from Sunshine and the others. With his back to them, the old man questioned, "Were any of the Ra killed?"

Claw answered, "No, but most all of them were wounded. Some worse than others."

With his back still to them, the old man said, "After the Ra get over the shock of what you have done, they will come to the jungle seeking to kill each of you. For now, go home. Visit your families. After one moon, be at my home. I will train all of you. If given enough time, things will be different when next you meet the Ra."

The old man turned and faced them. He sternly said, "Now, go!"

Claw and the others walked over to the old man and lowered their heads, one at a time, as they passed him. When Hearts got to him, she lowered her head and then gave him a hug. She whimpered, "Grandpa!"

The old man let Hearts hold him for a moment and then he grabbed her by both her shoulders. He pulled her back and said, "Get yee, now! Come to me in one moon!" Hearts whispered, "Yes grandpa."

Hearts looked at Sunshine and then walked away. Sunshine walked over to the old man, waiting to be instructed. You see, Sunshine wasn't going home. She wasn't permitted there. Sunshine lived with the old man. He was the only one who could deal with her volatile personality. The only time her family would let her visit was when the old man came to visit.

The old man looked at Sunshine. He could see that she had been sliced with an ax several times. He also saw that none of the wounds was life threatening. The old man ordered, "Go tend to your wounds! When next day comes, you start training!"

Sunshine didn't think it fair that the others got one entire cycle of the moon before they had to start training. Sunshine yelled, "But, grandpa!"

"Go, now!" the old man yelled.

Sunshine's face twisted in anger. She turned, growled and then walked away. Sunshine didn't like the way he the old man treated her. He always seemed to be tougher on her than anyone, else. But he was the only family member willing to put up with her, no matter what she did, when she became uncontrollably angry. So, although it bothered her, Sunshine went and did exactly what the old man told her to do.

Hearts, Claw and the others gathered their things and were off to their different homes. The Shinmushee Butchers lived in a separate area of Shinmushee. In fact, all three lived in different areas. Claw was the top Warlord in the area where he was from. He came here for the same reason that Hearts and the others did. To avenge the deaths of family members that fought against the original Butchers in the war against the House of Ra. After the stalemate in that war, the Ra were watched closely by scouts. All of their tendencies were noted and used in training. Still, it seemed that wasn't enough to defeat them.

Hearts was affected by her loss to Dan. She was the top female warrior in her region of Shinmushee and as good as any of the men. She was sure she would kill the young King of Ra. When the old grandpa suggested she take Sunshine with her, Hearts almost declined. She only did it out of respect for her old teacher. Hearts was glad Sunshine came. If she hadn't, well, Hearts didn't want to think about that, right now.

Hearts and Claw traveled together, until it was time for them to split up. They knew they would see each other soon. Both had trained under the jolly old man, before, but at different times. They remembered training with him was pure torture! They were resigned to the fact that it would be well worth it, in order to defeat the Ra.

When the body of the Hellcats' teacher the Hayee, Master Deen arrived at the main city there was a ceremony honoring him. He was loved by many, so the ceremony was packed. Everyone paid their respects and then his body was burned. This was the saddest the Hellcats were since their Grandmother died.

The next day sadness turned to anger. Ramala had a meeting with

Tara and Wana. Something had to be done about the situation at the First Lower House of Ra. Since, security had been compromised, it was a military situation. Ramala said that Wana should take whatever steps necessary to insure this never happens, again. Wana had a military caravan put together that day. When next day came, Wana was on her way to the First Lower House of Ra.

Besides a host of bodyguards, regular guards and Elite Guards, Wana had Elder Dan, Syn and Mangler come with her. She wanted to see first-hand what her nieces and nephews were up to.

Dan and La were well aware that their aunt Wana was on her way. After what happened, La knew there would be tough questions. She was just glad her mother wasn't going to be the one asking them. La planned on putting on a presentation for her aunt Wana, which would show that she and Dan had everything under control.

However, when Wana got to the First Lower House of Ra, she put off meeting with her niece and nephew. Instead, Wan met with the highest ranking members of the largest families here. She wanted to see what they thought happened and get their opinions. That didn't bother Dan, but it pissed La off that she was put off like that. La's spies told her that Wana was not only visiting the most important members of this House, but that she was also interviewing them. La wondered if her aunt wanted detail on what happened, why didn't she just come to La and Dan?

To make matters worse, Wana stayed at and had her meals with those families. La's suspicious mind thought the worse. She questioned her father and Syn Jara. Neither of them knew what Wana's intentions were.

After two days, La tried to enter one of the meetings Wana was conducting. No one was willing to tell La she couldn't enter. So, when guards alerted Wana that La was there, Wana went to meet La. Wana saw all three of her nieces smiling at her. La had on one of the fakest smiles that Wana had ever seen. Still, Wana was nice when she told her nieces that she would meet with them, later.

When La lightly begged, Wana was stern in her refusal. La

stared at her aunt Wana, until Shaya pulled on La's ponytail and said, "Alright, aunt Wana, we'll go. But don't keep us waiting too long. You know we miss you. You don't have to be all business on your visit."

"I'll see you soon. Just, not now." Wana said.

All three girls lowered their heads to their aunt. La quickly turned in a huff, because this had not gone as she planned. The three Ra girls left after that. Wana smiled to herself. She thought it was good that La had Shaya to be her voice of reason, much like Ramala had with Tara.

Young Dan knew there was nothing he could do, until his aunt Wana came to them. He wondered why La couldn't just stay calm and wait, like he was doing. Dan talked to La once more at last day meal. She listened and seemed to be calmer.

When next day came, messengers told Dan and La that Wana would have mid days meal with them and then meet with them directly after that. The early part of the day seemed to drag, but soon came mid-day's meal. Everyone filed into the eating hall. All three Ra girls took their seats and looked around the room. La studied her aunt Wana to see if she could guess what was going on. Yaya was there, but Wana ignored her as usual.

After everyone finished their meal, Wana waved her hand, signaling for Dan to remove the servants and guards from the room. Dan did that right away.

After the guards were gone, Wana stood up and looked at all of her nieces and nephews. She asked each of them their version of what happened. All of their versions were remarkably the same. Wana figured as much. After all, they had rehearsed what they were going to say.

Wana looked at La and then at Dan. She said, "I have met with the Elders of this Lower House as well as the other Lower Houses. I questioned them on your behavior. It seems they all are consistent in their assessments."

Wana paused for a moment. Her face was stern when she said,

"Dan, being warlord over this territory, you are solely responsible for everything that has happened. You have been partying and whoring around recklessly, while security was compromised. You and your warlords are to blame for the deaths of my master Deen and many others! I want the heads of all your warlords, so that I can show your queen mother that the situation has been resolved. They will be replaced with my warlords."

"You can't kill Bo! He saved my life! Do what you will with the others, but spare Bo! I would not be here, if not for him!" La pleaded.

Everyone stared at La, until she stopped talking. Then their eyes slowly moved back to Wana.

Dan couldn't believe this was happening. He looked at his siblings. They were warlords under Dan, while in the Lower Houses. Dan hoped his aunt wasn't including them. All of his siblings, except for Ram, looked panicked.

Wana saw the looks on their faces and said "Of course, that doesn't include any of you. Dan, you will return to the main city. Once there you will be committed to the custody of the palace, indefinitely. La and Shaya, both of you will return to your territory. You will be given the opportunity to run them, properly. If they are not controlled properly, the territory will be stripped from you and you will be banished to the main city. The rest of you will help La and Shaya. Fight me on any of these verdicts and you will be stripped of every title you have in the House of Ra."

That verdict hit Dan like a ton of bricks. It hurt, because he felt it was his fault. Dan thought he was doing enough, while having some fun. He knew if he had been more focused on running this territory, he might have been able to defend this Lower House, better.

Dan slowly stood up and looked no higher than Wana's chest when he asked "May I have permission to speak as warlord of this territory, before my title is stripped."

"Permission granted." Wana said, while staring at Dan.

Dan lowered his head to Wana and then said "You are right, aunt Wana. I am to blame for this travesty. I have behaved recklessly and should be punished, however you see fit. I gave my warlords orders that didn't give them a chance to succeed in defending this Lower House. So, my last standing order as warlord over this territory is to grant clemency and release all of my warlords from any death sentence. I also submit that they are valuable to the House of Ra and should be retrained to serve in whatever capacity they are best suited for. I am willing to do whatever is necessary to make this happen."

Wana stared at Dan. He still had his head lowered. After staring at Dan for a moment, Wana said "I will take this recommendation to your queen mother. If she has no objections, you ruling will stand."

Wana stared at all of nieces and nephews. Now that she had put them in their place militarily, she was going to give them a lesson as an aunt. She asked "How is it that our most hated enemy could march in here and set up all of you at the same time, before you knew it?"

Dan said, "They fought their way through our forces. Before we could react, they were right on top of us."

Wana shook her head in disappointment at Dan. Wana turned to La and asked, "Is that your interpretation, also?"

La wasn't here to be interrogated, she just wanted to know what her aunt intended on doing, so she would know how to react. She wasn't going to risk saying anything that might get her territory taken away from her. La just sat there staring at Wana.

Wana looked at everyone, else. No one said a word. Wana said, "If anyone attacked the main city of Ra, it would take weeks, if not many cycle of the moon, before they got to any of the palaces. It could never happen before first day's meal!"

Wana paused for a moment to see if any of them knew where she was going with this. They didn't so, Wana said, "It's true that I have more guards in the main city than you have here. However, if all your guards had fought, you would have had plenty of warning. And enough time to get together and formulate a plan!"

A light finally went on in La's head. La stood up and said, "She's right! Some of our guards must have let those Shitmushee walk in here and set us up! Probably hoping we'd all be killed! It's mutiny! How can we be responsible for that? I'm going to take the heads of every…..!'"

Wana interrupted with, "Hold on La! Sit down! You're not going to do anything, except listen to what I have to say!"

La couldn't believe her aunt would dare talk to her like this. Wana ordered in a more stern voice, "I said, sit down!!"

Shaya grabbed La by her arm and pulled her down into her seat. La let it happen. She stared at her aunt.

Wana wasn't going to get into a staring match with La. She composed herself and said, "While you are wildly popular with most of the young Ra, you are not as popular with many Hayee and their Elders. I blame all of you here for not mending the relationships you broke here, a long time ago. Another thing you need to realize is if the Shinmushee didn't kill their way getting to you, it's because they know some or all of the Elders here and have a sort of truce with them. Living so close to the jungle, that's probably why a lot of them haven't been killed by Shinmushee Butchers. They're getting along as best they can, in order to survive. Now, think about that."

Wana paused for a moment and then she said, "Don't take your failure out on anyone here. They're your family. Besides, if all they see you doing is partying and then blaming others when things go wrong, how does that reflect on you? We have to take the Southern Jungle, or except the fact that all of the Lower Houses have to survive, by getting along with the Shinmushee."

La calmly said, "Aunt Wana, everything you said is true. I see that now. Something has to be done to improve security and further our progress in taking the Southern Jungle. I take full responsibility for my part. I will secure my territory and with Shaya's help we will make a plan to take the Southern Jungle. With you support, of course."

Wana stared at La. She was caught off guard by La's calm demeanor. Although shocked, Wana knew La's strategy probably had ulterior motives. Wana said "First things, first. You and Shaya secure your territories and then we'll talk. For now, pack up and prepare to leave. My warlords are already securing this territory."

The Hammer-Axe Six stood up and lowered their heads to their aunt Wana. Wana stood up and left. The Hammer-Axe Six stared at each other in disbelief. Then they turned and stared at Dan. Dan was devastated, but put on his best face.

La looked at everyone, before looking at Dan. She said "Things could have been a lot worse. We got off easy. Once I and Shaya secure our territory, I'll request your help, Dan. After that, I will make you warlord. When you become warlord, Shaya and I will assist you in taking back these Lower Houses. Once you've secured the Lower Houses we'll take the southern Jungle, just as we planned. Dan, all you have to do is be patient. Living in the palace will be like having a vacation. You will just have to deal with mom and dad. You can do that, can't you?"

Dan watched La and everyone else as she talked. They all seemed to like La's plan. Dan could see hope in their eyes that after a short period of time, everything would go back to normal. Dan forced a fake smile on his face and nodded in agreement.

The next day, Dan put on his warlord butcher wardrobe. His brothers and Yin saw that and did the same. Don sent a messenger telling his sisters they should get here as soon as possible. La and her sisters were there in no time flat.

When La walked in she saw her brothers dressed for battle. She looked at Dan for an explanation.

"I've decided to stay a few more days." Dan said. Ram quickly pulled his Hammer-Axes and twirled them in one super-fast revolution. Ram looked at Dan and then slowly looked at La. La looked at Ram and knew that meant big trouble.

"We need to stay with the original plan. If we stay here, my territory will be taken." La explained.

"We are staying with the plan. I'll be the only one staying. I don't need any of you babysitting me. All of you will go and secure your territory. That means you too, Ram!" said Dan, as he turned and looked at Ram.

Ram looked at Dan and slammed his Hammer-Axes into their holsters. Ram's voice boomed with bass, when he said, "You'll be attacked!"

"He's right, you know. It's not safe here." La said.

"That's it, I'm staying!" Yin insisted.

Dan walked away from everyone and then turned towards them. With a stern look on his face, Dan yelled, "No one stays, except me! Go and take care of the business at hand! I'm the Hammer-Axe Champion, Chopper Ra! I can defend myself! No harm will come to me! I need time alone! I'm not going to have that if any of you stay!"

Everyone silently stared at Dan, not knowing what to say. Dan stared back. La broke the silence by saying, "Time alone he says! Let me know how it works out!"

La held out her hand, palm up, waiting for Danaaa's ponytail to bounce into it. Danaaa ran to Dan and hugged him, tightly. Once Danaaa let go of Dan Shaya quickly came over and hugged Dan. La was next. She hugged Dan and when she released her arms La pushed Dan backwards, with a good amount of force. With a hurt look in her eyes, La said, "I hope you know what you're doing!"

La raised her hand, palm up and this time Danaaa's ponytail jumped into her hand. La and her sisters left. Don, Yin and Ram walked up to Dan. They gave him a smile that was more nervous than reassuring, as it was meant to be. Then they left.

After hearing of Dan's plan to stay, Elder Dan, Syn and his aunt Wana came to talk with him. Young Dan was determined to stay. Later, Elder Dan and Syn met with Wana. They talked about the best way to deal with young Dan. Wana reluctantly agreed to their plan.

The next day young Dan was awakened by his father's voice calling him. Young Dan put on his clothes and walked out of his room. He saw his father and Syn, Jara staring at him.

"Syn is going to instruct you. I'll add something when necessary." Elder Dan said.

Syn smiled at young Dan. He remembered that smile meant the hell of being punished by the Syn, Jara. Young Dan wondered if he should just leave for the main city with everyone else.

The Syn, Jara started training young Dan, right away. She surpassed every hellish expectation that young Dan thought her training would be. His father stayed two days and then returned to the main city, along with Wana and his children. Elder Dan was satisfied that the Syn, Jara was doing a fine job with his son.

Syn trained young Dan from sun up to past sun down, every day for three weeks. She only gave young Dan breaks for meals. Young Dan didn't protest, because that was something Syn wouldn't allow from any of queen Ramala's sons. After the first week, young Dan finally asked, "Why is my training, nonstop, all day, every day?"

"Because, that's how much I care about you. When I leave you are going to be prepared. Remember everything I'm teaching you now, as well as in the past. You're going to need it." Syn said.

That was the only time young Dan questioned Syn. He thanked her for his training on the day she was leaving. Syn hugged young Dan and smiled at him. She said "Use this time, wisely."

Because the Syn, Jara had favor everywhere in the House of Ra meals were provided for her and Young Dan. Once Syn left, Dan was faced with the consequences of being stripped of his warlord title. That meant no servants, or maids. If Dan wanted a meal he had to eat when the guards were fed. That was a slight inconvenience to Dan.

This day Dan ate with the guards. He noticed that everyone looked at him, differently. Others pretended not to notice him, while some looks had a hint of challenge to them.

After a decent, but not as extravagant meal as he was used to, young Dan went back to his place. He lounged on some cushions, looked up at the ceiling and thought about his situation.

From the time he could remember, Dan was told he was going

to be King of Ra. He believed it, because everyone said so. It also was expected of him from his Queen Mother. Now, young Dan wondered if that was ever what he really wanted.

Then came the Hammer-Axe championships that he won three times. Young Dan was on top of the world with confidence in his skills, after that. The near defeat at the hands of a Shinmushee Butcher put doubt in his mind. Dan was saved when Danaaa helped him.

That and other near defeats made Dan question his title of Hammer-Axe Champion. With every challenge that came, Dan was determined to prove he was worthy of his title. The jolly old fighting master and his students Deadly Hearts and Sunshine crushed that dream.

The second Dan thought about Hearts and Sunshine he became angry. In his mind, they were the blame for him losing everything. Dan got up, walked over and picked up his Hammer-Axes. He went to his training courtyard and had an intense workout. Dan got cleaned up and waited for a couple of females to arrive.

After waiting a while, Dan wondered if the girls were coming. Usually he would send guards for them, if they were late. Dan couldn't because he had no guards. Dan refused to go chasing after those females. It angered him when they didn't show up. Didn't they know who he was? Dan remembered he was the man with no title. He wondered what other changes would affect his normal routine. Young Dan didn't like the changes he experienced, so far.

Dan didn't have to wait long to find out another change that came in the form of challenges. They started soon after the other Hammer-Axe Six left the First Lower House.

On this Day, young Dan was on his way to the guards' eating hall. He saw other guards on their way there, also. That wasn't unusual. They started making slanted comments towards Dan and then laughing afterwards. Dan knew what they were building up to. He was going to help them.

"So, this used to be the Hammer-Axe Champion." One guards said.

"Still am, until I'm beaten. However, I do give lessons. I can give you and your friends one for free. After that, it'll cost you!" Dan said.

None of these guards had ever seen young Dan in battle. They considered themselves pretty tough. There were twelve of them.

"If this lesson doesn't go as planned, we wouldn't want you running back and telling of our involvement." another guards said.

"I can guarantee that won't happen. I'll need the same guarantee from you, as well." replied Dan.

"Don't say we didn't warn you!"

Dan didn't remember any guards warning him. That didn't matter. They started circling Dan. Dan didn't pull his Hammer-Axes, until after the guards did. Once they'd done so, Dan fiercely attacked the guards. He beat them with the hammer side, without killing any of them. All of the guards were on the ground, incapacitated from the blows they received. Several more guards came up and were offended enough to go on guard against Dan. He put them on the ground as quickly as he'd done the others.

That morning Dan put down forty guards, before first day's meal. He had to put down twenty-five more after the meal. Before night came, Dan wounded ninety-seven guards. Each day after that, more guards attacked Dan. As the weeks went by, the attacks, although more intense, became less. The guards were learning the hard way not to provoke the Hammer-Axe Champion, Chopper Ra!

CHAPTER 18

Yaya was big sister to The Ra Rulers. They let her spend time with them after the Shinmushee crisis. Yaya mostly kept her mouth shut and didn't give any input. She was just happy to be able to spend time with her Ra family.

When Elder Dan, Syn and Mangler came to this Lower House, the first time, Yaya met them. Because it was a military emergency, Syn and Elder Dan only briefly greeted Yaya, before they got down to business. Elder Dan gave Yaya a quick hug. When Elder Dan held Yaya she felt her knees go weak. Yaya wanted to cling to him longer, but didn't. She feared someone would see her true intentions. She'd always had feelings for Dan when she was younger. Yaya was twenty-six years old. Yaya was going to let Elder Dan know how she felt. Elder Dan left before she had a chance to.

When Elder Dan returned, Yaya greeted him with a hug, just as she'd done before. This time Yaya pushed her body close on Dan and when he moved away to greet someone else, Yaya protested, wrestling Dan for a brief moment with her body. It was subtle, but Dan noticed it. He ignored it as he went about his business.

It bothers most women when a man does not notice her when she's trying to get his attention. Some women take that as a challenge. Yaya was no different. At first, she was subtle in trying to get Dan's attention. When that didn't work Yaya went further, while trying not to be obvious.

However, Yaya wasn't getting any results. No matter what she did, Elder Dan's attention always seemed to be elsewhere. Yaya thought that maybe Dan still saw her as a child. That had to be it! She decided to change her strategy.

That night, Yaya crept into the building Elder Dan was staying. Once there, Yaya listened to see if females were with Elder Dan. Yaya knew the Elder King liked female company most nights. Yaya didn't hear anyone, so she walked to Dan's room.

When Yaya got to the entrance she looked in. She saw Dan lounging on the bed. His chest was exposed and she could see the rest of him outlined by the sheet covering him. Yaya stared, until Dan turned and looked at her. When he did, Yaya walked into the room.

Nothing Yaya did all day trying to get Dan's attention was missed by him. He wondered what she would do next. Once she entered his room, he knew how far she was willing to go. Dan was going to give Yaya a chance to think about what she was trying to do. Something he wouldn't normally do when a female entered his room, looking as vulnerable as Yaya was.

"What's up?" asked Dan.

"I came to see you." Yaya replied.

Dan paused, before saying, "You should go back to your room. Clear your head with reasoning and then get some rest. When next day comes, you'll see things differently."

Yaya started slowly unbuttoning her blouse as she said, "You've always looked at me as a child. Well, I've loved you since I was a child. Now, I'm a woman. Can't you see that?" After that last sentence, Yaya's blouse came off.

Dan wasn't blind. He could see that. He noticed Yaya's body when he saw her last time he was here. Now he was looking at Yaya's young firm body, again. Dan wanted to do what was best for Yaya. He tried again, saying, "Sometimes a person can build things up in their mind, thinking it's what they want. Only to realize, later, that's not the case. Find you a good young man and give yourself to him."

Rejection! That's what Yaya felt. Dan's logic could have been the best in the world. That didn't matter to Yaya. What she wanted was right here in the same room. Why couldn't she have him? All Yaya's life she'd been taught, as a fighter, to never give up in battle. Yaya thought that maybe she wasn't trying hard enough, was why Dan was rejecting her.

Yaya slowly pulled down her pants. As she did, her flat rippled stomach muscles flexed from top to bottom. Dan saw all of that and more. Dan could have most any female he wanted. He didn't have to have this one. The trouble this could cause with his Queen Ramala wasn't worth it. Dan said, "Put on your clothes and leave."

Yaya only looked at Dan for a moment. She jumped on him from where she was standing. When Yaya landed on Dan he forcefully turned her over and pinned her down. He looked Yaya in her eyes and ordered, "Put on your clothes and get out!"

Dan moved off of Yaya and pushed her towards the edge of the bed. When he did Yaya whimpered in protest as she moved back towards him, wrapping her leg and locking it around Dan's leg. She quickly wrapped her arms around Dan's back, clinging tightly to him. While holding Dan, Yaya whimpered and made pouting moans in protest. Dan grabbed Yaya and tried to peel her off of himself. That made Yaya whimper, pout, moan and beg even more, while her body squirmed in protest. Yaya was young and very strong.

Dan fought off Yaya's physical begging as best he could. The sexually charged whimpering didn't help. Before Dan could stop it, his stick had risen to rock hard status. Yaya noticed that and wrestled to get a better feel of it. Once she'd done that, Yaya slowly grinded against it.

All of that was too much, even for a seasoned King such as Dan. He gave in and gave Yaya the experience of her lifetime. When Dan was done, he thought about what was going to happen when his Queen Ramala found out. He knew she would. Dan thought, 'No good is going to come of that!'

When next day came Dan found that Yaya had left his room. He was glad he wouldn't have to kick her out. Still, he knew there was going to be trouble. He hoped she wouldn't go telling his daughters. La definitely would take offense. Dan got up. He knew he shouldn't have let Yaya take advantage of him, even though she didn't. Dan was going to get cleaned up and then see how this all would play out.

Yaya was young and strong, so after a short nap she woke up in the middle of the night. She left and bathed herself. She tried to process everything she went through this night. After thinking about it, she came to the conclusion that it was all good! Yaya wanted Dan to do that to her, again.

When next day came Yaya went to meet the Ra girls for first day training. Yaya watched her sisters get ready and then all four girls walked towards the training courtyard. While they were walking, Danaaa stepped in front of Yaya and started walking backwards, in front of Yaya, while Yaya continued to walk forward.

La and Shaya watched Danaaa and thought she was acting silly. They weren't going to be bothered by her so early in the day. Shaya knew La would stop Danaaa if she went too far. Danaaa stared into Yaya's eyes. It wasn't a playful stare. It was stern and serious. Yaya instantly realized Danaaa's stare meant Danaaa might have smelled her father on Yaya. Yaya's eyes begged Danaaa not to say anything, without totally admitting guilt. Yaya could see that Danaaa had La and Shaya's attention. Yaya didn't need that kind of attention. Yaya nervously said, "Baby, quit playing around!"

Danaaa moved with lightning fast speed when she pointed one finger at Yaya indicting her. Then, just as quickly, Danaaa balled up the fist of that hand pointing at Yaya. Danaaa pointed that fist towards Yaya's face. She then moved it away as quickly as she put it there. It was a direct warning to Yaya. Everyone saw it. La was already annoyed that her aunt Wana had yet to meet with her. She didn't want Danaaa to get out of control so she yelled, "Baby, enough of this nonsense!"

Danaaa quickly turned her body in the direction that everyone else was facing. That jerked her ponytail and it lashed violently on Yaya's arm. Both La and Shaya stopped walking. La grabbed Danaaa's arm. La yelled, "What's wrong with you!?"

Danaaa snatched her arm from La. Danaaa peeked at Yaya and then looked back at La. Yaya's heart dropped to the floor. What would she say if Danaaa told La and Shaya what she did? Danaaa yelled, "First, we go to training. Then we have first day's meal!"

La, now confused, said, "We do that every day!"

"Then why is this day different?!" Danaaa yelled.

"What's different about this day?!" questioned La.

"That's what I want to know!" replied Danaaa.

La's lip went crooked and then it went straight. That was the first time that ever happened. La calmed herself, while staring at Danaaa. Shaya begged, "Can we please just go and train! I want to have first day's meal!"

La's eyes moved to Shaya's eyes and then back to Danaaa. Neither, La or Danaaa wanted this to escalate into an all week fight. But in the same breath, both were willing to do their part to make that fight happen. La calmly said, "Time for training. Enough of this. Let's go."

La had done her part to make this go away. The next move was on Danaaa. Danaaa jerked her head violently to the left and then to the right. Danaaa's ponytail jumped up in the air, just high enough for La to catch it. They turned and headed for training. Just like that, disaster had been averted.

Danaaa spared Yaya by not telling her sisters who she smelled on Yaya. Danaaa knew if she told, Yaya could possibly be killed. Danaaa didn't want that. At the same time, Danaaa didn't like that Yaya and her father had sex. She wondered why they would do such a thing, knowing the trouble it could cause. As a result, Danaaa was conflicted. That conflict going on inside Danaaa manifested itself in unruly behavior.

Training went as usual. Afterwards the Ra girls got cleaned up and went to meet Yin and their brothers. They all met up halfway to the eating hall. Young Dan noticed Danaaa staring at Yin.

Danaaa use to always start fights with Yin whenever she saw him. Dan got tired of that and always put himself in front of Yin, forcing Danaaa to fight him, instead of Yin. After many fights with Dan, Danaaa decided it wasn't worth fighting Dan and still not getting to fight Yin. So, Danaaa just watched to see if Dan would let down his guard, so she could attack Yin. Dan knew that, so it never happened.

Looking at his baby sister, Dan could tell something wasn't right with her. La and Shaya saw Dan curiously looking at Danaaa. Shaya said to Dan, "Baby's in some kind of mood. Leave her be. I really think that's best for everyone."

Dan knew his baby sister could be hell when she had an attitude. He wasn't going to be the one to set off the powder keg that was his sister, this time. Still, he thought, someone would. Dan looked away from Danaaa and looked at La. That meant it was time to eat.

The Hammer-Axe Six and Yaya arrived at the eating hall and sat at their usual table. Minutes later, Elder Dan walked in and scanned the room looking for his children. He wanted to see if word got out about himself and Yaya. After seeing his children, he knew it hadn't.

Shaya and Danaaa ran over to greet their father. Shaya hugged and smiled at him. Danaaa had a look on her face that Elder Dan couldn't describe. When Danaaa reached Elder Dan she was rough in her affection. Danaaa sniffed Elder Dan and looked up at him. He refused to look into Danaaa's eyes. He hugged and then smiled at Danaaa. That's when their eyes met. If there was any doubt whether Danaaa knew what happened, there wasn't now.

Danaaa quickly turned back towards the table and walked to her seat. When she did her ponytail lashed out at Elder Dan, slapping him across the shoulder. La immediately jumped up with her face full of anger, staring at Danaaa.

Elder Dan didn't want things to escalate so he warned, "La, take your seat. It was nothing. Don't get started!"

La slowly sat down. La and Danaaa watched each other closely as Danaaa sat next to La. For some reason that La didn't understand,

Danaaa was begging for a beating. La planned on giving it to her. Both knew they would be fighting, sometime, this day. Elder Dan saw his daughters staring at each other and said, "La!"

La looked at her father. Dan said, "We are going to have a civilized meal. I expect nothing less."

Dan stared at La, until she said, "Yes, father."

However if Danaaa did anything else, La was going to pummel Danaaa, until they pulled her off Danaaa.

The meal was uneventful. Everyone, except for Elder Dan and Yaya, were trying to figure out what was causing friction between La and Danaaa. It seemed Danaaa was purposely pushing La into a fight. They knew if they waited, Danaaa would let everyone know what was bothering her, after she had a good fight with La.

After Danaaa finished her meal, she put her elbows on the table and rested her face in her hands. She then stared at her father. At first no one said anything. Then La reached her boiling point. She said in a slow measured tone, "If you do one more thing!"

Danaaa quickly stood up and turned her back to the table. When she did her chair went crashing to the floor. Danaaa yelled, "One more thing!"

Danaaa said to Elder Dan, like she was giving an order, "Father, please excuse me from the table! I think it best!"

Without reservation, Elder Dan quickly said, "You're excused."

La couldn't believe what she just heard. It was like her mother was here giving Danaaa special treatment, as usual. La's father was hers alone to manipulate. How dare Danaaa tread on her territory! La stood up and turned towards Danaaa with bad intentions. Elder Dan stood up and said, "So help me Ramala if you take another step, I won't be responsible for what will happen! Take your seat!"

La slowly turned and stared at her father. She couldn't ever remember him threatening her like this! Elder Dan looked from La to Shaya. He said, "Go and make sure your sister is alright. La, you stay here!"

La incredulously looked at her father. She loved him, but she'd had enough of being ordered around. La said, as calmly as she could, "I'm not going to fight her, if that's what you think. Father, this is between sisters. It's best if you don't involve yourself."

La turned and walked out of the room, while everyone watched. After that they turned and looked at Elder Dan for his response. Elder Dan acted as if nothing had happened. Once Yaya saw that, she jumped up and ran after her sisters.

After catching up with her sisters, Yaya told them she was going to make sure her Wa family was alright. Yaya hugged La and then she hugged Shaya. When Yaya got to Danaaa she hugged her from behind, because Danaaa had her back to Yaya. Yaya held Danaaa and rubbed her stomach. That was something Yaya used to do to Danaaa when Danaaa was very young and upset. It always calmed Danaaa. Yaya whispered so that only Danaaa could hear, saying, "Thanks for not saying anything. Baby, please forgive me. I didn't mean to hurt you. Whatever I did, I couldn't help it. Please don't be angry with me. I couldn't bear that."

Danaaa turned and hugged Yaya. Yaya started crying. Shaya came over and said, "We're going to miss you, too. Just don't stay away too long."

Yaya wiped her eyes and left. Soon after that, Danaaa's attitude returned to normal. Danaaa still looked suspiciously at her father from time to time. Danaaa just couldn't figure out why they did it, knowing the trouble it would cause. Danaaa didn't tell her sisters what she knew about Yaya and her father. It was tough on Danaaa keeping that secret.

The main city of Ra was the most stable place in the Ra kingdom. No Shinmushee or rebels had ever been close to penetrating the city. Queen Ramala hadn't been out in the field in a very long time. Sometimes she missed it. The time off, while having and raising children showed her the down side of warring. That some come home disabled and maimed. Others were killed and didn't make it back, period. Ramala learned letting others fight for her wasn't a bad thing.

While waiting on Wana and her children to return, Ramala was enjoying time with her nieces, Tara's daughters, the Terrible Two. Yani and Tammy spent most of their time at Ramala's palace once Dan went with Wana to the First Lower House of Ra. This day everyone was having mid day meal. It was mostly the same people every day at this meal. Ramala, Tara, the Terrible Two, Jett, Anne, Trina and some of Ramala's closest cousins. Ramala invited different cousins to first day's meal and rotated them, depending on who needed a conference with her.

Everyone was watching little San-Jett run around like a mad man. It kept the Terrible Two from getting out of control when their younger brother put on a show for them. Jett wasn't like his sisters, who Tara had to negotiate and fight in order to get them to do things. Jett was a good boy for Tara and did most everything she told him. Tara could manipulate most anyone to do what she wanted, except for her daughters. Jett was easy for Tara. Tara was tough, but loving with Jett.

Guards came in with a message for Ramala. After hearing it, Ramala dismissed her cousins. Tara questioned Ramala as to what the guards told her. When Ramala told Tara, Tara ordered, "San-Jett, come to mommy!"

San-Jett turned and looked at Tara when he heard her voice. He walked over to her and wrapped his arms around Tara's leg. Tara looked at her daughters and then looked at Ramala. Ramala said, "They can stay."

"Good!" Tara replied and then left with San-Jett.

Ramala instructed and talked to the Terrible Two as she escorted them to their next training session. The Terrible Two listened, without interrupting. Once they reached the training center the two girls hugged their favorite aunt. After that, they looked at Ramala with begging eyes. Ramala smiled at them and said, "Alright, I'll come get you when you're done. If you do well, I'll have a special treat for you both!" that got the girls excited. They ran into the training center. Ramala loved these girls. She wondered why her own daughters weren't this easy to deal with.

Ramala went to one of her meeting halls. When she entered she saw Yaya. Yaya was fit and trim. She looked very athletic, but was healthy in the right places. Yaya looked like the perfect female warrior. Ramala was impressed!

Yaya saw Ramala and her eyes lit up. She lowered her head to Ramala and yelled "Mother!"

After that Yaya raced to Ramala and hugged her. Ramala hugged Yaya and was happy to see her. It had been a long time since Ramala had seen Yaya. She wondered why she was visiting.

Ramala pulled Yaya back and looked at her. Ramala said, "You look well! How have you been?"

Yaya excitedly said, "I've been well! I didn't know how much I missed you, until now!"

Ramala said, "Same here!"

Ramala and Yaya talked, until it was time to pick up the Terrible Two. Yani and Tammy were instantly jealous of the bond they saw between Ramala and Yaya. The second Ramala saw their behavior change, she put them in check. Ramala was the only one who could instantly stop these girls from acting out and creating havoc. When Ramala lightly scolded them once, they got in line. They knew Yaya had to be important for their aunt to do that.

Even though Yaya lowered her head to Tara at last day meal, she could see that Tara barely acknowledged her. Tara wasn't as rude to Yaya as she'd been in the past. Tara put up with Yaya for Ramala's sake. One thing Tara told Ramala before last meal was to ask Yaya why she was here. Tara didn't believe this was a random visit. She knew Yaya had a reason for coming here. Tara told Ramala to find out in private, as soon as possible. Ramala said she would.

Tara took her daughters to her palace after last day meal. Ramala and Yaya went to one of Ramala's gardens. After being out there for a short while, Ramala noticed Yaya was getting restless. Yaya gave Ramala a nervous look. Ramala asked, "What's on your mind?"

Yaya said, "I came here because….. I want to say something… It's just that….I don't know how."

Ramala said, "You know I love you very much, don't you?"

Yaya looked at Ramala and said, "I do. I love you, as well."

Ramala said, "Say what's on your mind. I'm sure we'll figure it out, once you've said it."

Yaya said, "Alright."

Yaya took two deep breaths before looking at Ramala. She took another one after that. Yaya said, "Alright mother, here it is. I.... I went into your King's room last night. I got into bed with him. He tried to talk me out of it. He even tried to physically resist, but I was persistent. Eventually he succumbed to my advances."

Yaya looked down and away from Ramala. She never looked up while saying, "I've always loved him, that's why I did it."

Ramala asked, "How do you feel, now that you've had him?"

Yaya said, "I don't know. I feel guilty....but... but."

Ramala said, "But what?"

Yaya whispered, "I'm sorry for what I did, concerning you."

Yaya looked into Ramala's eyes and said, "That makes me a bad person that I would do this to you, doesn't it?"

Ramala said, "I can't say that. That's for you to figure out. What you did, you didn't do to me. You did it to yourself and Dan. You have not been disrespectful in telling me this. I have no ill feelings towards you"

Yaya said, "But, I liked it.....I liked it a lot!"

Ramala said, "I know."

Yaya said, "But I still love him!"

Ramala said, "I know."

Yaya lowered her head and said, "I'm probably going be with him, again, if I can." Ramala said, "I know that, as well."

Yaya paused and said, "I will be very respectful, if I do so."

Ramala said, "We'll see."

It made Yaya nervous that Ramala was so calm about her having sex with Elder Dan. So much so that Yaya left that same night. Even though a great weight had been lifted off Yaya's shoulders by admitting to Ramala what she'd done, Yaya wasn't going to take the chance that she might not make it out of the main city of Ra, alive.

Of all the women who had sex with Dan, none of them came and told Ramala face to face that they had. That Yaya would take the chance that Ramala wouldn't have her killed was worthy of Ramala's respect. That Yaya was in no way disrespectful made it easy for Ramala to hear her out.

Ramala thought about it afterwards. She found it funny that Yaya left right after telling her. Ramala could see that even though Yaya was willing to admit what she'd done, Yaya was smart enough not to stay long enough to find out it wasn't the right thing to do. Ramala loved Yaya. She would let her live, for now. Ramala knew if she decided differently, Yaya would never suspect anything, until it was too late.

—— CHAPTER 19 ——

La and her siblings were on the lead caravan and didn't stop until, they got to the main city of Ra. Wana decided her caravan would camp for the night, instead of arriving very late. They set up camp and everyone got situated for the night. Wana felt she made progress at the First Lower House. She got a couple of her secret servicers to work her over sexually.

Elder Dan and the other men in the camp heard Wana's cries of passion. The men who had females with them, took it to those girls and had them join in the symphony of sounds. Elder Dan was going to wait until he got to the main city. Ramala was there, along with most any female he might want.

Elder Dan was daydreaming when a guard stealthily called him. Dan got up and walked out of his covered platform. He saw Yaya. Elder Dan remembered how forceful Yaya was convincing him to let her have her way with him. If she caused a commotion Wana would find out, right away. Elder Dan motioned for Yaya to join him. Pretty soon she was just as loud as the other females in the caravan.

Yaya was twenty-six. Dan took it to her, heavily pounding her into an orgasm, knowing that would get their encounter over as quickly as possible. However, at twenty-six Yaya had remarkable recovery time of less than five minutes. After that, Yaya was right on top of Dan, again. Every time Yaya came back for more, Elder Dan pounded her into orgasm, after orgasms. He was sure that would put her to sleep and keep her off of him for the rest of the night. Since

Dan was a master at not giving up his seed, he was ready every time Yaya was.

Elder Dan laid waste to Yaya at least four or more times, that he could remember. When day came she was gone. Dan was surprised at Yaya's go power. He wondered if the threat of Wana killing her when day came wasn't there, how long would she have gone? In a way, Dan was glad he hadn't found out. In a way he wished he had. Dan knew that kind of thinking was going to make a bad situation, worse. He already knew after what he'd done to Yaya she'd definitely be back for more. Heck, if it wasn't Yaya, Dan would be looking for her, after last night!

Dan tried to stop himself from thinking about last night. If Ramala found out about this, well, he didn't know what her reaction would be. He just knew there'd be one. He put Yaya out of his mind and hoped she would do the same with him.

Once Syn, Jara returned to the main city, she started training the Hammer-Axe Six. Soon they would be going to their territories and Syn wanted them to be at their best. Because La and her siblings were so advanced in their skill set, Syn refused to spar with them as a way of training them. She devised a way to give each of them specialized training. Syn used all of the torturous training techniques she'd used, while training them in the past. She learned most all of those techniques from her father and grandfather. Syn also invented new ways to push the royal Ra to their limits. When the Hammer-Axe Six adjusted to her training, Syn would switch it up on them.

One way Syn did that was by making each of them fight without weapons, while their opponents fought with weapons. The Hammer-Axe Six adjusted to that training and excelled after only three weeks. Syn decided to put a twist in that training. She would be the opponent with the weapon.

Once Syn did that, she found that La and Shaya would basically run from her. Danaaa would try to avoid Syn, until Syn cornered Danaaa with a kill shot. Don, Yin and Ram did the same as Danaaa, with the same results. But at least they were trying to figure out how to avoid the weapons, until they could counter-attack.

After two days of chasing La and Shaya, Syn decided to change things. She took them into a small room where they couldn't run. This worked out better than Syn expected. Both Shaya and La were forced to fight, so they did.

Syn would pressure them, with axes, up to the point where she had a clear kill shot. Syn would back away at that point and instruct the girls on what they could have done, better. Eventually, La and Shaya started to improve to the point that they were counter-attacking. The small room training technique worked so well with the girls, Syn used it with Don, Yin and Ram. Just like the girls, after being force to fight in a small enclosed area, the Ra men excelled, also.

Syn spent almost three moon cycles training the Hammer-Axe Six, minus young Dan. She pushed them and herself over their limits. When she was done Syn told the Hammer-Axe Six to keep training hard at the techniques she taught them. She instructed them to never think they're at the top of their fighting game, no matter how good they got. She told all of them, as good as you are there's always someone who is better. Then it becomes a test of who can adapt and do what it takes to win that battle. Syn was proud of her students. It would be near impossible to beat them. But, as Syn told them, no one is unbeatable. You just have to make sure you are prepared to win each and every battle.

Ram was the first of all the royal Ra to overcome Syn's technique of avoiding being attacked by her with axes, while using no weapons. Of course, Danaaa was the second. It only took Ram two and a half weeks to figure it out and mount an offensive attack on Syn. It surprised the Syn, Jara that Ram was that good and adaptable to fighting strategies. Syn tried to figure out a new way to challenge Ram's talents. Syn didn't have to, because just like everyone else, she discovered Ram gone, when next day came.

The night before, Ram stealthily got out of bed. He looked at Don and Yin. They all were deep in sleep. Ram thought, only for a split second, that if they were enemies they would be dead. Since, they were his brother and cousin, Ram quietly left the room.

Ram stealthily crept into the building where La and her sisters were sleeping. He looked at his sisters. Even though they annoyed him, he still loved them. Ram disappeared without being noticed. After he was gone, La jumped up out of her sleep and looked around. She felt like someone was watching her. When La jumped up, so did her sisters, even though they weren't in the same bed. They looked around, also.

La and her sisters used to always sleep in the same bed together. Shaya and Danaaa still slept together, but La slowly started sleeping separately from her sisters. Most times she still slept in the same room with them, but even that wasn't always. Danaaa smelled a slight hint of Ram. She figured he was outside prowling around the city. Since he'd never come into their room at night, before, Danaaa didn't figure he had this time. After looking around again and not detecting anything, all three girls went back to sleep.

Ram was at the First Lower House of Ra when next day came. He walked into the dwelling where he and his brothers stayed while here. There were no servants or maids. The place was messy. Ram stealthily made his way to Dan's room. Ram stood in the doorway and quietly watched young Dan.

Dan felt someone watching him. He slowly moved his hand towards his Hammer-Axe handle. Once he grabbed it he opened his eyes and saw Ram. With a big smile on his face, young Dan happily shouted, "Hey, Ram! Where's everyone else?"

"I'm alone." Ram's deep voice bellowed.

"Why are you here?" Dan suspiciously asked.

"To see you."

"Why?"

Ram shrugged his shoulders. Young Dan stared at his brother, figuring there was no telling what Ram was up to. Dan was happy to see Ram, so he got dressed. Afterwards, Dan said "Alright, let's get something to eat."

When they stepped outside, a group of young men and teenagers approached. They all had weapons drawn. Ram quickly pulled his Hammer-Axes. Dan stepped in front of Ram and put his hand up, stopping Ram.

"I'll handle this! Just watch." ordered Dan.

Ram put his Hammer-Axes back in their holsters and went on guard. Dan saw Ram wasn't going to attack, so he turned his attention to the others. That's when they attacked young Dan. At first, Dan fought them without using his Hammer-Axes. He pulled them when the battle intensified. Nevertheless, Dan beat all of the combatants into submission, without killing them. After that, food was brought to Dan and Ram.

While they were eating, Ram questioned, "You fight for meals?"

"I fight for pretty much anything I need, these days." replied Dan.

"Just take what you want. I'll help." suggested Ram.

Dan paused and looked at his youngest brother. He knew the only way Ram would help was by slaughtering as many people as possible. Dan smiled at Ram and said, "After all of you and Syn left for the main city, I faced attacks night and day. I ferociously put down those attacks. I was very angry because my titles were stripped from me. I still am, just not as much."

Dan paused and then said "I got to thinking about whether I really wanted to be king in the first place. No one ever asked me what I wanted, you know. I really don't care about being a warlord, or a king. All I wanted was to be the best Hammer-axe Champion, ever. So that's who I'm going to be!"

Ram listened, while Dan continued to talk. Ram looked around and could see this place hadn't been cleaned, properly. Ram wondered why a Hammer-Axe Champion doesn't have maids and servants. He also wondered why he has to fight for his food. Ram knew Dan never had to do that when he was warlord and king. Ram was beginning to think his oldest brother was making a bad career change.

Dan and Ram spent the entire day together. Ram realized that all the advantages of being a Hammer-Axe Champion were far less than being warlord and king. Even the women that Young Dan brought back to his place were different. Ram was used to seeing Dan with the highest ranking women. Once young Dan was stripped of his titles all those women conveniently avoided him. Ram could see that these women didn't have any rank and very little social training.

Ram looked around. He couldn't take any more of this. He motioned for Dan. Dan walked over to Ram. Dan had a happy and devious look on his face. Ram hugged Dan. When he let go of Dan, in his deep bass voice, Ram said "Being a warlord and king is better than this."

Ram turned and walked away. Dan stood there for a moment staring, confused by what Ram said. He didn't want to think about that, right now. Dan wasn't going to let Ram mess up his fun night. When Dan turned back towards the women there, the confused look was gone. It was replaced with a devious smile. The women giggled, knowing that smile meant a night of fun.

Ram walked down the roads of this Lower House, thinking. Ram wondered if Dan was a lost cause. The way Dan was living, Ram couldn't tell. He hoped his parents and siblings wouldn't see Dan like this.

Ram noticed guards and other people watching him. Usually, it never bothered Ram when people stared at him. It bothered Ram seeing Dan like that. That made these people irritating to Ram. He knew if he pulled his Hammer-Axes they all would stop staring. Ram wanted them to give him a reason slightly above staring at him. Then he would have no problem killing everyone in this Lower House.

No one gave him a reason, so Ram walked past the last guard post facing the jungle. He could see that four of the guards were sleep and six others were barely conscious, while scanning the tree line. Ram smiled to himself. He could kill all of them, before they knew what happened. So much for Ra security! Ram crept in the shadows, until he was in the cover of the jungle.

The next day Shinmushee scouts spotted Ram walking through the jungle. They alerted their superiors, who alerted the nearest Shinmushee Butcher. The Shinmushee Butcher got all of the fact on Ram's position. One thing the Shinmushee Butcher realized was that Ram hadn't attacked anyone. He just seemed to be walking through their territory, not looking for anything in particular. Scouts were told to follow him and give regular reports on his whereabouts.

Ram walked for a while on the ground. He didn't climb up on the platforms that went from tree to tree, through most of the jungle. Ram saw a small group of Shinmushee a little further away. They were cooking food. Ram was hungry. He saw no reason why he should be hungry when there was food, ahead. Ram moved closer, stalking his prey.

Scouts in the distance saw Ram and alerted their Butchers. Just as Ram came out of some thick bushes ten Shinmushee Butchers and a host of warriors came from the opposite direction, from behind the small group that was cooking. Ram kept walking towards the group cooking. He wasn't going to let Shinmushee Butchers keep him from getting a good meal. If he had to kill them, before eating, so be it. As he was walking forward Ram put his hands in a quick draw position next to his Hammer-Axes. Two steps later, Ram quickly pulled his Hammer-Axes and twirled them in one super fast revolution. It was time to see where this was going.

As Ram got closer an old woman quickly moved ahead of the Shinmushee Butchers and motioned for them to stop. She walked quickly towards Ram. Some of the others called out to her, but she reached Ram before anyone could react. Ram looked at the old lady as she stepped right in front of Ram, blocking his path. Ram was a half second from splitting her open when she said, "You look hungry."

With lightning speed that startled Ram, the old lady extended her arm presenting a pastry to Ram. Ram's unusually keen sense of smell told him that pastry was of the highest caliber and wasn't poisoned. Ram looked at the Shinmushee Butchers as he put one of his Hammer-Axes back in its holster. He then ate the pastry, while on guard. The old Lady said, "Good, isn't it?"

Ram looked at the old lady not saying anything, even though that pastry was excellent.

The old lady said "There's more where that came from!"

She reached with lightning fast speed, again. This time it was for the arm that Ram had his ax in. Ram quickly moved his arm and avoided the old lady. They both stared at each other for a moment. Ram didn't detect any hostile intent coming from the old woman. He slammed that ax in its holster and waited to see if this old lady would make a move he considered threatening. The old lady looked at Ram and put her arm between his arm and said, "Come on! I told you there's more over there! One can't be enough for you!"

The old lady pulled Ram closer to the Shinmushee Butchers and their warriors. Ram watched them, closely.

Ram saw the Shinmushee Butchers motioning for their warriors to move back. After that, the Butchers and their guards moved back. Ram looked down at the old lady who was forcefully pulling him with her. Ram bellowed in his deep voice, "You're fast and strong."

The old lady peeked up at Ram and said, "I feed men like you all the time. I have to be strong!"

Ram had a good meal, while the old lady talked. She didn't ask Ram questions. She could see he was the type of man you don't question. But she did say, "Are you looking for that old man you fought here a while back?"

Ram didn't remember seeing this old woman back then. He thought it must have been because he was too busy getting his ass kicked. Ram nodded he was. The old lady said, "There are scouts that can take you to him."

Ram looked around. The old Lady said, "Relax and finish you meal. They'll take you when you're done."

The old lady winked at Ram and said, "I'll give you a few pastries for the road!" then she smiled at Ram. Ram didn't want to, but a slight smile showed on his face for a half second, before disappearing.

Scouts informed their Butchers that Ram was looking for the old man. The Butchers sent messengers asking the old man as to what they should do. Those messengers wouldn't reach the old man for a while. The scouts that were leading Ram took him on a goose chase, until they were informed what to do. Ram followed the scouts for two days. Still, he saw no signs of the old man. The Shinmushee scouts stopped at different villages and Ram was fed well, before continuing his journey.

On the third day scouts came and had conversation with the scouts that were leading Ram. The old man decided to see Ram. That's when they took Ram directly to the old man. It was another half days journey before they reached a small city. This city was on the ground. Ram realized not all of the Shinmushee lived in trees.

Once they got to the city. All of the Shinmushee stared at Ram. Ram was use to people staring at him. His own family stared at him everywhere he went. They walked onto a large courtyard where Ram was asked to wait. About twenty minutes later, a throne with the old man on it was carried onto the courtyard.

Ram recognized two of the guards next to the old man as the ones he saw in the jungle when he was on his way back to the first Lower House, after his beating from the old man. He didn't know their names, but it was Claw and Deadly Hearts. Sunshine was in the comfort of a darkened room.

The old man stared at Ram. Ram got down on one knee and then stood back up. No one could believe he dared to come here by himself. The usually jolly old man wasn't surprised. He knew if he hadn't killed Ram, Ram would come back. The old man didn't waste any time. He unenthusiastically ordered, "State your purpose for being here!"

Ram's voice boomed with bass as he said 'Training."

Everyone was confused as to why this Ra thought he could come here to be trained, so that he could turn around and kill them. They thought Ram was insane.

The old man asked, "Why should I give you training?"

"I'm Ram."

"And you think that's good enough?"

"Yes." replied Ram.

The old man studied Ram for a moment and then said, "You've had a long journey. Go get cleaned up. I'll let you know your fate, when first day comes."

Ram lowered his head. He was led out of the courtyard and shown to a private bathing house. After he left the courtyard, everyone there turned and looked a question to the old man. They knew they couldn't say it with their mouths, so their eyes questioned, 'Are you really thinking about training that Ra scum, when we should kill him?'

The old man's eyes never answered that question. He just motioned with his hand. When he did guards lifted his throne chair and carried him off.

Ram was led to a room with a bed in it. He was told that he should stay there and not leave. Someone would come for him when the next day came. Ram didn't say anything. He understood, perfectly. If he left that room, he was going to have to kill some Shinmushee. That was the gist of the story. It was late. Ram didn't know what the old man would decide next day. Ram was going to rest so he could best deal with, whatever.

—— CHAPTER 20 ——

Sunshine mostly trained after sundown and at night. That meant she slept and rested most of the day. Hearts told Sunshine about Ram. Sunshine didn't get a chance to see Ram before he went to his room for sleep. Sunshine waited until after her first training session, after dark. She quietly crept to the doorway of Ram's room. She could see he was sleeping, on his back, with his Hammer-Axes resting on his chest.

Sunshine had seen killers sleep with their weapons close, but none like this. Still, Sunshine told herself that she could creep up on Ram and kill him, before he raised his axes. She was sure of it. The only reason she didn't was because she thought it might anger the old man she called grandpa.

What she didn't know was Ram was totally aware that someone was there. He heard and smelled Sunshine before she got to the doorway. Ram was waiting on her to move closer. He was going to cut her to pieces, without opening his eyes. Lucky for Sunshine, her curiosity was fulfilled by watching Ram in the doorway. After studying him for a moment, Sunshine left.

When next day came Ram was taken to a large eating room. There were Shinmushee of all ages. All of them stared at Ram as he was led to his seat. They continued to stare, without saying a word to Ram. Ram watched them, closely. To Ram, every situation was a chance to evaluate how he could kill, everyone in his vicinity. So, as he waited on his meal, that's what he did.

Ram was sitting at a table that had what looked like three families. This was different to Ram, because in the House of Ra children sat at tables separate from the grown-ups. In fact, everyone was separated. Teenagers ate together. Children ate together. However, here, all age groups ate together.

While thinking about that Ram saw a young girl staring at him. She seemed to be about four or five years of age. She walked towards him and stopped, while staring at him. She said, "You look different. Where do you come from?"

The girl's mother, who had lost track of her for a second, looked at Ram and then warned her daughter, saying, "Leave him be!"

The mother looked at Ram and said, "I hope she's not bothering you. She's just curious."

Ram barely paid attention to the woman, never looking at her. The mother watched her daughter to make sure she didn't annoy the stranger. The young girl heard her mother, but also heard what she said to the stranger. The stranger didn't think she was out of line. She was still curious. Ram hadn't answered her, so she said, "My name is Hannamobaya. They call me Hanna. What's your name?"

Ram looked around the room. He made sure no one was using this girl to distract him, so they could attack him. When he was sure that wasn't happening Ram said, "Ram." she then asked, "What do they call you?" Ram said, "Ram." the girl giggled and said, "That's funny! They call you the same as your name."

The girl moved closer to Ram and said, "Your eyes look funny!" the girl's mother warned, "Hanna, be respectful!"

"Well, they do!" the girl said.

Ram, who had not looked directly at the girl, turned and looked into her eyes. The girl turned, ran and took a flying leap into her mother's lap. She turned and looked at the strange man. She watched him, but she didn't want to talk to him, anymore.

Ram ate and was taken to the same courtyard he was at the day before. The old man was there waiting on him. He had warriors and Butchers with him. Hearts and Claw were also there. The old man didn't waste any time. He said, "I won't instruct you in fighting. However, I am willing to instruct you on being a slave. Can you learn that?"

Ram only looked at the old man for a second, before looking at the guards around him. Obviously, the old man was insane, if he thought Ram was slave material. Ram said, "No!"

"That's what I thought. You only want to learn what you want. That's not how you learn. If you know what you should learn, then teach me something." the old man said.

Ram only knew one thing, well. It was killing. Did the old man really want that? Ram stared at the old man. Ram moved his hands to a quick draw position near his Hammer-Axes. The old man saw that and said, "If you were good enough with those axes, you wouldn't be here begging me to teach you!"

Ram instantly took offense. He was going to kill all the old man's guards and then try to kill the old man. The old man said, "Look at you! All you know is killing. If you learn how to be a good slave, who knows what else I might instruct you on."

Now, they were getting somewhere! Ram knew he could learn anything, if he put his mind to it. Ram could learn how to be a slave, if the old man would train him in fighting techniques. That was Ram's interpretation, even though that's not what the old man said. Ram thought, 'Why didn't he say that in the first place?'

Ram relaxed his arms and hands. He nodded his head in agreement. The old man said, "So you agree to let me instruct you on how to be a slave." again, Ram slowly nodded in agreement.

The old man said, "Alright, we start, now. If you refuse, or rebel, I instruct you no more. Is that understood?"

Ram nodded in agreement. The old man then said, "Slaves don't carry weapons. Take all of your weapons and drop them to the ground!"

Ram hesitated. His Hammer-Axes and gutting knives were special gifts given to him by the famous weapon's maker the Hayee, Tagowa. Besides, that would leave him naked. That's what Ram thought about being without any weapons.

The old man raised his head and looked down his nose at Ram. Ram slowly reached for his Hammer-Axes. One at a time he dropped them on the ground. He then did the same with his machetes and gutting knives. Ram looked down at his weapons, before looking back up at the old man.

The old man said, "Take your weapons and put them in your sleeping quarters. No one will touch them. After that, return here. Someone will give you tasks to complete. As a slave, you are expected to complete all your tasks. If you feel you can't meet the challenge of being a slave, you can take your weapons and leave. Remember, the moment you use your weapons here, is the moment you're no longer welcome!"

Ram lowered his head and said, "Yes, Teacher."

The old man seemed annoyed when he said, "Teacher! Don't call me that!"

Ram asked, "What then?"

The old man paused for a moment and then said, "Call me what everyone else calls me!"

When the old man said that, Claw, Hearts and several of the guards looked at him in astonishment. Ram thought about what he heard everyone call the old man and questioned, "Grandpa?"

The old man nodded in agreement. Without realizing it Ram shrugged his shoulders, like whatever and then picked up his weapons. He took them to his sleeping quarters, like he was told.

Once Ram was gone Hearts turned to the old man. Her face looked confused when she respectfully said, "Grandpa, I don't understand. He's our enemy, yet you let him stay amongst us. Once he learns from you, he'll have the ability to kill many Shinmushee. Grandpa, please help me understand!"

The old man looked at Hearts. He could see she was trying to be as respectful as possible. The old man took a deep breath and sighed. He said. "You call him enemy. Also, you say he's learning. Well, if he's here you can study and learn him, just as well. If he learns more about us than you learn about him and the ways of the Ra, then he is the better student and you deserve whatever you get. Your training has already started! He has traveled alone through Shinmushee to come here for training. What does that tell you about him? What do you know of this Ram? That's what you should think about!"

The old man turned away from Hearts, letting her know he was done instructing her. Hearts said, "Thanks, Grandpa."

Ram hurried back after putting his weapons in his room. When he returned he found that the old man was not there. Instead, he saw several men who were instructing others. When those men saw Ram they walked over to him. Ram asked, "Where's the old man?"

The men curiously looked at Ram. Ram said, "Where's Grandpa?"

The men stared at Ram for a moment. Finally, one of them said, "He's busy. Don't worry about him. We have work for you. Come."

Ram had never been talked to like that, before. Nor had he ever done menial tasks. Ram stared at the warriors, mapping their positions around him. Ram knew he could easily kill them all and whoever came after that. He was going to make them pay for that disrespect with their lives.

While contemplating killing theses warriors, Ram thought about what the old grandpa told him about if he killed. Ram decided to comply, for now.

Today Ram removed and sorted trash, swept and cleaned. He ground grains into a flower like powder, using one-hundred pound cylinders of wood to grind it. He repaired dwellings and cleaned up the mess, afterwards. He chopped trees and fashioned the wood for whatever was needed.

All of this was different, but Ram was willing to do it, if he could learn from the old man. When mealtime came was when Ram became angry. Ram was use to eating until he was full. Here, they fed Ram like a slave. Ram put up with it for mid-day meal. However, he became even angrier, after last day meal.

Ram was in his quarters that night. He knew he would fail the test of being a slave. It wasn't because of the work. It was because he wasn't being fed, properly. Ram sat there thinking. He didn't want to give up. He wondered how he could get more food. His stomach kept interrupting him with strong growls for food. He couldn't blame it.

Ram could smell the food that he wasn't getting. That bothered him even more. Then he heard footsteps. Ram looked at his weapons. If they thought they were going to have him clean up after the people eating they had another thing coming!

Ram decided this wasn't for him. Whoever walked through that door, depending on what they said, was going to get a healthy dose of his axes. Ram watched the doorway and waited.

A girl walked through the doorway with a tray of food. She looked Ram over and then walked towards him with the tray. Ram jumped up and stared at the food. The girl nervously looked around and whispered, "Please, we have to be quiet! If they find that I've brought you food I will be beaten!"

Ram barely heard her. Once she got within reach, Ram grabbed her and the tray. He slung the girl towards the bed, while relieving her of the tray. Ram tore into that food like he hadn't eaten in days.

The girl got on her knees and watched Ram. She'd seen men eat like savages before, but never like this. She stared until Ram was finished. There was a cup of water that Ram washed down his food with. He would have rather had a tall glass of fresh warm blood. He turned and looked at the girl. Ram grabbed the girl roughly by her arm and pulled her close to him. He twisted her arm and asked, "Who sent you?"

The girl winced in pain. She said, "No one sent me! I came on my own!"

"Why?" asked Ram.

"I saw you, earlier this day, working hard. What they gave you, I knew it wasn't enough. I knew you needed more. That's why I brought it." The girl replied.

Because Ram was raised that way, he hated the Shinmushee. This girl was one. He grabbed the tray and gave it to the girl and then slung her out of the room. He could hear the girl running down the hall, after that. Ram felt tightness in his head. He got in the bed and tried to get some rest.

This was the longest Ram had gone without drinking blood. The tightness in his head was the beginning of withdrawal symptoms. Ram twisted and turned, until he finally fell asleep.

The Ra and Hayee drank blood, regularly. They believed it strengthened their mind, bodies and spirits. The higher in rank, the more blood you could afford to drink. Being the son of the Queen of Ra, Ram usually drank blood with every meal.

Ram woke up the next day with a strong craving for blood. It annoyed him because there were no Hayee, or Ra to get blood from. Ram wouldn't drink blood from a Shinmushee. They were considered savages and heathens. He was taught that drinking the blood of heathens and savages can turn your blood against you and make you insane.

The warriors hadn't come to get Ram, yet. The Shinmushee didn't seem to get up as early as the Ra. Ram would already be training with his brothers, by now. Ram decided if the old grandpa wasn't going to train him, right away, he was going to train himself, until that time came.

Sometime later, the Shinmushee guards came to get Ram. They took him to a small clearing. Ram could see a girl tied to a tree with her back exposed. After looking at her for a moment, Ram realized that was the girl who brought him food the night before. One of the Shinmushee looked at Ram and said, "This girl brought you food last night. That was forbidden. Nothing will happen to you, but she will be beaten."

A man with a whip came out and started lashing the girl. She took most of them without making a sound. But the last four made her cry out. After that the warriors took Ram to his first task. Ram was unaffected by the girl getting beaten. Ram shook his head. He knew he wouldn't be getting anymore meals at night. He just knew it!

They worked Ram hard that day. He saw the same girl several times. He thought she must be a slave, or close to it. She and others with her seemed to be working hard, also.

However, Ram wondered where the old man was. He wasn't here training Ram to be a slave. He had others doing it. Ram thought that was the deal. Ram started getting angry. Was the old man and the Shinmushee playing him for a fool? Where they trying to weaken him, by not feeding him properly, so they could kill him in his weakened state? That's what Ram was starting to think as he toiled through the day.

That night after a meal that Ram considered an insult, Ram was on his bed, staring at the ceiling wondering if he should kill as many Shinmushee a possible and then go home. While thinking that, Ram heard someone sneaking quietly towards his room. He put his hands on his ax handles. It was just as he suspected! They thought him weak enough to try to kill him this night. Well, they were wrong!

Then Ram smelled food. Seconds later, he saw the same girl put food inside the door and then leave, without even looking at him. Ram walked over and looked out the doorway down the hall. The girl was gone. Ram looked down at the food. He sniffed it for poison. After that he ate it. Again, that night, Ram had withdrawal symptoms from not drinking blood.

The next day when the warriors came to get Ram they saw the tray the girl left. They picked it up and escorted Ram to that same clearing. A few minutes later, several warriors showed up with the girl. She never looked at Ram. She was tied to a tree and beaten, again. Ram was still unaffected by the beating, but wondered why she kept bringing him food, knowing she'd get beaten. He couldn't help it, but hoped she would bring more food, despite the beating she might take.

That day Ram was worked harder than the day, before. Ram wiped sweat from his forehead. He still hadn't seen the old man. When was his training going to start?! That night Ram was in his room, thinking. When next day came, he was going to confront the old man and negotiate a better deal. If he couldn't Ram was going to leave.

Then that familiar smell and sound came. It was that girl sneaking through the hallway. Ram got up and quietly hid on the inside of the doorway. When the girl came and put the tray inside the door, Ram grabbed her arm and pulled her around the tray and inside the door. Ram looked her in her eyes and said, "Why do this?"

The girl struggled to get away, but couldn't. She said nothing. Ram turned her so that he was blocking the doorway. He let go of her. Once he'd done so, she took a few steps back from him. Ram said, "Answer me."

"Don't you want the food?" questioned the girl.

Ramala taught Ram that if someone does something for you, they usually expect something in return. Ram knew this girl wasn't taking a beating for nothing. He asked, "What do you want?"

The girl stared at Ram for a moment. She looked down and away, before saying, "I'm used by a lot of the men here, whenever they want. That also means that none of them will take me as a mate and protect me from the others. I see the fear they have for you. I just want protection. I'm tired of being used, like that!"

The girl picked up the tray of food and handed it to Ram. Ram took it. He said, "Sit."

Ram ate the food without saying a word. When Ram was done, he said, "I'll do it."

The girl smiled and said, "Just so you know, my name is Zararee. They call me Ree."

"I'm Ram."

"Everyone here knows your name and who you are. You're the one who fought Grandpa almost an entire day! No one's ever done that, before!"

Ree jumped on Ram's bed. Ram looked at her. She said, "I'm staying the night. If we're quiet, I won't be discovered. I'll leave before day comes."

Ram looked Ree's body over. She looked to be about twenty

years old. Whatever those men were doing to her body, it was still tight, although softer than the females from the House of Ra. Ram said, "If you stay, you won't be quiet."

Ree got excited and she said, "About that, I don't care!"

If she didn't care, neither did he. Ram put the tray down and got on the bed with Ree. They took off their clothes and got started up. After a few minutes, Ree was moaning. Soon after that she was howling like a banshee. It wasn't long before Shinmushee warriors showed up. When they came through the doorway, Ree backed up against the wall on the bed behind Ram. Ram watched the warriors as he put on his pants.

The warriors stood there, until Claw, Hearts and Sunshine appeared. They looked at the girl like they were ready to kill her. Ram heard a conversation outside in the hall. One of the warriors said, "Leave them be. They'll be dealt with when day comes."

All the Shinmushee left after that. When they were gone Ree questioned, "I wonder what made them leave?"

Ram didn't answer. He wasn't going to put up with Ree questioning him. He got back in the bed and looked her directly in her eyes. Ram said, "Quiet, I need sleep." then he turned on his back, facing the ceiling and closed his eyes.

A jolt of fear went through Ree's entire body when Ram looked directly at her and the bass in his voice vibrated in her ears. She decided to do what she was told. She moved close to Ram and went to sleep. When Ram woke up, Ree was still sleep. So much for her leaving before day came. Ram got up and started his daily training. A few minutes later, Ree woke up and started watching.

Shinmushee warriors showed up as usual. The warriors escorted them to that same clearing. This time Grandpa was there, along with Claw and Hearts. Once Ree saw him, she went down on her knees and pleaded, "Grandpa!"

Ram just went down on one knew and stood back up. He too said, "Grandpa."

The old man barely looked at them.

A warrior walked up with several other Warriors and said, "Do you claim this woman?"

"No." Ram replied.

Ree quickly turned and looked at Ram, angry and confused. One of the warriors pulled out his whip. Another grabbed Ree roughly by her arm. No sooner than he grabbed Ree's arm, Ram plowed his fist into that warriors jaw. Ram followed that up with two super-fast and powerful kicks. The first was to face. That kick snapped the warrior's head backwards. Before his head moved forward Ram's second kick plowed into his throat. That warrior fell to the ground. He grabbed his throat and died seconds after that. The other three warriors quickly turned on guard against Ram. Ram wasn't one to wait around. He destroyed those three warriors before they had a chance to react, without killing them.

After seeing that, Claw moved aggressively towards Ram. The old man said, "Hold it!"

Claw stopped in his tracks. Still, he stared at Ram, letting Ram know that the old man wouldn't always be around to hold him back. Ram didn't care about looks, he loved killing. If this guy wanted some, Ram would oblige him, anytime.

The old man waited a few second to see if anyone would disobey his order. Once he'd seen that not even Ram moved, he turned towards Ram and Ree. The old man said, "Ree, move your things into the dwelling where Ram stays. It seems no one, accept Ram, will defend you. Because he has chosen you, your actions will not be punished."

The old man looked back towards the Warriors and said, "Take Ram to his task. Ree, you go to yours."

Ram lowered his head to the old man and said, "Grandpa, teach me fighting techniques."

"What do you think just happened here? You fought those men without using weapons. I was the one who told you if you used weapons you were no longer welcome here. You, at least, learned that much!" said the old man, as he looked at the one warrior that was killed.

"You killed, not for pleasure, but to protect that girl." the old man said as he paused to let that sink in. He then said, "See, you're learning and you don't even know it. If I weren't here to tell you that, you'd probably be ready to leave. If you leave, you won't get what you came here for!"

Ram was irritated and angry as he stared at the old man. Why couldn't this fat old fart just teach him fighting techniques? Ram was sure he wouldn't need this other stuff the old man was trying to teach him. Yes, he might have saved that girl. But he only did it because she fed him when he knew they wouldn't! Besides that, Ram had no use for this girl. She was a Shinmushee and Ram was taught to hate them.

The only thing Ram could think of was to be straight forward about what he wanted. Ram said, "Teach me fighting."

The old man looked annoyed when he exclaimed, "I already am! You can't even tell when you're learning! You might as well leave! You're hopeless!"

While staring at the old man a strong withdrawal hit Ram. Ram's reaction was visible to everyone. The old man knew the Ra were blood drinkers. He said, "Look at you Blood Drinker! I'm showing you things you never knew about yourself. You're weakened from not drinking blood. Not drinking blood can make you just as strong as drinking it. I thought you were strong enough to take this training! Yet, here you are sulking like a baby! You're useless! This is nothing! Once you become self-aware, that's when you'll absorb greater fighting techniques!"

Ram felt insulted. He wasn't a quitter like this old man was making him out to be. Ram decided to stick with this a little longer. He would show the old man that he was tougher than he gave Ram credit for.

Ram looked at Hearts and Claw, just before warriors took him to his daily task. He didn't like them. They were always staring at him. First chance he got, Ram decided he was going to kill them. He didn't have a good reason. He was going to kill them, because he was pissed at how the old man was treating him!

Claw and Hearts didn't like Ram, just the same. They didn't understand why their grandpa allowed Ram to stay, even if he was treating him like a slave. Ram was a Ra. Why not just kill him? Ram had defiled one of their Shinmushee sisters. Even though Shinmushee warriors had treated Ree far worse than Ram had, that was Claw, Hearts, Sunshine's and every Shinmushee's interpretation of what happened. They didn't care about Ree's treatment by her own Shinmushee family.

They decided they couldn't let Ram leave with any training he might get here. One way, or another, Ram had to be killed. Since, their Grandpa strictly forbid Claw and Hearts to have any contact with Ram, without him present, they were going to have to do it without Grandpa's knowledge.

Ram's work load doubled. He not only did his tasks, he had to do the tasks of the man he killed. The others that Ram wounded, he also had to help. Ram didn't like it, but it was the way of the Shinmushee.

Ram chopped wood and carried it high up the trees to the platforms. After getting the wood on the platforms, Ram had to carry it to where it was needed. That wood was used for building and repairing the walkways up in the trees that ran throughout the jungle. Ram would then return and get more wood. On his many trips, Ram wondered when the construction would be finished.

Carrying the wood up the side of trees was the hardest balancing act Ram had ever done. All the bundles of wood were over one hundred pounds. Many were over two hundred pounds. Ram's legs were shaky every evening after climbing up and down those trees with all that weight strapped to his back.

Ram wasn't alone. He would also see Claw, Hearts and some of the other warriors carrying wood up into the trees. They seemed to hate it as much as Ram did. He watched as they struggled trying not to fall to the ground. That made Ram smile from time to time, knowing someone besides himself was being tortured.

Ram was glad Ree was around to bring him extra food. No one

bothered Ree because she was protected by Ram. They also didn't stop her from bringing Ram extra food. She was allowed to bring Ram extra food at lunch and later in the evening. No matter the work load, Ram would get up early and train himself, before his daily grind. After getting use to his slave routine, he started training at night, also.

As time went on Ram would see the old man watching him, Claw and the others as they performed the grueling tasks that they were given. Later, in the early evening, the old man would talk to Ram, Claw and the others.

Claw, Hearts and Sunshine would sometimes ask the old man questions. The old man would answer their question, although they didn't always like his answers. Ram didn't ask questions, at first. However, after still not being taught fighting techniques, one evening, Ram shocked everyone by asking, "When do I learn fighting techniques?"

Grandpa looked annoyed as he stared at Ram for a moment. After that, grandpa said, "Any idiot can learn fighting techniques! You've already proven that!"

Claw, Hearts, Sunshine and a few others laughed, until Grandpa cut his eyes towards them. Ram's eyes slowly moved and looked at Claw and the others, before slowly moving back to the old man. The laughter offended Ram, but not as much as the old man's words had. Now, Ram had enough anger to throw caution to the wind and kill everyone here. Ram started formulating a plan of attack.

The old man could see that Ram was beyond his ability to control himself. While looking indirectly at Ram, in a slightly calmer voice, the old man said, "I'll tell you a secret that all the greatest fighters have in common."

Finally! This was what Ram was waiting on. The old man instantly had Ram's full attention. The old man continued, saying, "They don't fight unless they have to. They rarely let anger determine when they fight and they never kill, unless absolutely necessary. It's easier to find a reason to kill, although that reasoning may be flawed.

It's tougher to think of a reason not to kill in a situation that others would. Once you kill someone, you can never reverse that."

What grandpa said completely baffled the natural born killer, Ram. However, Ram did think about what grandpa said, even though it sounded crazy to him.

Ram only wanted to learn more fighting techniques so he could be more efficient at killing as many people as possible, whenever he wanted to. Ram didn't want to have to think about why he killed, every time he killed. That might lead to less killing. Ram wasn't looking for that!

Grandpa could see that even though Ram looked confused, he listened intently. That made grandpa talk and instruct Ram even more with words, over time. Ram listened to everything the old man said. It sounded like the old man might be teaching him not to fight so that Claw and the other Shinmushee could kill him. Ram continued to train himself, just in case that was true. The crazy thing was that the more Ram listened to grandpa, the more Ram found that information to be sound. That confused Ram even more!

——— CHAPTER 21 ———

It was four weeks after Ram's visit. Young Dan was slowly coming out of sleep. He was alone, with only his Hammer-Axes and other weapons for company. Dan wiped his eyes and then he heard something. He rolled on his side and listened.

Someone was definitely inside this dwelling. Dan put on his pants and picked up his Hammer-Axes. He walked down the hall and into the main room. That's when he saw Trina cleaning. She had cleaned up most of the mess that had accumulated over time.

"I was going to clean that up, sometime, this day." Dan said.

Trina stopped what she was doing, smiled at Dan and then continued cleaning. Dan watched Trina for a moment. He was happy to see her. Dan slowly started helping.

"When did you get here?" asked Dan.

"I got here late last evening." Trina replied.

Dan stopped and looked at Trina, wondering why Trina didn't come to him, then. Trina, while watching Dan, said, "I stayed with my uncle's family. Because it was so late, I didn't want to disturb you. I asked my uncle and he said we could have a meal with his family, if you like."

Dan walked over to Trina and put his arms around her. They looked into each other's eyes.

"I missed you." Dan said.

"I missed you, as well."

"Let's have a pre-meal work-out."

Dan pulled Trina towards the hall leading to his room. Trina pulled away, saying, "That's not what I'm here for."

"What are you here for?" Dan questioned, with disappointment in his voice.

Trina slowly backed away from Dan. She said, "I thought I might be able to help out. If I was wrong, let me know. I'll leave when next day comes."

"I never said I wanted you to leave." Dan quickly replied.

"Then you will have a meal with me and my family?" questioned Trina.

Dan looked at Trina for a second and then nodded in agreement. They went back to cleaning. After a few seconds, Trina turned to Dan and said, "You will have to go through the mating process with my family, if you want me as your mate. I will not have sex with you, until then."

"You would mate with me, even though I lost all of my titles?" questioned Dan.

"I want you, not titles." Trina said, as a matter of fact.

Afterwards, Trina smiled and Dan saw her emerald green eyes light up with a fire that made him want to take her here and now. While contemplating that, Dan decided he would do this Trina's way. Trina stuck to her word and didn't have sex with Dan for four nights. During that time young Dan courted Trina and her family. After that, they officially became mates.

Trina also made deals with the families of the guards who would come and, as Trina put it, get free training from Dan. That deal made Dan a training instructor for this Lower house. In return, Trina bargained for maids, servants, food and clothing. Young Dan realized Trina was a great negotiator.

Early one day, while they were resting, Dan and Trina heard someone moving around down the hall. They looked at each other acknowledging that.

Moments later, all of Dan's siblings, except for Ram, walked into his sleeping room. Danaaa and Shaya ran over and jumped on

Dan. Trina moved back, giving them enough room. La, Yin and Don stopped and looked around. They analyzed the room and then Dan. Yin and Don walked over to Dan, while La stood with her arms folded at her chest staring at Dan.

"Still living like a peasant, I see!" La said.

Dan turned and looked at La after she said that. He calmly said, "I didn't ask you to come."

La unfolded her arm and then started pacing back and forth, as she said, "No, you didn't. However, that's not the point. We have secured our territory. Now we are going to secure these Lower Houses. It would be nice to have your help. Could you possibly break away from your new lifestyle and help us?"

Dan didn't answer. Don turned to Dan and said "Ram is missing. He was last seen when he visited you. Do you have any idea where he might be?"

Dan was shocked by that news. He assumed Ram had returned to the main city, after his visit. Dan looked around at everyone there and then shook his head no.

Shaya looked at Dan with concern in her eyes as she said "We think he may have gone into the Southern Jungle. Help us secure the Lower Houses so that we can go into the Southern Jungle and find our brother. We don't know what's happened to him. Help us find Ram!"

Dan could see the fear and concern in Shaya's eyes. Even though La had on her poker face, Dan could see she was worried about Ram, also. Dan wondered if he had paid more attention, when Ram was here, would he have been able to pick up on something.

Dan didn't mind living as a no title Hammer-Axe champion. There was no pressure on him. However, Dan knew he couldn't live with himself if he didn't help find his youngest brother. Dan stood up and said, "I'll help find Ram. However, I don't want any titles. After we find him, I'm returning here."

"Whatever, you say, dear brother." La said, sarcastically.

"Alright, let's make a plan!" said Dan.

Shaya sent a request to her aunt Wana for Bo's help. Because La and Shaya had impressed Wana securing their territories, Wana gave them permission to secure the Lower Houses of Ra. If Shaya needed Bo to do that, Wana was willing to send him.

Once Bo arrived, Shaya told him he would be working for Dan. Shaya told Bo not to refer to Dan as his king. Besides that, Bo was told his duties would be much the same as before. Bo was proud to have his previous position. He vowed to do better than, before. Shaya was confident Bo would.

After getting all of her Elite guards in place, La declared herself supreme Warlord over the Lower Houses of Ra. Once La established that with warlords of each of the Lower Houses, La offered the title of warlord over the Lower Houses of Ra to Dan. Young Dan turned down that title. Instead, he told La and Shaya he should be referred to as the Hammer-Axe Champion, Chopper Ra.

Young Dan and La came up with an excellent security plan. The Hammer-Axe Six would split up into groups and rotate, on security rounds for one night.

This was the longest time Ram had ever stayed away from his siblings. Dan, Don and Yin were concerned, but thought Ram could make it out of any situation. La and Shaya were worried about Ram, even though Danaaa told them Ram was unharmed. Danaaa didn't know how she knew that. She just knew it!

That wasn't enough for Shaya. She wanted to search the Jungle for Ram. La talked Shaya down, saying if Ram was in the Southern Jungle, he could be anywhere. La convinced Shaya that once they established security protocols, they could confidently search the entire Southern Jungle. Shaya reluctantly agreed.

Dan also said that Ram would show up any day. After two cycles of the moon, Dan stopped saying that. Scouts searched for Ram, while the Hammer-Axe Six carried out their security plans. If someone harmed Ram the Hammer-Axe Six were going to deal with them in the harshest way, possible.

Everything was going as planned. This day Hammer-Axe

Six were starting security details. Dan said they wouldn't do any strenuous training, on their patrol day. They would warm up when first day came, is all. The rest of their energy would be reserved for patrols and possible attacks.

On Dan's first day of patrolling he had twenty bodyguards, twenty Elite guards, along with Bo and his guards. There were already a multitude of guards at each of the outposts Dan visited. Dan stopped at each of the outpost and had short meals. He rested and then was on to the next on. He stayed overnight at the outpost closest to the Southern Jungle. When first day came, Dan headed back to his compound. He slept half the day, after being up on patrol all night.

Dan realized whoever stayed up all night on patrol would need half of the next day to recover. After that, they could resume their training schedule. That was the first change Dan made to the daily patrols.

Don went on patrol the next day after Dan. He went through the same rituals as Dan. The only difference was that Don decided to get some sleep. He had enough bodyguards and Elite Guards to wake him if trouble came. Don, like all of the Hammer-Axe Six slept with their weapons at arm's length. He knew he would be well rested and ready for any challenge.

Next it was Yin's turn. Yin had been in a foul mood, lately, because he missed his cousin Ram. Yin was angry because Ram hadn't taken him along. Yin was angry at the scouts and guards because they couldn't find Ram. Lastly, Yin was angry at Dan. He knew if Dan ordered it, they all would be combing the Southern Jungle, until they found Ram. He couldn't understand why Dan hadn't.

That night, Yin was at one of the outpost facing the Southern Jungle. He was restless and decided to go for a walk. His bodyguards and Elite Guards followed. Yin turned and looked at them. He picked three bodyguards and three Elite Guards to walk with him. He told the others to stay on alert and watch for anything that looked suspicious.

After that, Yin walked until he reached the edge of the Southern Jungle. He looked off into the darkness of it. He knew his cousin was somewhere in there. Yin knew Ram prowled at night. There might be a possibility of running into him. Yin started walking into the jungle. The bodyguards and Elite guards cautiously followed.

It was pitch black dark in the jungle. That made it very slow going. All of them had to keep a hand on each other, just so no one got separated. Yin didn't go too far. He just needed to know he was doing something to find his cousin. When next day came, Yin didn't tell the others that he ventured off into the Southern Jungle. Each time Yin went out on patrol, he took the same six men. And each time Yin took them a little further into the jungle.

Next was La's turn. La went with her bodyguards, Elite Guards, her Executioner Hoban, her Warlord Ali and their guards. It was a small army. La also had four personal assistants. They were the four girls that rescued her when she was injured, fighting Claw and the Shinmushee.

One was Sheena the liar. La liked that this girl could think fast on her feet and come up with lies that you might not believe, but were enough to stall you. La was also impressed with Sheena's fighting skills, which were much better than her lying skills.

The second one was Shara, the nervous farter. La didn't like that fact that Shara couldn't stop herself from farting when she was nervous. After seeing Shara fight off the Shinmushee, Shara's fighting skills couldn't be denied. La wanted Shara fighting like that for her.

The other two girls were Hesta and Lana, her childhood friends. Both were high caliber killers. La promoted all four girls to be her personal assistants soon after her rescue. They'd been with her since then. It surprised Shaya and Dan that La's new assistants were with La more than La's Executioner, Hoban. Also, when La needed a break from her sisters, her four girls were there.

That annoyed Shaya, at first. Shaya didn't mind if La needed time alone. Shaya just didn't understand why La's four assistants could be present, when she and Danaaa couldn't. Shaya let it go, because after being away from her sisters for a night, La was extra nice to them the next day. It was like that after La went out on security patrols without her sisters, too. Shaya equated that to La missing her and Danaaa. If it took that to make La nicer, Shaya would put up with it.

Tania, La's female Warlord, was on high alert, but didn't go with La on patrol. Instead, she was ready with the forces under her command, just in case La ran into any trouble. La had maximum protection as she walked on patrol. She ate well and rested at the checkpoints.

La decided she didn't want to stay at any of the checkpoints closest to the Southern Jungle. She stayed at another checkpoint closer to the Lower House. Scouts and guards surrounded her position all the way to the checkpoint closest to the Jungle. It was almost like she was there. If anything happened La would know, immediately. La got a good night's rest and returned when first day came. She even went to first day training session with her sisters.

La liked doing security patrols. That's because, besides studying all the processes, she really didn't have anything else to do. It was like a mini vacation from her brothers and sisters.

Last in the patrol rotation was Shaya and Danaaa. They had almost as much security as La. Shaya took the patrols very seriously. She watched and studied everything having to do with security. On the other hand, Danaaa excitedly played around and pestered Shaya. Danaaa knew she would see, or smell any trouble coming. She was bored is why she amused herself playing with Shaya.

Danaaa had to worry about pushing Shaya too far and bringing out Angry-Ax, Shaya's alter ego. No one wanted to deal With Angry-Ax, not even Danaaa! So, Danaaa pestered, but watched Shaya closely to make sure she didn't push her too far.

Besides Danaaa's antics, their patrol was uneventful. They stayed at an outpost closest to the jungle that night. It didn't bother them one bit. They slept like babies huddled close to each other.

When next day came, they went back and had first day training with La.

The security patrol rotations were going well. La and Dan assured everyone that all of the Lower Houses were free from the threat of Shinmushee. They backed up their words with the heavy presence of their military. Everyone, including all of the most important people felt completely safe. Any Hayee, or Ra could travel through out the Six Lower Houses, safely, seeing nothing but the Ra military at every turn.

The training for moving into the Southern Jungle was also going well. The Hammer-Axe Six all felt they had improved their skills to a higher level. They decided they would start their assault when the next full moon came. That gave them twenty-eight days to tighten up their plans. None of their plans included Ram.

Ram had been gone for over four moon cycles. By the time the Hammer-Axe Six planned on moving into the Southern Jungle it would be over five. One day, while digesting first day's meal, Danaaa told Dan and La that sometimes she would have crazy dreams about Ram doing slave tasks. No one believed that!

Ram's siblings knew he would die in battle, before becoming a slave. Dan, La and Don joked and chuckled about how absurd it sounded, dismissing Danaaa's dreams.

During a round of laughter from Dan, La and Don Yin quickly stood up, lifting the table and flipping it over. Even though Dan, La, Don and Shaya were quick enough to jump up and not get hit by the table, blood from the cups and food from the table splashed all over them. Danaaa did a quick tuck and roll to her left and was missed by all the flying debris.

Before anyone could react, Yin, with his eyes blazing and an angry evil grin on his face, yelled, "Ram is missing and you sit here making jokes! Make another joke and I beat the hell out of all of you!"

Danaaa stared at Yin. Everyone else wiped debris from their bodies and faces. Afterwards, they stared at Yin. There was a brief moment of silence and disbelief, while they all got over the shock of what Yin did and said.

All the Hammer-Axe Six were hit hard by Ram's disappearance. None more than Yin. At first, Yin was angry at Ram for not taking him along. As the days went by Yin's anger was joined by worry as he became concerned for Ram's safety. More time passed and all Yin heard was excuses why they weren't out searching for Ram.

Ram's disappearance somehow triggered thoughts about Yin's father in his mind. One day Yin's father left and after time away, he was dead. Yin didn't think they were doing enough to find Ram and it had him on the edge of his limits to control his anger. The last straw was when they joked about Ram, not knowing whether Ram was dead, or alive.

Shaya knew she had to react, or Yin could end up dead. Shaya quickly grabbed La's ponytail and pulled on it. La quickly turned her back to Yin and folded her arms at her chest. That let Shaya know La would allow her address Yin. Shaya knew whatever she said would have to be good.

Maids quickly ran over to La and started wiping the food from her face and clothes. With La's ponytail in her hand, Shaya had a concerned but stern look on her face when she said, "Listen Yin and listen well! Your actions here are unacceptable! Raging out of control will serve no purpose and could possibly lead to your death!"

That surprised and everyone, except for La. Now that Shaya had shocked Yin like Yin shocked everyone else, Shaya said, "None of us want that! However, you made one undeniable point. Ram is still missing. There will be a renewed urgency in finding him. Make no mistake about that!"

Shaya paused and then said, "Yin, you know we love you. That's why you're forgiven, just this once. With that being said, never rage against, or threaten us, again. That won't be forgiven. Now then, my sisters and I are going to get cleaned up. When next we see you I expect your attitude will be acceptable. If not, you don't want to know what happens then!"

Shaya turned her back to Yin, same as La and put her head on La's shoulder. La turned her head to the side and looked in Danaaa's direction. The second she did Danaaa ran over to La's other side. Once there, Danaaa turned her head, peeked at Yin and then quickly turned her head back towards La. That sent the end of Danaaa's ponytail flying up in the air towards La. La caught it and all three Ra girls walked out of the room.

Dan and Don watched as their sisters left the room. Once they were gone Dan and Don turned back towards Yin. They both looked at Yin for a moment. They could see he was still angry and on guard. Dan smiled at Yin and said, "Calm down. You got away with that one."

"Yeah! Never do that, again!" Don said as he smiled at Yin.

Dan grabbed a chair, looked at Yin and said, "Need a moment?"

Yin didn't say anything, at first. He just looked at Dan and Don. Don grabbed a chair and said, "We can sit for a while if you need to."

Yin looked at Don and said, "Not really."

"Good! Let's get out of here so they can clean up this mess." said Dan.

Dan and Don stood up once Yin walked over to them. Dan slapped Yin on the back and then they walked out of the eating hall. Servants and maids rushed in to clean up the mess Yin made.

Because Yin had a better attitude the next time La saw him, she never mentioned the table incident. La was caught off guard and embarrassed for her part in joking about Ram. That allowed La to let Shaya handle a situation she, herself, didn't want to. Besides, Shaya said everything that La didn't say. If Yin didn't get the point from Shaya's words, the next time Yin did something like that, La decided it would be his last.

Now, the Hammer-Axe Six were more motivated, than ever. They planned on finding Ram, or at worse, finding out what happened to him. Dan tried to keep the others optimistic about Ram. Some days that was tough for Dan, because not only did Dan have to convince the others Ram was alright, he also had to convince himself.

It was about two weeks before the Hammer-Axe Six planned on heading into the Southern Jungle. It was La's turn for security patrol. This night, La's group was a good distance from the First lower House. And just like every other night La spent out on patrol, this night was uneventful.

Early, when next day came, La was getting ready to meet her sisters. Before they left the checkpoint a large group of Ra guards came up and surrounded La's guards. The captain of those guards came up and begged to speak to La. La quickly motioned for him to talk. The captain said, "I am here to escort you to King Dan. Something happened last night. I need to get you to safety, right away!"

La, with concern in her voice asked, "What about my brothers and sisters?"

"They are waiting on you at the main meeting hall." the captain said as he lowered his head.

La could see the urgency in his demeanor. She quickly said, "Alright, let's go!"

La's spies told her what they knew. La's face looked very nervous as she got closer to the meeting hall. She heard loud cries of sorrow. Groups of Hayee and Ra joined La's group as they headed towards the meeting hall. As soon as La walked into the hall the crowd parted. La's guards made a path and La marched up to the throne area under the watchful eyes of everyone there. Once La got to the throne area, Shaya and Dan told La what happened. As La was being told, everyone watching could see La's face slowly contorting in anger. They saw a crooked scowl come on La's face as her eyes scanned the crowd. La's eyes indicted everyone she saw.

Dan and Shaya told La that some Hayee Elders and Warlords were beheaded, overnight, while they slept. Several of their bodyguards were found dead, although, no battles had occurred. The dead totaled forty. Somehow all of them were stealthily killed in the night. Their bodies were only discovered when day came.

La looked Dan in his eyes. They both knew of only one person who could have pulled off something like that. In a low voice that only La and his sibling could hear, Dan said, "We don't know for sure it was Ram!"

While staring at Hoban and motioning with her hands, La angrily ordered, "Investigate this, thoroughly! Have all the facts gathered and witnesses interrogated! We have many here that want answers, including me! For now, get these people out of here!"

Hoban and his guards cleared the meeting hall, as well as the roads around it. The Hammer-Axe Six had a private meeting with their top Warlords. If they didn't get a quick resolution to this matter, it could push back their efforts to move into the Southern Jungle. No one wanted that. While Ali, Bo and Tania investigated, the Hammer-Axe Six went to meet all of the families who had members murdered.

It was a very long day. Things got worse when a report came from a checkpoint near the Southern Jungle that three young girls were missing from Hayee families that lived near there. Two girls were five and the third was six. They were out playing when it was noticed that they weren't around. A search followed. After getting word of the killings earlier in this day, they decided to get word to the Hammer-Axe Six. They didn't know if this was somehow connected.

Dan and La decided that since Shaya and Danaaa had security patrols this day, they should investigate the missing girls. Dan, La and the others would sift through the information on last night's killings and investigate, here.

Shaya said she wanted to have a private meeting with La and Danaaa. They went to their sleeping quarters. Shaya had all the maids, servants and guards leave the premises. She then had her bodyguards surround the dwelling for privacy.

Once that was done, Shaya looked directly at La and said, "There were those who opposed what we are doing here at the Lower Houses. They would have distracted us from moving into the Southern Jungle and finding Ram. They were a threat, so I eliminated them, quietly."

La stared at Shaya, shocked by this revelation. Even though Shaya said as much, La questioned, incredulously, "You had all those Elders kill? How did you do it?"

"It couldn't be avoided. How it was done is not important." Shaya calmly said.

"I could have helped! Why didn't you tell me?" asked La.

"I needed everyone to see genuine anger and concern coming from you. That turns suspicion away from us. You played your part perfectly!" Shaya said.

La didn't like that she had been played. That was her interpretation of what Shaya said. L stared at Shaya and said, "Be very careful that you don't do something that I don't approve of. Don't force me to do something that I might regret, later."

"La, I wouldn't want you to do anything you might regret, later. Both of us control large territories in the House of Ra. We both have warlords and guards very loyal to us. A fight between our forces would be pointless. I told you what I did because I want us to be united on controlling the House of Ra. I'm going to do whatever it takes to insure that you are going to be queen. Eventually, we have to convince Dan that he wants to be king of Ra, again. We already have Trina bringing him along, slowly, on that. Your idea to send Trina here was brilliant! For now, let's concentrate on taking the Southern Jungle. That would be the greatest prize you and Dan can give mother. She would surely make you queen after that, wouldn't she?"

La stared at Shaya. She knew Shaya was smart, but Shaya was far beyond anything La could have imagined. Fighting with Shaya was a battle La knew would take up valuable time. La was going to keep a closer eye on Shaya with her network of spies. She also was going to figure out more ways to use Shaya's secret assassins, whoever they were. A crooked smile came on La's face when she said, "You're right! How could she not? Also, work on a plan to help get Dan back to his old self. When you return, we'll talk more."

It was shortly after mid-day meal when Shaya, Danaaa and a host of guards headed towards the area where the missing girls lived.

When Danaaa and Shaya were together it was a show for their Bodyguards. Shaya talked endlessly to Danaaa, mostly about Chet. Danaaa was especially tired of hearing about Chet, one of Shaya's favorite subjects. Danaaa got fed up with Shaya's talking and playfully lashed Shaya with her ponytail. That would distract Shaya from talking for a moment. Danaaa would get out of control and push Shaya just short of anger. This time was no different.

Shaya was fed up with Danaaa by the time they reached the area where the two girls were missing. After a lash from Danaaa's ponytail that really hurt, Shaya pulled her axes in the blink of an eye. Before Danaaa knew what happened, Shaya's axes were pointed at her. Danaaa stared at Shaya, but didn't see Angry-Ax.

When Shaya was Angry-Ax is the only time she could give Danaaa a good fight. Danaaa watched Shaya because she didn't want to hurt Shaya, if she didn't have to. That's why Danaaa didn't move her hands to a quick draw position, next to her axes. If Shaya moved her axes against Danaaa, Danaaa knew she was fast enough to get her axes and block whatever was coming at Shaya. She just knew it!

After pointing her axes at Danaaa Shaya said, "Baby, I've had enough of you! We have serious business here! I'm not going to put up with anymore nonsense! Is that clear?"

Danaaa knew Shaya really couldn't stop her, but seeing that Shaya was close to the edge, Danaaa decided to cooperate. Danaaa sheepishly smiled at Shaya, while nodding that she did agree. Shaya only looked at Danaaa for a moment. She wondered if she should leave Danaaa at this checkpoint while checking on the girls.

Nevertheless, Danaaa went with Shaya and the guards to interview the parents of the girls and anyone else that might have helpful information. Afterwards, the Ra sisters had a meal. After the meal, they rested. Shaya thought about all the information gathered about the young girls.

However, Danaaa's playful annoying mood wouldn't let Shaya concentrate. She had to watch Danaaa, while trying to think about the situation at hand. It wasn't working. Danaaa was bored and asked Shaya to go for a walk with her. Shaya looked at Danaaa. This was a chance to get rid of Danaaa for a while. Shaya said, "You go without me. Don't go too far. I'll be here when you return. Then, we'll rest." Danaaa nodded in agreement and then left.

Danaaa walked out of the hut like building and looked around. Which way looked like the way for a good walk? Danaaa looked right and then she looked left. She turned to her left and started walking. From where Danaaa was she could see the tall trees outlining the jungle. Danaaa was a few miles from the jungle and walked parallel to it. As she was walking, she wondered what was in there. She knew there had to be many things in there, as large as that area was. At the least, she knew there were Shinmushee somewhere in there.

Danaaa looked at the sky. It was clear. After their run in with the so called Lightning Jinn, all of the Hammer-Axe Six kept a watchful eye on the sky for clouds. Danaaa was no exception. After checking the sky Danaaa turned towards the jungle. A couple of Ra guards spotted Danaaa. They walked close and one of them said, as if Danaaa didn't know, "That's the Southern Jungle. It's very dangerous. We don't go there."

Danaaa looked at the guard. He might be afraid of the jungle, but she wasn't. Danaaa rubbed her fingers on her ax handles and said, "I'm going to take a look around. If I find anything, I'll let you know."

Danaaa turned and left. After she was gone the guards went to alert Shaya that Danaaa was headed towards the jungle.

Danaaa didn't know why she was curious about the jungle. It just seemed like it might be interesting. She knew if she ran into some Shinmushee she could easily deal with them. Danaaa walked up to the tree line and then walked into the jungle.

While walking, Danaaa started thinking. It seemed, to Danaaa, although everyone knew the protocol they should be following they weren't. Danaaa couldn't understand that and it bothered her. She thought about what everyone close to her was doing.

First, was her mother who taught Danaaa every rule and protocol she knew. However, her mother did whatever she wanted, no matter the protocol she set forth. Then there was her father. In Danaaa's eyes, he always seemed to break protocol when it came to women. That Yaya and her father did what they did wasn't enough. Danaaa felt she was involved because Yaya asked her to keep that secret from her sisters. Something Danaaa would normally never do.

Her brother Dan was always starting fights with enemies and then letting them escape, afterwards. That was Danaaa's interpretation of that. Danaaa didn't know what that was all about.

Don and Shaya's activities certainly weren't according to protocol. And Danaaa didn't want to think about La. She really didn't understand what La was up to!

Danaaa knew protocols were helpful to herself and everyone else. If everyone adhered to the protocols life would be easier. However, for a second, Danaaa wondered how everyone would react if she forgot about protocol and did whatever she wanted. Danaaa knew that wouldn't be good for anyone.

—— CHAPTER 22 ——

The area of the jungle Danaaa was in was thick with under growth. Danaaa had to climb over, under and through thick foliage. The bright multi-colored leaves lit up the jungle. Danaaa saw rodents, snakes and other critters from time to time. As she got further into the jungle Danaaa wondered what she would see next.

It wasn't long before her keen sense of smell caught the scent of smoke. Someone had a fire going. Then her hearing caught the faint sound of voices.

Danaaa moved cautiously towards the scents and sounds she'd detected. She was going to sneak up on whoever it was and see what they were doing. Danaaa thought if she was really quiet, they would never know she was there. That tickled Danaaa. She thought it would be fun.

Danaaa got closer and could hear men talking. She heard at least ten, or more different voices. Her ears and nose were giving Danaaa information that she was using to map where each and every one of the men were. Finally, Danaaa reached a spot where she could see the camp in a clearing. As battle hardened as she was, what Danaaa saw shocked her.

Danaaa saw fifteen to twenty men sitting around a fire. Three of them were just finishing tying a young girl to a long pole. Her mouth was covered and she was naked. Danaaa looked at the fire and could see it had sturdy wooden handles, at both ends, to hold a pole for cooking meat. These were cannibals!

In an instant, Danaaa knew they were going to cook that girl. Danaaa was snapped out of her shock when two men lifted the pole and walked towards the fire. The other men cheered as they did so. That was enough for Danaaa.

Danaaa climbed over the fallen tree trunk she was hiding behind. She jumped off of it to the edge of the clearing. When she did all of the men turned and looked at her. They all lustfully looked at Danaaa like she was another delicious dish they could add to their feast.

Something caught Danaaa's attention from the corner of her eye. It was two more girls tied together, with their mouths covered. Danaaa looked at the girls. Their eyes weren't covered. Danaaa saw fear in their eyes through the tears that were pouring down their faces.

Moisture pooled in Danaaa's eyes. It wasn't enough to form a tear. Danaaa didn't shed tears. It was said she didn't know how. Her lip went crooked on one side and started shaking where it hung crooked. Danaaa wondered how these men could do such a thing. She thought she might never figure that out. Well alright, then! There was one thing Danaaa knew she could do. She could swing an ax, real fast!

One of the men saw the look on Danaaa's face and thought it was from extreme fear. He didn't want to scare her into running off, so he said, "Don't be afraid, little girl. We're just playing a game. Come and sit next to your friends and you can play, next."

That was one of the worse calming techniques ever used. A moment later, Danaaa watched as most of the men bolted for their axes. They quickly moved into position to cut off Danaaa's escape routes.

Another man said, "Don't run you're surrounded!"

Danaaa pulled her axes so fast it startled several of the men. When she pulled them, her left foot moved behind her. The ax in her right hand moved just under her eyes, with the blade pointed forward. The ax in her left hand moved straight down by the leg that was behind her, with the ax blade facing backwards. Danaaa looked at the men over her ax blade. Once she'd done that, the two men holding the pole the girl was tied to dropped it and quickly got their axes.

With the men staring at her, Danaaa said, "How dare you address me, when you don't deserve to live? Why you worthless lower than ant shit humans! When I'm done you will exist no more. Don't worry. It won't take long. I can swing an ax real fast! I Chop I!"

These men incredulously stared at Danaaa, not caring about what she said. They just wanted to get one of the girls cooked, before they got hungry. Four of them ferociously attacked Danaaa at the same time. Danaaa did several super-fast spinning moves and all four men fell to the ground, with mortal wounds to their necks and chest. Five more attacked right after that. Danaaa put them down as quickly as she did the ones, before. Several more attacked and were killed, instantly. Now there were only three left.

All three had their axes aimed at Danaaa, plotting their attack. Danaaa took a step towards them. That's when all three men took off running in the opposite direction. It shocked Danaaa how fast they were moving away from her into the thick jungle. Danaaa took a running start and launched herself in the air, towards a tree. When the foot of one of her legs landed on that tree, Danaaa launched herself to the closest tree ahead of her landing and jumping off of that tree to the next one in front of her.

Danaaa repeated that until she was just ahead of the man who was ahead of the others. Before he realized she was in the trees, Danaaa launched herself downward, spinning, taking his head and landing in front of his headless body. Danaaa sent a powerful kick to his chest, moving him out of her way.

The second man was just stopping his forward momentum, trying to change his direction away from Danaaa. Danaaa jumped at him and drove her axe through his heart. Her other axe came right after that and took his head clean off his body. After his body fell, Danaaa was facing the last cannibal. His eyes quickly darted from left to right, before focusing back on Danaaa. He didn't think he would survive running away. That didn't work the first time. He also didn't think he would survive fighting this girl. However, he had to try.

Danaaa didn't advance on the man. Instead she said, "You won't be eating anymore young girls!"

Danaaa charged the man. He brought his ax down to split her open. Danaaa avoided his ax and plowed her ax into his chest and through his lungs on his right side. Then she ducked under his arm, twirling behind him and shoved her ax blade through his spine. The man lost control of his motor functions and fell to the ground like a sack of potatoes.

Blood poured out of his chest and back as he coughed up blood trying to get air in his lungs. Danaaa marched in front of him and kneeled down. She grabbed a hand full of his hair and roughly yanked his head up high enough to where their eyes met. Danaaa yelled, "I told you it wouldn't take long! I can swing an ax real fast! I Chop I!"

After saying that, Danaaa slammed the man's face in the dirt. She stood up and walked away. To no one in particular, Danaaa growled and then screamed loudly, "I hate cannibals!!!" The last man choked, drowning on his own blood right after Danaaa screamed that.

Danaaa quickly made her way back to the clearing where the girls were. Danaaa, first, untied the girl from the pole. She then untied the other girls. The girls quickly put on their clothes. Danaaa, while watching the girls, said, "You're going to be asked about what you've seen and experienced. Remember this, if not for me, all three of you would have been cooked alive, dying a horrible death! That has not happened. Tell what you know of those cannibals, but speak not of what I did. That part, forget. That's how you keep your head around here! Understand!"

All three girls nervously and frantically shook their heads in agreement. A second later Danaaa's face became very pleasant. She said in a soft reassuring voice, "Let's get you girls to safety!"

These girls just wanted to get back to their parents. They wanted nothing else to do with the jungle, or the she devil that saved them!

Shaya had all the guards she could find come with her to where the scouts saw Danaaa go into the jungle. She quickly set up a command post there. It was close to dark, so the guards lit torches and set them up around the perimeter. Just as Shaya was about to lead her forces into the jungle, they saw Danaaa and the three girls coming from the bushes towards them. Shaya frantically called out to Danaaa. When Danaaa and the girls emerged from the jungle the guards let out a loud cheer. Probably, because they wouldn't have to go into the jungle.

Shaya grabbed, looked at and fussed over Danaaa. Shaya sternly asked, "What happened?"

Danaaa's eyebrows furrowed, as she looked to the side, checking her memory. Danaaa yelled, "Cannibals! Cannibals had these girls prisoner and were ready to cook them when I got there!"

Shaya lightly scolded Danaaa, exclaiming, "Cannibals! You should have told me what you were going to do! You know I would have come and helped!"

"I didn't even know myself, until I did it!" said Danaaa.

Shaya looked suspiciously at Danaaa. Was it Danaaa's Jinn that showed her where these girls were? If so, why did Danaaa's Jinn think these girls important enough to save them? Shaya didn't know and certainly wasn't going to question Danaaa about it. Shaya looked at the girls and ordered guards, saying, "Get these girls to their parents!"

Guards walked over to the girls. All three girls ran over to Danaaa and hugged her, clinging tightly to her. Danaaa was shocked by their level of affection. She said, "You're safe now! Go home and don't play near the jungle!"

They slowly let go of Danaaa and went with the guards. As they were leaving the girls kept turning and looking at Danaaa.

Once the girls were out of sight, Danaaa looked at Shaya, pointed towards the jungle and said, "There are more cannibals in there!"

"That's not our concern." said Shaya.

Danaaa folded her arms at her chest and said, as a matter of fact, "It's mine! I'm going to find them! When I do, I'm going to kill all of them!"

"Baby, you don't even know how many cannibals are in there!" Shaya reasoned.

Danaaa threw up both hands, palms facing Shaya and yelled, "Who cares about that?!! I'm not going in there to see how many there are! I'm going in there to kill them!"

Shaya was annoyed with Danaaa's attitude. She knew Danaaa's mind was already made up. La and Dan weren't here to stop Danaaa. Ram was already missing and no one knew what happened to him. Shaya didn't want Danaaa going into the jungle alone and disappearing, forever. Shaya knew she couldn't live with herself if that happened.

Shaya smiled at Danaaa and said, "Alright, I'll go with you."

Danaaa, in her soft voice, solemnly said, "You should stay here. It's going to be tough and very dangerous."

"I don't care! We're sisters! If you're going, I'm going!" Shaya blurted out.

Shaya paused for a second and then in a calmer voice said, "We'll eat and then get some rest. We'll go when first day comes. That way, we'll be ready for anything!" Danaaa nodded in agreement. She liked Shaya's plan.

The first chance Shaya got, she sent messengers to tell Dan and La what she and Danaaa were planning. She told them to tell Dan and La that it was Danaaa's idea and if she didn't go with Danaaa, Danaaa was going to go alone. Also, that it was imperative that they get here as soon as possible.

It was very late when the messenger arrived at Dan's sleeping quarters. Dan and his brothers listened to the message. Dan told the messenger not to disturb La. Dan said he would tell La, first thing, when day came. The messenger lowered his head and left.

Dan knew if he, or that messenger told La of what Danaaa and

Shaya were planning, La might make them travel this night to get there. Dan was tired. He didn't want that to happen. Dan knew it was important to stop his sisters from going into the jungle, but he decided he would take care of this when next day came.

La and her four bodyguards got up early when next day came. They were preparing to go to first days training when Tania was announced by La's servants. Tania came in and told La what happened the night before with Shaya and Danaaa.

While Tania was talking, La was examining Tania's body. Tania looked thicker and healthier than normal. Tania's stomach was poking out of her clothes. Because of the situation at hand, La wasn't going to question Tania about her obvious situation. When Tania was done speaking, La told her to take as many guards as needed and find her sisters. Also, that Tania should keep La informed, with messengers, of her progress. La said that she was going to get Dan and they would be there as quickly as possible. Tania asked, "Is there anything else?"

La looked over Tania's body once more. She then looked at her four bodyguards and then back at Tania. La said, "Whatever you can think of to help the situation. I expect whatever it is will also be reported back to me."

Tania said, "As you wish, my Queen." Tania left after that.

"My cape!" ordered La.

Shara grabbed La's cape and put it around her shoulders, tying the string in front. La ordered, "Attach my Ax Ball!"

Tagowa made La a metal ball with an ax blade that she could braid at the end of her hair, like her other metal balls. La had been training with it and knew how devastating it could be. She decided now was the time to use it.

Shara did as she was told. She then tucked La's braid under her cape. After Shara stepped back, La motioned for her girls to follow her.

As soon as La left her dwelling she saw her brothers and Yin. La still hadn't got use to not seeing Ram with them. She told herself that was a good thing, because it kept Ram on her mind. La walked up to Dan and could see he already knew. Dan didn't want to discuss when he found out, so he said, "Let's get a good meal, while supplies are packed. We'll leave right after that." La nodded in agreement.

It wasn't long after first day's meal that they were on their way. They traveled a short distance and were met by several guards racing towards them. Once the guards got to them, the guards went down on their knees. La impatiently said, "Speak!"

The guard quickly told La and Dan that Tania's forces were in a stiff battle against the Shinmushee near where Danaaa and Shaya went into the jungle.

La looked at Dan. That's when one of the forward guards pointed and yelled, "Shinmushee!"

Everyone turned to see Shinmushee warriors emerging from the edge of the jungle. They were a little more than a mile away. After seeing the Shinmushee La and Dan quickly looked at each other. They had to come up with a plan.

La said, "Dan you take Don and Yin! Break through and into the jungle! Find Baby and Shaya! I, Hoban, Ali and my girls will handle things here!"

Dan hesitated, with a look of concern on his face for La. He said, "We should stay together. That way we're stronger."

"I don't agree. Right now, Tania's forces are fighting at that checkpoint. We are here facing these Shitmushee. That means they're controlling where we fight. Let me and my people create a diversion, battling them here. You, Don, Yin and your forces fight your way into the jungle after they focus on us." La said.

Dan wasn't sure about that. He looked as the Shinmushee were getting closer. La also looked at the Shinmushee. She pulled her axes. La looked at Dan and said, "I can do this, Dan! Don't worry about me! I can't be dealt with! All you have to do is find Baby and Shaya! When I'm done here, I'll join you! Wait until I have their attention and then charge into the jungle!"

Dan looked at La without saying anything. He tried to come up with a better plan. Dan, grasping at anything he could, said, "What if you run into that Claw fellow? What then?" La didn't hesitate, but her lip was crooked on one side, when she said, "When I see Claw, rest assured, you won't see him, after that!"

La quickly moved close to Dan and kissed him on his cheek. She pulled back from Dan, looked him straight in his eyes and said, "Watch MesoCyclone in action!"

La turned and looked at her girls. They walked over to La. La, her girls, Hoban and Ali marched towards the Shinmushee, with their guards following.

Dan watched as La quickly turned away from him and headed towards the Shinmushee. Don and Yin looked at Dan. Dan said, "We'll let La have some fun before we join in and help her."

Don looked concerned. Dan looking at him said, "You don't think I'm going to let La get herself in trouble with this plan of her, do you? Once things get intense, she'll be happy we helped her." Don and Yin nodded in agreement.

They watched La giving instructions to her team as they moved forward. They couldn't tell what La was saying, but her hand motions made it look serious. Then, without warning, La took off towards the Shinmushee like a bolt of lightning.

Her four girls, took off, following a short distance behind La. All four girls left space between each other. Hoban, Ali and the Ra guards just marched forward towards the Shinmushee. Once La got within five yards of the Shinmushee warriors she started spinning extremely fast while still moving towards them. Her ponytail was in the air almost immediately, whirling like a helicopter blade. La was spinning so fast that Dan and the others couldn't figure out how she could see where she was going!

Several warriors measured when La would get close and aimed their axes at her. But the speed in which La was spinning was deceivingly fast. With her axes in hand and the ax ball on her ponytail all spinning at the same time, it gave the illusion that her ax blades were spinning slower than they really were.

That miscalculation by the warriors left a path of sliced open bodies as La got to the front line. La never stopped spinning and chopping as she carved a path into the Shinmushee. Her girls were right behind La, carving up anyone that thought they could move in behind La.

By that time, Hoban, Ali and the Ra guards were attacking the Shinmushee from the front. After a short while, Dan and the others saw La come out of the hordes of Shinmushee all the way on the other end. She was still spinning, moving in front of Hoban and the other Ra, while carving up the Shinmushee. La's girls were right behind her swinging their axes with devastating effects. Dan could see that La was carving circles through and around the Shinmushee warriors. La and her girls were like vortexes in a tornado, circling and destroying everyone within the circle. Dan was astounded by what he saw. La really was the MesoCyclone!

Dan snapped out of his astonishment. He could see Shinmushee from all directions moving in on La's group. Dan saw Hoban, Ali and their guards taking that heat off La so she could continue her path of destruction. The Shinmushee weren't paying Dan, Don and the others with Dan, any attention. Dan didn't want to leave La, but he knew he had to take advantage of what La was doing. Dan motioned to his team and they charged into the less protected part of the jungle.

Danaaa slept late when next day came. Although, Danaaa was still determined to hunt cannibals, she moved about, slowly. Shaya watched as Danaaa took her time at first day's meal. They ate earlier than normal, because Danaaa wanted to get an early start into the jungle.

After her meal, Danaaa seemed to perk up and have a sense of urgency. Shaya was sure with all of Danaaa's earlier slow poking around La and Dan would have arrived by now. Still, they hadn't. Shaya had to come up with a plan, before Danaaa made up one.

Shaya tried to get Danaaa to wait, until La and Dan arrived.

Danaaa told Shaya she was sure they wouldn't be for a while. Danaaa said Shaya should wait. Danaaa started towards the jungle. Shaya hesitated and then quickly caught up to Danaaa, moving to her side. When Danaaa saw Shaya moving next to her, Danaaa jerked her head back and forth, sending her ponytail slapping against Shaya's butt.

Shaya rubbed her butt where Danaaa's ponytail hit and yelled, "Baby, don't get started!"

Danaaa could hear anger in Shaya's voice. That meant Angry-Axe was close. Danaaa smiled at Shaya, playing nice. She would rather kill cannibals than get pummeled by the Angry-Axe, Shaya.

Moving through the jungle on the ground was quite an adventure. There was thick undergrowth intertwined with tree stumps and logs to climb over. There were also hills, steep valleys and rugged terrain. It was more like a hiking expedition, than a hunting one.

After a while Shaya grabbed Danaaa's arm and asked, "Are you sure this is the way?! How will La and Dan find us?"

None of the Ra girls liked being handled. Danaaa snatched her arm from Shaya and said, "How do I know? It's the only way I know! If you're scared, go back!"

"Who said I was scared?!!" yelled Shaya.

"Who knows? I didn't!"

Both girls stared at each other. They could see this argument was going nowhere, fast. Danaaa turned and led the way. Shaya and her bodyguards reluctantly followed.

The further they went into the jungle, the more guards Shaya left at certain points. Shaya wanted to make sure someone could tell La and Dan where they were. Because she left between fifteen and twenty guards at each place, now there were only eight body guards with Shaya and Danaaa.

They came upon a clearing that was underneath platforms that were high in the trees. They could hear activity, even though they saw no one. After listening for a moment, they moved on. They could see a large camp, on the ground, ahead. Everyone crouched down. Danaaa looked at Shaya and whispered, "Cannibals!"

Danaaa started to get up. Shaya grabbed her and sternly whispered, "Wait!" Danaaa quickly turned and looked at her arm that Shaya was holding. Shaya let go and smiled at Danaaa. She whispered, "Alright, now that we know where they are, let's go get La and Dan."

Danaaa slowly shook her head no. Shaya said that they should, at least send three guards back to give their location. Danaaa nodded in agreement. When Shaya turned to order the guards, Danaaa stood up. After ordering the guards, Shaya jumped up to join Danaaa with only five guards.

Shaya moved next to Danaaa and bumped her hard, saying in a stern whisper, "Wait for me!"

Danaaa in a calm, but concerned voice, whispered, "You should go back! Wait with the guards! I'll come back when I'm done! These guys are really tough!"

"I don't care! I'm going with you!" Shaya forcefully whispered.

"Alright, let's go!" replied Danaaa.

Danaaa, Shaya and their five bodyguards slowly and cautiously moved towards the camp. In an instant, Danaaa grabbed Shaya and pulled her closer. Danaaa yelled out, "Spears!"

The bodyguards pulled their axes and turned, going on guard, looking for threats. As they were turning they could see men swinging, on vines, towards them at a high rate of speed. They all had spears in their hands. They launched them when they were close, swinging past the seven on the ground.

From that close distance the spears seemed to be coming a hundred times faster than any of them had ever seem. One body guard was killed, instantly. Danaaa avoided and wildly swung Shaya out of the way of several spears. Then another bodyguard had a spear go through his right shoulder. Seconds later, two spears went through his chest.

After seeing the men on rope like vines, flying through the air with spears, Shaya yanked her arm away from Danaaa. She quickly grabbed and started throwing hammers. Shaya's eight hammers all hit their marks. Those Shinmushee warriors feel to the ground hard. Shaya and her bodyguards quickly finished them off, with their axes.

When Danaaa saw Shaya pull her first hammer, she knew she had to help stop the men on the vines. She ran to a tree and launched herself upwards into another tree. When her feet hit that tree she pushed off and sent herself flying towards one of the men on a vine.

The angle she had prevented him from throwing his spear at her. He tried to maneuver to a better position, but it was too late. Danaaa's ax sliced through his back and spine as they flew past each other. Danaaa launched herself off of several more trees and killed the other vine swingers that Shaya hadn't hit with her hammers.

Once they were done, Danaaa and Shaya looked around. They only had two guards left. Danaaa turned towards the camp. The battle just outside of their camp got the attention of this Cannibal tribe of Shinmushee.

The Cannibal tribe of Shinmushee was one of the oldest families of the Shinmushee clan. Long ago, just to survive, the Shinmushee turned to cannibalism. After making weapons, most Shinmushee stopped eating human flesh. This family of cannibals kept their tradition of eating human flesh, even though all other Shinmushee families stopped that practice, long ago.

Most Shinmushee distanced themselves from their Cannibal relatives. Most families have that person, or persons that no one wants to admit are family. The Cannibals were the part of the Shinmushee family that no one talked about. They were an embarrassment to the rest of the Shinmushee family.

The Cannibals moved together and formed a society, separate from the mainstream Shinmushee. They were allowed to stay in an area away from non-Cannibals, but still in the jungle. As long as they didn't eat Shinmushee, they were left alone.

Once Danaaa turned towards the Shinmushee camp, Shaya and the two bodyguards followed. When they got close they could see the Cannibals were armed and ready for battle. They looked like serious killers to Shaya, but something was different about them. Most serious killers have a certain look in their eyes. In the eyes of these killers Shaya also saw a lustful hunger. It was unsettling to her. She quickly regrouped. This was no time to let scary looks get to her!

The Cannibals sized up the four intruders as they came closer. The two women were healthy with a good amount of meat on their bones. They would cook up well. One of the girls was thick. That meant a tender and juicy meal. The other girl would be good enough, because most female flesh was a bit tastier than male flesh was. They stealthily moved around the four, without getting too close. They didn't want them to get away.

Shaya saw that they were being surrounded. She whispered to Danaaa, "Let's scream and get it over with. They're nothing, but worthless Cannibals!"

Even though the Ra drank blood, Blood Drinkers looked down on Cannibals as scum of the earth. Danaaa whispered back, "Yeah, they do look hungry. I'm going to feed them some ax blade! You can scream after that, if you want!"

Shaya was going to let Danaaa have her fun. But if things got close to getting out of hand, Shaya was going to scream.

One of the Cannibals got Shaya and Danaaa's attention when he said, "Look! A meal that we didn't have to hunt! Wouldn't it be great if all of our food just walked right up to us?"

Another Cannibal who looked meaner than the first said, "Don't talk! Just kill them so I can see what that one taste like!" as he pointed his ax at Danaaa.

While looking at that man, Shaya became very angry. How dare he talk about Baby, like that! Shaya quickly pulled her axes. She paused when she heard Danaaa speak.

Danaaa stared at all the men, before looking at the mean one, saying, "Cannibalism is dead and part of the past. That's what you'll be, because you won't last! I can swing an ax real fast! I Chop I!"

"A Chop A!" yelled Shaya in a very sensual voice, that wasn't meant it to be.

The mean looking Cannibal let out a slow sinister laugh. His face got serious after that and then he said, "Shut up, next meal! Fight while you can! I like it when my food struggles!"

Now, all the other Cannibals were in position. They attacked, immediately. Shaya was angrier than usual. She didn't know if it was that man talking, or just the fact that these were Cannibals. It didn't matter. As soon as the Cannibals moved towards Shaya and her sister, that's when Shaya's alter ego, Angry-Axe, attacked.

There were close to two hundred Cannibals in this camp. Danaaa and Shaya tore into those Cannibals, ferociously. The Ra bodyguards mostly got out of their way and fought clean up.

It only took Angry-Axe and I Chop I twenty minutes to kill all but four of the Cannibals. Three ran, earlier, while the others were fighting. The last one was the mean one who taunted the Ra girls. He fought hard against Danaaa. Danaaa managed to wound him when Angry-Axe, who'd just finished off her last Cannibals, attacked. Danaaa quickly plowed her blade into the chest of the mean Cannibal. Angry-Axe swung her ax to take his head from his body, but was blocked by Danaaa's other ax. After pulling her ax from his chest, the cannibal dropped to his knees.

Danaaa blocked several more powerful swings from Angry-Axe, meant to slice the Cannibal to shreds. The Cannibal saw Danaaa looking at him, while blocking every ax swing from the angry girl. He could hardly believe this girl's skill. The Cannibal finally fell over, while Danaaa was still blocking ax swings. Danaaa saw that and said, "But, I already told you! I can swing an ax real fast! I Chop I!"

The Cannibal mustered the last of his strength and said, "See… you…in….Hell!" "Trust me, you don't want that!" whispered Danaaa. She then slammed her ax through his neck, removing his head.

Danaaa blocked several more swings from Angry-Axe, before

she stood up, while blocking more ax swings. Danaaa then brought her ax to within an inch from Shaya's face. Shaya swung her ax to block, but Danaaa moved her ax out of the way and brought her other ax an inch from Shaya's face. Danaaa then stepped back and quickly said, "I can swing an ax real fast! You don't want me! You want Cannibals! I know where more are!"

Shaya realized she'd attacked Danaaa and calmed herself. She also realized that Baby had her axes in her face twice and there was nothing she could do about it. Shaya whispered, "I wasn't attacking you. Still, you're really fast with your axes!"

Danaaa peeked at Shaya's axes, before saying, "But, you already know that!" Shaya smiled at Danaaa and said, "Just lead the way!"

When Shaya and Danaaa moved into the jungle the guards at that checkpoint sent for more guards. When Dan, Don and Yin got there, guards had fortified positions going through the jungle leading to where Shaya and Danaaa had massacred the first group of Cannibals.

Dan realized that Shaya and Danaaa managed to gain a solid foothold into the Southern Jungle. Dan decided to take advantage of that. Dan sent for more Ra forces. He ordered Tania and Bo back to the First Lower House to set up a command post. Dan said he wanted all of the Lower Houses heavily guarded. Dan also ordered that a supply route should be set up going to their positions into the jungle and should be protected at all cost.

Bo protested, telling Dan that he should go into the jungle with him. That Tania was capable of running the command post. Dan disagreed, saying, "I've seen that when you two work together nothing gets by you. That's what I'm counting on. We'll handle the Shinmushee. You and Tania make sure they don't over run the Lower Houses and cut off our supplies and guards. That's more important to me."

Bo lowered his head to Dan. It seemed to Bo that although Dan liked to take unnecessary chances, his military tactics were sound. Bo walked off. As he did, he thought about what Dan said. It was true. Bo and Tania had always worked well together.

Bo and Tania left for the first Lower House. On the way they had a meeting. It was imperative that they keep the Shinmushee from advancing on the Lower Houses. They decided to send messengers to get Stacia and Jay to this Lower House for a meeting.

While that was happening they moved most of the attack elephants, under their charge, to the perimeters of the Six Lower Houses of Ra, facing the Southern Jungle. They fortified those attack elephants with guards and Elite Guards. Each of the Six Lower Houses of Ra were turned into military camps. Most of the civilians left for the main city of Ra. Besides the families that stayed, almost all of Shaya's and La's army was in those Lower Houses. They were cutting the possibility of the Shinmushee moving into Ra territory.

It only took two days for Stacia and Jay to arrive at the First Lower House. Stacia would have gotten there sooner, but wanted to make sure she found Jay before she did. As soon as they arrived, a meeting was set up.

Jay, Stacia and their guards walked into the military meeting. They saw Ra guards on the perimeter of all four walls. Bo and Tania were sitting at a large table in the center of the room. Jay and Stacia expected to see, at least, one of the Ra children, but they didn't.

Bo saw that and took control. He said, "Have a seat."

Once they'd done so, Tania ordered all the guards out of the room. The only ones left were Tania, Bo, Stacia and Jay.

Jay and Stacia lowered their heads to everyone and got the same respect in return. Once everyone was seated, Bo said, "Me and Tania have been put in charge of the Ra forces in the Six Lower Houses, on orders from your Ra Rulers. We are to keep a supply route going to the Ra forces that are already in the Southern Jungle. We also are responsible for turning back any counter-attacks by the Shinmushee."

Bo turned to the Warlords in charge of this area and said, "You two will maintain this area and give support as needed."

Bo then turned to Stacia and said, "Stacia, we need you to keep your area tight and free of Shinmushee. We need to know, right away, if they attack. Don't try to take them on with only your forces. Also, keep a strong messenger system to all Ra strongholds. We need to know the moment we are attacked."

Bo turned to Jay. He said, "I have been given orders that you and your warriors should be left to help where you see fit. Still, I need you to keep a close eye on the Lower houses, especially the First."

As Bo was addressing each of them, they nodded that they would comply. Tania looked around the table and then said, "I'm sure everyone here has heard about the massacre of the forty Hayee Elders, have you not?"

Everyone nodded that they had. Tania's face was serious, but concerned, when she said, "Assassins are at work here. We don't know who, or why it was done. All the Elders and warlords killed had high rank. That leads me to believe the killings might be politically motivated. Everyone should be careful. Stacia, just as a precaution, you should give uncle Benobu extra protection. Never leave him alone. If it is political, he might be a target. Jay, you should do the same with Uncle Ray and other Elders."

Stacia looked suspiciously at Tania. Jay was also uneasy, because his father and grandfather were Hayee Elders. Tania saw this and said, "I mention this so as to form a bond between us. I will give all of you here any information I think will help you and your families. This meeting is only for us. No one should know what we talk about. Not your families, or even the young Queen and her siblings. We're not plotting against them, but we are protecting each other. If any of you don't agree with me and think this treason, take my head and give it to my Queen."

Tania walked away from the table and started to get on her knees, but was stopped by Stacia saying, "Cousin, don't!"

Tania stopped and looked at Stacia. Stacia looked at the others at the table and said, "I agree with Tania. Sometimes we might have to protect our families from the immaturity of our young Rulers, as well as other threats. In those cases, I will do everything short of treason to help all of our family members, if you do the same for me. Is this agreeable?"

Everyone at the table looked at each other. Jay was the first to agree. Everyone else did so, after that.

Tania walked back to her seat, while Jay and Stacia stared in shock and disbelief at what they saw. Tania's stomach was poking through her clothes. It was obvious she was with child. When Tania saw everyone staring she smiled, looking at Bo, while lightly rubbing her stomach. The smile on Bo's face let everyone there know whose child it was.

Tania looked away from Bo and back at Stacia and Jay. She said, "La doesn't know, yet. I'd like to keep it that way, until I find the best way to tell her."

The looks of shock turned to looks of concern. Everyone knew that in La's mind Bo belonged to La. They wondered how La would react. They hoped for the best, but didn't think La would react favorably. Stacia, with concern inn her voice, said, "Take all the time you need in order to present this properly to La. We will not mention this, at all."

Tania smiled in appreciation of the consideration being shown her. She looked at everyone at the table and then said, "We all have an important part in insuring the young Rulers successfully complete their mission. I will accept nothing but your best! Now go, we all have work to do! This meeting is over!"

Everyone got up, hugged Tania and then left. They all knew they couldn't talk about what they'd seen of Tania being with child. They also knew how dangerous their pact was. If it was found out by anyone and was told, they all would be dead. It also could get most of their families killed, as well!

After everyone left Bo had food and drink brought to them. They spent a few hours going over every detail and making adjustments as needed, insuring their plans were sound. When they were done, both were proud of the results. Now, they would implement their plans.

Tania stood up and looked at Bo. Bo had been pacing the floor, while he and Tania where going over strategies. When Tania stood up, Bo walked over to her. Tania watched Bo as he moved close to her. Tania backed up a little, but Bo quickly put his arms around her waist and pulled her close to him. Tania struggled, a little, quickly looking around the room, even though they were the only ones there.

Bo sternly whispered, "Stop looking around as if we're doing something wrong. She's going to find out, eventually. You do know that, don't you?"

Tania stopped struggling and stared into Bo's eyes. She did know that. Tania didn't want to face that fact, if she didn't have to.

After a moment, Tania whispered, "I know, but.....!"

Bo tightened his embrace on Tania and said, "But nothing! Our families already know about us. It's time we tell the Royal Ra."

Tania pushed away, slightly, while staring into Bo's eyes. She said, "La's had a strong crush on you since she was a child. This is serious! I'm afraid of how she might react!"

Bo said, "I've already explained to La that I don't have those kinds of feelings for her. I made it very clear."

Tania stared at Bo. She wondered if whatever Bo said to La made any difference. Tania was sure it didn't. Still, Tania knew La would find out eventually. Tania didn't want to be around when La did.

Tania didn't know it but, Bo had already told Dan about his relationship with Tania. Dan suggested Bo hold off on telling La, until the time was right. Bo reluctantly agreed, although he knew that several guards and who knows how many others already knew about him and Tania. Bo and Tania had been close since they were young teenagers. Over time, their friendship blossomed into much more.

—— CHAPTER 23 ——

It was a hot and humid day in the jungle. The sun filtered down though the leaves. Areas where the sunlight managed to make it to the ground were much hotter. The early morning mist that cooled that air became a thick hot humid and uncomfortable soup filling the air. Even though everyone here was used to the humidity, it was uncomfortable.

Grandpa's students, including Ram, did the torturous chore of hauling wood. After that came the most the most torturous training from Grandpa to date. While being pushed to the limits of their abilities, all of the students silently cursed Grandpa for his cruel and unusual treatment of them. That was their interpretation of the situation, including Ram.

All of that happened before mid-day. As they slowly walked to mid-day's meal, no one said anything. They tried to conserve as much energy as possible, knowing the afternoon would be just as torturous, if not worse.

Because Grandpa ordered it and made them spend most of their day training together, Claw and the other students accepted Ram, even though they didn't trust, or like him. And although they didn't trust Ram, they saw the effects of Grandpa's training on Ram.

It was more than a week after the Ra invaded the Southern Jungle before word of the attack got to the village where the old Grandpa was training Ram and his prized students. Shinmushee warriors said that despite stiff resistance the Ra were slowly pushing further into the jungle.

The entire time the warrior was talking, Ram could see anger rising in Claw and the other students. Once the warrior was done talking Claw jumped out of his seat and said, "Grandpa, the Ra have gone too far! We'll leave at once! They'll pay dear....!"

Without looking at Claw, Grandpa harshly ordered, "Sit down!"

Claw protested, saying, "But....!"

Claw only got out one word, before Grandpa quickly turned and gave him an intense stare. The second that happened, Claw stopped talking and slowly sat down in his seat. He lowered his head out of respect. When Claw raised his head, he looked Grandpa in his eyes and respectfully said, "Grandpa, instruct us on the best course of action!"

Grandpa's stare was a little less harsh when he said, "The best course of action is to stay here and keep training. If they reach here, I'll instruct you further concerning them."

With a confused look on her face, before Hearts could stop herself, in almost a whisper, she said, "Stay here and do nothing?"

Grandpa was slightly agitated when he said, "I never said that! I said stay and keep training!"

Even though Grandpa corrected Hearts, in everyone's minds, they all heard, 'Stay here and do nothing!'

Grandpa's eyes went from Hearts to Claw's eyes, before moving to Ram's and then settling on no one in particular. None of that was missed by anyone here. For the rest of the day Ram stuck to his chores and training, while keeping a poker face that didn't show he was affected, one way or the other by the news of the Ra invasion. Still, all of the Shinmushee looked suspiciously at Ram. Ram could feel the stares, but didn't care. If they stated something, he would deal with it at that time.

Later, that evening, Grandpa had Ram walk with him. Grandpa talked with Ram well over two hours. They returned to the suspicious eyes of Grandpa's students. Ram saw them staring at him, even though he didn't look directly at them. Angry stares never bothered Ram. Ram could see that although they looked angry, none of them were motivated to action. That kept Ram from moving, aggressively.

Ram walked back to the small hut like home he and Ree shared. When he walked in Ree had a meal waiting on him. She looked at Ram and said, "I thought you'd be hungry. Looks like I was right."

Ram looked at Ree. He had always taken her for granted. Even when he was hungry and Ree brought him meals, knowing she would be beaten. Ram looked at her as one of his Shinmushee enemies. All Ram's life he had been taught to hate and kill the Shinmushee, whenever possible. Ram looked at living with Ree as a beneficial arrangement for both of them and nothing more. However, something that Ram couldn't explain changed in him and he said in his deep bellowing voice, "Thanks."

Ree stopped what she was doing and looked at Ram. Ram had never thanked her for anything she'd done for him, although she thought he appreciated what she did. Ree smiled at Ram and then quickly went back to what she was doing. She was just as surprised as Ram that he thanked her.

Late that night Ram stealthily got out of bed. He looked down at Ree and then looked over at his axes. While reaching for his axes Ram heard, "I thought you might be leaving soon."

Ram turned and saw Ree looking at him with concern on her face. Ram turned back towards his axes and picked them up. Ree got out of bed and walked over to Ram. She asked, "Will I see you, again?"

Ram looked at Ree and shrugged his shoulders. Ree jumped on Ram holding him tightly. Ram slowly put his arms around Ree. They held each other for a moment. Once they released each other, Ram saw a tear roll down Ree's face. She smiled at him and said, "See you, later."

"Thanks, again." Ram said.

He turned and walked out of the hut. Ree ran to the doorway

and watched, until Ram disappeared into the darkness behind the torch lights.

Dan and La's army pushed further into the Southern Jungle, day by day, with each and every bloody battle they fought. They had already been fighting here for a little over a month. In that time, all of the territory they took was completely rid of Shinmushee warriors and Butchers. The only Shinmushee that remained were women, children and old men. All of them were stripped of weapons and were under the penalty of death, if they were discovered with weapons.

Dan and La were proud of the progress they were making, even though it was slow. They reached the summit of a hill that allowed them to see that the Southern Jungle stretched for as far as they could see. It made them paused and stare, trying to take it all in. Everyone, except Yin wondered how long it would take to conquer all of that area. Yin wanted to search and kill every Shinmushee in that area, until he found his cousin Ram.

Although a little disheartened by how vast the area was, La didn't care if the Southern Jungle was twice the size of what they were seeing. She was determined not to leave, until she had total control of the Southern Jungle. La was unaware that the Southern Jungle was more than ten times the area they saw from this hill.

This day started out with everyone being on edge. Last evening La's spies finally got enough courage to tell her about Bo and Tania. La was tormented by the news. She had to be stopped from going to the first Lower House and addressing that issue, by Dan, Shaya and Danaaa. Dan instructed Shaya and Danaaa not to let La out of their sight. Her sisters tried to cheer her up, however Shaya realized time was probably the best cure.

After first day's meal everyone, including La, was focused on the strategy of this day's battle. Dan instructed the plans for today's attack, while La added comments where she thought necessary. The Hammer-Axe Six were met by their Warlords, Elite guards and advisers. On the way, they were updated on activities at the battle front.

When they arrived they could see skirmishes already taking place between both sides. The Hammer-Axe Six and their Warlords watched to see what areas needed help to push further into the jungle. They quickly identified one area. They sent Elite Guards there.

They soon realized Shinmushee Butchers were there backing a large number of warriors. If the Ra didn't move quickly to help, large numbers of Ra guards could be killed. Dan and La gave each other a stern look. That meant it was go time.

They looked at the rest of the Hammer-Axe Six as they always did before battle. Everyone looked ready. They all spread out walking towards the Shinmushee Butchers, with their Warlords and bodyguards flanking them.

Once the Shinmushee Butchers saw the Ra Warlords advancing they sent their warriors charging towards them. While looking straight ahead, Dan turned his head slightly towards La and said "Ready to take out some Shitmushee?"

"How ready I am, you don't even know!" La said, in a whisper.

Dan saw La's four female bodyguards directly behind her staring intently ahead. Dan took a few side steps away from his sister, so as to give her enough room to take out her frustrations on the Shinmushee, without accidentally removing his head.

After the initial push from the Shinmushee warriors, their Butchers moved forward to help. That's when Dan motioned for his Warlords to have their guards move aside. It was time for the big dogs to dance!

Dan, giving the Shinmushee an option, said "Put down your axes and then we can negotiate the terms of your surrender!"

Dan's words were met with a spear thrown directly at his heart. Of course, he blocked it with his ax. Although, Yin attacked as soon as that spear was thrown, that was enough for the rest of the Hammer-Axe Six to attack, seconds later.

The Hammer-Axe Six put in some ferocious work on those Shinmushee Butchers. They polished off close to twenty of them in a little over an hour. Normally, it wouldn't have taken that long, but it seemed the further the Ra got into the jungle, the tougher the battles with the Shinmushee Butchers got.

The Hammer-Axe Six killed those Butchers without the help of Danaaa. Danaaa followed, fighting clean-up or where ever she was needed. If she wasn't needed in the first battle of the day, she would fight the second battle, alone, giving her siblings a rest. Just like she would during their battles, they would give help when needed, which was rarely.

As in all of the battles before, when the last of the Shinmushee Butchers were killed the Shinmushee warriors retreated back into the thicker parts of the jungle. Dan called out, stopping Yin and La from pursuing the enemy further. Dan wanted to take a moment to regroup and formulate a plan, before charging into the thicker undergrowth of the jungle.

The Ra talked for a moment before seeing more Shinmushee approaching. It was a few seconds later that the Hammer-Axe Six recognized Claw, Deadly Hearts and Sunshine amongst twenty or so other Butcher looking fighters.

A crooked scowl instantly appeared on La's face, while Yin slowly nodded his head up and down with an evil grin on his face. Dan and Shaya watched Claw and the others, closely. Danaaa only looked for a moment. When Danaaa saw La and Shaya standing next to each other staring at the Shinmushee, she stealthily grabbed both of their ponytails and pulled hard on them. Both Shaya and La quickly turned to see Danaaa jumping back to a safe distance with a mischievous grin on her face. Both gave Danaaa a hard angry stare, before quickly turning back towards the Shinmushee.

La said in a stern voice, "Baby, don't start with your pestering! Can't you see we have serious business to attend to?"

Danaaa slowly walked up to La and stuck her tongue out at La. La didn't understand why Danaaa thought this was a good time to pester her. La sternly stared at Danaaa. Danaaa slowly retracted her tongue, turned and looked at the Shinmushee. La turned and stared at Claw.

When La and Claw's eyes met, Claw could see sadness in La's eyes. Claw taunted La by saying, "Don't look so sad. I know you missed me. Now that I'm here, you can rest easy knowing you'll die by my hands!"

La's bodyguards moved towards Claw, but were stopped by La saying, "Girls wait! I'll address this lower than ant Shitmushee, before I kill him!"

La paused for a second, before looking at Claw and saying, "Last time I let you escaped with your life, yet you confront me as if I'll let you live this time!"

Claw smiled at La and said, "You're delusional, if that's how you remember it!"

"You're Shitmushee! You act as if anything you say matters to me!" yelled La.

"Why are you still talking when we both already know what it is?" Claw calmly said.

La's smile was crooked when she said, "Well said, jungle trash!"

The smile left Claw's face. La could see she had finally insulted him enough to take her seriously. Now she was ready to cut Claw to pieces.

Suddenly, Claw and the other Shinmushee with him turned away from the Ra, pulling their weapons and going on guard. That's when the Hammer-Axe Six saw Ram walking towards them. Seeing Ram surrounded by Shinmushee, Shaya screamed, "Ram, look out!"

Ram heard Shaya's voice but was concentrating on Claw, Hearts and the other Shinmushee around him. Ram's hands were in a quick draw position next to his axes as he moved slowly through the Shinmushee, watching them closely.

All of the Ra watched and were baffled as to why the Shinmushee weren't attacking Ram and why Ram wasn't shredding their Shinmushee enemies with his axes. Ram was now in front of the

Shinmushee watching them while still slowly backing away from them. Hearts angrily stared at Ram and yelled, "That's right! Go over there where you belong!"

Ram looked at Hearts, Claw and the other Shinmushee, until he had backed to a reasonably safe distance from them. He then turned, facing his siblings. The Hammer-Axe Six all ran to Ram with the girls profusely hugging him, while Dan, Don and Yin stared at Ram with happy, but confused smiles on their faces. Still, Ram seemed different to them. Ram smiled while looking at his siblings. He hadn't realized how much he missed them, until now.

Danaaa sniffed and smelled Ram. Afterwards, Danaaa looked Ram in his eyes and said, "What's different about you, I can tell. You haven't had any blood in a while. I don't blame you. If I were in the jungle for as long as you were I wouldn't drink their blood, either!"

Danaaa took the blood pouch from her waist and extended it to Ram, saying, "Drink some, but not all of it! It's all I've got for now!"

Ram looked at the blood pouch and then looked back at Danaaa. He took a step back and looked at his brothers and sisters. They all stared at Ram, mystified as to why he wouldn't drink the blood.

Their thoughts were interrupted when Deadly-Hearts said, "What a happy reunion. Turn around and go home, before it quickly turns sad!"

Claw chuckled a bit. When he did La violently flung herself away from Ram, bumping and sending everyone close to her, stumbling a step backwards.

La stared at Claw with hatred in her eyes. She said, "Now that my brother is safely with us, I see no reason you should live any longer!"

"So far, all you've done is talk. Quite frankly, your voice is annoying! So, do us all a favor, just shut up and fight!" said Claw.

Claw managed to shut La up, because she realized he was right. Nothing more needed to be said. La and the Hammer-Axe Six all spread out, readying themselves for battle. Ram moved backwards facing his sibling. He said, "This is their home. Let's go back to ours."

The looks of happiness that greeted Ram earlier were now replaced by looks of bewilderment and suspicion. Shaya forced a smile on her face, while with a crooked smile on her face, La yelled, "This land belongs to me! If I have to kill every Shitmushee to prove that point, so be it!"

Ram took another step back away from his siblings and said, "Go home!"

Shaya slowly said, "What have they done to you that you would stand in our way?"

La said, "It doesn't matter! If he tries to stop us, he'll get the same as them!"

All of the Hammer-Axe Six turned and incredulously stared at La, while Shaya yelled out, "LAAA!!!!!!"

La felt everyone staring at her and said, "You know what I meant!"

No one did so they stared at La waiting on further clarification. La stomped one foot and then the other. She said, "I meant we'll deal with Ram, once we get him home!" La looked back at Claw and said, "For now, let's get rid of these Shitmushee!"

Ram turned his body sideways so that he could see his siblings as well as Claw and the other Shinmushee. Because of his field vision Ram could see all of them just as clearly as if he was looking directly at them.

Ram saw hatred and determination in Claw, Sunshine, Hearts and the other Shinmushee with them. He knew it would be a great challenge to stop them from advancing on the Ra. Ram was ready for that challenge.

Ram also saw that Dan, Don and especially Yin were confused by his behavior. Ram knew Don and Yin wouldn't attack him and he was pretty sure Dan wouldn't, unless absolutely necessary. However, they were readying themselves for battle and staring at him and the Shinmushee ready to chop them to pieces.

Ram looked at his sisters. La only looked at Ram for a moment, before turning her attention back to Claw. The look in La's eyes told

Ram that if he got in her way, she would treat him the same as a Shinmushee.

Ram could also see Shaya peeking at him. When she did, she had a hurt and angry look in her eyes like she was trying her best to figure out why he was standing between her and their family's most hated enemy.

Then there was Danaaa staring directly at Ram, studying him. Danaaa looked almost the same to Ram, but there was a big difference. Her stare was cold, hard and straight to the point. Danaaa seemed more aggressive than ever, looking at Ram for any weakness she could use to her advantage. Danaaa had never looked at Ram like that, until now. She reminded Ram more of La than she ever had.

Dan, who had been staring at Ram, decided La was probably right. It would be pointless to reason with Ram in his present state of mind. Dan looked past Ram at Sunshine and then at Hearts. He pulled his Hammer-axes from their holsters. Hearts quickly raised her arms and lowered then, sending her hooked blades out past her fist, locking them into position.

The rest of the Hammer-axe Six, except for Danaaa, all pulled their weapons after that. Everyone on both sides started moving to a better position, giving themselves enough room to maneuver.

Seeing that, Ram tried to get himself to where he could stop both sides from killing each other. He knew it would be tough, but he was up for the challenge. Dan, Shaya, Don, Yin and La paused and looked at Ram. They were conflicted and slightly confused on how to proceed. They knew it would be difficult fighting the Shinmushee and Ram, at the same time.

Just then, Danaaa walked past them and up to Ram. While staring at Ram, Danaaa yelled to her siblings, "Just take care of the Shitmushee! I'll handle Ram!"

That was enough to allow the Hammer-Axe Six to refocus, knowing they wouldn't have to fight Ram and the Shinmushee. They started moving towards who they knew they'd be fighting. La and her four female bodyguards towards Claw, while Dan inched towards Sunshine and Hearts.

Don and Yin turned towards Shinmushee Butchers that were headed towards Danaaa. That got those Butchers attention and they went on guard against Don and Yin. Yin, with an evil grin on his face, motioned with his axes for the Shinmushee Butchers to come closer.

Ram moved towards the action, however Danaaa quickly moved blocking his path. Ram sternly said in his booming bass voice, "Get out of my way!"

Danaaa put both her hands on her hips, so fast in defiance of Ram's order he thought she'd drawn her axes on him. Although startled, it only took Ram a second to recover from that.

Danaaa stared at Ram trying to figure out what was wrong with him. Why would he turn against his family, trying to protect their enemy? Would he harm her other siblings in doing so? It angered Danaaa that Ram would make her have to think about that. Danaaa knew she might never figure those things out. Well, alright then! There was one thing Danaaa knew she could do. She could swing an ax, real fast! She just hoped she wouldn't have to do it against Ram.

Trying to make Ram understand the situation, Danaaa yelled, "But, you already know you can't make me get out of your way! Look at you! Weakened by no blood and your time, away, in the jungle! You should have taken the blood when I offered it to you! You'll soon regret that! Without drinking blood, you don't stand a chance against me!"

Ram had almost forgotten how loud his baby sister's voice could get. Still, without breaking eye contact with Danaaa, Ram put his Hammer-axes back in their holsters and said, "I'm not going to fight you!"

"Good!" Danaaa yelled, as she quickly sent the blade of her ax at Ram. Ram, not believing Danaaa had it in her to cut him, waited until the last possible moment, before moving out of the way of Danaaa's ax blade. Before Ram could think he was frantically stumbling backwards to get out of the way of her other ax.

Once Ram felt he was a safe distance, he stared at Danaaa, offended that she would actually cut him, if he hadn't avoided her. Danaaa stopped her attack putting her fist, with axes in them, on her waist. She was pissed that Ram had put her in this position.

Danaaa stared at Ram and yelled, "Staring at me like that won't help you next time! Besides, I wasn't going to kill you! I just need to cut you enough so the healers can take you home! As slow as you move, if I really wanted to kill you I would have used the metal ball on the end of my ponytail to smash in your skull! Now that you know what I have planned for you, see if you can stop me, you wanna-be Shitmushee! You disgust me!"

Ram was shocked and highly offended by Danaaa's words. While staring at Danaaa, all Ram could think about was the last conversation he had with the old man, grandpa. Ram was startled by the clanging of axes, letting him know the battles he was trying to prevent had already started.

The old Grandpa told Ram that he had to stop both sides from fighting, or two of his siblings might get killed. Grandpa also stressed that he wouldn't be able to stop Claw and the other from joining the battles against the Ra. And that if they were killed, many more just as tough would come from further south, trying to kill the Ra. Grandpa told Ram it was imperative that Ram stop both his families from killing each other. Ram stared at Grandpa after he said both your families, not understanding that.

Grandpa could see that and said, "You have learned a lot while here. One of the toughest things for you to learn was not to kill. Not only do you have to practice that, but you also have to teach this to others. That will test you in ways you can't imagine. This is training on the highest level. However, if you're not tough enough for this training, I'll understand!"

Ram wasn't a quitter and was up for any challenge. That's one of the reasons he came to the Jungle. The other reason Ram went to the Southern Jungle was because he wanted to learn better killing techniques from the old grandpa. Ram was sure that had not happened.

While thinking about that, Ram had to avoid a dozen or more lightning fast swings from Danaaa's axes. Ram quickly pulled his axes and started blocking Danaaa's axes. He wasn't going to use his axes offensively. However, he decided he would never stop any of these battles running from Danaaa.

Once Ram pulled his axes, Danaaa turned the heat up on him. Ram was in what seemed to him a death battle with his younger sister. Ram shook that off and gave Danaaa the respect her axes deserved.

Ram inched his way towards the other battles, while avoiding an onslaught from Danaaa's axes. Ram wondered how you stop people who are intent on killing each other from killing each other. Ram didn't know how he would do it but he was going to try. If he could somehow stop these battles using his axes, later he might be able to say something that might appeal to the intellect of both sides. Ram couldn't imagine what that might be. He decided he would think about that when that time came. First thing first, Ram had to stop this battle at all cost!

At this moment Ram had a strong dislike for the old grandpa. He didn't hate him. It just was Ram didn't understand what he could possibly learn from this. However, Ram wasn't going to give up. With every swing of his axes to block Danaaa's axes, just like with everything else the old Grandpa taught him, Ram cursed the old Grandpa for this lesson!

Ram quickly surveyed the battlefield, before nearly having his head taken off by Danaaa's ax. He angrily looked at her, while blocking several more ax swings. Ram couldn't figure out how Danaaa was going to only wound him if she was swinging her axes at his neck. Normally, that removes your head!

Ram refocused remembering what he saw of the battles raging around him. Dan, Hearts and Sunshine were in an intense battle.

Dan was putting heat on them. However, because of their intense training with grandpa, that battle was only warming up.

Ram also saw that La and her girls were giving Claw a fighting puzzle that would take him a while to figure out, if at all. That Claw could fight all five of them impressed Ram.

Don and Yin seemed to be doing very well fighting at least tree Shinmushee Butchers, each. Ram could see they both were much better than when last he saw them fight.

Ram looked around again and saw that Shaya was battling three Butchers, with several more spying on her. Ram couldn't take the chance that they might get a lucky strike on her. He had to help Shaya, despite the onslaught of Danaaa's axes.

Ram instantly went on an offensive tear with his axes that caught Danaaa by surprise. She wildly blocked everything coming from Ram. Ram turned the heat up even further and Danaaa had to take a step back to regroup. When she did, Ram bolted in Shaya's direction.

Danaaa saw that and then ran, taking a running jump into the air. Danaaa was flying through the air, spinning in a tight ball, over and past Ram. Ram had just gotten to Shaya and blocked a swing of an ax from one of the Butchers spying on Shaya. In that same instant, Danaaa was coming out of the air swinging both her axes aimed at Ram's neck. Ram was able to block one ax, but couldn't get his other ax off the block of the Butcher in time to block Danaaa's other ax. Shaya's ax blocked Danaaa's other ax that would have taken Ram's head clean off.

Shaya's other ax came flying at the neck of the Butcher Ram blocked. Ram blocked Shaya's kill shot and then sent the hammer side of his ax into four of the six Butchers that had Shaya surrounded so fast that they stumbled backwards. The other two moved backwards to a better position. Shaya quickly moved towards them. After ducking under another one of Danaaa's powerful swings, Ram moved directly in front of Shaya, letting that Butcher escape from Shaya's axes. Shaya and Ram stared at each other for a split second, before Ram turned and ran in the opposite direction.

Shaya turned, angrily looking at Danaaa and screamed, "You almost took Ram's head off! You were only supposed to wound him! Watch what you're doing and be more careful!"

"He moved so fast I got carried away! I didn't know if he was going to attack you or not! It's hard to cut him, without killing him!" Danaaa yelled, whining.

"Do what you have to! Just don't aim for his neck!" warned Shaya.

Danaaa pressed her lips together in frustration and bolted over to where Ram was. Ram managed to make it over to where Yin was, before Danaaa caught up with him. Ram blocked four kill shots from Yin's axes that would have shredded a Shinmushee Butcher. Yin wouldn't stop his attack so Ram hit Yin in the chest with four hammer shots. That backed Yin up. Yin angrily stared at Ram. However, Yin didn't attack Ram. That gave Ram a chance to block another ferocious round of ax swings coming from Danaaa.

First chance Ram got he bolted away from Danaaa. That got him sliced lightly across his shoulder from Danaaa's ax. Ram arrived at La's battle just in time to block La's metal ball from smashing into the side of Claw's head. Ram stayed just ahead of Danaaa's axes, moving towards Dan's battle.

Ram arrived just in time to block a powerful swing from Dan's ax that would have split open Sunshine's chest. Nevertheless, Dan's ax swing was so powerful that Ram could only block it past Sunshine's chest, into her shoulder. Ram had to quickly block Heart's hooked blade, preventing it from plunging into Dan's chest, while blocking another swing from Dan that would have taken the head of the wounded Sunshine.

After Ram blocked Dan's ax that would have taken Heart's head off, he had to block Danaaa's ax, protecting his own head. Ram quickly grabbed hearts, shielding her from Dan. Dan and hearts took a step back. Ram angrily stared at Danaaa for swinging at his neck, again. Danaaa shrugged her shoulders at Ram like she couldn't help it.

After almost being hit with La's metal ball, Claw pulled his axes. He was instant heat, as La and her girls tried to avoid his axes. Claw charged hard at La, while keeping the other girls at bay. Hesta charged Claw trying to take some of the heat off La. Claw easily blocked Hesta and sent his ax to split her open.

"HESTAAA" screamed La.

Claw withdrew his ax before it connected, while sending a powerful kick to Hesta's chest that sent her flying backwards into La. Seconds before, out of the corner of his eye, Claw saw Ram helping Sunshine off the battlefield. Claw motioned for the other Shinmushee to move back, so they did. Claw looked up. It was getting dark. He wasn't going to continue this fight, tonight, unless the Ra kept attacking.

La, Yin, Don, Shaya and Dan watched as the Shinmushee all started backing slowly deeper into the jungle. It was getting dark. So the Ra didn't advance. Then they saw Ram helping Sunshine, tending to her wounds.

La turned and stared at Claw. She questioned, "Why didn't you kill her when you had the chance?"

"Because you begged me not to." replied Claw.

La's blood began to boil when Claw said that. She angrily stared at Claw because that wasn't what happened. She screamed in fear of what might happen to Hesta. La decided it was best if they got back to camp. If not for Ram, she would have smashed Claw's scull in. La was sure she could do it, again.

"Right!" La responded before backing up, while keeping an eye on Claw and the other Shinmushee. The other Ra joined La, after that.

Ram helped Sunshine, until healers took over. He then was told to leave, if he didn't want to be killed, this night. Ram looked at Claw and the others. Any other time he would have taken them up on that offer. This time Ram turned and walked away.

"Why did you help me?" yelled Sunshine.

"I wanted to." replied Ram

"We were going to kill you, first chance we got." admitted Sunshine.

"You would have tried." Ram said, as he walked away.

Ram walked to the Ra camp. Guards alerted the other Hammer-Axe Six. When Ram walked up his siblings were waiting, angrily staring at him. Those looks shocked Ram. He'd seen those looks coming from Shinmushee and other enemies, but never from his siblings. For a split second, Ram wondered if his mother and father would look at him this way. That would be devastating. How would his aunts Wana and Tara look at him?

Ram went to the Southern Jungle to learn better killing techniques, so he could kill more people, efficiently. Now, it seemed he was taught not to kill. That old grandpa had somehow tricked Ram into becoming something other than what he was. Ram hated the old grandpa, even though he didn't want to.

Although confused, Ram felt he'd done the right thing, trying to stop the two sides from killing each other. Judging from the cold hard stares he was getting from his siblings, Ram knew it would be difficult to explain why he did what he did.

Suddenly, Ram was aware of the many slices that he had received from Danaaa's axes. He went down on one knee as a wave of dizziness hit him. Ram was exhausted and weak from Danaaa's ax cuts. Ram tried to gather himself. He looked at his siblings, again. The last thing Ram remembered hearing was Shaya's voice summoning healers.

ROBERT DAVIS enjoys hiking, rock climbing, the natural sciences, and learning about different cultures. He currently resides in Ohio. This is his first book.